RIVER
of the
SUN

JAMES RAMSEY ULLMAN

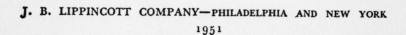

J. B. LIPPINCOTT COMPANY—PHILADELPHIA AND NEW YORK
1951

PRINTED IN
THE UNITED STATES OF AMERICA

W

To ELAINE
and also, of course,
to MAGGIE

AN ACKNOWLEDGMENT

The author expresses his thanks to Robin H. McGlohn, of Belem, and Robert S. Rau, of New York, who were of much help in setting him afloat on the Great River.

A NOTE

All the characters in this book are fictitious. Where names of real organizations are used, it is for the purposes of verisimilitude and does not imply that characters associated with such organizations have any connection with actual persons.

The locale of the book, on the other hand, is a blend of the real and the imaginary. There are, to be sure, an Amazon and an Amazonia, a country named Brazil and cities named Manaos and Belem. There is a jungle river flowing into the upper Amazon from the southwest that is known as the Juruá. But this is where the atlas ends. There are, at least to the author's knowledge, no actual streams called Yurima and Malaguay, no localities called Esperança and Graça de Deus, no Hills of Morning or River of the Sun.

As for storied and still-elusive El Dorado, Candide's speculation remains, after two centuries, as valid as any. "It is probably the country where all is well," he said, "for there absolutely must be one such place."

CONTENTS

Part I   THE RIVER   11

Part II   THE SHORE   183

Part III   THE FOREST   361

PART ONE

THE RIVER

1

THERE ARE THE seven seas, and one besides. From the Andes to the Atlantic, between the Isthmus and the pampas, rolls the ocean of the forest.

This is the ocean of earth's midriff. Its face drinks the fierce sun- and rain-beat of the equatorial sky; its floor is the red clay and brown loam of the equatorial earth. Between sky and earth it weaves a continental web of living tissue. It surges across the miles in a green tide of life.

Here is a screen of emerald. Push it aside. Beyond it is another screen; beyond that another and another; a labyrinth of screens, intertwining, multiplying, proliferating in an endless intricate fabric of growth and death. Far above the sun is shining, the rain is beating. But this is the ocean bottom. A thousand sounds fill the twilight, but beyond the sounds is stillness. Change is everywhere, but nothing changes. No clock ticks here; no seasons come and go. The creepers rise to the fronds, the fronds to the lianas, the lianas to the dark pylons of the boles. A minute has passed now, and now a century. Beyond the century is another emerald screen.

Here is a clearing. A billion sauba ants march through it, carrying the leaves of the forest like the banners of a destroying army. A horned triceratops, seeking a water hole, entangles itself in a vine, starves, and becomes a fossil. A naked man squats on the earth and builds a fire against the darkness and his fear. A plane flecks the sunlight with silver wings—circling, searching. But there is nothing there. Nothing but another billion ants carrying another billion leaves.

Here is a tree. One of a myriad and yet one alone. Its roots go down into the rich loam, the loam into granite and basalt, the granite and basalt into unimaginable depths of pressure and dark fire. And the tree thrusts upward. Its trunk rips through the mold and decay of the forest floor; its branches reach up with hungry arms toward the blue skylight above. The next tree coils a root around it in a death-grip. The lianas close in with their stranglers' nooses, and creepers, grubs and woodworms mantle it, gnawing its flesh and boring into its pulp. But still it climbs, struggling, carrying its enemies with it. It is not merely one tree, but every tree, every living thing in the forest-ocean, fighting to live. It is substance and energy, seed and spore.

And now at last it is the monarch, its crown broad and free against the sky. The sun and the rain strike down upon it, and then out of the rain the white blade of the lightning. A rending and splitting shake the forest, mounting to a roar, and crown, branch and bole topple in ruin into the shadows. Creepers and ferns close over them in a green shroud, and they are one with the mold and the ants. Where the roaring has been is now only the hum of the jungle. There is a whirring of wings, the laughter of an unseen monkey. Then these too are gone, and there is only the drip of the raindrops on the sodden web of the forest.

The rain drips down onto the fallen tree, onto the mold and moss, onto the tall black boles and emerald screens. It lies in dark pools in the hollows, sinks into the loam and clay, and moves in a seeping tide beneath the floor of the jungle. Slowly the tide swells and rises. And more rain falls. The green miles lie steaming under a veil of rain.

On the other side of the continent storms beat upon the crests of the Andes. Rain, snow and hail fall upon the ranges, and the ranges fall in glaciers and avalanches toward the plains. High on a treeless slope a thread of water trickles downward, funneling through its groove of rock. The groove becomes a gully, the gully a trench, the trench a gorge, the gorge a valley. Down the valleys pour the swift threads of a thousand streams, rushing to join the dark waters of the forest floor.

And presently they are no longer streams but rivers. The silver water of the mountain freshets has become the green water of the Tapajos and Xingu, the black water of the Rio Negro, the brown jungle-water of Madeira, Juruá, Putumayo, Ucayali, Marañon. From north and west and south the rivers flow; a thousand miles, two thousand, three thousand; tributaries and sub-tributaries, dark forest rivers and bright valley rivers, rushing, falling, flooding, twisting back on themselves, losing themselves, but always finding themselves again, always twisting on, flowing on; an empire of rivers flowing to the Great River and the sea. They are the currents in the ocean of the forest, the pattern in the labyrinth, the intestine and bloodstream of a continent.

Here at last is the flood of the Amazon. Yellow, coiling, gigantic. The tepid water lapping this mudbank comes from the snowcap of Chimborazo. It comes from the cataracts of Matto Grosso, the cliffs of Cuzco, the chicle swamps of Venezuela, the valleys and mountainsides of Bolivia, Colombia, Ecuador and Peru. It comes from the wet rotting leaves of a fallen tree in the deep heart of the rain-forest. It is part of all of them, and all of them are part of the Amazon.

An immense stillness broods over the rivers: over the mudbanks and sandbars, the shallows and channels, the wide reaches and dark inlets, and the opaque green curtain of the shore. It is the stillness of illusion. Behind the curtain, beneath the soft coils of the water, is a world locked in primordial struggle of beast against beast, plant against plant, life against life; a world forever dying and being born. Here is the jaguar's snarl, the peccary's charge, the cayman's snap, the anaconda's lunge. Through the bright fountain of the ferns crawls the strangler vine, and under the bland surface of the pool lurk the silver jaws of the piranha. Across the

mold and seed of the forest-ocean march the conquering
legions of the ants.

Out of the stillness a storm strikes, roars and passes. A
tree falls. There is the sudden shrill chattering, the beat of
wings, a warning whistle. And then stillness again. There
is no sound now. Nothing moves. . . . Nothing except the
lone boat that appears presently around a distant bend of
the river.

A man stands at the bow of the boat, his eyes squinting
into the distance. His clothing clings to him, sodden with
sweat. He is tired, hungry, lonely; his body aches, and his
flesh burns with the sting of mosquito, leech and pium fly.
But he is not thinking of these things. His thoughts, like his
eyes, are on the river ahead. On the gliding walls of the
riverbank that screen the secrets of a continent.

The man's name is Francisco de Orellana, captain-com-
mander of His Spanish Majesty's expeditionary corps, and
he and his conquistadores are the first civilized men ever to
look upon this jungle world. As he watches now, he sees the
vast and intricate foliage of the forest, the crowns of palm,
the pillars of mahogany, the lace of ferns, and beyond them
a vista of empire spreading away through the miles and the
years. He sees cities, fields, slaves, gold; gold in the earth
and the rivers, on the altars of temples and the helmets of
dusky kings; gold, wealth and power flowing unendingly
from a great equatorial kingdom, beside which the kingdoms
of Aztec and Inca will fade into nothingness.

The man's name is Father Samuel Fritz, gentle but res-
olute Jesuit from Bohemia. The green walls loom beside
him, motionless, lifeless; but he knows that deep behind
them life lurks and waits. Not only the plants and beasts of
the forest, but men of the forest as well. Cocomas, Mapari-
nas, Chepeos, tribes with no names—savage naked men with
blowguns, poisoned arrows and hatred of the white man in
their hearts. But the good father is not afraid. The Indians
will flee, and he will follow them. They will attack, and he

will bless them. In the Lord's time their war-cries will become the paternoster. The trees of the jungle will be hewn into crucifixes.

His name is Henry Walter Bates, English botanist, aged twenty-three, and in his hand is neither blunderbus nor rosary, but a long wooden pole with a net on the end. His quest is not for gold or souls, but for knowledge: thousands of nets, hundreds of chests full of knowledge. For eleven years he will thread the green mazes, following his prey. Tracking the fanged cat, the rainbow bird, the jewel-eyed serpent, the flickering butterfly. Searching out the runner and swimmer, the flier and creeper, the larva, the maggot, the pod. Surely those enchanted aisles into which he is now peering hold creatures stranger and more wonderful than the phoenix and the minotaur.

His name is Richard Riker, late of Stonewall Jackson's Second Corps of the Army of Northern Virginia. Three thousand miles to the north are the ruins of his farm, his countryside, the world he knew and loved. But he has put it all behind him. Defeat and shame and carpetbaggers are behind him. Ahead now are only the river and the green elbow of a promontory, and beyond the promontory, perhaps, a tract of arable land, a new homestead, a new life.

His name is Smith, Schwarz, Gulbransen, Wasniewicz, McGurk, and for three years he has swung his pick and shovel on the Panama Canal. Now the big ditch is finished, and he is free to go home to Akron, Hamburg, Malmo, Krakow, Londonderry. But he is not going home. He no longer has a home. He is going up to the Madeira, where they are driving a railroad through the jungle into the Bolivian rubber country. The black gum will soon be flowing down the rails like a stream of gold, and at the farther end will be the Big Bonanza, cases of White Mule—and a new life.

His first name is Pedro or Luiz or Manoel or Sebastião, and only his mother knows his last. Until a few months ago he was a farmhand on a fazenda in distant Ceará. Then the drought came; disease and starvation came; he would have

17

died with the others if the patrão had not advanced him a hundred milreis, given him a paper to mark with a labored X, and sent him up the river from Manaos. Now he will no longer be a plainsman but a woodsman, a seringuero tapping the caouchouc trees. His troubles are behind him. The patrão will provide. In the great forest there will be work, food, more milreis; a snug hut in which to sling his hammock; a plump Indian wife, perhaps; plump, laughing children. And a new life.

His name is Colonel P. H. Fawcett, D.S.O., Founders' Medalist of the Royal Geographical Society of London. Explorer, archaeologist and mystic, he has traveled for years through the remote and secret places of the earth, and now at last he is embarked on his ultimate adventure. It is not a new life that he is seeking, but an ancient and forgotten life—a lost world. For deep in this wilderness, he believes, are the ruined walls and dark vaults of a city older than Ur, greater than Nineveh and Tyre. Presently the prow of his boat will touch the riverbank, and he will enter the forest, pushing aside the first screen, and the next, and the next. He will disappear behind the emerald screens, never to return.

His name is Mistar Jones of Standard, Mistar Johnson of Allied, Mistar Jackson of Consolidated, Mistar Yanqui of the Estados Unidos Norteamericanos, and a week ago a silver stratoliner set him down on the airstrip in Belem. In his kit are his transit and theodolite, his DDT and atabrine, his wrenches, cables and drills. In his mind's eye, behind the forest wall, are sawmills, oil derricks, mine shafts, roadbeds, tractors, trim rows of bungalows and the long aisles of plantations. In his pocket is his letter of credit.

Or perhaps his name is my name: Mark Allison. And I remember the evenings when I stood with John McHugh and Christine Barna at the rail of the old *Dom Pedro,* squinting upstream into the sunset. I remember the slow pull and curl of the brown water among the reeds on the bank and the motionless green wall of the forest beyond the reeds. I remember raising my eyes and watching the immense brown tide of the river pouring toward us out of the silent miles. And presently the tide was no longer brown but yellowish tan, and then no longer tan but golden and flecked with gleaming red. The sun slipped down to meet the horizon; touched it, touched the forest, touched the river; and the great tide of sun and river streamed out from El Dorado across the darkening earth.

2

BUT THIS SIDE of El Dorado is the city of Manaos. And before the *Dom Pedro* there was the sidewalk café of the Hotel Joaquim Nabuco.

Eustasio Moranda had arranged the meeting the day before, but apparently he was uneasy about me, because he reappeared in the Panair office about a half hour before I was due at the hotel. As always, he was a trim immaculate vision in white linen, matching tie and handkerchief, and pointed patent-leather shoes that you could have used for a shaving mirror. He waited while I took care of a customer who wanted a round-trip to Santarem and then approached the counter.

"You have not forgotten?" he asked.

"No," I said.

"And you will come?"

I hesitated.

"Yes, you will come," he insisted. "You have promised." His small black eyes were fixed on my face. "Please—yes? This is a great thing for you, Marco amigo. It is all you have hoped and waited for."

I studied the counter. Then I said, "All right, I'll be there."

Moranda's face relaxed into a smile. "Good! Excelente!" He consulted his watch. "In twenty minutes—"

He waved and went out. And presently I too was leaving the office and walking the two sunbroiled blocks to the hotel. For the first block it was no different from any of the hundreds of times I had walked the route during the past two years. Then suddenly my heart began to pound. I stood still in the shade of a wall. I decided to go back.

But I didn't go back. I remained motionless where I was until the pounding had quieted a little; and then I went on. Christ, I thought, how I could have used a couple of gin-and-gingers. . . .

Not having them, though, had one minor advantage. The awning of the Nabuco's café was scaled to five-foot-six Brasileiros rather than to six-foot-one Californians, and every time I'd been drinking, which in those days was most of the time, I'd bump my head on the metal frame that supported it. Now, however, I ducked under safely, and there were Moranda and John McHugh at one of the round zinc-topped tables, waiting for me.

They stood up, and Moranda made the introductions and hissed authoritatively at the waiter. McHugh ordered gin-and-ginger.

"Beer," I said.

Moranda gave me an approving glance and ordered a vermouth and water for himself. "Cheruta, senhors?" he asked, producing a heavy gold case.

We each took a black ferocious-looking cigar, and the waiter brought the drinks. My hand, I noted with satisfaction as I raised my glass, was steady. Almost completely steady.

Moranda leaned his elbows on the table, cleared his throat and said, "I have, of course, already spoken to you, Senhor McHugh, about Senhor Allison here. And to you, Marco, about Senhor McHugh and the Companhia Cruzeiro do Sul. It is therefore not necessary to go again into the details." Whereupon he launched into the details.

While he talked, McHugh and I took turns sizing each other up. He was a compactly built man of about forty, with a broad, flat-planed face, cropped sandy hair and a fair skin that the tropical sun was in process of baking into a hectic brick-red. His eyes were gray and cool and I liked them, but

21

I wasn't too sure about the heavy forward-thrust chin and the thin, almost lipless line of the mouth. Everything about him gave the impression of—well—*direction*. If you were going his way, fine. If you weren't, there might be difficulties. Like Moranda, he was dressed in whites, but without the Latin style or flourish. Even in the shade there were dark stains on the shoulders and armpits of his jacket, and sweat glistened on his red forehead and among the thick yellow hairs on the backs of his hands.

So much for Allison on McHugh. But what about McHugh on Allison? If anything were to come of this beyond a free beer and a cigar, what he thought of me was obviously as much to the point as what I thought of him.

Tall—that was the first thing he would have noticed, of course. Long on bone and short on flesh; complexion an indeterminate compromise between coppery and sallow. Eyes: dark and fairly clear. Mouth: big and fairly firm. Other features: all in the right places and fairly well cut. But none of them so clear or firm or well cut as they had once been; all a little blurred and beveled and eroded by the years. Clothes: nondescript. Manner: casual and relaxed— or at least so you thought until you noticed the hand holding the beer glass. If I had been sitting in McHugh's chair with myself in the chair opposite, I would have said, five years ago—yes; now—no.

I put down the glass, pulled at my cigar and watched the blue smoke curl upward toward the awning.

The gist of what Moranda was now re-explaining was roughly as follows. McHugh was the field man for the Southern Cross Corporation, of New York and New Orleans, a new but rapidly expanding company that was specializing in the exploration and exploitation of various undeveloped areas in Latin America. Some six months ago Moranda had met the president of the company in Rio. There had been talks, negotiations, surveys. And the upshot was that Southern Cross had concluded a deal with the Brazilian Government whereby it was: (1) assuming the management of a rubber plantation called Esperança, near the mouth of the Juruá River; and (2) being granted one year's exploration rights to an area of almost unknown jungle country near the Juruá's headwaters. A party of engineers, technicians and assorted-ologists was currently on the way from New Orleans with a shipload of supplies and equipment, but McHugh, who was to be overall boss, had flown down in advance to make preliminary arrangements and get the lie of the land.

Moranda, who had become the company's local agent, had met him in Belem and accompanied him up-river to Manaos. On the way he had apparently talked to McHugh about me; and as soon as they arrived he had talked to me about McHugh. He had argued with me, pleaded with me. Until now, more than half against my will, here I was. . . . "Senhor Allison, yes, he is the man for you," Moranda was saying to McHugh. And then, turning to me: "The Company of the Southern Cross, it is the answer to all our hopes, Marco. They think and believe as we do. About the Amazon and its future. About the Juruá country. About the Rio do Sol. . . ."

He paused, and McHugh regarded me across the table and rubbed the blunt wedge of his chin. "You and Moranda were partners, Mr. Allison?" he asked.

"Yes," I said.

"In the investigation of this Juruá country?"

"Yes."

"You were the field man, I understand."

"I suppose you could call it that."

"Know anything about this Esperança place?"

"I've heard of it, of course. The Rubber Development Corporation ran it during the war and then pulled out about two years ago."

"But you've never been there?"

I shook my head.

"Not to the plantation, no," Moranda put in. "But of the country beyond it—of the Juruá and its tributaries—Senhor

Allison has great experience. He has flown over them many times."

"You're a professional pilot?" McHugh asked me.

"I *was* a professional pilot," I said.

"With Pan American, Moranda tells me."

"Yes."

"For many years," said Moranda, "Senhor Allison was a foremost aviator with Panair. It was from that distinguished position that he became partner with me in our enterprise; but unfortunately, as I have told you, it did not last for long."

"And now you're back with Panair?" said McHugh.

"Yes."

"But not as a flier?"

"No."

"Now as an executive," said Moranda quickly. "As chefé of the Manaos office, in charge of—"

"Now as a clerk," I said.

Moranda looked at me with a pained expression.

"The details don't matter," said McHugh. "It wasn't as flier that Moranda suggested my speaking to you. It was about this upper Juruá region. About the River of the Sun."

"Yes, of course—the Rio do Sol," said Moranda eagerly. "That is the important thing."

There was a pause, and I was conscious that both men were waiting for me to speak. But no words came. Steady now, steady, I thought. I felt my hand tighten around my beer glass.

Then McHugh was saying: "You've flown over this river—is that correct?"

"Not over it," I said. "I've seen it from a distance."

"How great a distance, would you say?"

"It was hard to tell. There was a range of hills—and mist—and then—"

I stopped. From the corner of my eye I could see Moranda's expression, encouraging me to go on. But I couldn't go on. "It's all pretty vague in my mind now," I told Mc-Hugh.

McHugh's cool eyes smiled and he took a sip of his drink. "I see your point," he said. "I think I'd be a bit vague myself, if someone were trying to get valuable information from me without offering anything in return." I started to speak, but he raised a hand and went on quietly. "That isn't the way my company does business, Mr. Allison. It was Moranda here who first interested us in this Juruá project, and we've made him our local agent. You happen to have information and experience which we think will prove important to us, and we're prepared to pay for that too."

"I have already told you this, Marco," Moranda put in.

"To be specific," McHugh went on, "I'm also offering you a position with Southern Cross. In your case, a field job: to go up-river with us. As base pay I can offer you at least what you're getting from Panair. And if we find what we're looking for, you'll make—plenty."

"What you're looking for?" I repeated.

McHugh smiled again. "Now it's my turn to be vague," he said. "You had your reasons to be interested in the Juruá country. We have ours. Suppose we let it go at that until you make your decision."

There was another pause. The two men were watching me. I took a drink of beer. . . .

And when I raised my eyes again, there was Christine Barna.

She wasn't Christine to me then, of course. She wasn't anything at all to me except a complete surprise, as she came in under the awning and stood in front of our table. The three of us got up, and McHugh introduced me.

"I'm afraid I'm early," she said. "Perhaps you'd rather I—"

But McHugh shook his head and Moranda pulled up a chair.

In the long months since, I have come to know Christine Barna so well that it is hard to remember just how she appeared to me as I saw her then for the first time. I was aware

25

that she was tall, but not too tall; and slender, but with the slenderness of a woman, not a girl. I saw her wide green-gray eyes, I know that. I saw her straight full mouth and the warm brownness of her skin and the soft glinting brownness of her hair. And that, I rather think, was all I saw. But it was enough. It was something new and astonishing under the Amazonian sun.

I had obviously been staring at her, for suddenly our eyes met, and she looked away. "Please go on with your talking," she told us.

"We've about finished," McHugh said. "Mr. Allison here may be going up-river with us."

I caught the *us* and looked from one to the other.

"My husband is at Esperança," Mrs. Barna said. "I'm joining him there."

And now suddenly I was staring at her again. But differently.

"You're joining him—?"

The words hung in the air. Mrs. Barna and McHugh looked at me curiously, and Moranda touched me gently on the arm.

"Does that seem strange to you?" she asked.

I got hold of myself. "No," I said. "No, of course not." I looked at Moranda and then away again. "I was just—surprised."

A thought struck her. "You don't know my husband, do you?" she asked eagerly. "Dr. Barna? Nils Barna?"

"No," I said. "I don't know him."

"Dr. Barna was a consulting agronomist for the Rubber Development Corporation," McHugh explained. "He stayed on at Esperança after it disbanded."

"Is he with Southern Cross?" I asked.

"We hope he will be soon."

"Mr. McHugh and I found ourselves leaving New York at the same time," said Mrs. Barna, "and I'm afraid he's been pressed into duty as escort."

"A grave hardship, I am certain," Moranda put in with an

26

elaborate Latin smile. "But it is an arduous trip for a senhora, escort or no—particularly on the upper Amazon."

"I've come well armed with romantic illusions," she assured him. "And Kleenex."

McHugh and Moranda laughed. Then there was a pause. "You're going to this Esperança place first, then?" I asked McHugh.

He nodded. "That will be our jumping-off place for the country beyond. Besides, we can't do much except the preliminary planning until the rest of our men arrive."

"How are you getting there?"

"By river-boat. Something called the *Dom Pedro*."

"The *Dom Pedro Segundo*," Moranda amended. "Yes, it is loading now at the wharf. In three or four days it will sail."

"I thought it was two days," said McHugh.

"Two, three, four. Certamente not more than a week."

McHugh bit his lip. There was another pause, and I stood up. "Well, thanks for the beer," I said. I nodded to Mrs. Barna and turned to McHugh.

"Do you want the job?" he asked me.

His eyes were steady on my face, and I looked back into them for a moment, and then at Moranda, who was registering enthusiastic approval. I may have looked at Mrs. Barna too, but I couldn't swear to it. Then I said: "I'll have to think it over."

"All right, think it over," McHugh said. "Let me know in the morning. I'll be here at the hotel."

I nodded again, ducked safely out under the awning, and walked the two blocks back to the office. It was empty, except for Manoel, a languid eighteen-year-old who served as combination assistant clerk and office boy. "Any customers?" I asked him.

"One one-way to Obidos," he said.

"Cash?"

"He say maybe tomorrow."

Having discharged my duties to Messrs. Trippe and Associates, I sat down at my desk and took out the deck of cards. Early in my stay in Manaos I had worked out a complicated solo version of casino, which I played endlessly to fill out the intolerable blank emptiness of the days. Sometimes it worked almost as well as gin-and-ginger. But not this time. And after a few minutes I pushed the cards away. Manoel, his elbows propped on the ticket counter, was performing his well-practiced feat of sleeping standing up. The electric fan in the corner whined and clicked. Behind my head an enormous blue bottle-fly batted itself against the window.

I put the cards away, got up, and crossed to the door. Manoel didn't move. Then I went out again into the street. The sun was still high and bright above the mango trees, but the ferocious heat of midday was lifting, and shreds of breeze flickered along the pavements from the direction of the river.

"Shine, mistar! Shine, mistar!"

A crowd of ragged brown boys followed me for a block and disappeared. I walked another two blocks—past cafés, offices, shop windows—turned a corner, and a second—and now presently the whitewash and red tiles and green mangoes were gone, and in their place were the mud walls of warehouses, the tin and thatch and rotting timber of slums. There were few people about, and the streets sprawled hot and empty in sunlit torpor. A small mange-eaten dog limped from an alley, twisted suddenly around and bit savagely into its rump. From behind a mud wall a rooster crowed.

As I walked on, the paving grew rougher, buckled and gaped open into long slits of grass and weed. Here and there in the dusty green were the bright yellow pinpricks of tiny flowers. I stepped on one and looked back, and it was gone. But tomorrow, I knew, there would be another flower in its place, and the next day another. All the concrete and all the footsteps in Brazil could not hold down the jungle. In the streets of Manaos you could feel the warped curve of the paving under your soles. You could feel the dark equatorial earth thrusting up from below against the thin sheath of stone.

After a while the pavement ended, and there was a dirt road, grass, reeds. Beyond the reeds was the river.

This was not the Amazon proper, but the Rio Negro—black, swift-flowing, enormous, yet scarcely more than a trickle compared to the great yellow mother-river which it joined some fifteen miles to the southeast. To the right of me spread the harbor. There was a single Booth Line freighter riding at anchor. There were two or three dingy riverboats, the masts of fishing smacks, a few wharves and cranes, and beyond them the crenellated white curve of the city. Above the city, high above the rooftops and the green crowns of the mangoes, the mosaic dome of the Opera House burned like a flame in the blue oven of the sky.

Somewhere, sometime, you must have heard of the Manaos Opera House. Built in 1910, at the height of the Amazon rubber boom, it was man's most spectacular gesture of defiance to the wilderness of the jungle ocean. World-renowned divas sang there. The Corps de Ballet from La Scala danced there. In the parterre boxes sat the Lords of the River, cavalheiros in boiled shirtfronts and their senhoras in lace and amethysts, secure in the belief that their city was the gate of the world's richest treasure-house, confident that as the years passed it would grow as great as Rio or Buenos Aires, Paris or New York. But of all they had they were proudest of their Opera House. Rising vast and ornate on the black river in the deep rain-forests, it was the very incarnation of the Amazon Dream.

Five years later rubber was dead. And Manaos was dead too. For a quarter of a century the Opera House stood dark and empty, while mold grew on its frescoed walls and the weeds pushed up through the cracks in its mosaic floors. During the middle forties it was opened briefly to house certain of the offices of the Rubber Development Corporation, a joint Brazilian-American enterprise devoted to high-pressure wartime procurement. And when the R.D.C. left

29

it reverted again to the mold and the weeds. If you should ever find yourself in need of an apt and not too shopworn symbol of *vanitas-vanitatum-sic-transit-gloria-etc.*, I commend to your attention The Opera House That Rubber Built.

There was a low bare hummock among the reeds by the riverbank, and I sat on it and looked at the city.

"I'll have to think it over," I had said to John McHugh. All right, I told myself—think.

I tried to focus and direct my mind, but this was an accomplishment no longer easy for me. Once, perhaps, I had been, like McHugh, a Man of Direction. But no longer. For almost two years now I had lived in a vacuum of my own devising, my life as aimless and planless as the gyrations of the droning bottle-flies in the Panair office. I knew no yesterdays and no tomorrows. I drugged myself with sun and heat, with liquor, with solitaire card games, and with the endlessly repeated round of routine mindless work. To judge, to decide, to act: these were functions I had deliberately relinquished. And as I sat there now by the riverbank, my thoughts glinted, flickered and splintered like the sun's rays on the dome of the Opera House.

I looked away from it and out across the harbor. The Booth freighter, I saw, had steam up. Later in the day, or perhaps tomorrow, it would head down-river for Belem; and, beyond Belem, for Liverpool or Glasgow, Norfolk or New York . . . . Did I wish that I were on it? No, I did not. I had not come to this place, as had the rubber hunters, with either ambitions or illusion. . . . "Manaos? Good God, why Manaos?" they had said when I went back with Panair and they asked where I wanted to go. "Maybe because it's the end of the line," I had told them. And that's what it was. And I was content with it.

Near the freighter, at the wharves, were the riverboats. One of them must have been the *Dom Pedro Segundo* . . . All right—think, I said. How about that? How about the Southern Cross Corporation and a plantation called Esperança and a river called the Juruá, and a Man of Direction called McHugh? For that matter, how about a slender, green-eyed and mildly mysterious young woman called Mrs. Christine Barna? And her husband, the agronomist?

Yes, he was part of it too, now. Her husband. *The husband she had come to join. . . .*

"Does that seem strange to you?" she had asked. "No, of course not," I had answered. But I had not answered the truth. I had not told her why I stared. I had not told her that I once knew another woman—oh yes, an equally young and lovely woman—who had come to this jungle-world to join her husband. Or that the woman's name was Joan Allison.

During the past few months I had finally succeeded in shutting Joan out of my mind. The drone of engines, the glinting of a river, the roaring and the darkness—I had shut them all out, far and deep beyond the walls that I had built around myself. But now they were back again, vivid and terrible. They had come up the river with Eustasio Moranda; with John McHugh; with a woman called Christine Barna. And after two long years they still possessed the power to set my heart to pounding—to close my hand tight and nerveless around a beer glass—to pierce the shell of my emptiness as with the thrusting blade of a knife.

My eyes moved out across the harbor, across the dark river, to the rim of forest beyond. . . .

And the sun was already dipping low toward the Opera House dome as I walked slowly back through the streets of the town. I went briefly to the office, closed up, and ate my usual solitary dinner at the usual down-at-heel, half-empty restaurant. Generally I spent the rest of the evening at the bar of the Nabuco, but tonight I walked on past it to the Pensão Alberti, which had been my home since I came to Manaos. And there in the shabby downstairs sitting-room was Eustasio Moranda, waiting for me.

"You have decided?" he asked eagerly.

I shook my head.

31

"You must decide, Marco. You must go." And now presently, he was arguing again, pleading again; and I sat there half listening to him and half to the sound of the rain that had begun its nightly drumming on the street outside.

When he walked into the Panair office the previous day it had been almost two years since I had seen Moranda. After the collapse of our brief partnership he had gone back downriver, first to Belem and then on to Rio and São Paulo. There had been a letter or two, in which he wrote vaguely of reorganizing and refinancing. Then silence—and I had assumed that our ill-starred vision of the River of the Sun was as dead for him as it was for me. But it wasn't dead for him. He had gone on planning, negotiating, promoting. And finally he had sold his dream to the Southern Cross Corporation, and here he was, back once more on the Amazon, all but begging me to join up with him again. Partly, to be sure, he was acting in the interests of Southern Cross, for he realized that, in practical terms, I could be of more use to them than he. But even more, I knew, he was doing it for my sake.

Why? you ask. What did he owe me?

The answer is that he owed me exactly nothing—and that was the remarkable and rather wonderful thing about Eustasio Moranda. He was, to use the antique phrase, a "good man." He believed in God, Brazil, Family, Friends, the United Nations, the Perfectibility of Man, and practically everything else in the book, with the single and signal exception of hard work. Carrying things to the final extreme, he believed in me; believing in me, he wanted to help me; and wanting to help me, it pained him that I was showing so little enthusiasm for helping myself.

"I'm better off on the beach, Eustasio," I told him.

"The beach, bah! What kind of talk is that—the beach? You have always worked, no? You are working now, no?"

"I have to live."

"So—that is just the point," he said, waving a finger at me. "You have to live, yes, and to live you do something about

32

it. The beach ones, they do not do something, no. It is for the other fellow to do something. They do not care." His finger froze and pointed. "You, Marco," he said, "you care. Do not say no to me, because I see it. I know it. And the one who still cares, he is not yet lost."

"I took my gamble once, Eustasio."

"But I am saying to you this is not a gamble. No—not like the last time. For this time we have with us a great corporation. The money. The men. I have told you of all these enginheiros and scientistas who are coming after Senhor McHugh. And more than that—yes. You know how it has always been in Amazonas, Marco: always the fine plans—but no men to do the work. This time we have a great project that will give us the men."

He was leaning toward me, his dark pointed little face alight with excitement. "Do you know what it is we are doing? We are bringing them from Europe. *Refugiados*—how do say it?—Unplaced Ones. Czechs, Poles, Jews. Craftsmen, workmen, peasants. Through the International Refugee Organization we are doing this; and the Brazilian Government and the Companhia Cruzeiro do Sul."

This, too, was something new under the Amazonian sun. "When?" I asked.

"Soon now. Very soon. When Senhor McHugh has left for Esperança, then I go down to Belem. I meet the enginheiros and scientistas from New Orleans and then the Unplaced Ones from Europe, and then I bring them all up-river in a boat which we have chartered."

"To Esperança?"

"To Esperança, yes. To the Juruá. To the Rio do Sol. Everywhere where there is need for them in our enterprise. This time you will have help, Marco. You will not be alone but among other men. As director; as leader. . . ."

"As D.P. Number One," I suggested.

There was a pause, and I got up. I crossed to the door and opened it and stood looking out at the dark, rain-filled street. But it wasn't the street that I saw. It was a zinc-topped table at the café of the Nabuco, and Moranda on one side of me and John McHugh on the other, and beyond the table, standing there, suddenly and incredibly, a woman called Mrs. Christine Barna.

Then I heard my voice saying to Moranda: "Joan brought Kleenex with her too. A whole damn suitcase full of Kleenex. . . ."

Moranda rose. He came over and stood beside me and laid a hand on my arm. "I know how it is with you, Marco," he said gently. "And why you are afraid of this thing. But you cannot go on with such thoughts forever. Do you understand? You cannot."

I didn't say anything.

"Joan herself, she is the one who would want you to go on with it. You know that—yes. She more than anyone."

"Perhaps," I said.

"Then you will say the word?" he pleaded. "In the morning you will go to Senhor McHugh. You will forget these things that are behind you. You will find a new work and a new life. . . ."

But when, a while later, he left, it was still without drawing "the word" from me. To forget what is behind, you must look steadily at what is ahead. To find a new life, you must crawl out from under the ruins of the old.

I climbed the stairs to the bare cubicle of my room. I took a bottle and glass from a shelf and began pouring myself a drink, and then I stopped and poured it back into the bottle and, pushing aside the mosquito netting, sat on the edge of the bed and looked out the window. The Pensão Alberti was built on the side of a hill, and the window faced inland, away from the river. Beyond it, through the rain, I could see a scattering of yellow lights and the faint outline of a road. And beyond them, darkness: the darkness of the night and the jungle ocean. For a long time I sat looking out at it.

Across the jungle. Across the years. . . .

3

IT HAD NOT been dark and rain-drenched the first time I looked out across it, but bright and shining in the sun. Even after twelve years I could remember the Clipper droning in from the Caribbean, and the coast of South America below, and beyond the coast, the green immensity of the forest. I could see it still, as I saw it then, streaming away mile after mile, hour after hour, through Venezuela, the Guianas, Brazil, across the heart of a continent. And I could still see myself, Co-pilot M. Allison, aged twenty-four, sitting motionless in the cockpit, staring downward, and feel the thrill that ran through me then, like the deep trembling of the plane itself, as we drove on across the midriff of the earth.

I remember Ted Hegstrom (he was my Senior then) watching me and smiling and saying, "Big."

Yes, big. Big and green. Big and still.

"After a while it will get smaller," Ted had said. "It will be a milk run."

But it never became a milk run for me. Not the tenth time I flew it; nor the hundredth. I was very young then, and an incorrigible romantic, and I suppose I felt about that tropical wilderness as some youngsters feel about the sea. What did it mean to me, you ask? What was there? As well ask Columbus what was beyond the Azores or Dan Boone what was west of the Alleghenies. Mystery and promise were there. The future was there. Everything was there. In those long-gone happy days the vast jungle and the tiny plane

35

streaking above it seemed to me the very symbol of man's destiny—and my own.

But it so happened that that was the year 1938, and it was not long thereafter that destiny was using other symbols, and other jungles were streaming past under the silver wings. Presently I moved on from Pan Am to the Army Transport Command, and from there to the Twelfth and then the Fifteenth Bomber Groups. I moved on from the wilderness of the Amazon to the wilderness of Tunis, Naples, Foggia, Vienna, Toulon. *Major Mark Allison,* said the *Oakland Tribune* one late spring day in 1945, *returned home yesterday after four years of as wide and varied experience as perhaps any pilot in the Army Air Force.*

Yes indeed. Very wide. Very varied. I had dropped bombs on airfields, fortifications, factories, power plants, office buildings, street corners, tenements, museums, churches, kindergartens and hospitals. I had killed Germans, Italians, Frenchmen, soldiers, politicians, grocers, linotype operators, cripples, schoolchildren, great-grandmothers and nursing babies. By the time the war ended I was an honored mastercraftsman at my trade. "I'll tell you something off the record, Allison," my commanding general confided to me on the day I was separated. "If the show had lasted a little longer in the ETO, you'd have been one of the first to carry an A-bomb."

Sometimes, lying there on my bed in the Pensão Alberti, I would try to think back to those days; but there was nothing much to think about. What I had done in the war was neither more nor less than thousands of other men had done, and that of course had been the thing that made it possible. The lines were drawn clear; you knew what your job was; and the fact that that job was destruction on a scale never before known in history made very little difference. Once in a while—not often, but once in a great while and after a great many drinks—you would try to talk about War and Death and Fear and Guilt and the other upper-case abstractions that nibbled like mice at the margins of your mind; but even then there was nothing much to say. The terrible part of it was that you lived in a world in which you could do such things without guilt. That was the way it was. You did what you had to do. Another bourbon, Mac, and light on the water. *Do not judge me, Lord God; I only work here.*

Yes, you had worked there: at your trade. After a while you worked superlatively well. It was not until later that you began to realize that you would never work at anything so well again; that in piloting your bomb-loads you had reached a height of effectiveness and importance compared to which the rest of your life would be an aimless mediocrity. As a flier—an instrument of destruction—you were an integrated purposeful mechanism, performing its appointed function. As a civilian, you were something quite different. As a human being.

And as a husband.

Time for a drink, I thought. When I reached this point it was time for a drink. I went to the shelf and poured myself one, and this time I didn't pour it back, but drank it down; and then I undressed and lay on the bed and hoped that I would fall asleep and Joan would go away. But she didn't go away. She was still there in the darkness of the room, beside me; there beyond the window behind the darkness and the rain. . . .

We had been married in the late summer of '43, when I was home for bomber training between Africa and Italy, and for the first two years it had been no different, I suppose, from any number of other wartime marriages: a thing of letters, plans, hopes, dreams—and utter unreality. We had been prepared for that. We knew it was inevitable. But what we were not prepared for was the unreality that followed, when at last the war ended and I came back for good. For even then, we soon discovered, we were not so much man and wife as a man and woman who had—well—happened to be married. We wanted each other, but scarcely knew

37

what to do, now that we had each other. We were in love, yes. But we were strangers.

What fault there was was mine, not hers. Call it "veteranitis"—I don't know. In the beginning I was convinced that I was through with flying, and I tried a succession of other jobs. We lived for a while in Oakland, then in Los Angeles, then in New York. But it was no good. Or more accurately, I was no good. I was a flier, and apparently that was all I was, and after six months I decided to go back with Pan American.

"Couldn't it be with one of the domestic lines?" Joan suggested. "Then we could at least be together more."

"I have my seniority at Pan Am," I explained. "And besides—"

Besides—and that part of it wasn't too easy to explain—the memory of those days in the equatorial skies was, somehow, the one meaningful thing that remained to me in the aimlessness that had beset my life. More than I had ever wanted anything, I wanted to fly those skies again; to see again the wide horizons and great tawny rivers; to look down again on the forest-ocean of the south.

Pan Am took me back, and we went to live in Florida. Or rather Joan lived in Florida, while I went back to my old Miami-Rio route and averaged a week at home with her out of every month. She didn't complain. If it was what I wanted, it was what she wanted too. Or at least what she wanted to want. But as the months went by I became increasingly aware that we still had neither a real marriage nor real happiness.

Even the flying was not what I expected it would be. Or what it once had been. Perhaps the war had something to do with that, too; or perhaps it was simply that I was older. I took my plane off and held it straight and climbed over the thunderheads. I turned the controls over to my Junior (for I was a Senior now) and went back and asked the passengers if they were enjoying their creamed chicken and tomato salad. I brought the plane down and hurried off for the three permissible drinks at the Plaza or Grande or Royale or Copacabana. Outwardly, I suppose, my life was little different from before, but within myself everything had changed. What had once been adventure was now routine. What had once been promise and mystery was—a milk run.

Only one thing remained for me the same as it had always been: the land, the continent, the sweep of the jungle and the rivers that threaded the jungle. More and more, as time went on, I found myself thinking about the Amazon country, reading about it, studying maps of it, talking to whoever was interested about its nature and possibilities and future. And finally the day came when I found myself sitting in the café of the Grande Hotel in Belem, listening with growing fascination while Eustasio Moranda, promoter and visionary, discoursed to me earnestly of his own version of the Amazon Dream.

It was not the Amazon proper that interested him ("that has all been picked over long ago"), but a remote tributary of the Amazon. Not the jungle ("that is only trees and vegetables and the accursed rubber"), but the higher open land beyond the jungle. Had I heard of the Juruá country? Vaguely—yes. Well, up toward the headwaters of the Juruá River there was a range of hills called the Serra Aurora, and beyond the hills an immense tableland, spreading away almost to the eastern slopes of the Andes. For four hundred years men had known of this plateau, and of a great river flowing through it, which the early explorers had called the Rio do Sol. For hundreds of years, too, it had been believed that this region was one of fabulous mineral wealth; but it was so remote and inaccessible that only a few stray wanderers had ever been there, and even in modern times it had been completely neglected, on the theory that, no matter what might be found there, it would be impossible to get it out.

I remember Moranda pausing and looking around him, almost conspiratorially. "But here is what I am talking to you about, Senhor Allison," he said. "I do not believe it is impossible to get it out."

The River of the Sun was known to exist, he went on; but no one knew where it flowed to. He, Moranda, on the other hand, was sure he *did* know. No, he had never been in the region himself, but he had talked to one or two men who had. He had read old histories, studied old maps, thought about the problem for years. He was convinced that the River of the Sun flowed down through the Serra Aurora into one of the upper tributaries of the Juruá. And equally important, he was convinced that both rivers were navigable for boats of fair size, almost all the way to their source.

"The key of the enterprise, of course," he said, "is to find the joining of the rivers."

That was a big order, wasn't it?

Yes, it was a big order. Too big for Moranda himself, and he had found it impossible to attract the backing for an expedition, without more evidence to support his theories. That was what he was after now: more evidence. And there was only one practical way of getting it. He himself had enough capital, at least for a beginning; but he needed a partner. He needed a plane to go up the Juruá and survey the country. And he needed a man to fly the plane. . . .

That had been the gist of our first conversation. There was another when I returned to Belem a week later. And still others over the succeeding weeks. The whole enterprise, I knew perfectly well, was the wildest sort of gamble. It was dubious, shakily financed, quixotic. It meant loss of security, hard work, dangerous flying, long weeks of living on the ragged fringes of civilization. And yet I knew in my heart that here at last was the thing that I had always wanted: the chance really to penetrate and pioneer that mighty wilderness. For another month or two I went through the motions of flying the milk route for Pan Am. And then, abruptly, I made my decision.

It seemed almost fantastic, talking about it to Joan in the prim little living-room of our bungalow in Miami. But she listened quietly and when I had finished made no objection, nor even at first asked any questions, but simply came over to me and kissed me and said, "I love you."

I remember standing there and staring down at her and not finding anything to say.

And then, just for an instant, a worried, questioning look came into her face, and she asked: "It isn't just for money, is it, Mark?"

"There may be a lot of money in it," I told her, "and there may be nothing. But—"

"But apart from money, it's something you really want to do?"

"Yes," I said.

"I know. I can tell it from your voice. Your face."

"And you don't mind?"

"No, darling. I don't mind. I'm happy—because at last you're happy." She raised her eyes to mine, and I saw that there were tears in them. "This is the man I married," she murmured. "This is the man I'm proud of."

"It won't be for too long," I told her. "You'll hardly know I'm gone."

"I won't know you're gone at all," Joan said. "Because I'm coming with you."

So I went. . . . And she came after me. . . . And two months later, with all the preliminaries behind us, there we were in a tiny godforsaken village called Fonte Boa on the remote reaches of the upper Amazon. It could have been dreadful, but it wasn't. It was wonderful. More wonderful, even, than our first days together, for then we had been little more than a boy and a girl and now we were a man and a woman, husband and wife. She took the broken-down shack that Moranda had found for us and turned it into a livable home. She bent with me over my maps and charts. She kept me company and handed me tools while I tinkered and fussed with the engine of the pre-war Sikorsky seaplane which I had half-rented, half-borrowed for the job ahead. And as

41

the days went on I found myself thinking: yes, this is it at last; not strangeness any longer but togetherness; not the end of our marriage but the beginning.

An aerial survey may sound like no more than flying to an objective, inspecting it, and flying back again. But that is not an aerial survey on the Amazon. Our equipment was rudimentary, the distances enormous, and the country an endless changeless labyrinth of jungle, floodland and twisting rivers. On the first series of flights we got no nearer than three hundred miles to our goal; on the second perhaps a hundred miles closer. And finally Moranda had to go downriver and bring up an auxiliary fuel tank—and more fuel—and we began all over again.

But, strangely, the delays and frustrations did not bother me. Joan was there. Hope and purpose were there. And each time I lifted my plane into the air the magic of those still, green miles was even stronger than it had been before. Sometimes, as I flew, I would think back to those other jungles I had known a few years before—the gray man-made jungles of rubble and death. And then I would thank God that they at last were behind me; that I had found a part of the earth, still young and living as He had made it, still untouched and unfouled by the hand of man.

Moranda, I soon discovered, was strong on plans and strategy but weak on long plane flights, and after the first few sorties he contented himself with supervising our jerry-built base. Joan, on the other hand, was constantly asking me to take her along. For several weeks I put her off on one pretext or another; but she kept on pleading; and in the end I gave in, because I too wanted her to go with me—wanted her to share everything that was a part of our new life together. "I'll bring you luck," she promised me. And I kissed her and grinned at her. And a few mornings later I led her down to the landing jetty, helped her into the old Sikorsky, taxied out to midstream and took off.

Now, lying on my bed in my room in the Pensão Alberti, I listened to the sound that filled the darkness. It's only the rain on the roof, I told myself. But it wasn't only the rain. It was the sound of a plane's engine. And Joan and I were sitting side by side in the little cockpit, setting out on our first flight together over the jungle.

We had flown together before, of course. But never like this. Never with the sky so blue and the sun so golden—with cities and men and the whole world of men behind us—with only stillness and silence before us, and the great yellow coils of the river beneath us, and the forest-ocean spreading on into the ends of space. We were climbing now and I was pulling back on the wheel, and with the other hand I reached out and touched Joan's hand, as it rested beside me on the leather seat. She did not speak, but merely smiled at me and then turned and looked down at the wilderness below. And I thought exultantly, yes, she too is seeing it now—she too is feeling it; and presently I leveled off, and the roar of the engine diminished to a soft humming, and the little plane raced on through the shining sky.

By this time we had reached a fairly advanced stage in the survey, and I was convinced that we were either approaching close to our goal, or that the goal was non-existent. I had long since followed the main stream of the Juruá to its highest navigable point—and found nothing. Then, in order, I began following its tributary rivers, first on the left and then on the right, but so far with the same result. All of them, I discovered, were blocked by obviously impassable rapids or simply petered out in trackless jungle swamps. And I had seen no sign of a range of hills, beyond which was reported to lie the fabled plateau and the River of the Sun.

On my last flight I had investigated a remote tributary called the Yurima, which flowed into the Juruá some three hundred miles above its junction with the Amazon. The outcome had been the usual one, but I was not yet quite through with the Yurima area, for, almost a hundred miles up, at a point where it was still broad and deep, I had come upon the junction of two sub-tributaries, which remained to be explored. From what I had been able to see of their

43

courses, both of these streams seemed to penetrate farther to the west than any of the other affluents of the Juruá. But even more interesting than this was the fact that, whereas one of them was the same yellow-brown as the Juruá and Yurima, the other was black—and blackwater rivers are very uncommon in that part of Amazonia. My maps gave little information about either. One called the righthand fork— the black one—the Malaguay, but another gave that name to the brown one on the left. Most gave them no name at all. And on none was there an attempt at accurate rendering, but only two dotted lines snaking off into a blank space labelled *Região Inexplorado*.

In any case, this is where I was headed for on the morning I took Joan with me.

For two hours we followed the Juruá, for almost another hour the Yurima, and not once in that time did we see a village or a boat or indeed any sign of life at all in the wilderness beneath us. Then we came to the forking of the tributaries, and on a hunch, no more—a hunch and a certain curious fascination—I followed the blackwater stream to the right. We covered fifty more miles. A hundred. The dark water below remained broad and rapid-free. But the forest ahead and on all sides was still the same as ever, spreading flat and featureless to the horizon's rim. I glanced at the fuel gage and saw that it was only a little above the halfway mark. In another few minutes we would have to turn back.

Then I looked up and saw that Joan was pointing. Her lips were moving and her eyes shining with excitement. And straining my eyes into the distance, I saw what she saw: a low bank of mist on the horizon ahead, and through the mist, all but shrouded behind it, the faint dark outline of what appeared to be a range of hills. I remember looking once, quickly, at Joan, and our eyes meeting, and then my body tense in my seat, my hand tight on the wheel, and the plane droning on over the jungle river. Slowly the mist drew closer. Slowly the dark outline behind it emerged and took form. And yes—I was sure now—it *was* a line of hills, low

44

and dark and wooded, rising out of the jungle; and below us the river we had been following seemed to bore on, straight ahead, into the very heart of the range.

A moment later the mist was around us. It closed in, and the earth was blotted from sight. For a while the plane bumped and swayed through opaque grayness, and I knew we were crossing the crest of the hills. And then suddenly it was brighter again. There was blue sky ahead—a rent in the mist—a great window in the mist—and beneath the window, the land on the far side of the hills. It was a vast sweep of land, stretching as far as the eye could see. Not jungle land, but open savannah land. Through its heart flowed a great river that shone like gold in the flooding sunlight.

In the same instant the sun glinted closer—on the dials of my instrument panel. And raising my eyes, I looked again at the fuel gage. . . .

We almost made it back to Fonte Boa. By leaving the rivers and cutting straight across the jungle, we made it within three miles. We could already see the Amazon when the propeller froze and the forest rose to meet us, like a slanting green wave. And when Moranda and the others reached us, the flames were still crackling in the blackened shell of the cockpit.

In the darkness now I lay listening again to the flames. Their sound faded, rose, receded again, farther and farther, deeper and deeper . . . . and now presently there was only the sound of the rain, as it drummed on the roof of the Pensão Alberti.

I got up and poured myself another drink, and this time I turned on the light and sat on the edge of the bed, drinking slowly. On the back of my right hand, which held the glass, was a small irregular patch of scar tissue, where a few drops of burning gasoline had touched me, as I tried to pull Joan out of the cockpit. And now I sat looking down at it for a long time. It was all the damage I had suffered in four years of war and twelve years of flying. Otherwise I was quite untouched. Quite whole.

"Joan would want you to go on," Moranda had said.

"Perhaps," I had answered him.

But it wasn't perhaps. . . .

By now I was feeling the liquor a little, and as I filled the glass once more and drank from it, I thought: "Here's to Mrs. Christine Barna, the lady who has come to the jungle to join her husband."

Presently I put the glass away again, turned out the light again, lay down on the bed again. After a while I slept a little. And at nine the next morning I presented myself at the desk of the Hotel Joaquim Nabuco and asked for John McHugh.

4

EVEN MANAOS SEEMS long ago now: the café; the room at the Alberti; the *Dom Pedro II* alongside the wharf, its whistle hooting and the woodsmoke pouring in brown jets from its funnel. It was early morning when we boarded it, and above the smoke and the red rooftops the dome of the Opera House flashed against the rising sun.

Eustasio Moranda, of course, was there to see us off. . . . Was our baggage aboard? Bom! Did we have the mosquito netting, the water-purifying tablets, the evaporated milk? Excelente! . . . How he wished he were going with us, *but*— eloquent shrug. First he must fly down to Belem to meet the scientistas from New Orleans and the Unplaced Ones from Europe. He must make the final arrangements for the chartered boat. Then he would bring them all up to Esperança. That would be in three weeks. Possibly four. Certainly not more than six.

"It is a great adventure on which you go," he declared, his dark eyes shining. "And a great day for Amazonas." He shook hands with us for the fifth time. "Felicidade! Go with God. Senhor—senhora—Marco amigo . . ."

Then he was gone—a tiny white waving figure on the receding wharf. The wharf was gone. The city was gone. A green elbow of shore nudged in behind us, and the dome of the Opera House sank like a phantasmagorical island into the sea. The *Dom Pedro* bore down the black waters of the Rio Negro into the yellow flood of the Amazon.

McHugh was on the bridge with the commandante, and

47

Christine Barna and I stood together at the rail. I had seen her only occasionally during the past week in Manaos, and then merely to say good morning or good evening or to make a casual suggestion about purchases and shops. What she thought, what she felt, what manner of person she was, were still wholly unknown to me. And now I tried to break the shell a little. As the ship moved along, I pointed out to her the passing sights of the river: the red- and blue-sailed fishing smacks, the thatch-roofed canoes, a steer being pulled through the water after one of the canoes by a rope around its horns. Each time she nodded or answered briefly, and now and then she smiled; but not once did she speak of her own accord, and in the silences between my comments she stood gazing down at the water, intent and withdrawn.

McHugh beckoned to me from the bridge, and I went up to him, and when I returned after perhaps half an hour she was still standing where I had left her. Her eyes were fixed on the now distant shoreline, and her hands were pressed flat against the rail.

"Why not come up forward?" I suggested. "You can see the whole river from there."

"Not right now, thank you," she said.

"It's cooler too."

"A little later perhaps." She looked at me, and then away again, and suddenly she murmured, "I—I'm a bit tired, I think. Would you excuse me if I—" Her voice trailed off, and she turned away.

And that was my first intimation that something was wrong.

Through the long hours we stood at the rail or swung idly in our hammocks on the afterdeck. The green shores opened silently ahead and closed silently astern. The *Dom Pedro* crept on into an immense sunlit stillness.

We were not, to be sure, the only passengers aboard. The little ship swarmed with caboclos, the casuals and home-steaders of the river. They were white, black, red, white-

48

and-black, white-and-red, red-and-black; dark of eye and hair; short and yellow-toothed and lean, with the deep inner leanness of lifelong hunger. A few would travel on with the *Pedro* to its ultimate destination, the remote town of Tabatinga on the Brazilian-Peruvian frontier. More came and went at the endless riverbank landings, carrying their hammocks, their baskets and paper satchels, their gourds and pigs and chickens and babies. The *Dom Pedro* sucked them up into the grimy iron shelves of its decks, held them briefly in its tight crowded vortex of clamor and stench, and spewed them out again onto the same green banks from which they came.

Nor was humanity the ship's only freight. There were the cattle in their lower-deck stalls, patiently awaiting slaughter. There were hogs, goats, hens, geese, turtles; and piled around, among and beneath them, were the bales, crates, stacks and heaps that formed the *Pedro*'s inanimate cargo. On this, an upward journey, it carried little local produce, but, rather, a weird agglomerate of commodities from the outside world: oilcloth, knives, nails, cotton dresses; fuel oil, cigarettes, tinned food, cartridges; shoes, engine parts, bracelets, safety pins. Over it all crawled the cockroaches, under it the rats, and the air was alive with blackflies and chiggers, seeking out the droppings of animals and the sweating faces of men. The whole of it—human, animal, inanimate—seemed less a haphazard accumulation than a single organism; the entrails of the ship; a kingdom of heat, stench, and confusion, swarming with dirt, with decay—and with life.

Even the black carcass of the *Pedro* had a life, and a life-history, of its own. On a bulkhead behind the pilot's wheel I one day found its nameplate, but it did not read *Dom Pedro II.* It read *Glen Mutrie, Glasgow, 1903. Pedro* or *Mutrie*, Brazilian or Scotch, it was an ancient groaning hulk of iron and wood, rust and grease. Originally designed as a coal-burner, it had long since been converted to wood, and most of its side-plates above waterline had been ripped out to leave the decks open. As a result of the latter operation it looked, from a distance, less like a ship than a sort of macabre three-decker sandwich, from the top of which projected the long and lopsided toothpick of its single funnel. Miraculously, the apparition moved. Quivering in every plate and bolt, it beat its patient way against the current of the river: tacking, churning, scraping against mudbanks, pausing ever and again at the shore to draw great stacks of firewood into its voracious maw. It hissed steam. Its whistle bellowed. Paint a face on its bow and Walt Disney could have sued for infringement of copyright.

It was comic. It was dreadful. And at the same time it was grotesquely gallant. For how many years had the *Mutrie-Pedro* done battle with the river? Thirty-five at least—perhaps forty; since the lost golden days of the rubber boom. Over how many flowing miles had it carried its burden of men, beasts, produce, sounds, stenches, hopes and dreams? The figure staggered the imagination. Yet it was still carrying them, still tacking, churning, scraping, struggling. A sullen iron-bowelled Caliban, it served its master, Man, in a world in which all else was Man's enemy. Black, limping and verminous, it crept along on its unending journey and hooted its defiance at the wilderness.

King of our tiny world was the commandante, a short solid old man of almost pure Indian blood, who boasted a small English vocabulary, an enormous gold toothpick, and a wardrobe of candy-striped pajama tops which he changed on an average of three times a day. Our chief contact with him came at mealtimes, when we sat at his table, together with the mate, the engineer, and such local dignitaries as came aboard for a free meal at the innumerable stops. He was friendly and obliging and a marvellous river pilot. Indeed, his only apparent failing (which he shared with some forty-five million of his countrymen) was a complete unfamiliarity with the concept of calendar and clock.

"When will we pass the mouth of the Purús?" McHugh asked him . . . "In an hour, senhor" . . . And it was three hours. Or: "When do we reach Coary?" . . . "Tonight, senhor." . . . And it was tomorrow.

As for Esperança, he would not even venture a guess, when we asked him one evening at dinner, but contented himself with "Cedo" . . . Soon . . . Then he finished his dried fish and farinha, brought out his gold toothpick and went to work on the remains.

"It is too bad," he added presently, "that you have not visited Esperança more earlier. Three, four years ago, with the war, then this Esperança was something, yes! With big boats, with jeepcars, with frigidarias. Always there were men up and down, in and out. From Belem, Rio, Nova York. Enginheiros, rubber men, doctor men, chefés politico, chefés militario—" He broke off and sighed. "Now what is it? Pouf! Nothing again. A jongle again. . . ."

By this time, of course, Esperança had become something more than a mere name to me. The commandante talked of it; McHugh talked of it; and back in Manaos he had given me a descriptive pamphlet that had been published by the Rubber Development Corporation. The only trouble with the pamphlet was that it was now three years old, and the R.D.C. had been gone from Esperança for over two. Meanwhile, until the deal with the Southern Cross Corporation, it had been operated jointly by the State of Amazonas and the Brazilian Department of Agriculture. But apparently it was a half-hearted sort of business, and the question was, how much of the old setup was left? By McHugh's estimates, not much. According to the commandante, still less. As far as I could figure it, we would find a hundred-odd thousand diseased rubber trees. Tracks without trains. Bulldozers without engines. Faucets without water.

And Dr. Nils Barna.

At first I had assumed that Barna was in charge. Apparently he wasn't, however, but had simply elected to stay on when the other R.D.C. people pulled out. The present chief, according to McHugh, was a Brazilian named Fontazar, who had been put in by the State some few months before.

"Will you keep him on?" I asked.

"For the time being, I suppose," said McHugh. "We'll see what Barna thinks of him."

I soon gathered that he wasn't much interested in Esperança, one way or the other. "The only way we could get the Juruá grants from the Brazilian Government," he told me, "was by agreeing to take on this white-elephant plantation of theirs." When the agronomists arrived, he added, they could start worrying about it. The rest of us had more important business up-river.

From the first morning when I had agreed to go along he had been questioning me about the Juruá and the country beyond; and I told him all I knew. I still had some of my old maps—or, rather, Moranda had had them and given them to me in Manaos—and for long hours on the *Pedro* we sat studying them, discussing them and comparing them with McHugh's. The great question, of course, was whether the River of the Sun and the Juruá system actually *did* connect. My observations from the plane had indicated that this was almost certainly the case; but the mystery within the question was how, if this were so, the river on one side of the Serra Aurora could be black and, on the other, a shining yellow-gold. One possibility, we agreed, was the action of mineral or vegetable deposits in the area where the stream cut through the hills. Another was that the gleam of the farther river had been merely an optical illusion.

The sun had been full on it when I saw it: was that correct? McHugh asked.

Yes, that was correct.

There had been a strong refraction?

Yes, very strong.

And I had seen the river for only a few moments?

Perhaps ten seconds, at the most.

McHugh stroked his chin meditatively and then went on to other matters. How much Moranda had told him about the ending of our venture, I didn't know; he kept the conversation wholly impersonal. And also, I noticed, he was still not talking about what, specifically, he hoped to find on the River of the Sun. By this time I had begun to have my own ideas on that subject, but if he preferred playing the Man of Mystery it was all right with me.

"The first thing is to *get there*," he told me. And then he added: "I have an idea this Barna may have a few suggestions about that, too."

Other than conferring with McHugh, there was practically nothing for me to do on the *Dom Pedro*. With the commandante determined to speak English, there wasn't even much interpreting. Most of the time I lay in my hammock, leaned idly on the railing, or played casino with Christine Barna.

The casino had begun on the second day out from Manaos. I suggested it when I once again found her standing alone and staring out at the river; and at first she declined, but suddenly changed her mind and smiled, and we tried it. And every day after that we played by the hour. The cards slapped briskly on the packing case we used for a table. The scoring sheets followed one another over the ship's side. Presently, as we played, she would seem almost a different woman—talking, smiling, even laughing over the hands. And one day, as we stopped playing, she looked at me and touched my arm with her hand and said, "Thank you, Mark. You've been good company."

Little by little, as the days passed, I learned a few things about her. Her maiden name had been Henshaw. She came originally from Cleveland but had spent most of her recent life in Washington and New York. She had been married for seven years, of which her husband had been in Brazil for the last three.

"And you haven't seen him in all that time?" I asked.

"No," she said, "I haven't seen him."

From the very beginning I had felt a curiosity about Barna —if for no other reason, then simply as "the husband she was going to join." But now gradually I was beginning to sense that there was something—well—strange about him, and whenever the conversation touched on him she veered gently away. She obviously preferred not to talk about him, and I did not press her. After all, there were a few subjects that I preferred not to talk about myself.

Each day was the same as the last, and the next. The green shores glided past. The yellow-brown waters poured down toward us out of endless distance.

At long intervals we would come to a town, a huddle of baked earth and colored tile set on a lonely mud-shelf above the river. And between the towns were the smaller way-stations of village and collecting-post: a raw gash in the green forest walls, a rickety dock, a tin-roofed warehouse, a few thatch-roofed hovels. And the vultures. In other parts of the world men seek out their own kind by other portents—by fire, smoke, dust or the gleam of lights—but on the Amazon the one infallible signal of human habitation is a cloud of circling urubu-vultures in the sky above.

Usually I would pick them up as minute black specks far ahead and watch them slowly grow until, a half hour or an hour later, the village or trading-post itself hove into sight. Then the *Pedro-Mutrie* tooted wildly and churned in toward the dock. Off went a passenger or two, a hog perhaps, a box of tools and a bale of yard-goods; and on came a new passenger, a cow, firewood, and a hundred-thousand assorted insects. Along the mudbank were perhaps a dozen or fifteen caboclos—men, women and naked pot-bellied children—staring, stolid and silent, at the moored ship. And on the dock, or in the warehouse behind it, were balls of rubber, blocks of balata, stacks of jaguar and peccary pelts, bananas and Brazil nuts and bound stalks of timbo. But these were not for the *Pedro* on her upward journey. Through the long hot hours a file of brown-skinned men and boys moved back and forth over the single plank of the gangway, and the firewood thumped and clanked on the plates of the lower deck.

Then at last there was the whistle again, the churning and trembling again, and the caboclos on the bank still staring at us as we moved out into the current. They had not spoken, indeed seemed scarcely to have moved, in the two or three hours we had been there. And now we could still see them silently watching, until the green shore shouldered in behind the ship; and then they were gone, and the village was gone, and there was only the jungle and the river and the black specks of the hovering vultures.

The settlements were the milestones of our journey; and so, too, were the storms. It was May now, and near the end of the rainy season, and every day, usually once in the early morning and again toward sundown, the equatorial sky struck down at us. There were no protracted warning signals, no slow massing of clouds, often no wind. The sky would simply turn with incredible suddenness from golden-blue to gray and from gray to a greenish black. Then out of it, quick and savage, came the wild torrent of the rain. For fifteen minutes, perhaps a half hour, the frenzy would continue. And then—as abruptly as it began—stop. The dark veil was ripped away, the banks reappeared, and sun and sky emerged, glittering. There had been no storm. There would never be a storm.

There was only the river and the shores.

Sometimes, lying in my hammock and staring out at them, I would become conscious of the same strange, almost hypnotic sensation that I had experienced in the old days of flying. We had left not only the world behind, but reality as well. The *Dom Pedro* seemed slowly to be shrinking in size; it had become a toy boat, and its passengers so many mannikins imprisoned in its tiny shell. And at the same time everything beyond that shell had also altered. The glazed sky, the coiling waters, the gliding shores had assumed the indefinable and ambiguous qualities of a dream. The dream unrolled before me in utter stillness. It would never change. It would never end. . . .

And then at last, on the eighth night, it ended.

The evening before the commandante had said we would arrive in the morning. In the morning he said it would be in the afternoon. In the afternoon he said "Cedo." And now it was night again, as McHugh and I sat down at his table for still another supper of dried fish and farinha.

"The senhora?" he asked.

"I believe she's changing clothes," McHugh said.

"Ah, so? For the arrival at Esperança—yes, to be sure. On our humble *Dom Pedro* we shall miss the lovely Senhora Barna. And the senhors too, of course," he added as an afterthought.

For a few minutes we ate in silence. The commandante crooked a finger and flicked a cockroach from the table. Mc-Hugh took a notebook from his pocket, made an entry in it and thumbed through the pages as he ate. A few stragglers came to the tables. And then Christine Barna appeared.

She came in quickly and slipped into her seat before any of us could rise. She had one smile for the commandante, who responded with a "Buenos noites, senhora," and another for the rest of us. Then she bent to her food without speaking.

As McHugh had said, she had been changing her clothes. Throughout the trip she had dressed almost indistinguishably from him and myself—in lightweight slacks and a khaki or cotton shirt, with the single feminine addition of a bandana about her head. Now, however, she was wearing a fresh print dress; there was a bright clasp at the V of its neck and a bracelet on her arm; and she had washed and toweled her now uncovered hair (God knows how, I thought, in the two-by-four squalor of the *Pedro*'s W.C.) until it gleamed brown and golden like a field of grain.

She's a damn good-looking woman, I thought. It was hardly a new discovery, of course, for I had known that from the first moment I saw her in the café of the Joaquim Nabuco; but I had forgotten it—almost—in the day-to-day routine of life on the *Pedro*. Now, watching her across the table in the dim yellow light of the overhead bulbs, I saw it again, and felt it again. I saw her green-gray eyes and straight full mouth and the warm glow of her hair. And then, presently, I saw something else besides: the thing I had seen that first day on the *Pedro,* when she stood alone and withdrawn at the railing, gazing down into the water. It was in her eyes—or behind them. It was in her lips and her shoulders and in the movements of her hands as she sat silently eating.

Yes, she's beautiful, I thought . . . .

And she's afraid.

The commandante harrumphed delicately. "The senhora," he said, "will be the loveliest vision that Esperança has seen in all its years."

Christine smiled her thanks. The commandante produced a bottle of wine for a farewell celebration. We drank and talked, and for a while she was almost gay.

But a little later, standing beside me on the foredeck, she was again silent and withdrawn, and I could again see the tightness in her hands as they rested motionless on the railing. We stood together, looking out at the river. The water flowed down out of the blackness ahead, flickered briefly in the glow of the *Pedro*'s wood-fires, and flowed on into blackness behind. I squinted my eyes into the distance, but there was no light. There was only the darkness and the black water and the immense changeless stillness of the night and the stars. I could feel the stillness pressing in upon us, and I struggled to break through it. . . .

But it was Christine who spoke first.

"I'm sorry," she said.

"Sorry?"

"To be—this way." She paused. Then—"Three years is a long time," she added.

I didn't say anything.

"Three years," she repeated. "And almost another three during the war. My husband and I have had just eighteen months together since we were married."

Up on the bridge the ship's bell clanked: twice, then once again.

Nine-thirty.

"In an hour the suspense will be over," I told her, smiling. "It will be as if you'd never been separated."

"Perhaps," she said. "And perhaps it will be—different." She had been looking down at the water, but now suddenly she raised her eyes to me. "Perhaps he won't be there at all."

"Of course he'll be there. He'll be waiting for you."

She shook her head. "No, not waiting for me. He doesn't know I'm coming."

I think I simply stared at her.

So that was it . . . .

"I could never quite bring myself to tell you or John," she said. "It seemed too—well—absurd."

"You mean you—" I stopped, groping for words. "Didn't he send for you?"

"No, he didn't send for me."

"But you must have written you were coming."

"No, I didn't write."

"But—"

She had again turned her head, and I could see only the curve of her cheek and the rigid line of her shoulder. I didn't know how old she was. Thirty, perhaps—or a little younger. Most of the time during the trip up-river she had seemed much younger: fresh and lithe in her slacks and gay bandanas; a girl rather than a woman. But she didn't seem a girl now. Youth had drained out of her.

Presently she murmured something about finishing her packing and went inside. And as I stood alone now at the *Pedro*'s rail, peering again into the distance, I realized with mild surprise that I was impatient. It had been a long time now since I had known impatience, because it had been a long time since I placed any importance on what happened to me; and I had come simply to recognize that it might be this or it might be that, and, whichever it was, it made no great difference. Surely it was of little consequence to me now whether Esperança was one way or another way, or whether Christine Barna's husband was there or somewhere else. Of no consequence whatever. And yet—

I smiled to myself. All right, I was impatient.

Also, I discovered, I very badly wanted a drink; and while this would ordinarily have been the last thing in the world to surprise me, it did a little now, because it was the first time I had really wanted one during the whole long voyage up-river. For the past week my life on the *Dom Pedro,* with its slow monotony of flowing river and gliding shores, had been its own narcotic; and now that the narcotic was about to be withdrawn, I was reacting as I had always reacted during the past two years when there was a step to be taken or a decision to be made. I wanted a drink.

Well, there wasn't any drink. Not a real drink, at least.

Going aft, I filled a cup at the iron water-tank near the dining tables, dropped in one of the tablets we had picked up in Manaos, and gulped the warm brackish brew that resulted. Most of the *Pedro*'s passengers had already strung their hammocks for the night, and the dim decks and corridors were a gently swaying forest of cord and wool. Apparently no one other than ourselves was getting off at Esperança. I got my already packed kit from my tiny cabin and went back to the foredeck.

Still only darkness.

And then . . .

I felt it in the new rhythm of the ship's engine. Looking up, I saw the wheeling stars. The *Pedro* had turned and was slowly moving in toward the southern bank of the river. In the blackness ahead a prick of yellow light appeared; then a second and a third.

Going to the bridge, I found McHugh and Christine with the commandante. "Yes, Esperança," the commandante nodded.

We stood without speaking as the dark line of the shore drew nearer. I could see the usual mudbank and clearing, the faint shapes of a few buildings, a wooden wharf, the three yellow lights . . . But no other lights. No movement.

"It looks deserted," said McHugh.

The commandante shrugged. "It is late," he said. Then, the shore gliding closer, he shouted to the helmsman, and the *Pedro*'s paddles churned the black water to a foaming glow. The iron plates of her bow nudged the wharf; there was the thud of ropes on planking, and a moment later the thud of bare feet as the deckhands leaped from the boat. Then the *Pedro* lay still. There was no sound at all.

The commandante smiled again. "Bem, senhors, senhora—"

In the darkness below us a file of men moved from ship to shore, laden with bales, crates and our few pieces of luggage. They set their burdens down and returned to the ship. Whorls of minute insects spun around the yellow bulbs that illuminated the wharf. Then in the darkness beyond there was another flicker of light.

"Someone's coming," Christine said.

A figure detached itself from the shadows and came slowly toward us along the rough planking. As it approached the ship I could see that it was a barefooted caboclo, brown-skinned and very old. He carried a lantern in his hand, and around the lantern swarmed still another cloud of tiny insects.

He and the commandante exchanged a few words in a dialect that I could not understand.

"What does he say?" McHugh asked.

"He says that it is a fine night," the commandante said, "but that later it will probably rain."

"Ask him where everyone is."

There was another brief exchange.

"He says there is only he," said the commandante.

"Damn it, don't they even meet a boat when it comes?"

I leaned over the rail toward the old man and spoke in slow careful Portuguese. "This is a rubber fazenda?" I asked.

"Como, senhor?"

"This place is called Esperança?"

"Si, senhor. Esperança."

"Who is in charge here?"

The man looked at me blankly. Then he spoke to the commandante again.

"He says he is in charge," the commandante said.

I made another try. "There is no one else here?" I asked.

"No, senhor."

"There is no Senhor Barna or Fontazar?"

The old man's face brightened. "Yes. Is a Senhor Fontazar. Is chefé of the fazenda."

"You can take us to him?"

"Yes, senhor."

I turned to the others. "Well—" I said.

But Christine Barna had suddenly leaned out over the railing. "Senhor Barna?" she asked. "Senhor Barna is here too?"

The old man merely stared at her.

"Ask him where we will find Dr. Barna," I told the commandante.

There was another colloquy.

"He says there is no Dr. Barna," the commandante said.

"Barna," Christine repeated. "Scientista. Senhor Barna."

The man shook his head.

"Come on," said McHugh. "We'd better get on to Fontazar."

The commandante accompanied us to the lower deck and out onto the wharf. Then he shook hands ceremoniously with each of us in turn. "Senhors—Senhora, it has indeed been an honor," he said. "Go now with God and the Virgin."

He went back onto the boat, and the deckhands loosened the mooring ropes. Presently there was a clanking of bells, followed by a blast of a whistle. McHugh and I picked up our gear and the old man shouldered Christine's. When, halfway along the wharf, I turned to look, the *Pedro* was already well out toward midstream.

Leaving the wharf, we followed a muddy path for perhaps fifty yards across a weed-grown clearing. Then a low tin-roofed building appeared ahead, and the old man opened a door. In the faint light of his lantern I could see the bulking shapes of crates and bales. There was a strong odor of mouldy earth and uncured rubber.

The old man set down his lantern, pulled three straw mats from a corner and spread them across an open space on the floor. Then he picked up the lantern again.

"Senhor Fontazar?" I said.

"Yes, Senhor Fontazar," the man said. "Is chefé at Esperança."

"You will take us to him?"

"Yes, senhor. Amanha. In the morning."

"No, now."

The old man shook his head. "Is not possible now. There are seven, eight kilometers. And much mud."

McHugh swore under his breath.

Then there was a silence. In the flickering light I could see the outline of Christine Barna's face, no longer glowing brown, but white and taut, as she stood silently listening. Now suddenly she spoke to the old man. "Senhor Barna—" she said again.

The man stared at her.

"Doctor Barna—scientista. You can take us to him? Please."

The old man shook his head. Then he pointed at the straw mats, picked up the lantern and went to the door. McHugh took a half step after him and stopped. The old man went out the door, closing it behind him.

Now it was almost totally dark in the warehouse. The only light was the faint glitter of starlight on a window at the far end of the room. The stench of raw rubber enveloped us.

After a few moments McHugh went to the door and opened it, and I followed him out. There was no figure to be seen. No lantern. I turned and saw that Christine was also standing beside us.

"Wait inside," McHugh told her.

"No," she said. "I'll come with you."

To our right, across the clearing, were the three yellow lights of the wharf and beyond them the blackness of the river. Ahead and to the left was the looming blackness of the forest wall. Following the wall, we came presently to an opening in it—a road or path. This we followed for perhaps five minutes, our hands groping before us, our feet slipping in mud and stumbling over invisible roots. Then we stopped. An enormous humming and buzzing filled the darkness, but there was no vestige of motion. The boles and fronds on either side of us stood rigid as lacquered screens. I was suddenly aware that it had grown cold. Looking down at Christine, I saw that she was shivering.

"No use going on through this muck," McHugh conceded.

We retraced our steps to the clearing, and then to the warehouse. Pulling the three mats to a corner, we sat down on them with our backs against the wall. McHugh brought out a pack of cigarettes and we smoked. Then we sat silently; and presently the humming subsided, and there was a closer louder sound, and I sat listening to the beat of rain on the tin roof.

After a while I looked at Christine, and she seemed to be shivering again. Or was she crying? McHugh went to the door and came back and sat down again. "Don't worry," he told her, "we'll find your husband in the morning."

Christine didn't answer. We fell silent again. The rain drummed on the tin roof.

5

The next thing I knew, the warehouse was filled with gray twilight and a man was standing in the open doorway. "Better get up easy-like," he said in English. "It ain't gonna feel so good."

But McHugh, I saw, had already risen and was crossing to the door; and rising creakily, I followed him. "Should of used more of them mats," the man added. "They stink, but a stink's better than a sore tail."

In the doorway he had been merely a silhouette. Now I saw that he was a slight scrawny man of sixty or more, in dirty duck trousers and a striped pajama top. His face was thin and his nose even thinner, jutting long, sharp and crooked between small watery-blue eyes. He had wispy gray hair and a three-or-four-day growth of grayish stubble, cut through by a broad white scar that extended from one ear to his chin. The rest of his face was of the color and texture of baked brown clay, except for his eyelids, which were blue-veined and hooded and gave him a vaguely reptilian appearance.

"Are you an American?" McHugh asked.

"Could be," the man said. Then, as an afterthought: "Name's Cobb."

McHugh told him our names. Cobb nodded briefly, then stared with sudden interest as Christine Barna came out of the shadows and joined us.

"This is Mrs. Barna," McHugh said.

"The watchman told me there was a woman," said Cobb.

"Only he didn't say it was a real senhora." He grinned, showing the brown stumps of teeth.

"Can you take us up to the fazenda?" McHugh asked.

Cobb shook his head. "Nothing to take you in."

"Didn't you come from there?"

"No. I sleep on my boat. Keep it in the inlet over there. Less bugs."

McHugh stepped quickly to the door and swept his eyes over the clearing and the river beyond.

"This *is* Esperança, isn't it?" he asked.

"Oh yes, it's Esperanzy right enough. Know what that means, mister? Hope—that's what it means." Cobb laughed.

"We have to get up to the plantation."

"There'll be a truck along soon. Someone always comes down in the morning."

"Why didn't they meet the boat last night?"

Cobb shrugged. "Reckon they wasn't expecting it yet. It was only two days late this trip. That's the same as being early."

"Is there a phone?"

"Sure—phones, wires, poles, the works. Only one thing missing: juice." While they were talking, I noticed, Cobb had been busy sizing us up. Now he drew a bony finger along the white line of his scar, and his small eyes became even smaller. "Look, gents," he said, "maybe we ought to lay our cards on the table before we start getting any chummier. Neither of you is with Singer, are you?"

"Singer?" McHugh repeated.

"Or any of the other companies?"

"What are you talking about?"

"I'm talking about sewing machines, mister. I've had the Singer franchise from Manaos on west for damn near three years now. Signed, sealed and tied with pink ribbons. So if you're peddling Singers you better be taking the next boat down; and if it's some other kind you better be taking it too, on account of one sewing machine salesman around here is plenty—and I'm it."

McHugh laughed. "What gave you that idea?" he said.

"Nothing gave me the idea," said Cobb. "I'm just asking."

"All right, then—the answer is no, we're not sewing machine salesmen. I'm a—well—suppose we say I'm an engineer. Mr. Allison here is my assistant."

"What sort of engineer?" said Cobb, still suspicious.

"For the Southern Cross Corporation."

The effect on Cobb was instantaneous and astonishing. His little eyes opened wide. He grasped McHugh's hand in a bony claw and pumped it violently; then he pumped mine and Christine Barna's. His long nose positively quivered as he looked from one to another of us. "Southern Cross!" he repeated, almost smacking his lips. "The Grande Companhia Cruzeiro do Sul, by God!" . . . It's you they all been waiting for. And me, too. Should of been off about my business a week ago, but I been waiting around for Cruzeiro do Sul. And then bingo, here you are, and I'm so dumb I don't even know it." He paused for breath, and a note of puzzlement came into his voice. "Only we was expecting more of you," he said. "Lots of men. Lots of machines. A big ship."

"The ship will be here soon," McHugh said. "I've come ahead to look over the ground."

"They've sure been waiting for that ship." Cobb shook his head slowly. "Well, they can wait a while longer, I guess." Suddenly he brightened and grabbed McHugh's hand again. "Anyhow, the new boss is here. Senhor McHugh, by God—the big new chefé of Esperanzy!"

"Just an engineer," McHugh said. "Fontazar will still be the chefé."

"Well then, the chefé who gives the chefé his orders. God knows, that fat greaseball could use some. . . . Begging your pardon, lady," Cobb added to Christine Barna.

While they talked, the quick equatorial dawn had brightened into day, and now through the doorway we could see the sun, like an enormous orange, cushioned on the treetops to the east. "Let's get out of this stinkhole," said Cobb.

"Come over to my boat and I'll cook up some café-con-something. You can see the truck just as well from there."

We followed him out the door and across the clearing, and now I saw that, even in the freshness of early morning, it was a place of blankness and desolation. On our right was the wharf, pointing like a rachitic finger into the empty river; on the left, a semi-circle of tin-roofed sheds; between them, weeds and a rutted path. There was no one in sight, not even the old caboclo of the night before. Passing the fork in the path which we had taken off into the forest in the darkness, we came upon a collapsed loading platform and a length of rusted track, almost hidden by the weeds. Beside the track, a little farther on, were stacks of rails, a litter of corroded iron plates and the black shell of a boiler. McHugh slackened his pace and looked slowly around him, but he did not stop nor speak. Christine Barna, behind him, walked with her eyes fixed on the path. Her shoes and legs were mud-caked and her dress soiled and wrinkled, but the sunlight gleamed and flickered in the brown aureole of her hair.

And now, presently, the weeds ended and before us was the stagnant brown water of an inlet. Here was another, smaller wharf and moored to it, an ancient gasoline launch.

Cobb pointed to the name painted in faded letters on its stern. *"Cantora,"* he said. "That means Singer in Portugee —a lady singer. Get it?" He gave a cackling laugh. "Scrounged her from the R.D.C. people when they pulled out," he explained as we clambered aboard.

Clearing a heap of litter from the seats on the afterdeck, he unearthed a place for us to sit down. "Now breakfast," he said, rubbing his hands together. "That's it—breakfast." He stood looking around him for a moment, then, with sudden inspiration, opened a locker and brought out a half-filled bottle of Barbadian rum. "But first a small shot of Dr. Cobb's Liver and Kidney Tonic. Guaranteed eye-opener and eye-closer. Full of vitamins and electrons." He offered the bottle to each of us, but looked surprised only when I declined. I suppose you can always tell a fraternity brother.

"Much healthier than solids in this climate," he told us disapprovingly. "Oh well—" He raised the bottle with careful formality. "To the Senhor Chefé—Senhor Allison—and the most charming Senhora—er—"

"Barna," said Christine.

"Sure, Barna."

He allowed himself two good gulps, wiped his mouth on his pajama sleeve, and then looked at Christine again. "Barna?" he repeated.

I could see her body go tense. "You know the name?" she asked.

Cobb nodded slowly. "Yep, seems to me I do." Then he snapped his fingers. "Sure, Barna. Some kind of an -ologist feller. He was right here in Esperanzy."

"Was?"

"Yeah, with the rubber crowd. He was a Swede or a Dutchman or something. I used to call him The Perfessor."

"You're sure he isn't here now?"

"Sure I'm sure. It must be—let's see—five or six months since I seen him last."

"Where did he go?"

"I dunno. Cleared out with the rest, I guess. All of 'em clear out sooner or later." Cobb grinned, showing his brown teeth. "Except me."

He took another drink from the bottle and sat down. He had obviously forgotten about breakfast.

"That's the way it is in this country," he said, waving a hand. "One comes—one goes. Government fellers go—Southern Cross fellers come. The perfessor goes and the beautiful senhora— Say!" he interrupted himself. "You and the perfessor, you must be related, eh?"

"I'm Dr. Barna's wife," Christine said.

Cobb blinked at her with his watery eyes. "Well, now, what do you know? His wife. The perfessor's wife! Never'd of thought you was a Swede or a Greek. Had you down

68

sure for a real Yanqui senhora. . . . Well, I'll be damned!"
Christine started to speak, but he raised his hand quickly.
"No offense, lady. No offense at all."

He took another drink.

"You're not here all the time, are you?" McHugh asked.

"At Esperanzy? Hell no, mister. I'm a traveling man. A
commerciante." Cobb waved his hand again. "I come and
go—come and go."

"Isn't it possible then that Dr. Barna is still here and that
you simply haven't seen him lately?"

Cobb shook his head. "No, it ain't possible," he said.
"Back a few years ago there were so many senhors
and doutors and general-commandantes around that you
couldn't tell who was which. But now, outside of the work-
ing-spiks"—he began counting on his fingers—"there's only
Fontazar—he's the chefé; and Davidyan—he's the storekeeper;
and Frei Ambrosio, the padre; and O Touro, the foreman—"

"O Touro," McHugh repeated. "What kind of a name is
that?"

"That's what they call him. O Touro—The Bull. He ain't
a Brasileiro, though; he's a nigger from the States. Works as
sort of assistant chefé and field boss." Cobb spread his
hands. "And that's it," he added. "Not a real white man in
the lot of 'em, let alone a perfessor."

Christine Barna was staring down into the muddy water
of the inlet. McHugh got up, walked slowly back and forth
among the crates and sacks that strewed the deck, and sat
down again.

"Hey, we forgot breakfast!" Cobb exclaimed.

He set down his bottle and started for the cabin; but before he reached it there was a sound from the shore, and a
truck nosed out of the forest road into the clearing.

Now the sun climbed the sky over the jungle and the river.
It was no longer soft and golden, but a hard brassy disc of
yellow fire; and the air, which earlier had been light and
clear, lay motionless upon the earth in a thick glaze of heat.

As the morning advanced, the glaze condensed into clouds, and the clouds into rain. The rain beat down in torrents on the river and riverbanks, churning the water into yellow foam; and the water, slowly rising, spread inland inch by inch, yard by yard, through the deep forests of the river's margin. Then, as abruptly as it had begun, the rain stopped. The sun burned down again through a shimmering haze, and insects rose from the pools and swamps of the forest, like puffs of dark smoke.

On the higher ground back from the river the rubber trees of the Esperança plantation ranged in long columns across the miles. Some were full-grown trees, some mere seedlings, but all were young, the oldest having been planted perhaps six or seven years before. And almost all were sick. Their thin tapering boles were scarred by the ravages of worm and grub, and armies of insects had clipped their leaves into ragged festoons of lace. From the trunks of some of the older trees hung cups or gourds, fastened by wire to the bark beneath the spiral slash of the rubber-gatherer's knife. A few were full of latex; more were half-full; most were empty. Some no longer had cup or gourd at all, and the wires that once held them hung loose and rusted against the scarred boles.

The files of trees were long, but once they had been longer. At the end of each rank rose the green wall of the forest, and behind this wall, I was soon to discover, were more miles of rubber trees, which a few years before had also stood free in plantation groves, but which the jungle had since reclaimed for its own. Brown men with machetes patrolled the green walls, hacking and slashing, but for each stalk and vine that they cut, two new ones grew. Day by day, week by week, the walls pushed forward; and ahead of them, like the outriders of an advancing army, the weeds pushed upward out of the earth. Weeds twined themselves around the roots of trees and seedlings, and surged in a green wave over the open ground between them. They sprouted from the muck of roads and paths and between the rotting ties of abandoned railway tracks. They grew in the crevices of walls and the roofs of warehouses and through the planked flooring of the huts of Esperança's two hundred caboclos. They spilled over like a tide onto the very porch of the plantation's main house, and Jorge Fontazar, sitting there later that morning with McHugh, Cobb and myself, stared at them, drew a long pull from his cigar and shook his head slowly.

"There are not enough men for the work," he said. "Always with the Amazon it is the same story: there are not enough men."

"Two hundred doesn't sound too bad," said McHugh.

"Two hundred, bah! The two hundred is with the women, the children, the old ones, the no-good ones. Seventy-five there are maybe who are workers." Fontazar's chair creaked, as he shifted his bulk forward and spread his plump brown hands. "You tell me please how it is possible to take care of two hundred thousand acres with seventy-five men?"

"There'll be more coming soon."

"More—sure. Always they are sending more. Seringueros from Fordlandia. Fieldhands from Bahía and Ceará. Convicts from the jails. Now it is refugees from Europe. Always they are sending them—and what comes? Nothing comes. No men, no ships, no machines, nothing." He waved a hand at Cobb. "Only this one comes, with his name-of-a-name sewing machines."

"By fast freight," Cobb said. "F.O.B., Matto Grosso."

Fontazar shook his head again. "You will see," he told McHugh. "When O Touro comes—that is my foreman—we will drive around the plantation, and you will see." He took another long pull at his cigar, let the smoke out slowly, and watched the thick blue coils drift upward toward the ceiling.

He was a fat and slovenly man, the pro-tem chefé of Esperança, with a round brown face, fat black-nailed hands and a belly that bulged out above his belt like a badly filled sack of flour. He had still been in bed when the truck deposited us at his headquarters, and it had taken him the better part

71

of two hours to change to his daytime pajamas, show us our rooms in the nearby guest house, and produce a semblance of breakfast. When at last it was over, I had walked Christine Barna back to the guest house and then rejoined the other three men on the porch of the office.

Now Fontazar spoke to me for the first time. "The senhora is comfortable?" he asked.

"She's resting," I said.

"She is upset, no?"

"Yes, she's upset."

"It is great shame," Fontazar murmured. "Six thousand miles she has come—six thousand miles to such a place as this, only to be with her husband. And her husband—pouf —he is gone."

"I don't get it," said McHugh. "She was sure he was here. My home office said he was here. We were expecting him to work for us."

"That is what I too am expecting, Senhor McHugh, when I come to Esperança four months ago. The Norteamericanos are gone, I tell myself. The militarios and the scientistas they are gone, and the machines will have rust on them and the frigidarias will not work. But at least there is still the most distinguished Dr. Nils Barna. With him the latex will flow and the trees will not have their illnesses. With him Esperança will grow rubber and be O.K." Fontazar shook his head. "That is what I say to myself. What happens is— pouf—I come, and he has gone up-river."

"You're *sure* it was up-river?" McHugh said.

"Yes, senhor. Up-river is what they all say. Up the Amazonas. Up the tributaries."

"But which tributaries? Where?"

"Where—ha! You know how long the Amazonas is? Three thousand miles. You know how many tributaries it has? No, nobody knows. Tributaries, and tributaries of tributaries, and tributaries of tributaries of tributaries. The country west of here, it is the greatest jungle of all the world. No villages—no fazendas—nothing. Alongside, this Esperança is like Rio, like Nova York."

"What do you think he was after?" I asked.

"After?" Fontazar shrugged. "Who should know what a man is after in this country? Gold? Rubber? The big bonanza? El Dorado?" He turned to Cobb, who was sitting with his eyes closed. "You tell them, Senhor Mordecai. You have been the great go-after one. What is it that one seeks up these godforsaken rivers?"

But Cobb did not answer. His hooded lids remained shut, and the breath rasped loudly in his bony nose.

"Everywhere this Mordecai has been. For forty years, everywhere in Amazonas. With the rubber, the gold, the El Dorados—so many you cannot count them. And look at him now, senhors; look what he has for it." Fontazar sighed gently. "No," he said. "I cannot tell you why this Dr. Barna has taken himself up the rivers. Myself, you see, I have never met him. And the others—those who were here before—they say they do not know either. He has gone up the rivers, they say. 'Where?' I ask . . . 'Quem sabe?' . . . 'Why?' I ask . . . 'Quem sabe?'"

There was another silence. Fontazar studied the blue clouds of smoke that hovered above him, and his brown moon-face was clouded.

"Yes, it is too bad for the senhora," he repeated presently. "What will you do with her now?" He looked at McHugh and then at me, but neither of us answered. "Ah well, we shall worry about it later. When we have finished worrying about the rubber that does not grow and the workers who do not come, then we shall worry about the Senhora Barna who cannot find her husband." He took another puff at his cigar, and his face cleared. "Anyhow, to worry is a foolishness. There is trouble, and sometimes the trouble stays and sometimes it goes, according to God's will. *Deus e Brasileiro*—you know the saying, hey? . . . God is a Brazilian . . . When He is ready for the rubber trees to flow, then they will flow; and when He is ready for the senhora to find her husband, then she will find him."

We sat for a little while without speaking. Cobb's head dropped down onto his chest, and his mouth fell open. Swarms of insects buzzed in the weeds outside. Then a man appeared around the corner of the house and came up onto the porch.

He was one of the biggest and blackest men I had ever seen, and he moved with the slow powerful grace of an enormous cat. He spoke a few quick words to Fontazar and then turned to McHugh and me and said "Good morning" in unaccented English. Getting up, I found that my own six-foot-one came barely to the level of his eyes, and as we shook hands mine seemed as small as the hand of a child.

"This is my foreman," Fontazar introduced him. "O Touro. The Bull." It wasn't hard to see how he had picked up the name.

He smiled a little, showing teeth as big as sugar cubes. "We were expecting more of you," he said.

"There'll be more soon," said McHugh.

"There's a jeep around at the side—any time you gentlemen are ready." (It was not 'genelmen,' I noticed, but 'gentlemen.' There was no more Georgia in his voice than Barbados or Bahía.)

"We're ready now," McHugh told him.

Fontazar frowned at the white glare beyond the sheltered porch. "It is now the heat of the day," he pointed out. "In an hour or two—"

"In an hour or two we can be back," said McHugh.

Fontazar shrugged and reached for his broad-brimmed straw hat. Cobb, sprawled in his chair, did not move.

The sun struck down at us like a mallet as we descended the steps, but the canvas top of the jeep provided a tiny rectangle of shade, and, once we were under way, our motion generated a faint stirring of air. McHugh and I sat in the rear, with O Touro driving and Fontazar beside him. The Negro's back and shoulders were so broad that his plump chefé seemed no more than a homunculus beside him, and his knees jutted out above the dashboard almost to the level of his eyes.

We swung out through the weeds and jounced slowly along a rutted mud road. This was obviously the center of the plantation, and at intervals on either side stood the sheds, warehouses and thatch-roofed cabins that were the work- and dwelling-places of its inhabitants. There were only a few of these to be seen, however: an old man hoeing a vegetable patch; two women at a pump, washing clothes; a brown boy, naked and pot-bellied, carrying a chicken by the legs. The old man and the women did not even look up as we passed; and the boy merely stared and scratched his scrotum. Only an occasional dog showed active interest in us, following the jeep with wild barking and bloodshot glare until it disappeared in the dust behind.

We came to what had once been a mowed field, with a soccer goalpost at one end and a half-collapsed bandstand at the other. And, beyond the field, to a long row of small quonset huts. "Empty," said Fontazar. "The R.D.C. engineers, they built them for the caboclos to live in, but the caboclos like better their own cabins. When the Europeans come—the Unplaced Ones—these will be the home for them."

A few hundred yards farther on was another row of huts. "Empty," said Fontazar.

Then we found ourselves in what amounted to a small village, with buildings clustered at the four angles of a crossroads. Fontazar pointed out a church, an infirmary, a school, a store.

"All empty too?" McHugh asked.

"Only the infirmary, senhor. Because we have no doctor and no sister. In the store there is Aram Davidyan—he is a Syrian; and for the church and school is Frei Ambrosio. You will meet them later."

"Not much seems to be going on."

"Going on?" Fontazar shrugged. "What is it that could

75

go on in such a place as Esperança? And besides, it is now siesta time," he added, a little wistfully.

Beyond the crossroads the houses and sheds straggled on for another half-mile or so. Then the last of them dropped away behind, and the jeep jolted on between geometrical rows of rubber trees. Occasionally, as we topped a slight rise in the ground, we had a distant view of the river, weaving like a yellow snake through the jungle below. When the river disappeared, there were only the long files of trees stretching into the distance. And at the end of each file, rigid and changeless, rose the green rampart of the forest wall.

Presently, we came to a grove of seedlings, and at a signal from Fontazar O Touro stopped the car and we got out. "I will show you what it is like with the young ones," the chefé said. "It is sad—very sad."

He walked ahead with McHugh, moving slowly from tree to tree, pointing and explaining. O Touro walked behind them, with myself last, and as we moved on I found my attention focussing less and less on bark and leaves and more and more on the figure of the Negro. Hunched in the jeep, he had seemed merely huge—a grotesque and awkward bulk—but now I was conscious again, as I had been when I first saw him, of the power and grace of that great blue-black body. Suddenly it occurred to me whom he reminded me of; it was of certain of the giant Senegalese Troopers whom I encountered with the French in North Africa. But in the next instant I realized that there were as many differences as there were similarities. The Senegalese were all giant, all flesh and bone, with the flattened faces of apes and the minds of children. O Touro, on the other hand, had the face and manner of an educated, even cultured man. His features, though wholly negroid, were clear and strongly cut. His gestures were controlled, his few words well-chosen, his eyes quick and aware. About his mind I knew nothing yet, except that I was sure he had one. It might prove interesting to find out more.

We drove on, stopped again, drove on again. Fontazar talked and pointed, and occasionally the Negro added a brief explanation. McHugh did not speak much, but his lips gradually compressed until they formed a thin whitish line across the pink sunbaked flesh of his face. I could see that the state of the plantation was even worse than he had expected.

When we stopped for the third time it was at a stand of older trees. "With them it is just as bad," Fontazar said. "Even worse—for these, they were once healthy. Is it not so?" he asked, turning to O Touro.

The Negro nodded. "Yes, even up until last year they were all right. But then—"

"Last year?" McHugh repeated. "You were here last year?"

"I've been here many years," said O Touro.

"Then you knew Dr. Barna?"

O Touro had been examining the bark of one of the trees, and for a moment he continued his inspection. Then he turned to McHugh. "Yes, I knew Dr. Barna," he said.

"How long ago did he leave here?"

"About six months ago."

"Why did he leave?"

"I don't know."

"Where did he go?"

"I don't know that either."

"Senhor Fontazar here says it was upstream."

"It may have been. I couldn't say."

McHugh would have continued the questioning, but at that moment a caboclo carrying a pail and a long knife appeared down the aisle of trees, and the Negro beckoned to him. "Here, Miguel," he said in Portuguese, "show the senhors how it is with the latex."

We watched the man cut and probe at the sapless tree. Then we returned to the jeep. As we drove on, the sun blurred and receded, and presently it began to rain.

For two hours the rain beat down on Esperança. Then it stopped, and the sun beat down. When night came it rained

77

again, but the darkness was no cooler than the light, and the black sky lay clamped on the land like the lid of an oven.

McHugh, Christine and I sat with Fontazar on the porch of the main house, talking desultorily and sipping warm beer and guaraná. Then Christine and I played casino for a while. Whatever was going on inside her as a result of that past day's happenings, she had kept tight control on her emotions; but it was still early when she excused herself and said she was going to bed.

"I've called a meeting for tomorrow morning of all the people here," McHugh told her as she left. "Don't worry— out of two hundred of them someone's going to know something about your husband."

But in the morning, as it turned out, it wasn't necessary to hold the meeting. For shortly after breakfast, as McHugh, Fontazar and I sat in the office going over the plantation accounts, the Negro, O Touro, appeared in the doorway.

"May I speak to you, sir?" he asked McHugh.

"We are busy now," Fontazar told him with a wave of the hand. "We will discuss later your problems with the trees."

"This isn't about the trees," the big Negro said. "It's about Dr. Barna."

McHugh jerked his head up. "What about Dr. Barna?" he asked.

"I know something about where he went, and I think I should tell you."

"Go on."

"He went up the River Juruá," said O Touro.

6

THERE WAS A short silence. McHugh's eyes were full on the Negro's face. "The Juruá—" he repeated.

"Yes," said O Touro.

"Where on the Juruá?"

"To a place called Graça de Deus."

"What is it?"

"It means, in English, the Grace of God."

"I don't care what it means. What do you know about it?"

"I don't know anything about it," said Touro. "I don't even know if Dr. Barna got there. There's been no word from him since he left here six months ago. But a place called Graça de Deus is where he wanted to go."

McHugh looked at me, but I didn't know anything about it either. No such name as Graça de Deus appeared on any map of the Juruá that I had seen.

Fontazar slapped the desk with his hand. "Why have you not told us this before?" he demanded of Touro angrily. "When Senhor McHugh asks you yesterday? When you know that the Senhora Barna herself is here?"

"Mrs. Barna is what has been bothering me," Touro said. "I would have told you right away, except that—" He hesitated.

"Except what?" said McHugh.

"That Dr. Barna asked me to tell nobody."

There was another pause. "Why did he tell *you*, then?" McHugh asked.

"Because he wanted me to go with him," said the Negro.

"And why didn't you?"

"Because I have a wife and child here. Because Esperança is my home."

"What was he going for?"

"I don't know."

"He asked you to go along with him," said McHugh, "and never told you why?"

The Negro shook his head. "He was going with an American Baptist missionary called Lassiter. Lassiter had a small boat, and he was heading up the Juruá, to live with the Indians."

"And—?"

"And that's all I know. Late one evening Dr. Barna spoke to me about coming. I told him I couldn't. And the next morning they were gone."

"Was Barna a religious man?" I asked.

"Not that I know of," said Touro.

"Never talked about saving Indians, or any of that?"

"Not to me."

McHugh opened a drawer, took out our most detailed map of the Juruá country, and spread it on the desk. For a full minute he, Fontazar and I bent over it, but there was still no Graça de Deus to be found among the twisting black lines and broad green blanks. "It is something that you have made up out of your head, this place," Fontazar said accusingly to Touro. "It is no place at all."

"You're sure *you've* never heard of it?" McHugh asked him.

Fontazar rolled the name on his tongue and shook his head. "No, I have never heard of it." Then suddenly a thought struck him and he waddled toward the door. "Senhor Mordecai! Hi, Mordecai!" he called. . . . "This Cobb," he said, turning back to McHugh, "he is on the porch now, and maybe he will know it. All the no-place-at-all places this Cobb knows. . . . A Graça de Deus, you know it, hey?" he asked, as Cobb appeared, "A Grace of God place up the rectum of the Juruá?"

Cobb stopped dead and stared at him.

"What?" he said.

"Do you know of a place up the Juruá River called Graça de Deus?" said McHugh.

Cobb's eyes went from Fontazar to McHugh; then to me; then back to McHugh. It seemed a long time before he spoke. Then he said quietly, "Yeah, I know it."

"You see, it is how I have told you!" Fontazar announced triumphantly. He seized Cobb by the shoulder. "Come, you will show it to us. Here on the map: show it to the senhors."

Again Cobb looked curiously from one to another of us and then walked slowly over to the desk. He picked the map up, held it away from him and squinted. Then he spread it out again and bent over it so closely that his long nose almost touched it. "Can't manage so good since I lost my glasses back a while," he said. "Where's Esperançy?"

"Here," said McHugh pointing. "With the circle around it."

Cobb fixed a claw-like finger on the circle. Then the finger moved slowly up the Amazon to the mouth of the Juruá . . . . up the Juruá to the tributary marked Yurima . . . . up the Yurima to the sub-tributary marked Malaguay. At the point where the thread of the Malaguay stopped and green space began his finger also stopped. "That's where Graça de Deus'd be," he said. "About there."

There was a silence. I glanced at McHugh, but his face was impassive.

"What is it?" he asked. "A village?"

Cobb shook his head. "Used to be a Jesuit mission way back in the old days. Then it was a sort of Indian trading-post. Don't reckon it's much of anything any more."

"When were you there?"

"There?" Again Cobb shook his head. "I never been there, mister."

"You talk as if you know it."

"Yeah, I know it all right—in a sort of way. There was a time once I was on my way there; only I never made it." He

81

was silent a moment, staring down at the map. "That's a hell of a long time ago now," he said.

"*Why* were you on your way there?" McHugh asked. "What did you expect to find there?"

"At Graça de Deus, nothing. That's just a kind of jumping-off place for the country behind."

"What sort of country?"

"Hill country," said Cobb. He pointed at the map again. "You see all that blank space there, after the rivers stop? Well it ain't blank space—not really. It's hills. A whole damn range of hills rising out of the jungle . . . . and beyond the hills open country . . . . and in the open country *another* river. . . ."

"Called the River of the Sun?"

Cobb raised his head, and again his pale little eyes studied McHugh curiously. "That's right—the Rio do Sol," he said. And after a pause he added: "Whatever set you thinking about that?"

"For one thing," said McHugh, "O Touro here says that this Graça de Deus is where Dr. Barna has gone."

The effect on Cobb couldn't have been greater if the roof had cracked open and snow had poured in. For a moment he just stared. Then his mouth began to work, but no sounds came out. Then suddenly he was almost shouting. "Yes! Christ, yes—that's it! Why in hell didn't I smell it out before?"

Touro and Fontazar stared back at him in astonishment.

"That much we know," McHugh said. "Or at least that Barna started for there. What we want to find out now is *why.*"

But Cobb had bent over the desk again, and his brown birdclaw hands were fumbling with the map. "That's it," he mumbled. "That's it all right. Where else would a man go, once he headed up the Juruá?"

"But why?" McHugh persisted. "Why, for instance, did *you* want to go there?"

"For gold, that's what for! Years ago, in Belem and Manaos, that's all they was talking about: gold on the Rio do Sol. In the hills—in the open country—in the river."

"But you never got there?"

Cobb shook his head. "Nor no one else, far as I know. Must of been hundreds tried; and not a single body made it in there and out again." He gave a cackling laugh. "Bodies is right," he said. "If you think the upper Amazon is God's green hellhole now, you should of been here then. Yellow jack, scurvy, fuzzy-wuzzies with blowguns, snakes that could swallow a canoe. Bodies—ha! They came floating down the rivers like balsa logs. Least I came down paddling—and I got farther up than most."

"And you've never tried to go back?"

"Tried? Christ yes, I've tried. It's damn near forty years now I been looking for someone to grubstake me back there. Traders, Yanks, politicos—anyone who'd listen to me. Only they wouldn't listen. Sure, gold in your eye, they'd say. And bugs in your brain." Cobb shook his head again. "Then at last another guy comes along, and he's got bugs too. One guy in forty years, and I been talking to hundreds of guys, only I'm too dumb to talk to this one. . . . The perfessor. Holy cow, the perfessor! . . . Damned if I thought he knew the difference between gold dust and farinha."

McHugh had listened to him quietly, but now he slowly shook his head. "From what little I know of Dr. Barna," he said, "I don't think it was gold that interested him."

"What then?"

"I'm not quite sure yet."

He walked to the window, and in the silence I could hear the buzzing of insects in the weeds outside. Then, presently, he turned and spoke to Touro. "Please go over to the guest house," he said, "and ask Mrs. Barna to come here."

The Negro nodded and left the room.

"And you may as well call off that meeting of the cabo-clos," McHugh told Fontazar.

"Yes, senhor," said the superintendent, and went out too. Cobb, I could see, wanted to talk some more, but McHugh obviously didn't, and after a moment Cobb reluctantly followed Fontazar. McHugh returned to the window, and the insect sounds became audible again. Also, I was suddenly conscious of the heat in the office. The thermometer on the wall showed ninety-eight degrees, and as I bent again over the map on the desk, the sweat dripped down from my wrists and stained the paper.

After a few minutes McHugh turned back to the room. "Interesting," he said.

"Yes."

"What do you make of it?"

I thought it over and then I said: "I agree with you. Barna doesn't sound like the sort to be looking for gold."

"No," said McHugh, "he's not looking for gold. I rather think he's looking for the same thing we're going to look for."

"Meaning oil?" I asked.

McHugh hesitated briefly and then nodded. "I thought you had a pretty good idea," he said. "But it seemed to me better not to talk about it until we were off the *Dom Pedro* and I was sure you were staying on."

"How do you know there's oil there?"

"We don't, specifically. You never do know until you actually drill and hit it. But we do know there's oil in the Upper Amazon valley: the Ganso Azul wildcat outfit over in Peru proved that a few years ago. Also, it's been known for some time that the upper Juruá country is built up on very old sedimentary beds, which are the best kind of petroleum-bearing formation. And finally"—here McHugh paused and smiled a little—"finally your own reports of your flight, as we got them from Moranda, sounded very much—whether you knew it or not—as if you'd been looking down on a chain of surface oil domes."

I stared at him. For a moment I think I half smiled. Oil, it so happened, was one of the things Moranda and I had thought we *might* find in the River of the Sun country. But

84

it was only one among many possibilities. Only the wildest of hunches. . . .

"But what about Barna?" I said at last. "How could he have known any of this?"

"I don't know. But I've a damn good idea he did. For one thing, he's been knocking around the Amazon for quite a while. For another, he's a lot more than just an agronomist, you know. Originally he was a chemist, I've been told, and back before the war he used to work in all sorts of fields."

"What about Shell and Standard and the other big oil companies?" I asked. "If everyone else has wind of this, how is it they haven't?"

"They probably have by now. And that's exactly what I'm thinking about: that Barna may in some way be in with one of them."

"But Southern Cross has the rights, hasn't it?"

"The *exploration* rights, yes. But if the exploring's already been done—"

McHugh broke off and rubbed his chin with his big yellow-haired hand. Then he said thoughtfully: "Of course we don't even know if he got up the river."

"Not yet," I agreed.

"In fact, we don't even know if he's still alive."

He went over to the desk and looked down again at the outspread map. The insects buzzed beyond the window. And presently O Touro came in with Christine.

She listened quietly and intently, but the only sign of emotion was in her hands, which she held tight and motionless against the arms of her chair. And when McHugh had finished it was she who now began asking questions of O Touro about her husband's life at Esperança.

The big Negro, however, had little to add to what he had already told us. In those days, he said, Dr. Barna had been only one of many outlanders at the plantation. He had spent most of his time in the laboratory or out alone in the forest, involved in experiments of his own. Touro, as a foreman, had had little occasion for contact with him.

"How long was he here?" asked McHugh.

"About two years, I'd say—on and off."

"What do you mean, on and off?"

"He was away a good deal," Touro said. "On exploration trips."

"Exploration? For what?"

"Rubber, I suppose. The R.D.C. people were always looking for new rubber areas."

"Where did he go on these trips? Up-river?"

"Yes, mostly up-river, I think."

"To the Juruá?"

"I don't know."

"To this Graça de Deus place?"

"I don't know," Touro repeated. "As I told you, I only knew him slightly."

"If you knew him so slightly," said McHugh, "why did he ask you to go with him?"

"That was when the R.D.C. was breaking up, and everyone else was going home. Senhor Fontazar had not arrived yet, and outside of the caboclos I was the only one staying on."

"What about this Reverend Lassiter?"

"He wasn't located here. He simply happened to pass through about that time and apparently agreed to take Dr. Barna with him."

"And then Dr. Barna asked you to go?"

"Yes."

"In what capacity?"

"He said as a helper."

"A helper in what?"

"He didn't go into details."

"Did you at any time, either then or before," said McHugh slowly, "hear Dr. Barna say anything about oil?"

"Oil?" The Negro shook his head. "No, I never heard him mention oil."

McHugh was silent for a few moments, his eyes on the wall above Touro's head. Then he turned to Christine. "As far as you remember," he asked, "has your husband ever been concerned with oil?"

"Yes," she said. "Nils has worked with oil."

"Where? When?"

"Soon after we were married, back in 1941, we went out to the East Indies, where he was to do some work for the Dutch Government. It was all very secret, and he could never tell me much about it. But partly, I know, it had to do with the investigation of new oil fields."

"How about before he came down here? Did he talk about oil then?"

"No," she said, "not then. All he mentioned then was rubber."

"You're sure of that?"

"Yes, I'm sure of it."

McHugh stood up and paced slowly up and down before he turned and spoke to her again. Then he said gently: "I don't want to pry into your personal life, but I think it's important that we find out as much about this as we can. Haven't you any idea why your husband went up-river?"

Christine looked from McHugh to me and then back to McHugh again. "No," she murmured, almost inaudibly.

"He wrote you nothing about it?"

"No."

"I have the impression—excuse me for pressing the point, but I have the impression that you were not greatly surprised when you found he was not here at Esperança."

Christine didn't answer.

"Were you?" said McHugh.

"No," she whispered.

"Why not?"

"Because he didn't know I was coming. Because I—I hadn't told him."

McHugh stood watching her silently. And I watched her too. "Why?" he asked. "Why didn't you tell him?"

"I was afraid he might not want me to come."

"Why shouldn't he want you to come?"

"I don't know."

"Because he had gone up-river?"

Now suddenly her control broke, and she jumped to her feet. "I told you I don't know," she cried. "I don't know any more about it than you do. . . ."

She turned quickly, as if to leave the room, but stopped, and McHugh went up to her and put a hand on her arm. "I'm sorry," he said. "I haven't wanted to upset you."

She stood motionless for a moment, struggling to get hold of herself. "I understand," she said quietly.

"And I'm sorry, too," McHugh added, going back to the desk, "that there isn't anything we can do about it until the ship arrives from Belem. Except be patient and wait."

"Yes, of course: wait—" said Christine.

And we waited. . . .

A week passed; then a second week. The sun beat down, and then the rain. The clay of the roads changed back and forth from dark oozing brown to dusty yellow, and the clouds of insects grew ever denser above the stagnant pools. A few miles to the north, below the plantation, the great river flowed on, empty, under a white-hot empty sky.

In the groves and huts of Esperança life crept on in its torpid pattern. The rubber-gatherers trudged their rubberless miles from tree to tree, ate their beans and dried fish and farinha, and lay through the long nights and breathless noons, half-sleeping and half-waking in their hammocks. The women stood by their earthen stoves or bent over the meager greens in their weed-choked vegetable patches. The naked pot-bellied children squatted in the mud of the roadsides and scratched the itching sores on their faces and bodies.

Frei Ambrosio, the fat and fair-skinned little priest of the community, shook his owlish head sadly and sighed. "For a few years during the war, senhors, it was another thing," he told us. "There was a doctor then, and a nursing sister.

88

There was an enfirmario that was open and pipes that held water and everywhere a fine cleanliness. But now—now you see it. The yellow fever is gone, yes; but that is all. The malaria, the dysentery, the hookworm, the sores and fevers and dirtiness, they are all back again as they were before. It is a sad thing, is it not, that it takes a war to make such betterment, and when the war is over it is all gone, all over?

"I do what I can," he said, shrugging. "The foreman O Touro—he is a fine man, this Touro, and of great humanity —he does what he can too. But it is not much. It is little. These caboclos, they are good people, but they have not the schooling for such matters. They are still close to nature, and nature is innocent and without sin, but it is also, alas, dirty.

"But when the big ship comes," he added, brightening a little, "then things will be better again—yes? There will be a doctor on the ship. There will be better food for the stomachs, soap for the bodies, shoes for the feet. Yes, with the Companhia Cruzeiro do Sul, Esperança will be better again—even without a war."

The padre, I soon noticed, had his troubles not only with his flock's cleanliness, but with its godliness as well. All the caboclos were Catholics, of course, and most were regular communicants. But they were obviously as "close to nature" in spirit as in flesh, and the genteel surface of their Roman faith was underlaid with rituals and superstitions that had had their origin far nearer the Congo than the Jordan. Macumba, the Brazilian variant of West Indian voodoo, had long since seeped up-country from the coastal "black belt" of Bahía. The singing that came from Frei Ambrosio's little church during Sunday services was half hymn and half chant. Virtually all the women wore at their throats the tiny carved ebony fists called *figas,* designed to ward off the evil eye.

For the latter the padre was inclined to blame Davidyan, the sallow, cadaverous Syrian who operated the plantation store. "It is you who sell them these abominations," he accused him indignantly.

"I sell them because they are all I have to sell," the store-keeper defended himself. "But when the big ship comes, wait and see—it will be different. I have ordered from Manaos a fine line of rosaries, crucifixes, medals, holy pictures. The people will buy them, and it will be good for their souls; and it will be good for me too, because I do not make any profit anyhow from these damnable *figas*.

"Yes, you will see. When the big ship comes, it will be different."

In the jeep, driving through the rubber groves, the Negro, O Touro, said: "The trees need grafting and insecticides and a new cover-crop. Most of them aren't dead yet. When the ship comes we should be able to bring them back."

In the office, Jorge Fontazar loosened his belt around his flour-sack middle and said: "The houses you have seen, they all need paint and roofings. The machines they need new parts and the electricidad new wires and a generator. When the ship comes we will have these things, and the fazenda it will go again."

On his launch down in the inlet Mordecai Cobb set down his bottle and said: "I should of been on my way a week ago; but what the hell—my business is selling sewing machines. And when that ship comes I'm figuring on selling a nice shiny Model B-32 to every damn refugee dame on board."

"After the ship arrives," Christine Barna asked McHugh, "will it soon be ready to go up-river?"

"Yes, soon," he assured her. "When the ship comes, things will start moving fast."

Thinking back, it occurs to me that I haven't yet said much about John McHugh. As a person, I mean. Perhaps that's natural enough, however, because up to this point, in Manaos and on the *Dom Pedro*, he had scarcely existed for me as a person. He was not a talker. Nor did he have any particular quirks of manner or personality that you could extract from the whole of him, hold up as Exhibit A or B, and say, "This was McHugh." On the *Pedro* he had been pleasant enough, a little remote, almost negative, and still I knew that "negative" was, at bottom, precisely what he was not. He was, in fact, a charter member of that cool-eyed and steady-handed fraternity of men who get things done in the world—as positive and integrated an organism as a radar range-finder or a diesel engine. No, I hadn't been so far wrong that first day at the Nabuco when, more or less with tongue in cheek, I had labeled Mr. McH. a Man of Direction. And now, in the heat and torpor and damp rot of Esperança, I could see that he was coolly and deliberately taking his bearings and winding himself up.

By this time, of course, I had learned a little about him. In theory—and by original profession—he was a construction engineer; in practice, a sort of non-political global trouble-shooter, whose work had carried him back and forth across the earth from Minnesota to Manchuria and British Columbia to Peru. Through more than three years of the war he had been an operations officer in the Navy's Seabees, bush-whacking through jungle, coral and mud across some three thousand miles of Pacific islands. And I'll make my guess that he had done a first-class job. It took all kinds to fight a war, of course, and in my day I think I had run into most of them. But McHugh's kind were the ones who won it.

Like surprisingly many men who lead his sort of life, he was married—with a wife and three daughters stowed safely, and presumably chastely, away in Upper Montclair, New Jersey. Mail, on the Amazon, was something that came and went about as often as the seasons, but McHugh neverthe-less wrote them a letter every three days, with the routine conscientiousness of a man dressing himself or brushing his teeth. Whether or not he was lonely, I don't know. My guess is that he was, but didn't know it, because he was a person who would not have approved of so subjective an emotion.

During those first days at Esperança he did what he could

to restore the place to a semblance of working order. Assisted by O Touro and myself—with the occasional reluctant addition of Fontazar—he jeeped tirelessly back and forth across the steaming miles of the plantation: observing, questioning, directing, and acquainting himself with its condition and its problems. He inspected, listed and rearranged the depleted contents of the warehouses. He prepared living quarters for the newcomers who would soon be arriving. He set crews to work clearing weeds, grading roads, repairing the wharf. But I knew that, however busy he kept himself, he, like the rest of us, was inwardly simply marking time until the arrival of the ship. He crossed the days off the calendar on the office wall. He waited. . . .

According to his calculations, both the Southern Cross contingent from New Orleans and the D.P.'s from Europe should have reached Belem, at the mouth of the Amazon, a few days after we left Manaos. Allowing a week there, for immigration and custom formalities and the transfer to the chartered boat, and another two for the voyage up-river, he had expected them to arrive toward the end of our second week in Esperança. But the second week passed, and then a third, and there was still no sign of it. The rain-swollen river still flowed by, huge and empty, under an empty sky.

Then at last, early one morning in the fourth week, there was a stirring in the emptiness. It was not smoke, but a glint of silver. Not a ship, but a plane. Its faint humming rose to a drone, its drone to a roar, as it swooped low over the plantation and then banked and circled for its landing on the river. And a little while later we stood at the wharf, while the plane taxied in and the door opened and Eustasio Moranda, in spotless whites, emerged and shook hands with us.

"It is a fine little plane, no?" he asked proudly, pointing to the COMPANHIA CRUZEIRO DO SUL that was painted in blue lettering on its fuselage. "It was delivered for us in Manaos just two days after you left on the *Dom Pedro*."

He smiled, and then his face clouded. "There have been certain small difficulties," he added apologetically.

7

"SMALL DIFFICULTIES" WAS one way of putting it. When, later that day in the main house office, Moranda recounted to us what was going on down-river, it made a jungle trail seem, in comparison, a paved highway.

"The day after you have left Manaos," he said, "I go down to Belem to meet the scientistas from New Orleans and the Unplaced Ones from Europe. The ship we have chartered for them—the *Fortaleza*—it is there. Good. The scientistas will arrive in three days. Good. But the Unplaced Ones? No one knows when they will come. No one in Belem has heard of them. So I arrange with my associates to take care of the scientistas when they come, and I fly to Rio, and in Rio I talk with Senhor Hieronimo Siquiros, of Siquiros y Companhia, who are the southern Brazilian representatives for Cruzeiro do Sul. I tell him there have been certain delays and confusions, and he says they would not have happened if everything had been handled by Siquiros y Companhia. Then he says, 'Come, we shall see what can be done.'"

During the next ten days, according to Moranda. . .

The Chief of the Bureau of Immigration said: "*Marcha para o Oeste*—on to the West. That is the Brazilian Dream, and it is our wish for other people to share the dream with us. These refugees from Europe? Yes, they will be coming soon. It is a question only of the arrangements for transportation, and that of course is a question for the Department of Commerce."

The Undersecretary of the Department of Commerce said: "We have been in communication with the International Refugee Organization, and I am sure that when a few problems are settled everything will proceed according to schedule. You must understand that an exception to the law is being made in the case of the Companhia Cruzeiro do Sul, to allow a foreign corporation such rights as they have acquired. It is because of these refugees that we are doing this, and the difficulty of finding both labor and capital for work in such country. But still we must proceed carefully, for the future of our country depends on keeping control of our natural resources in our own hands."

The Assistant Secretary of the Department of Labor said: "Yes, in matters such as this we must act with great caution, for the future of our nation depends on the rigid exclusion of European communists and other subversives. Also to be considered are the differing wage scales for various classes of workers and the availability of local Indian labor. On this last item I must refer you to . . ."

The Vice-Commissioner for Indian Affairs said: "The day of the ruthless exploitation of the Amazon Indian, senhors, is long since past. He is now the ward of the government. Therefore, before the Companhia Cruzeiro do Sul begins its operations on the Juruá and its tributaries, I must require of you that . . ."

The Assistant Secretary of the Department of the Interior said: "It is the one-crop rubber economy that has for years been the curse of the Amazon. And with the plantations it is no better than with the wild rubber. You have seen what has happened with Ford, and with the R.D.C. as well. Now it is on the other resources that we should concentrate: on timber, fibres, hides, fruits, minerals, and, most of all, oil."

The Undersecretary of the Department of Agriculture said: "Never will Amazonas attain a stable and prosperous economy until we forget these foolish dreams of El Dorado and concentrate on its one great natural resource: rubber. Plantation rubber is its only hope for the future, and all that is needed is sound financing, skilled scientists and reliable labor."

The Deputy Collector of Customs said: "Labor, yes, that is essential, but even more important for such regions are tools, machinery, vehicles, power. Much of these, of course, must still be imported from abroad, yet we must be vigilant to protect our own young and growing industries. On these matters of which you speak I should like to help, but they are unfortunately involved with many local regulations, and I suggest . . ."

The senator from the State of Pará said: "The Collector of the Port of Belem is locally appointed but operates under federal jurisdiction. Furthermore, the ultimate destination of the cargoes in question is not in the State of Pará but in the State of Amazonas, and I therefore recommend . . ."

The senator from the State of Amazonas said: *"Marcha para o Oeste*—yes, that is the Brazilian destiny. In the years to come the Amazon will bloom like a garden, and Manaos will be one of the great cities of the world. I must point out to you, however, that such enterprises are not under state control. Have you spoken yet with the Department of Labor? Or the Customs Bureau?"

The Trade Counsellor of the American Embassy said: "We'll see what can be done."

And on the eleventh day Eustasio Moranda had flown back to Belem.

"And there were no D.P.'s there?" said McHugh.
Moranda shook his head.
"How about the others?"
"The Cruzeiro do Sul people, they were there—yes."
"Still in Belem?"
"Yes."
"Why?"
Moranda reached into his briefcase and handed McHugh a batch of stapled sheets of paper. They were from one Edward Wooderson, in charge of the group from Southern

Cross, and across the top of the first sheet he had written: *I am simply enclosing copies of my last three weeks' reports to the home office. I think they will give you the picture without need of further comment.*

The reports followed:

June 2—Docked at Belem at 7 a.m. Moranda, who was to have met us, in Rio. Customs informs me there will be "a few formalities."

June 3—Customs House. Conference with U.S. Consul. Ditto with Board of Trade, State Employment Service and Immigration Bureau. Immigration says that European immigrants are expected within the week.

June 4—Further conferences. Carrick (botanist) and Matson (machine maintenance) sick and confined to hotel rooms. Moranda wires from Rio, will be back on 7th.

June 5—Four-way conference with Consul, Immigration, Labor Dept., Customs. Immigration says directive from Rio instructs that S.C. must post 5000-cruzeiro bond for each immigrant entering country.

June 6—Matson removed from hotel to hospital with dengue fever. Inspect *Fortaleza,* ship chartered for up-river journey. Size adequate, but undermanned and infested with rats. Phone N.Y. office about bond for D.P.'s, and they say they will call Moranda in Rio.

June 7—Moranda wires he will be delayed a few days. Arrange for fumigation of ship. Harper (junior geologist) and Thorbeck (surveyor) express disgust at delays and say they want to go home. After a long palaver they are dissuaded.

June 8—Immigration notifies us there has "apparently" been some delay about D.P.'s. Begin interviewing local applicants for crew jobs on *Fortaleza,* but must receive clearance from Depts. of Labor and Interior before hiring them. Carrick joins Matson in hospital. Both very ill.

June 9—O'Neill (in charge of bulldozers) arrested for selling five hundred undeclared Cuban cigars to a local merchant. Conference with consul. Wire from Moranda that he will arrive on tomorrow's plane.

June 10—Immigration says they have received word that immigrants sailed on the 6th from Bremerhaven, Germany. Meet Rio plane, but Moranda is not on board.

June 11—Moranda arrives. Conferences.

June 12—Conferences. Phone calls to N.Y. and Rio. O'Neill will be held in Belem for trial next month. Wire N.Y. for replacement. Labor Dept. clears local labor for *Fortaleza* crew, but must still get O.K. from Interior.

June 13—Receive final customs clearance on everything except trade goods and store supplies, which will be left here and sent up later. (We hope.) Thorbeck, without telling anyone, boards a northbound plane and flies home. Harper and a few others still disgruntled, but agree to stay on.

June 14—Immigration notifies us that D.P.'s did not sail on the 6th after all, but are now scheduled to leave Marseilles on the 17th.

June 15, 16—Conferences and phone conversations with N.Y., ending in decision to proceed without them.

June 17—Both Immigration and the Belem city authorities insist that we wait for the D.P.'s, claiming S.C. has undertaken to feed, house and transport them from the date of their arrival in Brazil. If we pull out in advance, they are afraid they will become public charges.

June 18—Further talks, which end in our guaranteeing to house and feed D.P.'s while in Belem and to charter another ship to take them up-river. Erickson (assistant paymaster) will remain here to handle arrangements.

June 19—Interior Dept. finally clears native labor for crew, but most of original applicants have meanwhile been signed on for coastwise freighter. Matson still seriously ill and will be sent home. Carrick improved, but must stay in hospital. N.Y. says replacements will be flown down.

June 20—Departure set for tomorrow. No word yet as to whether D.P.'s left Marseilles on 17th.

June 21—Departure postponed. Intensive drive for local labor, but to date total hired is less than thirty.

June 22—Departure scheduled for tomorrow.

"And when *did* they leave?" asked McHugh.

"Unfortunately," said Eustasio Moranda, "I cannot say exactamente."

"You mean they're still there?"

"No, no, senhor. I am certain that by now they have left. But on the twenty-second I myself flew up to Manaos to make the necessary arrangements, and after two days I have a telegram from Senhor Wooderson, saying it will perhaps be yet another week. So I know you are of course impatient to hear, so I fly up to tell you how it has been."

He went on talking, but McHugh seemed to have stopped listening. . . . And late that same evening, when the three of us were again together in the office, he was once more silent and abstracted, as he sat re-reading, for perhaps the third time, still another message that had come up to him from down-river.

Presently, however, he got to his feet, came over, and handed it to me. "This is from Blake, in New York," he said.

"Blake?"

"The president of Southern Cross. . . . Don't bother with the first page; start on the second. Here." He pointed.

". . . So much for our difficulties (I read), which I daresay are inevitable. On the brighter side, you will be pleased to know that our Juruá grants, particularly those in the Yurima-Malaguay area, have been arousing interest in *very* impressive quarters. Specifically, I have had calls during the past two weeks from high officials of both Shell and Soconoy-Vacuum. They were indirect and cagey of course—just a little pumping operation, I suppose you would call it—but it was obvious that we are no longer the only ones who think there is oil up the Juruá. Confidentially, I believe we could sell our exploration rights right now for half again what we paid for them, if (a) we wanted to and (b) our contract with the Brazilian government permitted it.

"Rather interestingly, I thought, both the Shell and the S-V man brought up the name of this Nils Barna, whose wife flew down with you. What they obviously wanted to find out, although they did not ask it in so many words, was whether or not he is working for us; and I gather that they consider him the one man who really knows the score down there. My comments were non-committal. By this time, however, I assume that you have met Barna, and I would appreciate a detailed report from you on his theories and findings. My own feeling is that the sooner he is actually in our employ, the better; but I leave this to your own discretion, as well as the terms of whatever deal you may work out with him.

"In view of all this background, one thing obviously becomes of increasing importance, and that is that we actually get up into this Juruá country as quickly as possible. As you know, our contract for exploration rights extends for only one year. If we find oil during that time we are all right, because we then automatically acquire ten years' exploitation rights. But if we do not, the Brazilian Government is then free to deal elsewhere, and I am afraid that Shell, S-V, or any of the other really big outfits could, and would, outbid us. In other words, time is of the essence. Go to it!

"We shall eagerly be awaiting word from you. Cordially, Harrison Blake."

McHugh gave the letter to Moranda, and we sat silently while he read it. "It is a shame," he said, when he had finished. "Yes, a shame that we cannot move more quickly. But what is there to do now—except wait?"

McHugh did not answer him at once, but instead walked to the window and stood silently staring out into the darkness and rubbing his jaw with the back of his hand. When he turned back to the room I could tell from his eyes that he had made a decision.

99

"We can go ahead up there," he said.

"Before the *Fortaleza* comes?"

"Yes, before it comes. Now."

"How can we?" I asked.

But again, instead of answering, McHugh went on with his own thoughts. "Blake's letter speaks for itself," he said, "and it may be a month or more now before that damn ship arrives. Obviously nothing much can be done here until the agronomists and the equipment come. Up on the Juruá, on the other hand, there's plenty to be done."

"But you have no boat," Moranda pointed out. "And no men."

"For labor we can take along some of the caboclos from here. The first job up there will be to get a base built and look over the ground, and they can help with that sort of work as well as anyone. Also, I agree with Blake that the sooner we put a finger on Friend Barna, the better."

"It all sounds fine," I said. "But how do we get there? Swim?"

McHugh smiled a little. "I don't think that will be quite necessary," he said. "You've seen those two old rubber-barges down in the inlet, near the wharf?"

"Yes, I've seen them. But it would be quite a trick, I'd imagine, to get them to drift upstream."

"I don't think that will be necessary either." He paused a moment and then added: "Come along with me."

The three of us went outside and got into the jeep, and McHugh swung it out onto the main road and then off to the left, toward the river. And it was only then that I realized where we were going.

Mordecai Cobb was lying on his bunk in the dimly lit cabin of his launch, with a tattered comic book on his chest and a half-consumed bottle of rum on the floor beside him. "Well, by God, the chefés!" he welcomed us. "Sure is an honor to have a social visit from the big chefés."

He hoisted himself up and offered us a drink, but Mc-

Hugh shook his head. "Where do you go when you leave Esperança?" he asked.

Cobb blinked uncomprehendingly.

"In this launch of yours, with your sewing machines. Where do you go next?"

"Wasn't figuring on going much of any place. Leastwise not until after that ship arrives."

"How would you like to change your plans and go up the Juruá?"

"The Juruá?"

"Yes, the Juruá—the Yurima—the Malaguay. Right up to the hills and the River of the Sun, where you've always wanted to go."

Cobb looked from McHugh to me to Moranda, and then back to McHugh. "You mean—" He stammered and stopped. "You mean you want me to—"

McHugh told him what he meant.

And I sat there in that dim, yellow-lit cabin, listening and watching them; and Cobb sat across from McHugh, listening too, but with his gaze fixed on a porthole behind McHugh's head, and on the night and the river beyond. The river was black. The river was empty. But I knew it was not empty to Mordecai Cobb, as he stared upon it now across the miles and the years. For presently, his lips began to move soundlessly, and his pale watering eyes seemed somehow, very slowly, to be deepening into a clear, almost burning blue.

8

THE FOLLOWING MORNING McHugh outlined his plan to Christine Barna. She had her choice, he pointed out, of remaining in Esperança until the *Fortaleza* arrived and then coming with it when it proceeded upstream, or of returning to Manaos on the plane with Moranda and waiting for the boat there. Of the two, his own suggestion would be the latter. There were almost certain to be further delays, and it would at least be more comfortable for her back at the Joaquim Nabuco than in the frowsy guest house of the plantation.

"But it's up to you," he told her in conclusion. "I know how upsetting all this must be for you, and I want to help in any way I can."

"Then let me come with you," Christine said.

"On the launch?"

"Yes."

I knew that this possibility, too, had occurred to McHugh. In fact, he had pointed out to me the night before that Christine might conceivably be of great help to us, if Barna, who now loomed so large in our plans, proved in any way "difficult." But there were hazards, too. And responsibilities. McHugh thought it over and then he said, "It won't be anything like this, you know. Or even like the *Dom Pedro*."

"That doesn't matter," she answered.

"This country we'll be heading for is about as wild as anything left in the world. Going in on a decent boat, and after something's been built up there, is one thing. But now, this way—" McHugh shook his head. "It's no good for a woman."

"There'll be other women along, won't there? The caboclo women. Wives and daughters."

"Yes, possibly. But—"

"Then one more woman shouldn't bother you," she said quickly.

McHugh didn't answer.

"Please," she said. "Please, John."

He was silent for another moment, his gray eyes fixed on her face; and I can make a fair guess that with half his mind he was thinking of Nils Barna and with the other half of his own wife back in Upper Montclair, New Jersey, and wondering what it would be like to have a wife who followed you up jungle rivers. Then at last his eyes smiled, and he said, "Well—" and I knew she was coming.

Next on the agenda was Eustasio Moranda, who was to return down-river that same day to rejoin the bedevilled Wooderson. McHugh gave him a brief note for Wooderson and detailed oral instructions to supplement it.

"As you know," he said, "one of the chief reasons we picked the *Fortaleza* was that it's a very shallow-draft boat. About the Amazon proper and the Juruá, of course, there's no problem at all, but with the Yurima and Malaguay we're not so sure. Allison here is certain, from his own air survey, that there are no rapids or other obstructions all the way in to the base of the Serra Aurora; and, also, our calculations show that there's plenty of depth, except possibly during the last half of the dry season. On that, though, we can't take any chances." McHugh indicated the calendar on the wall. "This is the end of June. The rivers will start getting real low about the end of September. Which means that the *Fortaleza* must be in, and *out,* of those tributaries within three months from now."

"It will require no such time as that," Moranda assured

him. "The boat will be at Esperança in a few weeks now—at the most, a month. And then—"

"Maybe it will and maybe it won't," said McHugh. "At least with the present plan it doesn't matter too much. Even if it doesn't start up the Juruá until the end of August, that will still give it plenty of time for the round-trip."

"Senhor, I assure you—"

"But one thing must be absolutely certain," McHugh went on, rapping sharply on the desk with a pencil, "and that is that the *Fortaleza* leaves here *no later than the end of August*. Is that clear?"

"Senhor, I—"

"Is it clear?"

"Yes, senhor, it is clear."

"And you can tell Wooderson that by the time he arrives we'll have everything ready for his geology boys."

"Yes, senhor," said Moranda.

Soon afterward he began his preparations for departure. And not reluctantly either; for, bemused though he may have been by the Amazon Dream, Eustasio Moranda much preferred to pursue it from the strategic vantage point of a comfortable office or well-shaded café. In the roughly twenty-four hours he had been at Esperança he had changed his white linens no less than three times. He patted his face and hands assiduously with his handkerchief. And after lunch, as we walked out to the jeep that would take him down to the wharf, he tiptoed through the mud and dust as gingerly as if they had been live coals.

"And with you, Marco amigo?" he asked. "How is it with you in this new life?"

"All right," I said.

"That I can tell from seeing you. It is as I have said, is it not?" He paused, his dark eyes studying me, and then went on: "Soon it will be even better than all right, Marco. Wait and see. It will not be like the last time. Even with the few difficulties that have risen, it will be a great success, this venture, for this time we are no longer alone but part of a great companhia. You have heard how Senhor McHugh speaks. How he acts. Behind us now there is purpose, power, money." He smiled at me, and suddenly his eyes were shining. "Yes, this time it is all different. When next I see you, amigo, your hands will be black with the oil of the Rio do Sol. . . ."

Fifteen minutes later McHugh, Christine and I stood on the wharf, bidding him goodbye.

"You will not change your mind, senhora, and come back to Manaos?" he asked her.

But she smiled and shook her head.

Then, presently, the engine was roaring and Moranda was waving and the little plane taxied out toward midstream. It turned, raced, rose—became a silver bird, a glinting speck, a mite, nothing—and where it had been was again only emptiness.

Driving back to the plantation in the jeep, Christine Barna seemed more relaxed and at peace with herself than I had ever seen her before.

During our three weeks at Esperança I had been busy helping out with odd jobs in the office and warehouses and had seen little of Christine except at meals and in the evenings. At first I assumed that she was spending most of the time in her room in the guest house, but soon I discovered that, with the help of the priest, Frei Ambrosio, she had been busy reopening and operating the plantation infirmary. One morning I brought her over a few of the meager medical supplies from one of the warehouses and then helped out as interpreter while she applied the iodine swab, castor oil spoon and thermometer to a reluctant procession of caboclo children.

"I didn't know you were a nurse," I said to her.

"I'm not," she told me. "At least not a real one. I took a little training before I came down here, on the chance it might be useful."

Now that she was occupied and of service, she showed almost no sign of the anxiety and fear that I knew were within her. In her makeshift dispensary, she was brisk, effective and cheerful, calling each mother Senhora and each child by its first name, laughing at her own struggle with pidgin Portuguese. At mealtimes in the guest house she was full of questions, suggestions and stories of her day's experiences. Sometimes she wore plain cotton dresses, like the caboclo women's, sometimes the shirts and slacks which she had worn on the *Dom Pedro*. But, invariably and incredibly, she appeared as cool and fresh as if she had just stepped from a bath and toweling, her brown hair gleaming, her eyes deep-green and clear. One of the astonishing things about American women, I thought, is that it *isn't* just in the movies that they do it. Whenever Christine was around Fontazar and Cobb gawped at her unashamedly. And I could well understand why.

In the light of all that has happened since, it is hard for me to go back and analyze my own feelings about her at that time. I was attracted to her, yes—as who wouldn't have been in the circumstances? I was curious about her and very much aware of her. But mostly, in those early days on the *Pedro* and at Esperança, I was conscious of a gradual and subtle change that seemed to be taking place within myself. For more than two years I had lived entirely inwardly. I had shut myself away from the world, coiling ever more tightly into the shell I had built around me. Not to want, not to care, not to know or feel or desire: that had been the Law and the Prophets—and what I lived by.

After Joan's death I had spent a few blank months in a furnished room in Belem. Pan American offered me my old job back, but the one thing I knew, clearly and absolutely, was that I was through forever with flying. Then they offered me an office job—in Belem or Rio or Miami—but I refused that too. I couldn't face the prospect of spending my life among people who knew what had happened. Finally I settled for the remote and stagnant backwater of Manaos.

And there I had not had more than the merest superficial relationship with a single human being.

There had been Ted Hegstrom, the "senior" of my early co-piloting days, who was now Pan Am's chief operation officer for northern Brazil. One day, after I had been there about six months, he walked into the Manaos office, and, although he didn't say so, I knew he had flown the nine hundred miles up from Belem solely to see and talk to me. Well —he talked. He said what anyone else would have said. And then we went to the Nabuco and had a drink and then another and then some more drinks, and then I guess he took me home and put me to bed, and in the morning he was gone.

There had been Manoel the office boy, and the mechanics at the hangar, and an occasional brown girl with whom I would spend a night and then not even recognize on the street the next day. There had been the white faces and brown faces and red faces and no-color-at-all faces with which I exchanged tickets and cruzeiros across the Panair counter. There had been the faces and voices at the bar of the Nabuco. And that was all anyone had been—a face, a voice.

Until, at last, the day on which Eustasio Moranda had come up-river. And with him, John McHugh. And Christine Barna. . . .

And now it was as strangely new and compelling an experience for me to feel interest in a woman and curiosity about a woman as for another man to fall passionately in love. It was as if a tree could speak, or a stone could feel, or a man long blind could see the flickering of light again. It was as strange as that. As unforeseeable as that. And at the same time I knew, most strangely of all, that it was not primarily desire for her, as a woman, that had made this thing happen. Oh, that was part of it, all right. Her eyes, her hair, her voice, her body, they were all part of it; for I had not, after all, seen a young and desirable woman of my own kind for almost two years, and whatever else had happened to me in that time, I was still, physically at least, a man. But far more than this, far deeper and more subtle, was the growing awareness of a kinship between us; of a—how shall I put it?—a lostness, an emptiness, a hope and a fear that we shared, and still could not share, because of our self-built walls and defenses.

Sometimes, after supper, we played casino, as we had on the *Pedro;* and on the night after Moranda left we played late, and presently the others had gone to bed and we were alone. We finished a hand, and I wrote down the score and picked up the cards to shuffle again. But I didn't shuffle. Instead, I held the deck motionless in my hand and looked at her for a moment, and then slowly around the room.

"Well, here we are," I said.

She smiled a little. "Yes, here we are."

"And pretty soon now, on we go."

She nodded, but didn't speak, and suddenly it seemed to me that she was waiting for something—and that I was waiting too.

But *why* are we here? . . . That was what I wanted to say . . . . And *why* shall we be going on? Oh yes, I know there is an easy enough answer for each of us. I am here, and going on, because I am employed by the Southern Cross Corporation, which is looking for oil. And you are here, and going on, because you are rejoining your husband. Yes, those are the answers all right, but they are not the answers I want. Those are the facts, but they are not the truth.

Tell me a little about yourself, Christine: about what you want and hope and fear. And tell me, too, about your husband, this Nils Barna, this eminent and elusive chemist-geologist-agronomist, whom you have not seen in three years; who came to the Amazon with the Rubber Development Corporation and stayed when the others left; who keeps moving on up the river, always farther, always deeper. Why did he not come home? Or want you to come to him? Why did you travel five thousand miles by plane and ship, only to end up on a warehouse floor, in the rain, crying? You are a very lovely woman, Christine. I like to watch you and stand at a ship's rail with you and play casino with you, and I would like to reach across the table now and touch your hand. But there is more to it than that. More than being with you, or even having you, I want to *know* you, and most of all—strangely and perhaps absurdly—I want to know your husband. For I too, you see, am a man whose wife once came to join him. And I have the growing conviction that when I know Nils Barna, I shall then also know much more about you—and perhaps even about myself.

Ah, myself. Well now, myself. Obviously I was going to get around to *that* subject sooner or later. . . . Why am *I* here? you asked. What do *I* hope to find up these jungle rivers? . . . It is very kind and polite of you, Christine, to be so interested.

Well, for one thing, I suppose, I am trying to find myself. The self that I once was; that hoped and cared and wanted and loved. Perhaps all that is gone irrevocably—with the war, with the bombs, with the droning of engines and the white still face of Joan. Perhaps I am not searching for anything at all, but simply running away from this self of nothingness and emptiness. Until a few weeks ago I would have said, yes, that is all I am doing. But now I am no longer sure, for now at last I have begun to feel again within me things I had thought were long since dead. Since Moranda and McHugh appeared. Since you, Christine, appeared. . . .

Call it the past I am looking for. Or the future. Call it an oil well on the Rio do Sol. The names do not matter, because they are only names. Just as Nils Barna is only a name. I am looking for oil, you for a husband; and although they are utterly different things, still they are the same thing. That much I know, and I think that you know it too, and that is why, even though we are scarcely more than strangers, there is a closeness between us. However different our beginnings and endings, here in mid-course the cores of our two lives have touched. And our two journeys have become one journey.

Perhaps that is why a few minutes ago, Christine, I wanted

to reach out my hand and touch yours. But never fear—I am not going to do it. Do you see this little patch of scar on the back of my hand? That is why I am not going to do it. You have come to this place to find your husband, and I shall try to help you find him, and I hope you have better luck than a girl called Joan Allison.

These are some of the things I wanted to say to Christine Barna, sitting there at night in a bare, yellow-lit room in the guest house at Esperança. What I said, dealing the cards, was, "96-89. Cards-and-spades or four aces and you're in."

That was the way it was with us through those first few weeks at the plantation. And then, a day or two later, it all changed.

I was working in the main house office along about mid-afternoon when word was brought to me that two of the caboclos had had a fight with machetes out in the rubber groves, and on my arrival I found that one of them had sustained a bad gash across the side of his face. Putting him in the jeep, I drove to the infirmary, where I found Christine alone with perhaps half a dozen patients.

"This is pretty nasty," I told her. "See if you can find Frei Ambrosio, and he and I'll patch him up."

"No," Christine said. "This is my job."

And while I stood by and tried to help, she went to work. It wasn't easy for her—I could see that—for her face was pale and her lips tightly compressed as she painstakingly cleaned and probed the bloody mess of the man's cheek. But she kept at it until the flow of blood lessened, and then we saw that the outer ear on the gashed side had been all but severed from the head.

"Give me a needle and sutures," Christine said, pointing to a cabinet.

"Can you do it?" I asked.

"Yes, I can do it. I can see exactly where the stitches should go."

I gave her the implements, and she threaded a suture into

the needle, her face tense but her hands steady; and then she bent over with the needle poised and took the drooping lobe of the ear in her fingers and was about to begin stitching, when the ear came off in her hand.

For a moment she stood looking down at it, almost as if it were something she had found and was curious about. Then her lips moved a little, and her face went from gray to dead-white, and I thought she was going to faint. But she didn't faint. A single shuddering tremor ran through her, and then, with slow deliberate movements, she put down the severed ear and set about bandaging the raw stump. I tried to take over for her, but she wouldn't let me. And when she had finished and I offered to drive her to the guest house, she refused to go.

"You've had enough for one day," I told her.

"No, I'm all right," she insisted. "And there are the other patients waiting."

And that was the end of the incident—until late that night.

I remember it had been even hotter than usual during the evening, and not a wisp of air stirred as I lay on my cot in the little room in the guest house. The sweat poured from my body onto the soggy sheet. The sound of the insects outside swelled from a hum to a drone—from a drone to a deep drumming. And finally, toward midnight, I got up, went down the corridor and out onto the verandah. All the lights in the house were out, but the full moon, just risen, hung red and enormous over the treetops to the east. In the soft glow I could see the mud path leading away from the steps, and the tall weeds on either side of the path, and beyond the weeds the files of a rubber grove, and beyond the long files the high rim of the forest. With the moon above and behind it, the forest was darker than the rest—dark with an absolute blackness that made it seem actually a wall, hemming in the half-lit circle of the plantation. For a moment it appeared to me to be slowly drawing closer along the aisles of the rubber grove. In the next, it wavered, stopped and receded again.

Then, turning, I saw that Christine was sitting on the steps at the far end of the verandah. I went toward her, but stopped halfway, realizing that I was wearing only a pair of shorts.

"That's all right," she smiled. "I'm not in full dress either."

I came closer and sat on the verandah railing and saw that she was wearing some sort of plain loose-fitting house robe, and that her feet were bare. They and her bare arms and the deep V at her throat seemed as brown as a native's in the darkness, and the moonlight flickered in her hair and eyes.

"Can't sleep?" I asked.

She shook her head.

"Sleeping comes hard in the tropics, when you're not used to it."

"And when you are used to it?"

"It's hard too."

We sat without speaking, looking out across the rubber grove.

Then I said: "You're still upset about what happened at the infirmary, aren't you?"

She didn't answer.

"Don't be. Don't keep thinking about it. You did everything you could."

"I suppose so," she murmured.

"Good God, you're not a surgeon. Or even a nurse. How can you expect—"

Christine shook her head. "It isn't that. I feel terribly about that poor man, of course, but I don't suppose anyone could have saved his ear." She paused. "It was the way I behaved about it. The way I—"

"You behaved marvelously," I told her. "You were dead game."

"Game—" she repeated. "Oh my yes—game." When she spoke again it was with a quiet, almost gentle bitterness. "Do you know what happened after you left? I was sick. Right there in the infirmary in front of the other patients."

"You shouldn't have forced yourself like that."

"No, that's just the point. I had to force myself. I had to do it. You see, Mark"—she hesitated—"you see, this isn't the first time something like this has happened. I've been in this sort of a place before."

"In the East, you mean?"

"Yes, in the East. In Borneo. And out there I—well—I just wasn't much good, that's all. Things like this happened, and I wasn't any good." I was about to speak again, but she forestalled me. "That's why it's so important; why, this time, I *have* to be good," she said. "I mean my husband to be proud of me this time."

She sat looking out over the moonlit grove, and it was a long time before she spoke again. But I knew that when she did it would be about Nils Barna, at last.

"I don't know whether you'd heard of my husband before," she went on presently. "Some have, some haven't—but he was really quite famous in his field before the war. Especially in Europe."

"Is he Dutch?"

"Yes. Or, rather he became Dutch. Actually his father was Hungarian and his mother Swedish. That's where the Nils came from. But he grew up in Holland, took his degrees at Leyden and Leipzig, and then spent half his time working around Europe and the other half all over the world. Nils was a scientist first, last and all the time, and nationality never meant much to him. He's the one man I've ever met who was truly a citizen of the world."

"Is he much older than you?" I asked.

"Thirteen years. I was twenty-two when we were married back in 1941, and he was thirty-five and, as I say, already famous."

Then she told me how they had met. It had been in the fall of 1940, when she was a senior at Ohio State University, in Columbus, and Barna, who had been in England when the Nazis overran the Netherlands, was serving as consultant in one of the great Ohio rubber plants. They had been introduced at the house of one of her teachers. They had talked, and he had seen her home. He had called her the next day. And the next.

"It would be easy to say now that I fell in love with him that first night," she said. "I really don't know. But what I did know, then and there, very surely, was that I had never met such a man before. It wasn't his continental worldliness or poise, either. It was mostly, I believe, that he was the first really *serious* man I had ever met. Not solemn, not heavy or pedantic, but simply serious, with a brilliance and depth of experience that I'd never before encountered. Above all —or perhaps I should say beneath all—he was a dedicated man. To science; to humanity; to the service of one to the other.

"What drew Nils to me is a little harder to say. Partly, I suppose, it was the attraction of the Great American Girl. I must have been something new and fresh and rather amazing to him. He used to say he could feel himself growing younger and happier each hour he was with me, and I believe it was quite simply the truth. Just as it was the truth that I felt myself becoming more of a woman and a human being each hour I was with him. Which is all another way, I suppose, of saying that we fell in love."

They had been married, she went on, in the spring of 1941. Then Barna's work brought them to New York, and from New York to Washington, where he was involved in research for various government departments. Presently he had been flown over to London for conferences with the Dutch government-in-exile, and the upshot was that he was asked to undertake an important scientific mission to the East Indies.

The Pacific war, of course, had not yet begun, and it had been all right for her to accompany him. They had gone first to Java and Sumatra, then to the remote eastern coast of Borneo, which was to be the scene of Barna's principal investigations. Their headquarters was the plantation of a Dutchman named Jakob Koppel, an old friend of Barna's who had lived in Borneo for many years and knew the country well.

Here Christine paused in her story and sat looking out into the darkness beyond the verandah. "Well—I flubbed it," she said presently. "As long as it was all romantic imaginings, everything had been fine; but when it became reality I simply wasn't up to it. As I told John the other day, Nils' work was concerned with the investigation of reported oil deposits. Most of them were far up in the interior of the island, and Nils and his crew were away a great deal, usually with his friend Jakob as guide. For weeks on end I was alone at the plantation, and after a while it began to get me down. I was terribly lonely and depressed; no matter how hard I tried I couldn't seem to adapt myself; and finally I took sick, first with malaria and then with some kind of intestinal parasite. By that time it was obvious that I had to leave, and it was decided that I would go back to the States and wait there until Nils could rejoin me. He flew down to Batavia with me, put me on a ship, and assured me we'd be together again within a couple of months. And that was the last I saw of him for almost three years."

The Japs had come?

Yes, she went on—the Japs had come. Pearl Harbor had come. She had tried every way she could think of to communicate with her husband—but it had been hopeless; and then, so quickly that it was unbelievable, the Japs had moved down into the Indies, and Barna might as well have been lost on another planet. Until she was well again she lived with her family in Cleveland; then she went to Washington and found herself a government job. No word of her husband ever came to her. And by the time two-and-a-half years had passed she had almost accepted the fact that she was a widow.

"Then suddenly, out of nowhere," said Christine, "there was a cablegram. Nils was alive, safe—and in Australia. A month later there was a second, saying that he was coming to America. And at last, one late summer evening in 1944, there he was, Nils Barna, my husband, sitting in my two-by-four apartment on Thirtieth Street Northwest, Washington, D.C., U.S.A."

"That must have been a tremendous moment," I said.

"Yes, it was tremendous. And terrible too. It was wonderful and terrible and happy and sad and strange, all mixed up together; but most of all it was strange, for the simple reason that, although we still loved each other, we had become strangers. Those three years of such incredibly different lives seemed to stand like a wall between us. Part of it, I knew, was my own dreadful feeling of guilt at having left him. I hadn't known the war was coming, of course; but still—I'd failed him."

Christine paused and went on. "But it wasn't only that," she said, "because I could see that Nils himself had changed. I don't mean just physically, though that had happened too, of course. He was much thinner than before; a little stooped; a little gray and bloodless. But the real change was inside him. It was as if—well—as if he'd been drained out. Whereas before he'd been a very intense man, he now seemed remote and detached. Where purpose and dedication had been, there was now just—emptiness."

The Japs had caught him, of course?

No—almost miraculously, they had never caught him. When the invasion came, he and his friend Koppel had been deep in the interior. They had managed to hide out for almost two years, working their way slowly toward the southern coast, and from there, at last, Barna had found a native boat which took him off the island. Then there had followed another six months of slow maneuvering eastward through the archipelago, until finally he reached the Australian-held section of New Guinea. He had never talked much about his experiences, but apparently they had involved the most frightful hardships and dangers.

What of this Jakob Koppel? Had he got out too?

Christine shook her head. "No," she said, "Jakob didn't get out. Something went terribly wrong there; just what,

Nils could never bring himself to tell me. I suppose he either died of hunger or disease—or was killed. I don't know. But what I do know is that what happened to him is at least a part of what changed Nils.

"Anyhow—" again she paused. "Anyhow, there we were in Washington, Nils and I, struggling to patch together the pieces of our marriage. I wanted so much to make it up to him for all he'd been through—to be a real wife to him at last. But there was still the war, of course. I was busy with my job, and Nils with reports and research for the government. On the surface we were reasonably happy, and he was kind and affectionate to me, always. But I knew that, deep inside himself, he was living a life that was meaningless; that even his work no longer interested him; that his mind and heart were elsewhere. More and more, as time went on, he withdrew into himself. I tried to get at him; but I couldn't. And when he was offered the chance to go to the Amazon with the Rubber Development Corporation—and he accepted —I was unhappy but not really surprised. This time, of course, there wasn't even the possibility of my going along. After a few months together, off he went, and I haven't seen him now for another three years."

She was silent again, and I brought out some cigarettes and lighted one for each of us. I remember how the smoke hung before us like a blue cloud in the windless air. I remember the humming of the insects in the weeds, and the moon, no longer red now but high and silvered, and the black wall of the forest beyond the files of rubber trees.

"Why didn't he come home?" I asked. "When the war ended, why did he stay here?"

"Well, for one thing, of course, the R.D.C. kept operating for quite a while afterward—"

"It's not operating now."

"No," she said.

"He must have written you about it, didn't he?"

"Yes, he wrote. At first, when the others were coming home, he said that he was staying on for a few months to

117

finish some experiments. Then in his next letters he didn't mention leaving at all, but only that he was well and I shouldn't worry. Then he stopped writing. For a while I assumed he was off in the bush somewhere. But as the weeks and then the months went by, I no longer knew what to think. It was like the first separation all over again. Only worse. Finally it appeared to me that there was only one possible answer. That he was never returning. That our marriage was over.

"And then his last letter came. . . ."

She paused.

"Go on," I said.

"He wrote that he had brought me nothing but unhappiness. That he belonged in one world and I in another. That I should divorce him and forget him."

"That's all?"

"No, not quite all. At the end he wrote: *Goodbye, my dearest. I shall carry your bright memory with me for the rest of my life.*"

Christine drew in on her cigarette, and its tip glowed orange in the darkness. "That's why I'm here," she said, her voice so low that I could scarcely hear her.

That was all she said. I suppose that was all there was. I left the verandah railing, where I had been sitting, and sat beside her on the steps. For a while we smoked in silence, and then I said, "You'll find him, Chris."

She didn't say anything.

"If he's gone up the Juruá, we'll find him. Wherever he went. Whatever he's looking for."

"Whatever he's looking for—" she repeated.

"You don't believe it's oil, do you?"

She shook her head slowly.

"What, then? Why did he go?"

A long moment passed, and still she didn't answer. In the faint light I could see that she had turned her head and that her eyes were fixed on my face. "I thought perhaps *you* could tell me why," she said.

118

"I?"

"Yes, you, Mark. . . . Why are you here? What are you looking for?"

"I *am* looking for oil," I said.

"Only oil?"

Now it was my turn not to answer.

"No, not only oil," she said. "That isn't all you hope to find on this River of the Sun."

"What else is there to find?"

"That's what you're going to tell me."

I looked at her long and curiously, and then away again, out at the night. "Why should I tell you?" I said.

"Well, for one thing because it's your turn. And for another, because you want to."

And she was right, of course: I wanted to tell her. More than any other time I can remember, I wanted to break down the barriers and bare my mind and heart to another human being. But how could I tell her my story, now that the time for telling had come? What was the heart of it, and the meaning? What was its beginning and its ending? For a while I sat looking down at the patch of scar tissue on the back of my hand. And then, almost to my surprise, I found that I had begun to speak. . . .

I didn't know then, and I don't know now, how long I sat there on the verandah steps, talking to Christine Barna. I didn't talk in any sort of chronological sequence, or with any pattern or plan, but simply spoke of this thing and then that thing, as it came into my mind. About flying and the flier's world, and bombing and the bomber's war. About the sound of engines, drumming, roaring, and the terrible stillness and emptiness that closed in when the engines stopped. About meeting Joan and marrying her. About Pan Am and the milk run and Eustasio Moranda and his visions. About my first flight over the jungle, and my last. About the twisting rivers and the empty horizon, and then the mist on the horizon, and beyond the mist the hills and the shining uplands, and all around, the vast untouched ocean of the forest. About another wife who had come to that forest-ocean to join her husband. About what had happened to her. . . .

And when at last I had finished, the moon was high in the sky, and there was a faint stirring of air in the weeds near the verandah, and I realized that it would soon be morning.

"Mark—" said Christine.

I looked at her but didn't speak.

"It was an accident."

"Of course," I said.

"Everyone has told you that, haven't they?"

"Yes."

"And it doesn't help?"

"No."

"What *will* help, Mark?"

"I don't know. Maybe this."

"This?"

"Going on. Farther. Deeper." I stopped and looked at her curiously. "Like your husband," I said. . . .

We didn't speak again, and after a few minutes we got up and went inside and down the corridor, and at her door she turned to me and we said goodnight. Then I went to my own room and crawled under the mosquito net and lay on my cot in the hot darkness, waiting for morning.

9

THE SUN BURNED down on Esperança. Each day it burned with a whiter intenser heat, and each day the morning and evening rains were briefer. Presently a day passed without its raining at all. The dust rose in languid billows from the roads and fields, as the caboclos stirred themselves to still another change in the ever-changing and yet changeless pattern of their lives.

The Brazilian of the cooler southern latitudes is a man of temper and temperament, vital and quixotic, half filled with laughter and half with tears. But the caboclo of the Amazon is another species entirely, wrapped in an almost impenetrable caul of dull-eyed lethargy. In part this is his largely Indian heritage; even more it is the legacy of years of heat and hunger, of malaria and hookworm and rickets and intestinal parasites. His possessions are the clothes on his back, a machete, a hammock and, if he is lucky, a wife. His pleasures are an occasional cockfight and, on payday, a gourd of cachaça, the indigenous raw rum of tropical Brazil. This, usually, is all he asks of life. And, invariably, all he gets.

With few exceptions, the people of Esperança did not care if they stayed where they were or went somewhere else. Esperança was where they lived, but it was not their home. Most of them had been brought there during the war by the Rubber Development Corporation. Before that they had lived now here and now there along the rivers, wherever there was work to be done and a cruzeiro to be earned; in this place and that place and the other place, but always, really, in the same place; always with the same thatched huts, the same mudbanks, the same rivers and forests and clearings. The names of the fazendas changed. The patrãos and chefés changed. But their own lives never changed. Whereever they were, the rains came and went, the rivers rose and fell, the latex flowed or did not flow, according to God's will. And if they were now to go from a place called Esperança to a place called Graça de Deus, that was God's will too. The rumors of the project that was being hatched by the new chefés caused no more than a ripple in the blank surface of their apathy.

On the morning after Moranda's departure McHugh called them together in a meeting. Using Fontazar and myself as interpreters, he outlined our plans and said that we would need thirty good men to go with us. The caboclos listened in stolid silence, and at the end there were only a few questions. Most of them came from one of the older men, a gnarled, pockmarked seringuero called João Batista, who, I gathered, served as a sort of assistant foreman to O Touro.

How long would they be gone? he asked.

That depended on what we found up-river.

What would the pay be?

Twenty per cent higher than at Esperança.

Could the men who went take their families with them?

Yes, they could take their families, if they were not too large. The barges, it had been estimated, could carry a total of seventy people, but thirty of these had to be actual workers.

There was a scattering of other queries, and then silence again. "Deus e Brasileiro," João Batista said, shrugging. "If He and the Companhia wish it so. . . ."

And therewith the meeting ended.

As for what McHugh referred to as "the staff"—Fontazar, of course, would remain in charge at Esperança until the *Fortaleza*'s arrival and then take his instructions from Moranda and Edward Wooderson. The one "must," McHugh emphasized to him, was that the *Fortaleza* start off for Graça de Deus before the middle of the dry season. . . . Did Fontazar clearly understand that? Yes, senhor, he did. Would he make certain that Moranda and Wooderson understood it? Yes, senhor, he would. . . . Fontazar, I knew, was contemplating our departure with neither sorrow nor envy. His idea of a proper plantation was not one in which crazy Norteamericanos inspected sick rubber trees and leaking barges at high noon. Nor was his notion of the Promised Land a camp on a mudbank at the headwaters of a jungle river.

Davidyan, the storekeeper, would also stay behind; and so too, we expected, would Frei Ambrosio. But, to our surprise, the little padre promptly presented himself at the office and announced that he would be going along. "To leave my little church will of course be an unhappiness," he said, looking earnestly from one to another of us with his round owl-like eyes. "But those who go will perhaps need me even more than those who stay; and furthermore I have heard that up the Juruá there are half-savage Indians who are still cut off from the mercy of God." It subsequently came out that he had also heard of a certain Reverend Lassiter, who had accompanied Nils Barna on his journey; and if heathen Indians were a source of distress to Frei Ambrosio, the thought of hardshell Baptist Indians was a full-dress abomination.

Whether or not God was a Brazilian, He had obviously called. And nothing either McHugh or I could say was going to make the good padre turn a deaf ear.

That left O Touro—and in retrospect it is hard for me to understand how we thus far had no inkling of what was going on in Touro's mind. From the beginning we had simply taken it for granted that he would be one of the upriver party. In fact, it had already become apparent that he would be one of its most essential members. He was not only an immensely strong man, but an intelligent and capable one as well. He understood and could handle the caboclos. And the caboclos, in turn, while they may have turned to Frei Ambrosio for their soul's comfort, obviously depended on the big Negro in most of the practical aspects of their lives. O Grande Companhia Cruzeiro do Sul may have been their new employer-in-theory, but O Touro was their chefé-in-fact.

"Get a gang down to the wharf," McHugh told him, "to start repairing the barges. And assign another to No. 4 warehouse to help Mr. Allison and Davidyan line up the supplies."

Touro nodded.

"Meanwhile," McHugh went on, "I'll leave it to you to select the men to go with us. They'll be working under you, anyhow, and I want you to use your own judgment."

The big Negro hesitated, and then he said: "I'm afraid there's been a misunderstanding, Mr. McHugh. I won't be going along with you."

McHugh stared at him. "What do you mean?" he asked.

"I prefer to stay here, sir."

"Why?"

"Because this is my home."

"But we've been counting on you."

"I'm sorry, Mr. McHugh," said the Negro. "I'm happy to work for the Southern Cross Company. I want to do as good a job for you as I can. But here in Esperança—not up-river."

"What's the matter with up-river?"

"This is my home," Touro repeated. "I have a wife and child."

"You heard me say the families could go. There'll be many wives and children along. Even Mrs. Barna is going."

"I'm sorry. But when Mrs. Barna's husband asked me to go with him eight months ago, I thought about it carefully and decided against it. I didn't want to leave my wife and son; nor did I want to take them from what little they have and put them down in some jungle wilderness. That's what I told Dr. Barna, sir, and I feel the same way now."

McHugh cajoled. He argued. His exasperation grew until his gray eyes became stone-cold and his mouth a white scar in the brick red of his face. But it was no use. Touro had made up his mind. And when, after a while, he left with a final "I'm sorry," the projected up-river party of the Companhia Cruzeiro do Sul was unmistakably minus a foreman.

All of which was bad enough; but even worse was still to come. For it soon became apparent that the caboclos, who, before, had been apathetically willing to go where they were told, were now no longer willing at all. "If Touro is staying here," Fontazar reported back to us during the afternoon, "they say that they will stay too."

We called in João Batista and argued with him. We set Frei Ambrosio to work. We drove around the plantation, from grove to grove and hut to hut. That night McHugh called another meeting. But it was no good. Of all the caboclos in Esperança less than a dozen were still willing to go. The rest merely listened to us with impassive brown faces and then murmured, *"Não, senhors. Muito triste, senhors."* If their beloved boss-man wasn't going they weren't going either.

Three times during those days McHugh closeted himself with the big Negro, and three times he came out with his face redder than ever. Fontazar tried his luck, and I tried mine, but with no more result. We were stymied. Even McHugh could think of nothing further to do. Late in the afternoon of the third day we sat on the main house porch, holding the warm beers that Fontazar had produced, and I could feel the hot lethargy of sky and sunlight pressing down on us like a suffocating pillow.

And then Mordecai Cobb appeared.

It was three days now since we had seen him—or, more accurately, since he had seen us, for McHugh and I had twice gone down to his launch, only to find him out cold in his bunk. Apparently he had decided after that first meeting that the situation called for a spree, and he had gone about it with a thoroughness that left even a junior fraternity brother like myself a little awe-struck. As he came up now onto the porch he looked like something that had been flushed up from the river bottom, but he had sobered up enough to see at a glance that something had gone wrong.

"Where's the body?" he asked.

And we told him what had happened.

Of all of us, I would have expected Cobb to be the most upset. But he simply sat there and listened, and when we were through he nodded a little, and his small eyes seemed to be getting smaller and smaller, and I'm damned if all of a sudden he didn't break out in a chuckle.

"Well, well, well," he said. And then again, "Well, well, well." I'd been wrong about the sobering up, I decided.

"You find it a joke?" McHugh asked.

"Sure," Cobb said. "That's it—a joke. A good one too. Only catch is—" he raised a finger and waggled it gently— "our old pal Touro don't know yet who it's on."

We waited for him to continue, but, instead, he reached into his back pocket, pulled out a bottle, and took a long slow drink. Then he set the bottle down and winked at us. At that time I still didn't known much about Cobb's past occupations; but I knew what one of them *should* have been, and that was a ham actor.

McHugh got up, walked over, and stood in front of him. "All right, let's have it," he said. "What are you talking about?"

Cobb stared up at him with his watering eyes. "Talking about?" he repeated vaguely. "Now what the hell *was* it we was talking about?" Suddenly he snapped his fingers. "Touro —that's it! We was talking about our old pal Touro." He took another drink, set the bottle down with a thud, and, to everyone's surprise, stood up. "Senhors," he said with dignity, "you will be so good as to excuse me."

"Where are you going?" McHugh asked.

"Going? . . . I am going, sir, to answer the stern call of dooty. To make a small sociable call on our old friend Senhor O Touro the Bull, formerly known—" he winked again and grinned at us—"as the old friend of a couple of other fellers."

McHugh started to speak again, then gave up and merely nodded. "All right, go ahead," he said. "Take the jeep that's outside." Then he thought better of it and added, "Allison here will drive you."

I got up and crossed to the screen door, and Cobb followed me. Halfway there he remembered his bottle and went back for it and stuffed it in his pocket. "For the road," he said. "For the long road that hath no turning and no saloons."

Then he chuckled again.

O Touro's home was a cross between a hut and a bungalow. It had the mud walls and thatch roof of the caboclos' dwellings, but the walls were painted a trim pinkish-white and boasted wide screened windows with flowers along the sills. The door, I noticed as Cobb knocked, was a manufactured one, with a knob and lock.

It was opened by a plumpish young woman in a print house-dress. "Senhora Touro," said Cobb with a flourish, and she smiled at him, a little nervously, and then at me. She was neither lighter nor darker than the usual run of North Brazilian women, but her skin had a fine, almost creamy texture, and her eyes were clearer and quicker than the eyes of the other women I had seen at Esperança. "This is Senhor Allison," Cobb introduced me. "One of the new chefés Norteamericanos." And smiling, she asked us in.

We entered a neat, almost attractive room that was furnished partly with homemade pieces and partly with the Brazilian equivalent of Grand Rapids. There were gay curtains and a clean hardwood floor. There were a few books and a small phonograph and, off in one corner, what looked like a brand new Singer sewing machine.

"Working all right?" Cobb asked, nodding at it.

"Yes, senhor—excelente!" Touro's wife went over and spun the wheel enthusiastically. "Had we yet the electricidade, it would be even better than marvilhoso." She spun the wheel again; then suddenly remembering her duties as hostess, she made us sit down. "My husband, he is in the garden. I shall get him for you."

She went out, and we sat waiting for a minute, and then a small boy poked his head through the doorway, stared at us, and came into the room. He was about ten, I'd have said, and darker than the woman, with a puckish face, bright, very round eyes, and a solid little brown body.

"Hi there, Bub," Cobb greeted him. If he was still drunk you couldn't tell it now.

"My name is not Bub; is Tourinho," the boy said with dignity. Then he turned his attention to me. "You are Yanqui senhor, yes? I will explain. My father he is Touro, the Bull; and I am Tourinho, the Little Bull. I speak the Ingles too," he added proudly; "and I am fan for José Di-Maggio."

"What?" I said.

"You do not know José DiMaggio?" he asked incredulously. "Who plays the beisbol."

"Well, yes, I guess I do," I conceded. "Are you a ball-player too?"

"Yes, senhor, am ball-player. With the Yanqui-men, when they were here, I play the beisbol all the time. They tell me about Teodoro Williams, Roberto Feller, José DiMaggio. You have seen him maybe, yes? You have seen José DiMaggio play the beisbol?"

"Yes, I've seen him," I said.

The boy's eyes shone with excitement. "You tell me about him, please? He is big, yes? He is strong? So big and strong as my father, almost—"

He was still talking when his mother reappeared, followed by Touro. The big Negro had to stoop to get through the doorway, and the ceiling of the room had apparently been built to allow him exactly an inch leeway. He had a friendly nod for Cobb and myself and then turned toward the boy. "You've been out barefoot again, haven't you?" he said.

Little Bull didn't answer.

"Haven't you?" he repeated.

His son nodded reluctantly, and Touro gave him a solid slap on the rump. "Get inside there and put on your shoes," he ordered.

The boy bit his lip and went out, his mother following him, scolding. "It's hookworm," Touro explained to us. "Every barefoot kid on the Amazon has rotten insides from it; but no, he won't listen. All he's worried about is that somebody'll think he's a sissy."

"Fine youngster though, Touro," said Cobb.

"Could be worse," Touro conceded.

"The senhora's looking fine too."

"Tereza's all right, I guess. A little upset, maybe, the last few days."

"Upset?" Cobb repeated. "How come?"

"For the same reason everyone else is upset."

"Oh," said Cobb blandly. "You mean this little business about the move?"

"Yes," Touro said. "That's what I mean."

Cobb nodded understandingly and was silent a moment, his eyes on the new sewing machine in the corner. Then he said: "You know, it's sort of a coincidence you mentioning that, on account of it's what I wanted to have a little chat about. Leastwise, Mr. McHugh wanted to have a little chat, but seeing as you and me are sort of old friends, I told him maybe I could do it for him."

Touro had taken a chair facing us and was sitting with feet planted on the floor and hands resting on his knees. He was looking steadily at Cobb now, but didn't move or speak.

Cobb cleared his throat. "I was thinking, old boy, that maybe you'd changed your mind."

"No," said Touro, "I haven't changed it."

"Can't tear yourself away from dear old Esperanzy, hey?"

"Esperança's my home."

"Yeah, yeah—sure. It's a lot of other people's home too, only all the rest got sense enough to want to get out."

"No," the Negro said. "The others want to stay too."

"Only since you been working on 'em." Cobb shook his head. "Damned if I understand what's come over you, Touro. You turning into a Red soapboxer or something?"

There was a long wait before Touro answered. Then he leaned a little forward in his chair and spoke very quietly and evenly. "Look, Mr. Cobb," he said, "I'm not a man that wants trouble. I've spent most of my life trying to avoid trouble, and that's one of the reasons I'm in Esperança. My family and I have been here a long while now, and so have some of the other families. We worked for the Oliveira Company, that ran the place before the war; and then for the Rubber Development Corporation and the Department of Agriculture; and we're perfectly willing to go on working for Southern Cross. But here. Where our home is. You can't pull up human lives by the roots, like so many weeds."

"Nobody's trying to pull anybody up. We're just giving you all the chance to better yourselves."

"What I'd like to see bettered first is Esperança. Back when the R.D.C. was here it was the best fazenda on the Amazon. And it can be again, too. Forty or fifty more families, a few trained plantation men, a doctor, a school-teacher—that's all it needs. That's what we thought we might be getting when Southern Cross took over."

"Sure, sure," said Cobb. "That's what you *will* be getting. All that stuff. The works. When the ship comes—wait and see. Only first there's this job to do up-river."

Touro shook his head slowly. "I know that kind of job," he said. "The old Amazon job. . . . Sometimes it's gold. Sometimes it's rubber or mahogany or timbo or something else. And now it's oil. Get there first—rip up the country—grab and run. That's how it is for the chefés—the big fellows —if they're lucky. But for the caboclos—the little ones— there's nothing to grab and no place to run to. I've seen them up and down the river, and so have you. Without a home. Without a cruzeiro. . . . No thanks, Mr. Cobb, that's not the sort of job I'm looking for."

Cobb ran his tongue back and forth over his lips. I knew he was slowly getting ready to spring a trap, but I had no idea as yet what it would be.

"You're dead wrong about that, Touro boy," he said. "Matter of fact, talking that way about a fine outfit like Southern Cross is downright insulting." He raised his hand amicably. "But let's forget it. If you don't want to go, okay; nobody's going to force you, and I'm sure it'll be all right with Mr. McHugh for you to stay right here. Of course I doubt if the Company could pay you a salary, seeing as how you're turning down their job. And maybe the senhora wouldn't be too good a credit risk any more on that nice new machine—"

Touro started to speak, but Cobb raised his hand again. "That's all beside the point, though. Okay, you're not going. But about the others now. Ain't it a little unfair to keep *them* from going?"

"I'm not keeping them," the Negro said.

"You advised 'em not to, didn't you?"

"They're simple ignorant people, and they trust me. When they asked my opinion I gave it to them."

"And you don't think maybe you could change it a little?"

"No, Mr. Cobb, I don't."

Cobb sighed and shook his head. "You're making things very tough for me, Touro boy," he said. "I'd sure hate to see this nice family of yours get all messed up because of a piddling business like this."

Touro's eyes narrowed very slightly. "My family?" he repeated.

"Yeah, the senhora and that fine kid of yours. It'd be a hell of a note to lose 'em, wouldn't it? Really a hell of a note if you—well—had to go away and leave 'em all alone."

"But I'm not going away."

"I'm not talking about upstream, old boy. There you can take 'em with you, of course. I was just thinking that one of these days you might find yourself heading downstream—so far down that maybe pretty soon you'd be all the way to Belem."

Cobb paused, and I saw the Negro's big hands close slowly over his knees. "Go on," he said.

Cobb blinked his watery eyes and cleared his throat again. "Well, to tell the truth, Touro boy, there's a little something been on my conscience quite a while now. Goes way back twelve years or so; to 'thirty-six I guess it was, or maybe 'thirty-five. Well, anyhow, I was down in Belem around then, tending to some business, and I remember one morning learning as how there'd been a hell of a ruckus on one of the U.S. banana boats that was loading down at the wharves. Seems one of the officers had got his head bashed in the night before, and a big nigger—no offense, old boy—a big nigger stoker had jumped ship and disappeared.

"It was none of my affair, of course, and I guess I'd of never given it another thought, only that a few days later the chefé of police in Belem—he's an old friend of mine—calls me in and says that, seeing as I got around the country more than most, maybe I'd keep an eye open for this creep. 'Is the officer feller dead?' I ask, and he says you're damn right he's dead, there's a hole in his head big enough to hold a papaya. 'And what's the colored gentleman's name?' I ask next. And he tells me; only it don't mean much of course, on account of the guy sure enough will be calling himself something else. So he gives me a picture. It was a damn nice picture too; must of been took by a real good photographer."

Cobb paused and ran his tongue between his lips. "Well, I told the chefé, sure I'd look around. Only you know how those things are. Pretty soon I forgot all about it. Never gave the whole business a thought until years later—must of been during the war when I started calling up here at Esperanzy—and then in a funny-like sort of a way my conscience started bothering me. That was a hell of a way to let down your old pal the chefé, I started telling myself. A good law-abiding citizen like Mordecai Cobb ought to be helping out the policia when they got problems on their hands."

He got slowly to his feet. "Yep, a conscience can be a damn pesky thing, old boy," he said, shaking his head. "Sometimes I get to thinking: hell, maybe that Bull Jackson feller is right here in Esperanzy and I don't do nothing about it. Maybe I could nose around a little and put the finger on him. After all, the *Dom Pedro*'ll be putting in here again in a few days now, on her way down river, and I could just load him aboard and ship him off F.O.B. to my old pal the chefé.

"Yep, a conscience is a hell of a thing, sure enough. Keeps a guy awake nights."

Touro hadn't moved, and he didn't move now. His hands were still on his knees and his feet still flat on the floor; but when I looked at his eyes, they were no longer the eyes of the same man I had been looking at five minutes before. The only thing I was glad about was that they were fixed on Mordecai Cobb and not on me.

I got up too.

"Well, it's been a mighty nice little visit," said Cobb, "and we'll be glad to see you any time you want to make us a return one up at the office. Glad the senhora likes the new machine. And, oh yeah—" He took a wrapped candy bar from his pocket and laid it on a table. "Here's a little something I brought for that fine kid of yours."

Touro neither spoke nor moved, and after a few moments we crossed to the door and went out. When we got to the jeep Cobb opened his bottle, which he'd left on the seat, and had a long drink.

"How about it?" he asked me.

And this time I took one.

That was—what? Call it Monday. Nothing happened that evening; nothing happened Tuesday; but early Wednesday morning O Touro appeared at the office and asked to see

McHugh. They were closeted for a bare ten minutes. The big Negro said simply that he had reconsidered and would go, and McHugh said good enough and gave him his instructions for getting things started. As far as I could gather, there was no argument, no unpleasantness. By evening fifty caboclos had signified their willingness to make the move, and the next day work got under way in earnest at the warehouse and the wharf.

I had of course told McHugh what had happened at Touro's house. And I told him, too, that I didn't much like it. Neither did he, said McHugh, but added that what might or might not have happened thirteen years ago needn't concern us now. Touro or Jackson or whatever, the Negro was obviously a first-class foreman, and we needed him.

"I wasn't thinking of what he's done," I said. "How about what he *may* do—to Cobb?"

McHugh shook his head. "I brought that up with him. And I've also talked with the padre here, who's known him for some time. He said Touro's the steadiest man on the plantation; the best family man; and by far the most intelligent. Besides, I like the man personally. I trust him."

"So do I," I said. "But how about the other side of it, then? Is it fair to him?"

"Is what fair?"

"Forcing him to go along if he doesn't want to?"

McHugh bit his lip and his gray eyes hardened. "Who's forcing him to go along?" he said. "You? I? The corporation? What goes on between him and Cobb is their business, not ours. All I know is that he's a good man and we need him, and the caboclos won't go without him. What am I supposed to do—go out of my way to wreck our plans?"

"You're the boss," I said.

But I still didn't like it as a way to start off the operation.

Nor did I much like another aspect of the situation which I'd been turning over in my mind since Moranda had left. And the following day I mentioned this also to McHugh.

"What about the D.P.'s?" I asked him.

"The D.P.'s?"

"They'll be arriving soon now. Shouldn't our first job be to get them settled?"

Obviously the refugees were the last thing in McHugh's mind. And the last thing he wanted there. "For all we know, they're not even in the country yet," he said. "We'll worry about them when they come."

"We'll be up in the jungle when they come."

McHugh looked at me for a moment and then said quietly: "Look, Allison, you were in the war, weren't you? Things didn't always work out just right, did they?—even in that infallible Air Force of yours. What did you do: lie down and give up every time there was a snafu? You tried to get out of the snafu, didn't you? You said to hell with the snafu and kept your eye on the main objective. . . . At least that's what anyone who was worth a damn did. And that's what I'm trying to do here."

Suddenly, for the first time since I'd known him, he was really angry. "I thought you wanted to go along on this thing?" he snapped.

"That's right," I said.

"Then why do you keep looking for an excuse to lie down and give up? First it was the Touro business. Now it's the D.P.'s. If you don't want to go along, don't. Pull out. Go back on the *Dom Pedro*. We'll get along all right up there. Barna'll show us the way. . . . But if you stay on, remember we're here for just one thing: oil. And that we're operating on just one principle, and that's two little words from the Seabees: *Can do*."

He stopped, mopped the sweat from his face with a handkerchief, and then stood staring belligerently out the window. When he turned back to me his voice was quiet again.

"Is that clear?" he asked.

I nodded, without speaking. Yes, it was clear all right, I thought. And one other thing was clear too. Touro Jackson may have been indispensable. I wasn't.

We let it go at that. We went to work. And for a week thereafter, in the dust and hot sunlight, the plantation hummed with an activity that I wouldn't have believed possible. Crates and tins and bales moved by the truckload over the rutted road from the warehouses to the wharf. The sound of hammering and sawing arose from the two barges in the inlet. A gang of caboclos worked on the reconditioning of three canoes with outboard motors, which McHugh had exhumed from storage for possible use in up-river exploration. And on his nearby launch Cobb tinkered alternately, and with equal enthusiasm, with his engine and his Barbadian rum.

A few days before the *Dom Pedro* was due on its return trip, he asked me to write a letter for him. It was to the Singer Sewing Machine agent in Manaos, and the gist was that he was about to open up the richest sales territory since Marco Polo visited Cathay—and that he might be a little while in the process.

"Not telling them about the Big Bonanza?" I asked.

"Hey?"

"About all that gold you're going to find."

"Time enough for that when I get back. Then they can take their damn machines and hemstitch their behinds."

I sat looking at him, trying to figure out what went on behind those tiny water-blue eyes. "You really think you're going to find gold, don't you?" I said.

"I'm going to find something, laddy—don't you worry about that. Up on that Rio do Sol there's something, sure as you're born. Maybe it's yellow gold, like I used to think. Maybe it's black gold—green gold—any damn color gold; that don't matter. But there's something—sure. I've known that for thirty-eight years, and now I know it better than ever."

"But—"

"But nothing," he said. "What do you think this Barna feller went up there for? A cure, maybe? He went on account of there's something there he wants. That's the

136

tip-off, laddy: Barna. And if it's something good enough for the Perfessor to go hunting after, by God, it's good enough for me!"

During that time I was keeping my eyes open for signs of trouble between Cobb and Touro. And so too, I think, was McHugh. But there were no signs at all. The big Negro went quietly about his work, treating Cobb as impersonally and courteously as he did everyone else; and after a while it was hard for me to recall, or even to credit, the terrible look which had come into his eyes that afternoon, as he sat silently listening while the trap sprang shut on him. Cobb, for his part, was as full of "Touro boys" and "old fellers" as ever and positively went out of his way to pay little attentions to the Negro's wife and youngster. He was a cute old cookie, that Mordecai Cobb.

McHugh was here, there and everywhere, tireless and effective, an old operations officer in his element. Christine divided her time between the infirmary and the homes of the caboclo families who were about to move, helping the women with their problems and preparations. Frei Ambrosio was busy. Davidyan and even Fontazar were busy. I was busy. For ten or twelve hours each day I shuttled back and forth between office, wharf and warehouse, taking orders, giving orders, assigning, checking, supervising; and when night came I was so tired that I fell asleep almost as soon as I crept into my cot. I thought of nothing beyond the day just past and the day to come. I did my job. I ate. I slept.

. . . . Until the night before the *Dom Pedro* was due on its down trip from the Peruvian border, and then suddenly, irrevocably, sleep was gone, and again I lay in the darkness, with the sheet a sodden rag under my body and the hum of insects seeming to rise to a roaring in my ears. And again I got up and went out onto the verandah, but on this night no one else was there. I sat alone for a long time. I thought for a long time. About Touro and Cobb. About the D.P.'s. About Christine and Nils Barna. About where I was and where I had come from and where I was going.

137

And presently I had decided, dispassionately, almost coolly, that I was not going. This thing in which I had involved myself was a fantastic and meaningless charade. From Manaos to Esperança and from Esperança to Graça de Deus; up the Amazon, the Juruá, the Yurima, the Malaguay; farther and farther, deeper and deeper . . . And for what? . . . It wasn't my job, my profession, as it was Mc-Hugh's. I wasn't looking for a husband, like Christine, or the Big Bonanza, like Cobb, or security, like Touro, or souls to save, like Frei Ambrosio, or a new and better home, like the caboclos. It was all fantasy and self-delusion and a futile searching for a dream that was dead and gone. It was without sense, without purpose or hope, and I might as well go back to the nothing-at-all of Manaos.

Yes, I decided—I would go back. In the morning I would speak to McHugh. . . .

But I didn't speak to McHugh. I went about my work at the office, the wharf and the warehouses. And in the late afternoon of the following day, when the *Pedro* pulled out from Esperança, there was no Mark Allison aboard, any more than there was a Bull Jackson. I remember I stood on the mudbank, near the jetty, watching the little boat until it was out of sight; and then I turned and stood looking upstream, while the afternoon flowed toward evening and the river flowed down out of the blazing sunset; and I knew then, once and for all, that upstream was where I was going, the Juruá, the Yurima and the Malaguay were where I was going, the River of the Sun was where I was going; where Nils Barna had gone and Christine Barna was going was where I was going too.

Why?

I smiled to myself. . . .

Perhaps Dr. Nils Barna, when we found him, could tell me why.

10

THE GIANT AMONG rivers is an unconquered river. The
Mississippi has long since been domesticated. The Nile and
Ganges, Volga and Yangtse have for thousands of years been
the highways and irrigation ditches of great civilizations.
Even the dark Congo has been largely tamed to the service
of man. But the Amazon flows on today as it has always
flowed, with scarcely an indication or acknowledgment that
there is such a creature as man upon the earth. It has met
no master, nor even a worthy antagonist.

March to the West, say the Brazilians, as the Americans
of all nations have said before them. But in Amazonia the
march is still a dream. Along fifty thousand miles of river
and tributary and sub-tributary there is not a bridge, not a
dam, not a power plant, not a reservoir, not a levee. Its
villages, missions and trading-posts are as widely spaced as
islands in the sea. Red man, black man and white man; conquistador, priests, homesteader, scientist, explorer, ex-
ploiter; ship and plane and machine and dream of empire—
all of these together have raised no more than a ripple on
the smooth surface of its yellow tide.

And now Mordecai Cobb's launch and two ancient barges
moved slowly up the main stream toward the mouth of the
Juruá. For a hundred miles there were no villages, no
fazendas, no boats, nothing. The path behind us flowed on
into the world we had left; past Esperança, Manaos, Belem;
across jungles and oceans; to Rio, to New York, to Europe,
to the parliament of nations; through capitals and sky-

scrapers and board rooms and quonset huts; into the hopes and fears of many nations and the minds and hearts of many men. But on the path ahead there was only a green and sun-lit stillness.

If the *Dom Pedro,* when we boarded it, had seemed a Disney creation, our new floating home was pure Dali. More or less in the center of things was Cobb's launch, the *Cantora,* straining, quivering and angrily spitting oil and grease. On the starboard side a barge, lashed to it, projected like a broad flat wing, and astern the second barge followed along as a sort of roped-on tail—the whole looking like nothing so much as a huge one-winged bird wobbling along through the water and unable to take off. Theoretically the launch was for—well—let's call it "the staff," the side barge for the caboclos and the stern barge for livestock, equipment and supplies. But within a few days our three-unit fleet was an indiscriminate welter of humanity, cows, pigs, chickens, crates, bales, cartons, baskets, tools, building materials, gasoline drums, hammocks and refuse. The caboclos alternately slept, grumbled, quarreled, and sang endless and unintelligible chants with the saddest sweetest voices I had ever heard. The children swarmed over the decks of the launch. The chickens roosted on its rails. God, with some slight aid from Mordecai Cobb and John McHugh, kept the incredible armada afloat and moving. By this time I needed no convincing that He is a Brazilian.

The distance from Esperança to Graça de Deus, we had estimated, was some six hundred miles. The *Cantora,* pulling the barges and with the current against her, averaged three and a half an hour, which would have figured out to a week's trip— if we have traveled twenty-four hours a day. But we didn't travel twenty-four. We traveled eight, ten, at most twelve, and each evening, at sunset or a little after, we pulled in beside a clearing or mudbank for the night. Soon the shore glittered with fires, built for the double purpose of cooking and repelling insects; and when supper was over the women and children returned to the barges to sleep, and the men slung their hammocks among the trees. At first Christine, McHugh and I tried to sleep with Cobb in the cabin of the *Cantora,* but the heat and stench soon drove us outside. For the rest of the trip we spent our nights with the men on the edge of the forest, swaying gently in our hammocks under the mosquito netting. The fireflies flickered around us, and beyond them the jungle rustled and stirred with the sounds of darkness. Usually, toward morning, I would awake to hear the pattering of rain on the treetops high above.

By the calendar, the dry season had now begun, but "dry," in Amazonia, means only less-rain, not no-rain. The rivers fall very slowly from week to week and month to month, and the tropical storms still come and go across the skies. Late the second afternoon a violent squall closed in on us, almost without warning. For perhaps ten minutes the river churned to the beating of a cloudburst; thunder bellowed, and great pulses of lightning throbbed across the sky. And then, presently, when the storm had passed, river and jungle were, I think, stiller than I had ever seen them before. A breathless glaze filled the void between earth and sky, and the jungle wall, a hundred yards to our left, seemed merely a painted canvas of black and green. Even the river, the launch, the barges and every living thing on them were as if held and transfixed in the stillness. In all the world only the sun moved, gliding slowly down the rain-washed sky toward the treetops in the west.

A third day passed. A fourth. And on the morning of the fifth there was at last a change in the river. The waters broadened, the south bank curved away; and, following it, we moved from the main stream of the Amazon into the mouth of the Juruá. On the far shore, barely visible between river and forest, were the huddled houses and sheds of a village—the first we had seen since leaving Esperança.

"Will we stop off?" Christine asked McHugh. And Mc-Hugh, in turn looked at Cobb.

"No point," said Cobb. "Nothing around but a few spiks

141

and some pigs and the wreck of an old plane that must onct of got bushed there."

And in half an hour the village of Fonte Boa had dropped out of sight astern.

In the beginning the Juruá was almost indistinguishable from the Amazon proper, but gradually it began to take on characteristics of its own. It was even yellower than the Amazon, more sluggish and meandering, and its course was broken up into a maze of channels, sandbars and wooded islands. Also, the forest on either side seemed lower than before, and we soon saw that the trees were not rising from solid earth but out of the water itself. *Igapos* are what the Brazilians call these flooded forests. During the rainy season they extend for thousands of miles along the Amazon's great tributaries, neither river nor land, untracked and impenetrable.

During the first three nights on the Juruá, we could not go ashore, but simply tied up to the trees in the *igapos* and slept as best we could on the launch and barges. They were no longer merely our carrier, but our world; hermetic and self-contained. And as everything beyond that world grew more dreamlike and alien, it became, contrastingly, more personalized and more real. This was true not only for "the staff," but for everyone in our floating community. At Esperança the caboclos, with one or two exceptions, had been simply—caboclos. Now they were Augusto, Domingos, Miguel, Sebastião; Emilia, Eugenia, Magdalena, Rosa. When a voice was raised in anger or song, we recognized it. When a child cried or shouted, we knew whose child it was.

More often than not, in the latter case, it was O Touro's. His mother called him Jayme, that being presumably his proper name; but to everyone else he was Tourinho—Little Bull—and he was far and away the liveliest, most ubiquitous and, I sometimes suspected, most intelligent passenger in our three-ply fleet. Whether or not he would eventually grow to the dimensions of his father it was impossible to tell. But even at ten he had a wonderfully strong and well-formed little body, and he was forever clambering and swinging about the launch and barges with the agile energy of a laughing brown monkey. He was full of questions, too: about the workings of the launch, the course of the river, the country through which we were passing, the nature of cities and trains and planes, the chances of the Nova York Beisbol Yanquis against the Detroit Tigres and the Cleveland Indios. . . . And almost equally full of answers. . . . One day he pointed out—correctly—to Cobb that a washer had worked loose in the carburetor of the *Cantora*'s engine. One night, when we were able to sleep ashore, he vanished alone into the forest and reappeared an hour later with a basketful of wild mangoes.

I remember watching him once while he was playing on the barge with some of the caboclo children and suddenly realizing, almost with a start, that his real name was Jackson. No one called him that, of course. In fact, I wondered if he himself knew the name; for his father, no less than his mother, lived wholly as a Brazilian, rarely spoke other than Portuguese, and never gave so much as a hint of his pre-Amazonian past. That the man called O Touro was, or had been, an American was obvious to me from the start, but what kind and condition of American was a good deal harder to say. According to Cobb's story, he had once been a ship's stoker—and his body looked the part. But his face, voice and manner were more those of—well—a professional man, or even a teacher or preacher. It seemed altogether incredible that he was wanted by the police, for murder.

On the *Cantora*, of course, there was little for him to do in his capacity as foreman; but his quiet control over the caboclos—and their respect for him—was as strong and manifest as it had been at Esperança. His relationship with Cobb, too, continued as it had been before: "Touro boy" on the one hand and "Yes, Mr. Cobb" on the other. Toward McHugh and myself, too, Touro was reserved, courteous, almost formal; toward Christine, perhaps a little gentler, a little

143

warmer. But it was only with his wife and his son that he really emerged from the shell of his isolation. Most of the caboclos ignored their children and treated their women as if they were a sort of inferior livestock. Touro, in contrast, spent long hours with Tourinho and obviously adored his plump and bright-eyed Tereza Carolina. Each day he removed the tarpaulin that covered their possessions and carefully oiled and polished the shining sewing machine that was her pride and joy. And often in the evenings, before sleep, we would see him lying on their barge with his head on her lap, listening to the singing of the men around him. Presently, without moving, he would join in with them, his eyes fixed unwinking on the star-sown sky, his voice slowly swelling, deep and full, beneath the high sweet singsong of the caboclos.

Touro was one of the two middlemen in the hierarchy of our little community. The other was Frei Ambrosio. And it would have been hard to find two men more widely different.

The padre was short and round, with remarkably light skin for a Brazilian, and in his heavy black cassock, which he wore even in the blaze of midday, he bore an unmistakable resemblance to a melting butterball. But he didn't melt. His energy never flagged. Day in and day out he was back and forth across the launch and barge, ministering to his flock, teaching the children their catechism, holding communion, hearing confessions, tirelessly exhorting to godliness and cleanliness. Austerity and self-righteousness, however, were as alien to his nature as was sin itself. Of lowly origin and meager background (he had never been farther afield from the Amazon than the monastery of his order in Recife), he was, by any other than frontier standards, far from an educated man. But I soon learned that he had qualities that served him much better than education, and among them were shrewdness, tolerance, devotion and a deep warm humanity.

Also, he was an accomplished and shameless politician.

When he felt that God's purpose would be best served by keeping his eyes open, he kept them open. When the situation was such that neither he nor God could do much about it, he shut them tight. He was equally ready, as occasion demanded, to exhort, admonish, threaten, cajole, flatter, bribe and lie, and at first I was half shocked and half amused to observe the yawning gap between his pious precepts and devious practices. Gradually, however, I came to realize that, in Frei Ambrosio, this was neither inconsistency nor hypocrisy, but simply a sound and practical working hypothesis. His faith was so strong that he could afford to be venal in small things. The ends for which he strove were so clear and sure that the means didn't matter.

Knowing the rigid regulations of his order, I asked him one day how he had been able to leave his post at Esperança without first obtaining permission.

"It was not easy, my son," he confided, "and for many long hours, there in my little chapel, I prayed the Virgin for guidance. Those who are staying need me, I explained, and those who are going need me; but is it not the poor Indians of the forest who probably need me most of all? . . . And in the end the Virgin understood and gave me permission to go."

"But the church?" I asked.

"The church, my son?"

"Your superiors in Manaos."

"Ah yes, of course, my superiors. Unfortunately it was impossible to exchange word with them in the short time available; but surely, when the Virgin herself has given consent, they would not withhold theirs." Frei Ambrosio paused for a moment's meditation, then added: "And besides, they will not know about it until my work is done."

How the good padre fared when at last he returned to civilization, I never found out. But one of his lesser stratagems began backfiring on him before the *Cantora*-et-al was a week out of Esperança.

From the night in the plantation office when Cobb had done his spellbinding, the caboclo João Batista had been one of the most eager of all the plantation-hands to start off on the new venture. A diabo com borracha! A plague and a malediction on rubber! He had given his life to the accursed gum, and what had it given him back? Misery, that's what. Poverty and a bent back and seared lungs and a great tiredness. But now at last he was through with rubber. By the blessed intercession of God and Our Lady and the Grande Companhia Cruzeiro do Sul, he was done with it forever. In the place to which we were going there would be no rubber, but only oil, and even an ignorant and unlettered caboclo like João Batista knew that in the craziness of things today oil was more precious than gold. What made him think that there would be wealth for him, poor John the Baptist, in *anything* he would ever do in this world was the secret of his own innocent mind. But think it he did. "Yes, amigos, it is a great thing we are going," he would say, his dark eyes shining in his thin pockmarked face. "To a new hope. And a new life."

Well, maybe. But first, as it developed, there were new problems—and that was where Frei Ambrosio came in.

João Batista's wife, a toothless dispirited drudge, had no more voice in family decisions than his hogs or his chickens; but their daughter Serafima was another story. In fact, *quite* another story. Serafima was sixteen; she had been the undisputed belle of Esperança, carried herself like a movie queen, and was exclusively interested in the three not-unrelated subjects of clothes, men, and going down-river to Manaos or Belem. When she discovered that she was about to head, not down-river, but up, she had almost literally raised the thatch off the Batistas' roof, and her father, in desperation, had called on the padre for help. What happened then was pretty well garbled by the time it got to "the staff," but the gist of it, obviously, was that Frei Ambrosio had told some whopping lies. His other blandishments having failed, he had, I gathered, taken a deep breath and described Graça de Deus as a veritable metropolis of the jungle, second only to Rio and perhaps São Paulo among the great cities of Brazil.

Serafima would love it there. She would be happy, gay, and undoubtedly Queen of the Mardi Gras. . . . "A slight exaggeration," he conceded later, "but one that the Lord will surely forgive. To keep a family together; to save an innocent child from the fleshpots of evil; surely that is a more important thing than a quibble over details."

"And when she sees Graça de Deus?"

"By that time, with God's grace, she will have seen, too, the error of her ways. And also, she will already be there, and it will be hard for her to go back."

Unfortunately for the padre, however, it took Serafima only a day or two on the river to discover that she had been hornswoggled, and the reverberations that shook the *Cantora*-and-barges, was only slightly less violent than the thundering of the tropical storms. Frei Ambrosio reasoned with her. (Loud recriminations.) João Batista shouted at her. (Tears and rage.) Cobb all but offered her a free sewing machine. (He knew what he could do with it.) And finally McHugh himself compounded the priest's perjury by assuring her that, with the arrival of the *Fortaleza,* Graça de Deus would become a boom town overnight. All to no avail. In the end, her anger blew itself out from sheer exhaustion, but merely to bide its time behind a haughty and sullen silence. Henceforward, heathen or even Baptist Indians were going to be a pushover for the padre compared to Serafima Batista.

The yellow-brown river glided past. The forest walls glided past. More often than not, now, they were scarcely walls at all, but, rather, thin lacy screens, and behind them we could see the still waters of the *igapos* stretching away into green gloom. The trunks of the trees showed that the river had already fallen an inch or two from its seasonal high. Their black oozing bark was sheathed with the larvae of generations of insects soon to be born.

Of actual animal life we saw almost none. With the water still deep in the *igapos* the earth-prowlers of the forest stay on the higher ground, farther inland; and the alligators

147

and turtles usually lurk out of sight until the falling river uncovers sandbanks for hatching and sunning. Frequently during the day we would hear the din of birds or monkeys, high in the trees, but all we would see was a sudden whirling of bright plumage or, at most, a distant shape rising suddenly up out of the forest and arrowing away into the sky. At night the darkness hummed and throbbed with incessant sound, but we saw nothing.

At intervals of twenty, thirty, forty miles there would be a low bluff or mudbank rising out of the flooded land, and on the mudbank, perhaps, a deserted huddle of cabins or a collapsed shed. It was hard to imagine what kind of men had once built and inhabited them, what they had sought and found there, and where they had now gone. Once the shores had closed in behind us, it was hard even to believe that these lonely ruins were not mere mirages of the heat and sunlight.

Often it seemed as if the river itself were a mirage, wavering and glinting around us, turning, curving, twisting back on itself, never ending, never changing, until I was all but convinced that we were not actually progressing at all, but simply circling around through an immense and intricate labyrinth, in which each day we exactly retraced the route of the day before. There was no longer any visible current, but only a slow deep coiling of the waters. There was no view, but only vistas. And every vista was empty, still, identical.

"As it was in the beginning—" Christine Barna murmured. And her gray-green eyes were quiet with contemplation as they moved across the sunlit miles.

The days glided into the nights and the nights into the days. We chugged on, stopped, ate, slept, woke up, and chugged on again. Nothing seemed to happen. And yet, I realized almost with surprise, one thing or another was constantly happening.

There were the storms.

There was l'Affaire Serafima.

And one day there was a fight.

Surprisingly, it had nothing to do with her. In fact, we never did find out what started it; but suddenly, one late afternoon while we were still underway, there was a thumping and shouting over on the starboard barge, and we saw that two of the younger caboclos were at each other with knives. McHugh and I made our way over as quickly as we could and pushed our way through the ring of men that had already surrounded them.

"Stop it," McHugh ordered.

But the two fighters paid no attention. Crouching, they circled each other, then leapt in, lunged and leapt away again. Their mouths were working with soundless curses, their dark eyes were bright with hate. One of them was already bleeding from a wound on his cheek, and the other had a long shallow slash on his forearm.

"Stop it!" McHugh said again, taking a step forward. But before either of us could interfere O Touro was there, suddenly and quietly, towering between them.

"Give them here," he said, extending his hands for the knives.

One of the men paused in his circling and looked at him, undecided. But the other, with a quick cat-like motion, tried to lunge past him, and when Touro blocked his way his rage shifted abruptly to the big Negro.

"Out of my way, son of a black whore!" he snarled. "Out of my way or I will kill you too, bull nigger!"

For a long moment Touro merely stood there, looking at him. And then, suddenly, I saw in his eyes the same thing I had seen on that afternoon in Esperança when he sat quietly in his bungalow and stared at Mordecai Cobb. The pupils seemed to be slowly contracting. The whites glinted. In the next instant, it seemed, he would leap forward in swift and terrible violence. . . . But, just as it had been in the bungalow, what happened next was not violent at all. Touro took a slow step forward, reached out a hand and took the knife from the man's hand as if he was taking a toy from a child. Then he turned and took the other man's knife. And then he walked to the edge of the barge and dropped both knives into the water.

The two caboclos stood looking at him without speaking. The crowd of watchers melted away. A half hour later the *Cantora* bore in toward the nearer shore and we tied up in an *igapo* for the night.

There were other incidents; constant incidents. The *Cantora's* overworked engines sputtered and died at intervals and had to be laboriously nursed back to life. We spent a day grounded on a sandbar. One of the caboclo children fell overboard and narrowly escaped drowning. Two revolvers and a shotgun disappeared from the cabin, and many hours of questioning and searching failed to turn them up.

But nothing that happened had any real cogency or meaning. None of it seemed to fit into a pattern of experience. The realities of Esperança were remote behind us, the realities of Graça de Deus still unknown. It was as if we were ferrying along some tropical Styx, with all normal activity suspended, life itself almost suspended, while we moved slowly and blindly from one world into another.

Most of all, I was aware of a state of suspension in the relationship between Christine and myself. In the tight confined community of launch and barges we were, of course, almost constantly together; but it was a togetherness merely of physical proximity, of shared experience, of mood. Since that night on the verandah at Esperança we had spoken neither of past or future. Nor of Nils Barna. We ate, slept, talked, played casino in the cabin, and sat crosslegged on the foredeck watching the endless changeless vistas of stream and shore.

We crept on through the days.

We waited. . . .

And at last, on our sixth day on the Juruá, the country around us began slowly to change. The river became a little narrower, the islands fewer, and there were now long stretches of mudbank and dry shore between the flooded miles of *igapo*. Toward midday we passed a tiny settlement of rubber-gatherers, the first inhabited place we had seen since Fonte Boa. And as we rounded the next bend in the river the forest wall to our right opened up, Mordecai Cobb spun the wheel of the *Cantora*, and we swung out of the Juruá into the darker clearer waters of the Yurima.

"Half-way to hell-and-gone," he murmured, spitting reflectively over the side. "Mebbe a bit more."

Looking back on my account of our journey thus far, I realize that I've not said much of Cobb. This hasn't been because of an oversight, but simply because there wasn't much to say. In terms of the trip itself, he was, of course, the most essential person aboard—the Charon of our Stygian ferry and the only one among us with even the slightest knowledge of river navigation. But in spite of this—or, rather, I suppose, because of it, and because he recognized his responsibilities—he was a far quieter and more circumspect Cobb than during the days of preparation at Esperança. For one thing, McHugh had exacted a promise from him that he would do no drinking during the voyage, and, at least as far as anyone could tell, he was keeping it. Late into the nights, after the rest of us had turned into our hammocks, he would stay up tinkering with the launch's engines or shuffling through his meager stock of maps; and during the long days, hour after hour, he sat hunched over the wheel, in his stained pajama tops and broad-brimmed straw hat, his pale hooded eyes fixed unwaveringly on the river ahead.

Sometimes his natural talkativeness broke through the surface and he would discourse ramblingly and profanely on everything from submerged sandbars to Getulio Vargas to the comparative merits of Barbados rum and Brazilian cachaça. On occasion he would comment on some feature of the river or shore that stirred his recollections of forty-odd years before. But for the most part he sat either in abstracted silence or humming to himself in a croaking monotone; and as the days passed I could almost see him, like some ancient barnacled shellfish, withdrawing farther and farther into himself.

. . . Until at last, now, we were creeping up the Yurima in the hot glaze of early afternoon, and he was sitting at the wheel beside me with his eyes slitted against the sunlight. And suddenly I realized that he was no longer watching the river, but the shore; and not merely watching it, but studying and searching it.

"Been this far before?" I asked him.

He didn't seem to hear, and after a moment I repeated the question.

"Yep," he said. "Yep, just about."

He didn't elaborate, but simply kept staring at the shore to our left; and, following his gaze, I saw the *igapo* gliding past, and beyond the *igapo* still another empty, desolate mud-bank. Presently we were opposite it. We were creeping past it. And then Cobb spun the wheel, and launch and barges swung slowly in toward the shore.

I didn't say anything, but a minute later McHugh put his head out the cabin door and asked: "Pulling in for the night already?"

Cobb shook his head. "Just want to go ashore for a bit," he said.

"Ashore? Where?"

Cobb pointed at the mudbank. . . . And now, watching it as we swung closer, I saw that it was not empty, as I had thought at first, but that in its center and a little way back from the bank were the charred ruins of what had once been a group of huts. McHugh started to speak but apparently thought better of it, and we nudged up against the bank in silence. The caboclos on the barge glanced up at the launch for orders, but there were none forthcoming. They and Mc-Hugh and I watched without speaking while Cobb left the wheel and clambered over the *Cantora*'s side.

No sooner was he ashore, however, than he paused and turned back to us. "Want to come along?" he asked me.

"Where to?"

"Only a little way. It'll just take a few minutes."

I looked at McHugh, but McHugh didn't say anything, and then I shrugged and said, "All right," and followed Cobb up onto the caked reddish mud of the shore. No one else left the boats.

"Guess mebbe with a thing like this it's better to have somebody along," Cobb said. He said it aloud, but it was himself he was talking to—not me.

We skirted the black ruins, and I could see from the almost disintegrated wood that they had been there a long time; a very long time. A toad goggled at us from the top of a rusted iron pot and flopped heavily away. Looking back, I saw that the launch and barges were out of sight beneath the rim of the riverbank; and the only sound now was the faint sucking noise of our shoes on the half-dried mud. After perhaps another fifty yards we came to the forest wall and stopped.

"Used to be a sort of path here," Cobb murmured. "Sure as hell won't be here now, though."

He stood looking from one side to the other, trying to get his bearings. Then he pushed aside a screen of ferns and vines and took a few steps forward; but presently stopped and came back again. After peering around once more, he made another try, a few yards to the right. This time he kept going, ducking and thrashing through the undergrowth, with myself close behind him; and presently we came out into what appeared to be a small half-overgrown clearing between the trees.

"Should have been a boy scout, sure enough," said Cobb.

He was standing still again, and, squinting through the shadows, I saw a black slab of wood that tilted up out of the moss and creepers near the center of the clearing. Suddenly I realized that I was looking at a grave.

"Reckoned it might last a while if I put it in here out of the rains," Cobb murmured. "And by Jesus, it has." For perhaps a minute he stood silently looking down at the slab;

then, bending, he began manipulating it gently and carefully, so that it would stand straight in the ground. "Massaranduba," he said. "Hardest wood in the world. It's thirty-eight years now since I cut and carved this."

Moving closer, I saw that there were letters chiselled in the wood—very faint but still legible. *Gizella Firosi,* they read. And underneath the name, *A Dourada.*

"The golden—?"

"Yep," said Cobb. "That's her. The Golden Gal."

I waited for him to go on, but he was silent again, maneuvering the slab until it was straight and firm to his satisfaction. When he had finished he rose and stood looking down at his handiwork. Then, to my surprise, he crossed himself awkwardly.

"Guess mebbe she'd like me to do that," he explained, almost apologetically. "She was a real Christer, that kid."

He turned away, and I followed him, and we made our way back through the undergrowth and across the mudbank toward the shore. After the cool gloom of the forest it was like stepping out into a blinding yellow-white furnace.

"Thanks for coming along," said Cobb. "All alone, that sort of place gives a feller the creeps."

"That's all right," I told him.

He didn't look at me, but kept his eyes fixed on the caked mud that stretched away before us to the river. "God almighty, that's a long time ago," he said.

11

PLENTY OF THINGS in Mordecai Cobb's life had been a long time ago. Sometimes you had the feeling that he had been floating on through Amazonia as long as the rivers themselves.

Like most men who lead largely solitary lives, he was alternately garrulous and silent, open and secretive. Thus far on the trip, as I've said, he had been for the most part quiet and withdrawn; but his visit to that ancient grave had obviously stirred up a host of memories, and, with them, the need to exorcise them by talk. That same night we were moored off another mudbank a few miles further up the Yurima. And Cobb, sitting with us on the *Cantora*'s deck, chewed meditatively on a wad of plug tobacco and felt his way back, gropingly, into the past.

By now, to be sure, I already knew a little about his history. Before Singer he had worked for the Rubber Development Corporation, before that on the Ford Rubber plantations on the Tapajos, and before that, as far as I could gather, on virtually every enterprise that had existed in that part of the world during the last half-century. For Mordecai Cobb had first come to the Amazon when he was thirteen years old.

"I'm kind of hazy on them earliest days," he told me once. But he remembered that his father had been a farmer in either Iowa or Nebraska—he wasn't sure which—and had come to South America with his family as a member of some sort of religious sect.

"Nobody ever told me much about it," he said, "but I know there was quite a few of them kind of colonies being set up down here in those days. Most of these spik republics wanted settlers pretty bad, I guess, and they were sending out all sorts of stuff about how if you didn't like it where you was living, why come right on down and cut yourself a slice of the Garden of Eden. Well, that was meat for my old man, sure enough, on account of he didn't like *anything* where he was; and pretty soon him and these lodge brothers of his—The Free Disciples I think they called themselves— upped with their families, and off we went to Peru. I reckon there was about three hundred of us at the beginning, counting women and kids. They called the place we were going to New Zion, and the general idea was that everybody'd grow bananas, go to church fourteen times a week, and not get kicked around by no bankers and politicians."

Cobb permitted himself a cackling laugh. "New Zion! Boy, you should of seen the place. It was way the hell and gone up the Ucayali River on the jungle side of the Andes, and it must of been where malaria and yellow jack was invented. The first week there they buried my younger sister, and a few months later the older one, and a year later my mother. I wouldn't want to upset the senhora by having her hear this, but that's when I first learned the Amazon ain't much of a place for the ladies."

Apparently his father, too, had died while Cobb was still a boy; the colony had broken up; and for the next few years he had drifted up and down the rivers, working in rubber forests, lumber camps, trading posts and fazendas.

"It was a tough life," he reminisced, "but I got along fine. It's funny how things work out sometimes. For most folks, coming to the jungle is like being set down in the center of hell. But me, I loved it, right from the start. I remember I used to go out into the forests with some of the Indio kids, and every time I'd come to a turn in the path or push aside a branch or fern my heart would start thumping and I was sure that the next minute I was going to find—Christ knows

156

what. A city of rubies, maybe. Or a harem of princesses with gold underwear. Not that I ever did, of course. Only thing I ever found was bugs or snakes. But nothing stopped me, no sir. Nothing was stopping Mordecai Cobb in them days. Whatever was hid in that jungle, I was going to find it."

But it wasn't about his boyhood that Cobb spoke that night on the deck of the *Cantora*. It was about a girl called Gizella Firosi. . . .

"This was back when I was about twenty-four," he said, "and I'd been working in the rubber camps on the Putumayo." He looked from one to another of us to see if the name registered. "Remember it? Sure you do. Even after all this time everybody remembers it. That was right at the top of the Amazon boom, and rubber was king, and the Putumayo was the king's storehouse. I guess every freebooter and wildcatter and highjacker this side of the Isthmus was in there on that half-acre of hell—tearing the jungle to pieces, tearing themselves to pieces, tearing the Indios to pieces. After a while it got so bad they had to send some sort of international commission down to clean things up. Three years I was there—yessir, three long years—and let me tell you, *I* remember it all right. If you hear me jabbering and howling in my hammock one of these nights it won't be the D.T.'s like you think, but only me dreaming about that Putumayo.

"Well anyway—" He paused and spat over the side into the dark water. "That's where I'd been, and even though I wasn't no mama's boy back in them days, at the end of three years I'd had a bellyfull. Besides, I hadn't done so bad for myself—had a real nice little pile salted away—and one day I just upped and got out of there. To another river? Another camp in the bush? Hell, no. When fellers made their pile on the Amazon in them days there was only one place for them to go with it, and that, by God, was where I was going too. Goodbye, jungle. So long, rubber and bugs

157

and Indios. Yessir, I bought myself a little canoa and started down-river for Manaos.

"Manaos . . . ." Cobb's pale eyes kindled. "What you seen on the way up here wasn't Manaos. That was a corpse; what was left when the urubus finished picking the bones. But Manaos *then*—Jesus! It was Rio, Paris, New York and the Land of Canaan, all rolled into one. Everywhere you looked there was paved streets, big houses, restaurants, hotels, swells with white shirts and gals with diamonds. The opera house had just been up a couple of years. They was talking about parks and railroads and theayters and a marble state capitol. But more than anything else they was talking about rubber. Yessir, rubber was it, by God—rubber was king of the whole goddam world—and if a few thousand poor slobs of Indios out in a jungle had to get chopped into little pieces on account of it, what the hell. Leastwise there was no Indios lousing up Manaos. Nothing was lousing up Manaos. It was going places, that town and nothing was stopping it.

"And there was me, one fine day, paddling up the Rio Negro in my little canoa, and there was the city at last, all big and shiny in the sun. Mind you, I was a grown man now, and since I was a kid I'd never seen a real town or a woman without lice in her hair. With twenty thousand milreis clanking in my jeans, that Manaos was like some big melon hanging there in front of me, ripe for the tasting. And I tasted it, all right. I bought myself clothes, food, liquor, women, even a fat gold watch with rubies in the back. I went to all the restaurants, all the cafés, all the gambling joints and cathouses, and then at last one night, after I'd got myself a boiled shirt and white tie, I said, hell, you'd better soak up a little edication too, and off I went to the opera."

Here Cobb paused to spit again and draw a long slow breath. "That's where I saw *her*," he said.

"Like I was saying, Manaos was some fancy place in those days, and the opera company had been brought over special from Italy. I never did find out what they were putting on that night—something about an E-gyptian princess, I think— but, anyhow, I just sat there a while wondering what in hell was going on, and then she came out, and I *knew* what was going on. She wasn't a singer or anything—just one of the gals in what they call the ballot—but far's I was concerned she might as well of been there all alone on the stage. She was a little thing, quick and light like a bird, with hair and eyes that looked like they were lighted by some kind of black fire; and she was wearing a sort of shiny gold robe around her that I guess was the same as all the other gals were wearing, only alongside her the rest looked like they was dressed in gunnysacks.

"Well, I just sat there goggling at her and not knowing if I was sitting in a theayter or looking through the pearly gates; and I went back the next night and the night after, and I couldn't sleep and I couldn't eat, and after a while I asked one of the fellers in the place I lived how you went about getting to know a dame like that. You send her diamonds, he said. I don't have no diamonds, I told him. Then you send her flowers, he said. So I send her flowers. I send her half the goddam orchids in Brazil. And then one night I take a couple of extra snorts to keep my knees steady and go around to the back door of the opera house, and when she comes out up I step just like one of those dudes in the pictures, and I say, 'I'm the feller that's been sending you the flowers.' I don't know what I expected her to do. Look right through me mebbe. Yell for the bouncer. But she don't do nothing like that. She just looks at me a minute and then smiles and says it's been very kind of you, senhor, and then I say how about something to eat or something, and she says she doesn't see why not, and that's how I got to know Gizella Firosi."

Cobb paused again and made a noise in his throat that was half grunt and half cackle. "Yep, that was her name," he went on. "Gizella. . . . Back at the beginning there I used to grin every time I said it. She was a wop, of course, like all of them with the opera, and she couldn't speak no Portuguee and I couldn't speak her lingo, so we got along in a sort of half-assed Spanish. But, Christ almighty, *how* we got along! I was a dead pigeon right from the beginning, of course: stark staring crazy in love. But the thing that's hard to get is that she fell in love with me too. Don't ask me why —I still don't know. Sure enough I wasn't the scarecrow then that I am now, but still no one was mistaking me for any fancy dan. Money? Yeah, I had a little, but it wasn't peanuts to what she could of picked up from half the guys in town. Like I said, I just don't know. All I know is that that gal loved me—and I loved her. Within a week after we met we was living together in the best hotel in town. We were food and drink and breath to each other, and outside the times she was up there on the stage of the opera house, there wasn't a minute day or night that we wasn't together. And then at last do you know what that fool kid did? When the rest of her crowd packed up and left for home she quit her job and stayed on with me."

I never got it quite straight how long Cobb and his Gizella were in Manaos together. As he told it that first time, it sounded like only a few weeks. When occasionally he referred to it later he made it seem much longer. But whether it was measured in months or weeks or only days, it had obviously been the great and unforgettable time in his life.

"You know what I got her?" he said to us. "A carriage, by God! A carriage and a slick bay stallion, and every afternoon we'd drive up and down the avenidas and then on to the cafés and the restaurants and the shows and the hotels; and every man-jack in that town, from the crummiest shineboy to the chefé of the rubber trust, would of given his eyeteeth to have something like that at his side. I tell you, she shone like the sun, that gal! Black eyes, black hair, yeah—a real wop. But all the rest of her light and quick and bright and shining. Like the sun, I say; like gold. That's when I started calling her *A Dourada*. The Golden Gal. . . ."

Another pause.

"Gold," said Cobb. "Sure. Gold—silver—milreis. . . . There we were, thanks to the little pile I'd made, and the world was ours, and everything I'd ever dreamed of was ours, and the jungle and black rivers and stinking smoke-houses and chained Indios, they were all gone and forgot and a million miles away. Only they wasn't of course, really. Ride a few blocks one way and there was the jungle, waiting. Ride a few the other and there was the river, waiting. They was still there all right, just where they'd always been; and pretty soon it was that pile of milreis that was going, going, gone, until at last the day comes when I take a couple of long ones to steady me down and then I say to Gizella, 'Honey girl, I'm broke.'

"Well, sir, I'd just took it for granted that that'd be the end of it, but all she says is, 'What is it you will do now, Mordecai?'

" 'Go out and try to make another pile,' I said.

" 'With the rubber?'

" 'No, rubber's all sewed up now by the big trusts. It's no good for a loner. This time I'm going after gold.'

"Then I tell her that I been nosing around a little, and how there's a boat leaving soon for 'way the hell-and-gone up some jungle river nobody ever heard of, where they say they've found gold-dust in the water. 'And I guess that's the deal for me, honey,' I say to her.

" 'How long will you be gone?' she asks me. And I tell her six months, mebbe a year; it's hard to say with this kind of thing. 'But I don't want to stay a year in Manaos alone,' she says. And I say, 'Of course not. You better get yourself moving and catch up with that opera crowd.' And she says no, she ain't going to do that either, she's going to go along with me."

Cobb shook his head slowly, as if even now, after thirty-eight years, the thought astonished him. "Imagine," he said. "This crazy kid. Never'd slept out of a bed in her life. Never'd got her feet wet outside a bathtub. And there she is, all set to go with me up into the very bung-hole of the world.

I should of had better sense, of course. I was only a kid too, and daffy in love with her, but still I should of had better sense. Only I didn't. I grabbed her and kissed her all over, and then we went out and blew in the last of my dough on a big night on the town. And then the next day, you know what that gal did? She upped and hocked her jools to raise the money for our passage and outfits, and a few days later there we was, she and I, on a cruddy old steam-launch, creeping up the rivers toward the Rio do Sol."

He gave another of his cough-like cackles. "You think this country's wild now?" he asked. "And the old *Cantora* not so hot? Boy, they're Fifth Avenoo and the *Queen Elizabeth* alongside of how things was then. Of all the things that could have happened to us we didn't miss one. Heat, rain, bugs, snakes, shooting Indios, food you couldn't eat, water you couldn't drink, fifty-seven kinds of shakes and fevers—we had 'em all. Fifteen out of forty on the boat was dead before we was three days into the Juruá, and the rest of us looked like something out of a cannibal's nightmare. The commandante said he was going back. But most of the passengers said no, they wouldn't go back. I guess it was the same for them as it was for me and Gizella. Without the gold there just wasn't nothing to go back to.

"Well, anyhow, there was a sort of fight, and we went on a few more days, and then there was another fight and the commandante got himself a knife in the chest. Them of us that was left took over the steering, and after a week or so we got up near the mouth of the Yurima. Halfway, we says. Ha! And no sooner do we say it, than bang, rip, the old tub hits something under the water, and in ten minutes she's sunk like a stone. I guess another ten must of drowned then and there, and a few more was chewed up by alligators. The rest of us got to shore, set up a sort of camp, and started dying more leisurely-like. Fever got most of them. Some went nuts and threw themselves in the river. And at last the few that was left began disappearing—into the jungle, down the river on logs—until there was nobody left but Gizella and me.

Just the two of us, mind you—me and this kid who used to wear gold skirts and put perfume in her bath—sitting there by the river alone.

"I don't know how long we sat there. A week—or mebbe two. Time gets sort of screwed up with things like that. We ate berries and fish. I tried to knock a raft together, but couldn't. Gizella prayed, and when she wasn't praying she just lay there in my arms and smiled at me. And then at last, by God, a canoe comes along, a little dugout thing with an Indio family in it; and they hear me yelling and paddle over, and I say for Christ's sake give us a lift. But they say they can't, they're full up already—which wasn't no lie, really—and we argue back and forth a little, only it's no use, and then I do what I got to do. I take my gun, which I'd managed to save from the boat, and knock 'em down like clay pigeons: one, two, three, four, five. No fancy business. No Putumayo stuff like putting out eyes or chopping off hands. Just a quick neat hole through each of them, and then I lay them out nice and orderly on the bank—one, two, three, four, five—and Gizella and I pile into the canoe, and off we go upstream."

Pause. Spit. . . . Cobb shook his head and smiled.

"Did you get what I said?" he asked. "Upstream. Not down, but *up*. . . . Yessir, even after all that happened we was still going on, still going for gold. Only by this time it was more than gold we was looking for; it was—well, I guess you'd have to call it a kind of dream.

"Anyhow. . . .

"We went on for three or four days in that canoe, and I must of been a pretty tough specimen back then, because I was still paddling all right, still feeling all right. And Gizella, she was all right too. All right, hell—she was wonderful. She was what one gal in ten million would of been like: not afraid, not squawling, always smiling at me. . . . Until one morning I wake up and look at her and she ain't smiling, she ain't all right, and all of a sudden I see she's sick with the fever. It was the yellow jack, I reckon—I never did find out for sure. But whatever it was, there was nothing to do but make her as comfortable as I could in the canoe and go on paddling. And that's what I did for another two days: paddled and paddled, and she got sicker and sicker, until soon she couldn't eat no more, and then not even move or talk or hear when I talked to her; and then at last we come to a place where there's people—on that mudbank it was, where we stopped a while back—only there was a village there then, and a few louse-eaten seringueros—and I carry her up and lay her down in the corner of one of the smoke-sheds that they use for curing rubber.

"I remember that shed like I was in it yesterday: hot, dark, stinking. Only there wasn't anywhere else to put her. I sat there beside her for a couple of hours, holding her hand and once in a while dripping a little water on her face; and then she sort of fell asleep and I went outside a while. A few of the seringueros were lounging around, and they asked me how she was, and I told them no good. Then they asked what the hell we were doing there, and I told them that too. 'Know of any gold up the river?' I asked them.

" 'Sure,' they said. 'Sure there's gold. Sometimes we can see the yellow dust floating down the water.'

" 'Think it comes from far off?'

" 'Yeah, pretty far off. Up the Yurima. Up the Malaguay. From the Rio do Sol it comes. You know the Rio do Sol?' they asked.

" 'Sure I know the Rio do Sol,' I said.

" 'Then you'll find the gold sure,' they said.

"That was when I wanted to laugh. But I didn't laugh. I went back into that black stinking shed, and I sat there the rest of the day and all that night. Sometimes Gizella talked a little, only it was in eyetalian and I couldn't understand. Sometimes she'd open her eyes and look at me, only she didn't know who I was. And then at last, as it was getting along toward morning, there was a minute when she *did* know, and this time she didn't say nothing, but just smiled a little, and I swear to you, as true as I'm sitting here now, that the inside of that stinking old shed turned all of a sudden from black into shining gold. . . . And then the next I knew it was sort of a gray greasy dawnlight, and the seringueros came in and said they was sorry but they had to start curing rubber, and I said that was okay, we was finished with the shed anyway, and I went out and started digging a grave."

Cobb was silent a moment and then grinned a little. "I sure did a good job carving that massaranduba wood," he said.

He shifted his tobacco from one cheek to the other and for a while sat staring down into the black water. "Yep, that was a long while ago," he murmured presently. "For a few years afterwards that was all I thought about. Gizella, the Juruá, the Rio do Sol—and how I was going back there again and this time make it. Only—well, you know how it is. Time sort of passes. You go here and you go there. You get to doing other things. . . ."

One of those "other things," I knew, had been working on the famous Madeira-Mamore Railway.

"Sure, the Mad Mary," he told me once. "That's what we used to call it—Mad Mary. The crazy iron bitch. And do you know what that railroad was, mister? That railroad was the greatest engineering job the world ever seen. Two hundred miles of track—that's what we laid down there; two hundred miles of shining steel through the worst hellhole on the face of the earth. And by the time we were through there was a corpse for every crosstie on the roadbed."

"Well—" He sighed. "The Mary herself's been a dead pigeon a long time now. I thought for a while I was going to make another little pile on her. But no. The rubber boom died—and she died. And I moved on again; tried something else again. . . ."

Keeping track of Mordecai Cobb for the next twenty years was like trying to find your way through the jungle itself. At one time or another, apparently, he had had a go at just about everything a man could do in Amazonia: looking for gold again; looking for rubber, balata, hides, timbo, Brazil nuts; trading with the Indians; working in a warehouse in Santarem, in a lumber mill in Iquitos, on river boats on the Negro and Ucayali; dreaming of the day when he would have a boat and an outfit and a few dollars in his pocket again and could head back for the Rio do Sol and the Big Bonanza. There seemed to have been one long blank period during which he may or may not have been in jail. There was another (sometimes he said it was three months, sometimes three years) when he had had an Indian wife and lived in a tiny native village up near the Ecuadorian border. Then there were the Ford rubber plantations on the Tapajos.

. . . And there, for eight years, was Mordecai Cobb—first at Fordlandia, then at Belterra—at long last a cog in the machine of progress, earning more and living better then ever before in his life, and hating every minute of it.

"I could of told them it all wouldn't come to nothing," he said, shaking his head and spitting reflectively. "All that scientific stuff's all right in its place, I guess, but its place ain't the Amazon. And the rest of the crap they set up—dormitories and cafeterias and schools and dentists and line-up-for-this and line-up-for-that—that's all right too, I guess. Only not on the Amazon. You can't turn this country into no factory, mister. Nor into a boy-scout camp neither. Wild and free: that's the Amazon. Sun and rain, jungle and river, rubber and gold—and let the pium flies eat the hindmost. Yep, I could of told them a few things all right. And one of them was that even Hennery Ford, with all his men and all his millions, wasn't going to tame this man's country."

No, even Ford hadn't been able to tame the Amazon. For fifteen years he poured money and men into it, and then at last gave up in disgust. He turned his plantations over to the Brazilians, and pulled out. End of Amazon Dream, Mechanized Version. The jungle grew on. The rivers flowed on.

Mordecai Cobb moved on. . . .

"By this time war was starting up again," he said, "and

there was all kinds of crazy things going on. You seen yourself what it was like. Generals and politicos all over the place. Soldiers building airports. Doctors sticking needles into people. Rubber Development fellers sticking needles into trees. That's when Esperanzy and a few other of those places got really started. It was Ford all over again, and, like I could of told them, it ended up like Ford too—everybody running like hell for home and leaving the trees to the worms and the bugs."

What had he done during the war?

"Me? Oh, about the same as always. Little of this, little of that. Somebody was always trying to hook me into some damn alphabet-outfit, but I said no thanks, I'd had all I wanted of that stuff with Mr. F. of Detroit. I'd been a loner all my life, and that's what I was aiming to stay." In the end, however, he had taken a job with the R.D.C. as a sort of guide-interpreter. "Figured it would keep me moving around at least," he explained. "And that it did all right. Best part of it, though, was that when the war ended and they pulled out they let me have the *Cantora* here almost for free. She had a different name then, of course. Like I told you, I changed it after I hooked up with Singer."

Why Singer?

"On account of I was busted again, like always. Sure—there I was for the first time in my life with a boat all my own. After all them years of hustling and half starving I was set up right at last. I could see that Big Bonanza shining on the horizon like the morning sun. Rio do Sol, here I come at last! ... Only I couldn't move an inch. I didn't even have the price of enough gas to move from one side of the dock to the other. So I hear that Singer's looking for a guy with a boat, to peddle for them up in the back-country. So I say okay, I'm your man. And one night about a year later, there I am tied up at a dump called Esperanzy, minding my own business with a friendly bottle, when a caboclo sticks his head in the cabin and says there's two senhors and a senhora sitting over in one of the warehouses; and, though I don't know it at the time, it's what I been waiting for these thirty-eight years."

Silence. A very long silence. . . .

Spit. Cackle.

I remember, on that first night on the Yurima the mosquitoes for some reason weren't as bad as usual, and we had stayed out late on the *Cantora*'s deck in the warm whispering stillness. I remember the trees along the bank to which we were moored, and how their branches overhung the launch, making a small pocket of deep shadow. But beyond the trees the moon was bright and silver on the river, and now and again as Cobb talked its reflected light winked and glittered in his eyes.

"It's funny how things go," he said at last. "I reckon in those years I been up and down every damn river there is between the Andes and the Atlantic. Excepting only one. Excepting the one out of all of them that I've always wanted to go up most of all.

"Sure, funny—" he repeated. "I guess I didn't tell you before, but back there long ago, while Gizella was lying in the smoke-shed waiting to die—all of a sudden then she opens her eyes and smiles a little and says to me: 'It wasn't God's will, Mordecai, that we should get where we were going. But *you* will get there—yes. Some day, with His help, you will get there for us both.' Like I've said, I ain't got much religion, but the more I think about it the more I get the notion that mebbe she was right."

Cobb paused again and got stiffly to his feet. "Yep, she was quite a gal, that little wop," he said. "Quite a gal."

That night, for the first time since we had left Esperança, he took a bottle with him into his hammock. McHugh didn't say anything. None of us said anything. And the next morning he seemed about the same as on any other morning. When we moved off up the Yurima, he was at his usual place on the *Cantora*'s foredeck, his bony shoulders hunched over

168

the wheel, his pale hooded eyes squinting into the distance. The sun rose, red and enormous, behind us. The green shores opened up ahead. And Mordecai Cobb set out on still another day of his lonely journey on the river that has no end.

12

THE RIVER TWISTED on into the green miles. Now that we had passed Cobb's place of ghosts, I was the only member of the party with any personal experience of the country ahead; but that experience, of course, was only of the sketchiest sort. The Yurima from the air and the Yurima from the deck of a launch bore little resemblance to each other, and nowhere in its shifting maze was there any landmark that stirred my memory to recognition. One thing that encouraged me, however, was that my judgment about the navigability of the route had thus far been correct. All the way up from the Juruá we had taken periodic soundings of the channel, and everywhere there had been enough depth for even the largest of river boats. With the river still high and free-flowing, it seemed highly improbable that it would present any major obstructions before we reached our destination.

"This here water won't be dropping much for another three months," Cobb assured us. And by that time the *Fortaleza* would long since have been in and out.

It was on our fourth day on the Yurima that we came to the one landmark that I *did* know. A fork appeared in the river ahead. The water of the lefthand fork was the same yellow-brown as all the rivers below it. But that of the right-hand fork was black. For a distance of perhaps a quarter-mile there was a swirl of mingling currents, and then the darker current disappeared. Beyond the junction, separating the two tributaries, was a bare mud promontory, and on it, squalid and lonely, a cluster of thatch huts.

The inevitable fleet of vultures circled patiently in the sky. The inevitable row of naked pot-bellied children stood staring as we swung in toward our mooring. Presently a few men and women emerged from the huts and joined them.

"Anything to trade?" we asked.

They went on staring.

"Fruits? Vegetables? Fish?"

A few heads shook: no.

"Where's your chefé?"

One of the men pointed to a hut, and we clambered ashore.

The villagers were darker-skinned than the caboclos from Esperança, with the straight black hair and equiline features that are the mark of the pure, or almost pure, Indian. Except for the children, however, they were dressed in store clothes, wore crucifixes and saints' medals around their necks, and spoke a recognizable, if distorted, Portuguese. *Indios mansos* —tame Indians—are what the Brazilians call these marginal people of the Amazon tributaries; and for many centuries now, since the coming of the early traders and missionaries, they have lived a twilit transitional life in the no-man's-land between civilization and the jungle. The old lores and skills of the days when they were *Indios bravos*—wild Indians— have been forgotten, and they had learned almost nothing to replace them. They trudge the long miles of the forest estradas, searching for the white man's rubber. They wait for their food and other meager necessities to arrive from downriver on the white man's boat. There is no naturalness in their lives, no independence, no self-respect. Ignorant, diseased, without hope or strength, they huddle in their desolate mudbank settlements along the great rivers, fearing the wilderness that was once their home, clinging precariously to the fringes of a world they never made.

The village chefé, to whom we were led, was an old man with the face of an Indian war-god and a body covered with the running pustules of yaws. . . . No, unfortunately there was no food in the village for trading. Almost all their food was brought in on the launch of the patrão, which came twice a year to collect their rubber.

"Have any other boats been here?" McHugh asked.

"No, senhor," said the chefé. "It is many moons now since another boat has come up the Yurima; and even then it was not a real boat, but only a little nutshell with two men in it."

"What kind of men?"

"They were *brancos*, senhor. White men, like yourselves, who talked to each other with a strange tongue. One said he was a priest, but he was not a true priest—not a Catolico. About the other I do not know, except that he was a tall man and quiet, with hair dark red like the achiote berry and circles of glass over his eyes.

We glanced at Christine; and though she said nothing her face spoke for her. It was Barna all right.

How long had they stayed at the village? Only a few hours, said the chefé. . . . Then where had they gone? Up-river. . . . Up which river? The old man pointed: not to the black tributary but to the brown. . . .

McHugh looked at me and then back at the Indian. "You're sure of that?" he demanded.

He was sure.

"The brown river—is that the Malaguay?"

"Yes, senhor, it is the Malaguay."

"And the black one—what's that?"

The old man shrugged. "It is the black river."

Nothing we said or asked could shake his story. The other Indians nodded and pointed. The two *brancos* had taken the lefthand fork.

"Where were they going?" we asked.

"They did not say."

"They didn't come back?"

"No, they did not come back."

"What is there up the Malaguay?"

The chefé shrugged again. "There is jungle," he said. "There are *Indios bravos*."

172

"And up the black river?"

"The same."

"Have you been up them?"

"No, senhors."

"Have you heard of a place called Graça de Deus?"

"No, senhors."

"Of the Serra Aurora? Of the Rio do Sol?"

"No, senhors."

Back on the launch we groped our way through the dilemma. There was the possibility, to be sure, that the old chief had been lying, but it seemed a remote one, for he had answered unhesitatingly, and the others, without coaching, had corroborated him. As for their being simply mistaken, that seemed unlikely too. Travelers were so rare in this remote place that the Indians would undoubtedly recall every detail of their coming and going.... What then? ... Barna and Lassiter had gone up the lefthand tributary. Why? Because they'd known something about it? ... I, of course, knew nothing about it, but only about the other branch— the black river. Yet there was no reason why the brown shouldn't also lead to the hills. It was perfectly possible. Almost anything was possible.

In the end it was decided to follow the brown. There was no reason to disbelieve the Indians. In our minds, the search for oil and for Barna had become almost synonymous. And also—there was Christine. After her long months and miles of journeying it would have been unthinkable, at this point, to disregard the word of men who had actually seen her husband and veer off on a tangent of our own.

Certainly, it was a responsibility I wasn't going to take; and when McHugh spoke out for the lefthand fork I raised no objection. McHugh wrote a brief note and left it with the Indian headman, to give to Wooderson when the *Fortaleza* appeared. Then Cobb spun his flywheel, the *Cantora* shook and spat, and we were on our way again.

The Malaguay (if it *was* the Malaguay) was indistinguishable from the Yurima. We saw no further settlements, no tame Indians, no wild Indians. For the first time, however, a thread of tenseness and anticipation ran through the monotony of the hours, because we knew that, for better or worse, we were on the final lap of the journey. And we at last knew, too, whereas before we had only surmised and hoped, that Nils Barna had preceded us on our route. In spite of the innumerable turnings, the river bore on gradually toward the southwest—which was the right direction. By afternoon of the second day beyond the village I estimated that we could be no more than fifty miles from the base of the Serra Aurora, and many times we climbed to a vantage point on the launch and swung our binoculars along the horizon ahead. But there was no sign of hills, nor even of the banks of clouds that presumably still shrouded them. Mile after mile, before and around us, the forest spread away flat and unbroken to the empty sky.

That night, after the others had gone to their hammocks, I sat alone in the *Cantora*'s cabin, poring over our maps. For a long time I looked down at the weaving line that marked our course: at the black ribbons of the rivers, the blank greenness beyond the rivers, the two ultimate threads that twisted out into the greenness beyond the farthest reach of the Yurima. Along one thread someone had pencilled the word *Malaguay*, along the other the word *black;* and beyond *black* was a circle, and in the circle, *Graça de Deus*. I erased it. I drew a second circle in the blank beyond *Malaguay* and wrote *Graça de Deus* there. . . . Or at least that was what I thought I had written, until a while later, waking from a doze, I looked at the map again and saw in the circle the word *Barna*.

Occasionally Christine and I still played casino. Sometimes we stood together at the *Cantora*'s rail. But that was all. We had been strangers. For an hour or two, once, our lives had met and touched. And now we were strangers again. Now and then I wondered how long we would have gone on being strangers, if it hadn't been for the night of the "party."

It was, I think, on our third day on the Malaguay and our eighteenth out from Esperança, and it was also one of the innumerable feast-days that dot the Catholic-Brazilian calendar. Not, to be sure, that there was much to feast on, nor that the caboclos usually marked their saints' days with any great festivity. But on this one occasion they did, for a few hours, break out of their usual shell of stolid apathy. Partly it was release from the tedium of the journey, partly, perhaps, the knowledge that we were at last nearing our destination. But whatever the cause, a spark was generated, caught fire and spread, and that evening, when we pulled into shore, the whole community threw itself into a celebration. A great bonfire was built in a cleared space between the trees. Each family selected its plumpest fowl for roasting. A guitar, an improvised drum and a dozen gourds of cachaça rum made their appearance from nowhere. And when darkness fell the night-sounds of the jungle were, for once, drowned out in a man-made din of shouting and singing.

I had thought that McHugh might object to the hubbub—and especially to the cachaça—but he was as full of good spirits as anyone, and after supper he, Christine and I sat close to the bonfire, each with a mug of Cobb's rum, and watched the younger caboclos dancing. Presently Touro's huge figure appeared among the others, towering above his plump wife, Tereza Carolina. Then a moment later there was another familiar figure—not towering this time, but lean and scrawny as a billygoat as it whirled and hopped against the bright background of the flames. And suddenly I was laughing out loud, as I hadn't laughed for a long time. For the billygoat was none other than Mordecai Cobb—and his partner was Serafima Batista.

Soon a group of caboclos was crowding around us. "You will dance too," they urged us. "Yes, the senhors and senhora will dance too!"

McHugh shook his head, smiling; and so did I. But suddenly Christine was on her feet beside me, her hands outstretched and pulling me up. "Yes, the senhor and I will dance too," she told them.

And then we were dancing. We were two more shadows among the other shadows in that jungle clearing, weaving and wheeling and stamping on the soft earth in what, as near as I could tell was a cross between a samba and a Virginia Reel. I heard the strum of the guitar and the thump of the drum. I felt the glow of the rum inside me, and I saw Chistine looking up at me, her brown face flushed, her eyes bright, her lips smiling. And I thought to myself: this is the first time you've ever seen her really smile, really laugh, really happy; this is the Christine you've never known but always imagined— light and dancing, young and laughing; and now I was laughing too, I was looking down at her, I was pulling her close to me, until I could feel the warmth of her body against mine, warmer than any rum, warmer than any flame. . . .

And then—it was all over. The music had stopped. The fire was dying. The dancers had gone. Christine had gone. The spark of the little celebration was extinguished, the singing and shouting were stilled, and the deep hum of the forest crept back into the clearing and reclaimed its own.

I lay for awhile in my hammock, among the trees. Then I got up and walked across the clearing, looking to see if perhaps McHugh or Cobb were available for a final drink or a snatch of talk. But there was no one stirring. After a while I went down to the shore and across the barge and onto the *Cantora*. I stood leaning on the rail and looked out into the darkness.

We were moored in a deep inlet of the river, and no current touched the water. The air hung heavy and still. Along the shore I could see the rows of hammocks sagging like enormous ripe fruits from the trees, and among them the quick darting arcs of fireflies. There was no sound now. Nothing moved. But when presently I turned a little I saw that there was another figure at the *Cantora's* rail, perhaps thirty feet away from me, gazing out over the stern. I approached it and the figure swung around toward me—and then I saw that it was Christine.

At first neither of us spoke. Then I came closer and stood beside her, and after a few moments I said, "Trouble sleeping again?"

She nodded.

"Hammocks take some getting used to."

"No, I like hammocks," she said. "They're clean and cool."

"Yes, they're cool," I agreed.

"Do you think we'll sleep in hammocks or cots at Graça de Deus?"

"Hammocks, I should think."

We were silent for a little while. Then—

"Mark," she said.

"Yes?"

"Will we get there tomorrow?"

"I don't know."

"I was thinking that perhaps we might. That perhaps tonight was the last—" Her voice trailed off, and there was another pause. "It's hard to believe, isn't it?" she said.

In the darkness I could see her eyes looking up at me, but they were not the same eyes that had looked up at me while we were dancing. There was no laughter in them now; no glinting firelight.

"Don't be afraid, Chris," I said.

She didn't answer.

"It will be all right."

"Yes, of course," she murmured. "It will be all right."

She had turned away, and I stood looking down at her without speaking. I felt the deep warmth rising again within me—filling my body, filling my brain. And now at last I knew, once and for all, what it was that had happened to me . . . and I wondered bitterly *why* it had happened.

No, that isn't true, for I knew that too. I knew exactly and clearly and perfectly. It had happened because it was the one thing still needed to complete the monstrously bad joke of my life. Not to want, not to care: that had been my only defense against its aimlessness and sterility, the shell I had substituted for arms and armor. And now that too was gone. Even the dull peace of apathy was gone. After all those months and years of nothingness I was alive again, a man again, capable of feeling, desiring, seeking, possessing. But instead of victory it was only another defeat. Instead of happiness it was only absurdity and futility.

It was a joke. If I had been back at my old corner table at the Café Nabuco I would have taken a long deep drink and laughed out loud.

But there wasn't any drink. There was neither laughter or tears, but only emptiness. Only the dark nothingness of the night around us and Christine Barna standing beside me at the rail.

"We're always standing at rails," I said. "Other people stand at bars or gates or altars. We stand at rails."

Christine didn't speak. A night-bird cawed and was still. The fireflies wove their tiny tireless patterns through the blackness of the shore.

Perhaps a minute passed. Perhaps only a few seconds. And then I did something I had not known I was going to do at all. I reached out my hand and touched Christine's. She did not withdraw it, but merely stood straight and still before me, not speaking, not moving, and for an instant there it was, naked and shining in the darkness between us: desire—hope —reality: the reality that was life itself, and yet more insubstantial and preposterous than any dream.

Then I dropped my hand.

"Goodnight, Mark," she said.

"Goodnight, Chris."

I watched her as she made her way across the shoreward barge and disappeared among the shadows along the bank, where the hammocks hung from the trees. I watched the shadows and the thin tracery of the fireflies and then, turning, I stood watching the still water of the inlet spreading away into the river, and beyond it the river spreading away between the forest walls, farther and farther, deeper and deeper, into the darkness.

"Goodnight, Chris. . . ."

We didn't reach Graça de Deus the next day. . . . Nor the next. . . . The stream broadened and narrowed again, twisted and straightened again, boring on endlessly into the green heart of stillness. And on the twentieth night of our journey we lay again in our hammocks at the forest's edge, with the dark water gliding beside us, as it seemed now it would glide on forever.

It was about four that I awoke, and I knew at once that it was a sound that had awakened me. But I had no intimation of what sort of sound it was. Raising myself on my elbow, I looked around, but saw nothing. Then I lay still and listened.

To one side of me I could hear the soft rise and fall of McHugh's breathing, and then presently a faint creaking of hammock cords on the other side, as Christine shifted in her sleep. That was all. Yet in the next instant I was sitting upright, because I knew it wasn't all. Another sound was there, deep behind the darkness, and as I listened now, motionless and straining, it swelled until it seemed to fill my ears and throb softly in the channels of my brain. It was low, persistent, pervading, and I had the impression that it was coming from very far away. It rose, undulated, fell, swept up again out of the stillness and subsided into it. Then it was gone.

It's the planes again, I thought. You've been dreaming and hearing the planes again. Lie down. Go back to sleep. . . . But I didn't lie down. For a few minutes I remained as I was, without moving. Then, bending over, I pulled on my boots, stood up, and walked toward the bank of the river.

Suddenly I realized that another man was standing on the

179

bank, and that the man was Cobb. "Heard it too?" he asked as I came up to him.

"Yes," I said. "What is it?"

"A cachoeira."

"Rapids, you mean?"

"Yep, rapids."

I listened again; and almost instantly I recognized that he was right. Soft and remote though it was, what I heard now was unmistakably the sound of rushing water.

"Why didn't we hear it before?" I asked.

Cobb shrugged. "Sound can behave in queer ways. Besides, everybody was moving around and talking."

"How far away would you say it is?"

"Four or five miles, I'd reckon."

"Then we're—" I hesitated, groping for the possible alternatives. But there weren't any alternatives. Hills or no hills, rapids meant the end of navigable water. "Then we're there," I said. "It's Graça de Deus."

"It damn well better be," said Cobb.

That last morning, for the first time on the journey, we pushed off before daylight. When we awoke the caboclos and told them why, a tremor of anticipation ran along the riverbank, and for perhaps half an hour, while we unslung our hammocks, ate a quick uncooked breakfast and clambered aboard the barges, the darkness was alive with movement and voices. But once we were underway, anticipation took another form: the form of stillness. There was no sound at all now, except the familiar stuttering rhythm of the launch's engine and, in the distance, the deeper rumbling rhythm of the cachoeira. The men and women standing on the rails and bales and windlasses and gunwales loomed like so many carved figures in the darkness.

And presently, with almost startling suddenness, night began to fade. The stars dimmed and receded, and the void beyond them turned to sombre purple and from purple to ashen gray. On either side of us the forest walls emerged from obscurity, their intricate tracery transfixed and clear, their foliage glowing with a pale ghostly green. An unseen bird cawed wildly and was still. And now, in the east, the sky gleamed with a great fan of light from the still-hidden sun.

I looked at Christine, standing motionless beside me. And then away again.

There was a bend in the river. The next reach. The next bend. There was yet another stretch of green-brown water and at its far end a strip of foaming white, where the river came down over a spillway of ledges and boulders. In the next moment, however, it was no longer the rapids at which I was looking, but a small clearing on the righthand shore, perhaps half a mile below their beginning. And now, coming abreast of the clearing, we swung around and nosed into its mudbank, and Cobb shut off the *Cantora's* engine.

I remember the sound of the cachoeira. I remember the single thatched cabin that stood in the center of the clearing, and the plume of smoke that rose above it into the windless air, and the figure of a man standing in the doorway. He was a tall angular man in faded khaki, hatless, with thick dark-reddish hair and a pale beardless face on which he wore a pair of steel-rimmed glasses. For a few moments he remained in the doorway and then walked slowly toward us across the clearing; and I watched him as he came closer and reached the mudbank and stopped; and then it was no longer he I was watching, but Christine again, as she left the rail and made her way across the shoreward barge to the bank.

She came up onto it and hesitated and then stepped forward again, and the man stepped forward and took her gently in his arms. For a long moment they didn't move. No one on the launch and barges moved. And presently, Nils Barna raised his eyes and looked at us, and the sun, just risen, glinted with sudden fire on the lenses of his glasses.

"Welcome to El Dorado, gentlemen," he said.

PART TWO

THE SHORE

13

AND NOW WE were there. On a mudbank called Graça de Deus: a pencilled legend on a map, a fleck in the forest-ocean. This was it at last. It was nothing at all . . . but it was the center of the world.

And in that center, on that first incredible morning, stood a man called Nils Barna, and of all the unreal reality that confronted us he was the most unreal of all. He was a tall, slightly stooped figure in faded khaki, appearing like a mirage on a mudbank. He was a fine-featured bloodless face, a shock of rust-colored hair, a pair of cool gray eyes behind glinting lenses. He was a voice speaking in quiet, almost unaccented English to McHugh, to Cobb, to O Touro.

"So you at last changed your mind about coming up the rivers?" he asked the Negro.

"Yes," said Touro, "I changed my mind."

"Perhaps I should take a few lessons in persuasiveness from the other gentlemen here." Barna smiled a little. "And you, Mr. Cobb?" he went on. "I presume you hope to sell some of those magical machines of yours to the Indians?"

"Indians—" McHugh broke in. "Around here?"

"Their village is about half a mile inland," said Barna.

"What sort of Indians?"

"They call themselves Tupari. They are a branch of the Tupi-Guarani family, I believe. You need not worry about their bothering you—unless, of course, you bother them first." Barna turned back to Cobb. "In the matter of your sewing machines, for example, I would not recommend too

—well—too aggressive a salesmanship. That was the Reverend Lassiter's lamentable error."

Yes, of course—Lassiter. Where was he? we asked.

"Unfortunately he is dead," said Barna.

"Dead?"

Barna nodded. "You have not yet had a chance to inspect the clearing. When you do you will notice over on the far side the remains of a burnt-down building."

"Well?"

"It was the Reverend Lassiter's chapel. The Tupari burned it down."

"And Lassiter?"

"They burned him inside of it."

For a long moment we simply stared at him.

"As I was about to mention to Mr. Cobb," Barna continued, "the Reverend Lassiter was a bit of what you Americans call a high-pressure salesman. He went about his work in very businesslike fashion. The Indians, however, had apparently had somewhat the same experience once before and were not inclined to repeat it. They were really quite patient about the whole thing; I recall no less than three occasions when their chief, Pombal, asked him to leave. But the Reverend Lassiter, unfortunately, was a stubborn man. And at last the Tupari found it necessary to take direct action."

"Good God," said McHugh. "And what did *you* do?"

"I gave the poor fellow as decent a burial as I could. The Indians helped too. Ironically enough, they were better acquainted than I with the Christian funeral ceremonial."

"Didn't you try to escape?"

"Escape? No. For one thing, there was no way to, because the Indians had also burned Mr. Lassiter's launch. Also, there was no reason to. The Indians, you see, were not hostile toward me."

"Not hostile—?"

"No—why should they have been? I wanted nothing of them. I was not interfering in their lives."

"You mean you've simply gone on living here?"

"Yes, I have gone on living here." There was another pause, and Barna, watching us, seemed again to be smiling. "Come, gentlemen," he went on, "there is really no need to look so shocked. It was an unfortunate thing for Mr. Lassiter, yes; but one cannot blame the Tupari. After all, we from the civilized world are scarcely innocent of violence, would you say?"

"But—"

"But this is different? I am afraid I shall have to disagree with you. The Tupari, you see, acted neither from bloodlust nor for conquest, but simply to preserve their way of life. And that, if I recall my modern political philosophy, is the most highly respectable of motives."

The cool eyes moved away from us to Christine, who was standing beside him. "But we can discuss these matters at some other time," he suggested to McHugh. "My wife, I am sure, has had a hard journey. And also we have not seen each other for a very long time. . . ."

He nodded, took Christine's arm and, while the rest of us watched in silence, led her across the clearing toward his cabin.

Here was Nils Barna. But where was *here?* Later on that same first morning we unloaded one of the three outboard-motored canoes, and McHugh, Cobb and I cruised the half-mile upstream to the lower limit of the cachoeira. How far the rapids extended we couldn't see, for a sharp bend in the river blocked off our line of vision; but what we could see, beyond any doubt, was that it was impassable—for the *Fortaleza,* the launch and barges, and even a canoe.

This in itself was no major setback, for it would have been too much to hope that there was no obstacle whatever at the point where the Malaguay emerged from the hills. . . . But where *were* the hills? Above the bordering line of the tree-tops, as far as the eye could see, there was only the unbroken blue of the sky. . . . Could it be that we had taken a false trail, after all? That we should have followed the black river instead of this one? The mere fact of Barna's presence seemed to disprove it. He obviously was here for a reason. After six months in the region it was inconceivable that he did not know what he was about. And yet ...

Where were the hills?

McHugh's eyes turned from the blank horizon and fixed on me, questioningly; but he was not the man for either premature judgment or quick discouragement, and all he said was, "We'll talk to Barna. He'll know what the story is."

When we returned to the clearing, however, he was still in his cabin with Christine. Cobb was for routing him out forthwith, but McHugh restrained him, pointing out that our reception had been cool enough as it was, without our further antagonizing Barna by breaking in on his reunion with his wife. Also, whatever the situation proved to be, this was obviously going to be at least our temporary base of operations, and there was plenty to do besides asking questions.

Accordingly, we called the caboclos together. And we went to work. For the rest of the day, and through the days that followed, men and animals and tools and machines and supplies moved from launch and barge to the shore, and then back and forth along the shore, in a welter of purposeful confusion. There was the sound of axes and machetes, and the green wall of the forest receded. There was the sound of hammers and saws, and huts and sheds began to rise along the open sweep of mudbank. There was the sound of voices everywhere: shouting, arguing, ordering, complaining. There was the voice of Serafima Batista, wailing shrilly, as she looked around her at the place that was to have been the metropolitan rival of Rio and São Paulo.

The site which McHugh selected for our camp was about three-quarters of a mile below the cachoeira, which meant some four or five hundred yards downstream from Barna's clearing. It was on an inlet that afforded good mooring for the launch and barges and was also sufficiently wide and deep, according to McHugh's estimates, to serve the same purpose for the *Fortaleza,* when she arrived. Furthermore it was on ground that had obviously been occupied before (by Indians? missionaries? rubber-hunters?), and was less densely overgrown than the rest of the riverbank. From it a path of sorts led up to Barna's cabin and the rapids beyond; and from Barna's clearing a second path forked off inland, presumably toward the Indian village.

During our first day at Graça de Deus we saw no sign of Indians. It was our plan, of course, to establish friendly relations with them and to elicit their help in our exploration of the country. But none of them appeared in our clearing, and McHugh felt that, for our part, it would be wiser to wait and make our first overtures through Nils Barna. Fortunately, no word of the Reverend Lassiter or his demise had seeped through to the caboclos. Strict orders were issued that everyone was to stay close to the river. And for the moment, if there was no contact, there was at least no trouble.

But there was also no Barna. Throughout that first day we momentarily expected him and Christine to come down to the launch, which still served as our headquarters. But neither appeared; and when, toward evening, McHugh dispatched a caboclo with an invitation that they join us for supper, Barna sent back a return message expressing his thanks, but declining. The night passed. The next morning passed. Then about noon, McHugh and I walked up the path to Barna's clearing. A plump, almost naked Indian girl was squatting beside a crude oven near the cabin. She watched us with slow dark eyes, but neither moved nor spoke, as we passed by her and approached the entrance.

I have called Barna's dwelling a cabin. Actually it was a cross between a hut and a small house, constructed, Indian-fashion, of thatch and woven fronds, but with a raised flooring, windows and a door. We knocked, waited briefly, and then Barna appeared, seeming even taller and more angular than before, as he stood framed in the low doorway. For an instant he looked at us blankly, as if not recognizing us; or perhaps it was only the harsh sunlight beating against his eyes, for the next moment he nodded, pleasantly enough, and asked us in. As we followed him, a second, inner door opened across the room, and Christine appeared.

"Hello, John. Hello, Mark," she said.

"I am sorry if I have appeared rude," said Barna in his quiet meticulous voice. "But my wife and I—after so long a separation—"

While a few more amenities went back and forth my eyes moved about the room. What I had expected to find I don't know. Books, perhaps; scientific paraphernalia; a laboratory of sorts. Nothing would have surprised me. But there were none of these. There were the thatched walls, a woven mat on the floor, a table, a few chairs, an unpainted chest and cupboard. Beyond the doorway through which Christine had come there was a second smaller room, in which I could see two slung hammocks, another chest, another chair. I looked at each object in turn, slowly and methodically, as if I were taking an inventory, and presently I realized that I was doing so because I was trying not to look at Christine.

McHugh was no hand for wasting time when he had something on his mind. "We're sorry to break in on you, Dr. Barna," he was saying as I turned back to them. "But, frankly, we're baffled, and I think you can help us."

"Help you?" Barna repeated. "How?"

McHugh told him briefly what we had expected and what we had found. "Or rather what we haven't found," he amended. "The range of hills called the Serra Aurora."

"Ah yes," said Barna. "The Serra Aurora—"

"You know them, then?"

"I have heard of them, of course. The Serra Aurora are rather famous in Amazonian legend."

"Where are they?"

"The Tupari say they are off to the southwest of here."

"Up the river?"

"Yes, in that direction."

"How far up?"

"The Tupari are vague about distances."

"How far would *you* say?"

"I really couldn't say. I have never been there."

McHugh's eyes narrowed slightly. I could see that he didn't believe Barna, but, for the moment at least, he allowed it to pass. . . . How far *had* Barna been? he asked. Only to the head of the rapids, said the latter. . . . And how far was that? About four miles. . . . Was there a trail around them? Yes, there was a trail of sorts, but badly overgrown. . . . And beyond these rapids were there more rapids? Barna really couldn't say.

There was a pause, and then McHugh leaned forward a little and said quietly: "We have reason to believe, Dr. Barna, that the Malaguay flows along the base of the Serra Aurora. And that there it joins another river, called the Rio do Sol. Or perhaps the upper Malaguay itself is known by that name."

Barna didn't say anything.

"You have heard of the Rio do Sol?"

"Yes, I have heard of it," said Barna.

"What do you know of it?"

"I have already told you that I have not been beyond the rapids."

"What have you heard of it, then?"

"The Tupari have their own stories, of course. Certain explorers and prospectors, I believe, have others." Barna looked from one to the other of us with a bland half-smiling expression. "I gather that you gentlemen have also heard certain stories," he added. "And that is why you are here."

McHugh nodded.

"I shall be most interested to hear the results of your investigation. In country of this sort the possibilities, of course, are almost unlimited. New flora and fauna. Mineral deposits. Primitive tribes. Perhaps even a lost city—"

McHugh hesitated a moment, and then he decided to say it. "—Or perhaps oil, Dr. Barna?" he asked.

I remember the silence that followed as we waited for

Barna's reaction. But, at least visibly, he showed no reaction. The thin long-boned hands remained open on his lap. The gray eyes behind the steel-rimmed glasses remained steady and opaque.

"Oil—" he repeated presently. "Yes, that is an interesting possibility too."

"Meaning that you think it's there?"

"There, Mr. McHugh?"

"On the plateau behind the hills. Along the River of the Sun."

"I was under the impression that I had already explained—"

"You've explained nothing, and you know it," McHugh interrupted; and I could see that his temper was wearing thin. "Do you expect us to believe that you've come all the way into this wilderness for no purpose? Or that you've been here for six months and still know nothing about the country?"

"I am afraid that my reasons for being here are my own affair," said Barna mildly. "And what you choose to believe, Mr. McHugh, is yours."

"You still deny that you have been in to the Serra Aurora?"

"That is correct."

"Or that you've ever been up the river beyond the rapids?"

"Also correct."

"How about the Indians here? Don't they go up in their canoes?"

"The Tupari do not have canoes," said Barna.

"Well, on forest trails, then. There are trails, aren't there?"

"Yes, there are a few trails."

"Do some lead as far as the hills?"

"I really could not say. But I rather doubt it."

"Where do they lead, then?"

"My impression is that most of them lead nowhere, but are merely hunting circuits. You really should accompany the Tupari on one of their hunting trips, Mr. McHugh. It is quite fascinating to observe their methods."

"I'm not interested in—"

"You will be when you have seen them," Barna assured him. "They have had to become particularly ingenious, because they no longer use poison on their weapons."

"About these trails, Dr. Barna—"

"Like most Amazon tribes, you see, the Tupari used to manufacture the famous curaré poison; but since their first contact with the outer world they have lost the technique, along with so many other of their jungle skills."

"Look, Doctor, all I'm trying to find out is—"

"Since I came here I have been trying to help them rediscover the formula. That is quite amusing, don't you think? —a European scientist struggling unsuccessfully to match the skill of jungle Indians. But it is also quite a serious matter for the Tupari, for curaré, I should say, is as important on their level of civilization as steel or oil, or even uranium, on our level. After all, gentlemen, any culture is only as powerful as its tools of destruction, and. . . ."

The quiet, modulated voice talked on. McHugh sat silently, his lips compressed into a thin line. I watched a shaft of sunlight that had slanted in through the screened window and was gleaming softly in Christine Barna's hair.

Mordecai Cobb was not the man to cool his heels on a mudbank. While McHugh and I were with Nils Barna he had set off to do some investigating on his own, and toward sundown he reappeared with his report. He had found the trail around the cachoeira, of which Barna had spoken, and followed it to the end. It was overgrown but passable, and came out on the river again just above the head of the rapids.

"And then what?" asked McHugh.

"It ends."

"And the river?"

"It goes on."

"Any sign of more rapids?"

"No."

"Or of hills?"

"No."

Cobb listened, nodding, as we told him of our conversation with Barna, and when we had finished he spat meditatively and said, "I could of told you as much."

"What do you mean?" said McHugh.

"What I mean," said Cobb, "is that if you was the perfessor—if you'd been scabbing around in a jungle for six months and put your finger on something big—would *you* go blabbing about it to the first Tom, Dick and Harry that came along?"

"We're hardly Tom, Dick and Harry," McHugh pointed out. "The Southern Cross Corporation happens to have the exploration rights to this country."

"Exploration rights in a pig's behind. Where do you think we are, amigo—in a law office or something? 'Rights' are about as important as snowballs in this piece of the woods."

McHugh slowly stroked his jaw. "What are you suggesting we do?" he asked. "Ignore him?"

"Ignore him, hell! Put the screws on him. Learn him who's running the show here. Look, Mac, just give me ten minutes with that perfessor and I'll guarantee you—"

He went on for a while, but McHugh seemed scarcely to be listening. "I doubt if anything like that will be necessary," he said, when Cobb had finished.

"If he's going to be tough, we got to be tough too."

"There'll be plenty of time to be tough later, if we have to. Meanwhile there's another tack to take."

"Softsoaping him, you mean?"

"No, not softsoaping him. Bypassing him."

"Bypassing? . . . For who? For what?"

"For the Indians," said McHugh.

Too large a group, we decided, might unduly frighten the Tupari; too small a one might put us in needless danger. In addition to ourselves, the contact-party included O Touro and two of the steadier caboclos. We carried rifles, but they were slung innocuously over our shoulders. We carried gifts and trade goods. At the last minute Frei Ambrosio, who had got wind of the project, appeared and pleaded to be taken along, but McHugh gently turned him down. Our relations with the Indians would scarcely be improved by introducing an immediate reminder of the Reverend Lassiter.

"You all know the Brazilian Indian laws," said McHugh, before we started off. "You can't use force on them, and you can't use the threat of force. That's one thing we're not going to get in trouble about. Understand?"

We nodded.

"Understand?" he repeated, looking directly at Cobb.

"Don't worry, chefé," Cobb assured him. "Me and them Indios are going to have a regular love feast."

Leaving the clearing, we followed the trail to Barna's cabin. There was no sign, however, of either him or Christine, and this time we did not stop, but turned off on the branch trail that forked inland from the river. For perhaps ten minutes we moved along, quickly but warily, between high opaque walls of frond and fern. Then the path mounted a slight rise in the ground, twisted and broadened— and we came out into the Tupari village.

It consisted of a clearing about fifty yards across, with a small stream running along one side and a ring of circular thatched huts huddled in the center. Only a few of the tribe, mostly women and children, were in evidence when we first emerged into the open, but as we advanced, slowly now, others appeared in the doorways of the huts, and all of them stared at us in motionless silence. As far as I could tell, they seemed a sort of crossbreed between "wild" Indian and "tame." Some were dressed in oddments of civilized clothing, others only in loincloths and beads. The flesh of most of the men was daubed either with whitish clay or the crimson stain of the achiote berry. A few wore parakeet feathers or necklaces of monkey teeth. Yet the overall effect they presented was not of colorfulness but of squalid drabness, not of barbaric strength but of distrust and fear.

We stopped as we approached the nearest of the huts, and Cobb spoke to the group gathered there in a dialect I could not understand. No one answered, and after a few moments Cobb tried again, presumably in another language. This time the Indians exchanged glances, and presently one of them raised a hand to indicate that we should follow him. Leading us to the far side of the ring of huts, he stopped in front of one that was somewhat larger than the rest, motioned us to wait, and went inside. We stood looking at the dark entrance and at the row of javelins and blowguns that were ranged against the thatch wall on either side of it. The other Indians, perhaps fifty in all, came up silently behind and formed a wide watching circle around us.

Then three men emerged from the hut. First the one who had brought us there; then a younger one; then an older one. The young Tupari, clad only in a loincloth, was a typical forest Indian of the best type: his skin a smooth cocoa-brown, his black hair cut in bangs across his forehead, his body as slim and straight as the bamboo blowguns along the wall. But it was on the other one, the old one, that my eyes were now suddenly fixed. For there was nothing typical of anything about the old one. Even before he had fully emerged from the shadow of the hut he appeared as a strange and repellent figure of a man, gnarled in face and body, warped and curiously lopsided in gait. And now that he was standing close in front of us, in full sunlight, I saw that he, indeed, *was* warped and lopsided. For where his left hand should have been was a stump, where his left ear should have been was a scar, and where his left eye should have been was an empty socket.

His one small dark eye looked at each of us in turn; then he raised his one hand, palm outward, to his forehead, apparently in greeting. There was a moment's silence, and McHugh gestured to Cobb to talk to him. But, to our surprise, the old man suddenly spoke in gutteral Portuguese.

"I am Pombal," he said, "chefé of the Tupari. This"—he indicated the young Indian beside him—"is Cambar, my son."

McHugh said something about the greatness of the Tupari tribe. He said something about the Companhia Cruzeiro do Sul. He said that the Companhia wished only to be friends of the Tupari.

Were we rubber men? asked Pombal.

No, not rubber men.

Or God-men?

Nor God-men either.

What then? Why had we come? Today we had come only to make friends, said McHugh. And to bring gifts. Look— He reached into one of the sacks we had brought with us and pulled out a handful of knives, matches and fishhooks. The circle of Indians around us closed in slightly to see, but their chief held them back with a gesture.

"And for these gifts, senhor," he asked implacably, "—what is it that you want in return?"

"We want nothing in return."

Pombal shook his mutilated head. "I am only a poor forest Indian, perhaps, but I am not a fool. When the white man comes up the rivers, it is not for nothing."

There was a brief silence, and then Cobb took a step forward. "All right, chefé, have it your own way," he said. "We want something. But all it is is the answers to some questions."

"Questions?" the old one repeated. "What questions?"

Cobb told him. McHugh and I picked up where he left off. But we might as well have saved our breath, for to every query Pombal replied with a negative shake of the head. He and his people, he insisted, knew nothing of the country beyond Graça de Deus. They hunted in an area only a mile or two back from the river.

Didn't they go past the cachoeira?

No.

Didn't they use canoes?

197

No.

Hadn't they ever been to the west? to the hills?—to the Rio do Sol?

No.

As the fruitless catechism went on I could see that Cobb was becoming restless. At intervals he fingered the butt of his slung rifle, and finally he turned to McHugh and said, "There might be a few ways to freshen the old boy's memory."

But McHugh shook his head. And presently he took another tack.

"You are friends of Dr. Barna, aren't you?" he asked the chief.

Pombal repeated the name as if it were meaningless to him. Then—"You mean Barnanda?" he said.

"Yes, Barna—Barnanda. The white man who was here before us. We know you are his friends."

Pombal didn't answer.

McHugh turned to the circle of Indians. "Aren't you?" he asked.

But no one answered.

"The others do not know Portuguese," said the old man. "Fortunately none of my people except myself has ever needed to know Portuguese." He paused, and the socket of his sightless eye seemed to be boring straight into us. Then he added: "Yes, we are friends of Barnanda."

"So are we. His good friends. And now we wish to be yours."

"If you are friends of Barnanda, why is he not with you now?"

McHugh hesitated—but only an instant. "We have brought his wife to him," he said. "He is with her now. He could not come."

"When will he come?"

"The next time."

"Then the next time we shall be friends," said Pombal.

A few minutes later we turned to go. The circle of In-

198

dians opened silently to let us pass. And that was the end of it.

Or, rather almost the end—for at the edge of the forest I turned and looked back. The crowd of Tupari had dispersed, but I could see the figures of the chief and his son still standing in front of their hut. And now, as I watched, they were joined by a third figure that emerged from the doorway: a taller figure in faded khaki, wearing glasses that glinted in the sunlight.

14

OUR THOUGHTS MAY have been on El Dorado. But our home was a mudbank. A week after our arrival the strip of land beside the Malaguay was at the halfway mark between a jungle clearing and a going community.

At its center, or thereabouts, was a palm-and-thatch shack that McHugh had designated as "H.Q." Close around it were—or would be, when finished—the "staff" bunkhouse, a storage shed, Frei Ambrosio's makeshift chapel, and an even more rudimentary open-sided structure that served as combination store, commissary and general meeting place. On one side, to the east, was the inlet and the river, on the other three the huts of the caboclos, ranged in a wide semicircle with the forest wall rising directly behind them. The single break in the wall was the entrance of the trail that led to Barna's cabin, the rapids and the Tupari village.

For several days after our first visit we had no further contact with the Indians. We did not go again to their clearing, and, though we suspected that they occasionally watched us from the cover of the forest, none of them actually showed themselves in ours. It would have been better otherwise; for the presence of these unseen neighbors made the caboclos suspicious and fearful—especially the women, who soon took to wearing their protective *figa* charms at their throats.

"These are wild savages who lurk in the jungle," they complained to their menfolk. "They will murder us one night in our sleep."

"*Tolice*," the men told them. "Nonsense. You mind your business and they will mind theirs." But I noticed that they kept a wary eye on the forest wall that ringed the clearing and slept with their machetes beside them in their hammocks.

There might, I think, have been overt trouble, even then, if it hadn't been for O Touro. He performed prodigies, not only of labor in directing the construction work, but also of leadership, in dealing with the constant apprehensions and complaints; and for the first time I was able to see in action the true measure of the man's worth. Frei Ambrosio, too, was a soothing influence, for, unlike his flock, he was not displeased with what he found in his new parish. The Reverend Lassiter, about whom he had been most concerned, had obviously moved on—where, he neither knew nor cared—and though he had yet to see a Tupari in the flesh, he was happy in the knowledge that at least there were no more Baptist heresies being disseminated among the heathen. He worked for long hours with the caboclos on the building of his new chapel and eagerly awaited the day when McHugh would allow him to begin his proselytizing.

Even more anxious for a go at the Tupari was Mordecai Cobb. "Look, chefé," he said to McHugh, "I been around a while and I know these Indios. I've lived with them, slept with them, fought with them—Chrissake, I've even spawned them—and I'm telling you there's just one way to handle them, and that's like Indios."

But McHugh had decided to let the Indians alone for the time being. And Nils Barna, also. "Let's get ourselves set first," he said. "Whatever we do beyond here, this is obviously as far as any ship can go; and the *Fortaleza* crowd will need a decent base when they arrive." To all outward appearances, he directed his entire attention to the planning and supervision of the work in progress. But I knew that inwardly—as had been the case back at Esperança when the *Fortaleza* didn't come—he was carefully taking his bearings and winding himself up.

As for myself, I too was working hard. I was trying to work so hard that there would be time and energy for nothing else. For a few days I was in charge of a crew that was bringing in timber from the forest, and several times I had occasion to use the trail that ran upstream past Barna's cabin. But never again did I stop to knock at the door of that cabin, nor even so much as turn to look at it. I walked straight ahead through the clearing. I quickened my pace. I went about the job at hand.

After we had moved our "H.Q." from the launch to the central shack, Christine and Barna occasionally had their evening meal with us, but those were almost the only times I saw her; and not once did I see her without others present. When she was there I tried not to meet her eyes, or even look at her. When she was elsewhere I tried not to think of her; and in this I was, for a short while, moderately successful. Or at least I was successful during the crowded, active hours of the daytime. But when darkness came it was another story. A very different story. And night after night I lay in my hammock under the mosquito netting, sweating and sleepless, while the images of Nils and Christine Barna appeared and reappeared before me and then at last followed me into my dreams.

It is hard for me to say just what I had expected Barna to be. Chiefly, I think, this is because my preconception of him had been less as an actual person than as an abstraction. He had been the man who went up-river before me; the man fleeing from something, hiding from something; *the man whose wife had come to join him.* In a way, I suppose, I had made him almost a projection of myself—a doppelgänger—and in so doing had failed to allow for his existence in the three-dimensional world.

And now—here he was. A body, a face, a human being. A tall, angular, rust-haired man walking slowly across the clearing or sitting opposite me at the trestle table in the staff shack. His manner remained as it had been on that first day we met him: polite, urbane and withdrawn. He spoke both

English and Portuguese,—and I am sure at least four other languages—in a quiet meticulous voice, and his movements, too, had a meticulousness and deliberation about them that at times approached the mechanical. Far from having gone to seed in his remote and lonely exile, he gave an impression of almost perfect inner control. By virtue of some mysterious chemistry of its own, his skin had neither tanned nor reddened in the fierce equatorial sunlight, but still retained its original northern pallor. Insects did not seem to bite him; nor did he seem to sweat. One could visualize him, looking little or no different, in a laboratory in Leyden, an office in Washington, a compound in Sumatra, a jungle hideout in Borneo. He was, I soon began to suspect, a man virtually impervious to outer environment, because he carried his own inner environment with him wherever he went.

Just what that environment was, it was considerably harder to tell. His attitude toward us, as far as I could see, was neither friendly, on the one hand, nor overtly hostile, on the other. His conversation was almost entirely limited to casual comments on our day-to-day activities. And when McHugh again began questioning him about terrain and routes, his answers remained oblique and guarded.

We had been to visit the Tupari, McHugh told him.

Yes, he knew.

"We're aware that you know, Dr. Barna. You were there at the time, weren't you?"

"I go to the village often. As I believe I have told you, I am trying to help them."

"Help them to do what?"

"To live a tolerable life."

"And to lead this tolerable life—is it necessary that they be antagonistic toward us?"

"Yes," said Barna with cool reasonableness, "I am afraid that it is."

The following night . . . .

"About those hills called the Serra Aurora, Dr. Barna—"

"Yes?"

"You say they lie to the southwest of here?"

"That is what the Tupari say."

"If they've never been there, how do they know?"

"It happens that they have various tribal legends about the Serra Aurora. And also—" Barna paused. "Also, they claim that they are occasionally able to see them."

"See them? How? From where?"

"From a certain high point of land near the upper end of the rapids."

"Have you been to this point?"

"Yes, I have been there."

"And *did* you see the hills?"

"I am not certain."

"What do you mean, you're not certain?"

"As you have possibly observed, atmospheric conditions over the forest are apt to be poor for visibility. What I saw may have been a range of hills, or it may merely have been a mirage."

The night after . . . .

"We went up to the head of the rapids today."

"It was a pleasant excursion, I hope."

"We couldn't locate this high point you spoke of."

"It is somewhat obscured by the trees. But even if you had found it, there is nothing to be seen except occasionally in the early morning, when the sun is just right."

"Will you take us there tomorrow morning?"

"Tomorrow morning, I am afraid, there will be mist."

"The next morning, then?"

Barna seemed to be thinking it over. "Very well," he said at last. "The next morning, perhaps—if tomorrow night is clear." He paused again and smiled. "It will be interesting to have a fresh opinion on whether the hills are reality or illusion."

It was five o'clock and still night when McHugh, Cobb

and I left the clearing two mornings later. The caboclos were asleep in their huts. There was no movement anywhere except the dark flow of the river, no light except the stars and the darting beams of our flashlights.

In spite of what he had said, I had my doubts that Barna would come with us; but when we reached his cabin he was standing in front of it, waiting. And beside him, tall and silent, was another figure, that I recognized as the young Indian, Cambar, the son of the headman of the Tupari.

"Did you tell him to come?" asked McHugh.

"I did not have to tell him," said Barna. "Cambar always accompanies me on my little excursions. I believe he fancies himself as my protector."

Entering the trail on the far side of the cabin, we moved on through a twisting tunnel of darkness. Barna went first, with the Indian behind him, McHugh next, and Cobb and myself bringing up the rear. The endlessly repeated shadow-pattern of tree-trunks, fronds and creepers glided toward us out of obscurity ahead, wavered and flickered in the yellow gleam of the flashlights and glided away into obscurity behind. As we had already discovered, the path here was considerably overgrown and obviously had been little used in recent years, but it was still passable for men in single file. On all sides of us the hum of the jungle insect-world was so vast and unbroken that it seemed not sound at all, but rather an encompassing vibrating silence. And through it, louder as we advanced, came the deep rumbling of the cachoeira.

We moved on for perhaps twenty minutes. Then the night began to thin into dawn. The beams of our flashlights paled, and we snapped them out. The insect chorus faded. As I looked ahead along the gray dimness of the trail, it seemed to me that we were moving not over land at all but across the canyoned bottom of a deep translucent sea.

Except that the sea-bottom is silent, and the world around us was now alive with roaring sound. Presently the forest to our left thinned, and we caught glimpses of white water and leaping spray; then the path curved sharply, and we came out beside the great cauldron of the cachoeira. At Graça de Deus, a mile downstream, the Malaguay was a placid smooth-flowing river perhaps three hundred yards across. But here it was no more than fifty, and no longer a river at all, but a boiling torrent funneled into a steep rocky trench. To our right—upstream—it came down over a series of precipitous ledges in a great cascade and plunged into a deep basin below. Here for an instant it became a still green pool; then it moved forward again, at first slowly, then faster and faster, as if spewed forward by a huge pump, until it was a swelling racing tide. It struck the rocks again, shattered into hundreds of gleaming ribbons, whirled and crisscrossed in a frenzy of foam and spray, and finally plunged out of sight among the trees below. Along its entire visible length it seemed almost to tremble with the power of its own sound and movement—a wild vortex of life in the encompassing stillness of the forest.

There was only this one point at which the path came out on the cachoeira. Beyond it the trees closed in again, the river was hidden, and its sound diminished gradually from a roar to a rumble and from a rumble to a distant murmur. High above us the sky showed brighter beyond the interlacing branches of our tunnel's roof. Up ahead Barna turned and gestured that we should quicken our pace. The sun would soon be coming up.

I could feel the ground rising gradually beneath our feet; and presently Barna swung off the path to the right and disappeared among the trees. At first I thought he was simply plunging into the forest, but when I reached the spot at which he had turned off I saw that it was another path he was following. It was far more overgrown than the main trail—the merest thread of a route, choked and screened by rank undergrowth—and it was easy to see how we had missed it during our search for the high point two days before. It twisted and turned a few times, steepened abruptly, leveled off again, climbed again; and then, suddenly, there was sky ahead of us, as well as above. The screen of jungle fell away, and for an instant, as we stopped, I had the sensation that we had come out on the rim of space.

It was not even a hilltop on which we stood. It was a mere mound or knob in the forest. But the ground before us angled down with sufficient steepness so that we could see over the tops of the nearest trees, and beyond them the green miles of the forest spread in an immense arc into the distance. Close below us, and a little to the south, was the Malaguay, but the cachoeira was hidden from view, off to the left, and there was no hint of the wild turbulence that filled the river a few hundred yards farther on. Like the lower river, the upper was yellow-brown in color and sluggish in current, its channel fringed by the promontories and niches of flat lowland forest. From our vantage point we could see it twisting away for a distance of perhaps five miles. Then it dwindled, flickered, became simply a crease among the treetops, and vanished in the forest-ocean. In itself, it was no different from any of a thousand jungle rivers. It was a tributary-of-a-tributary-of-a-tributary-of-a-tributary of the Amazon, the merest microscopic capillary in the gigantic anatomy of a continent. But now, as my eyes moved out across green distance, I saw, with a sudden lifting of the heart, that it wasn't just "any" river. For off beyond it, broad and deep on the horizon from which it flowed—unmistakable and unforgettable—was a great bank of white low-lying cloud.

McHugh glanced at me, and I nodded.

"Wait," said Nils Barna. "Perhaps in a few minutes now we may see beyond it."

We waited. No one spoke again. Silent on our island in the wilderness, we watched the miracle of a day being born.

The dawnlight that lay over the earth was no longer gray but living silver. There was no cloud, no mist, no whisp or shred of wind, but only a great gleaming clarity that, moment by moment, grew purer and more intense. In all the world spread before us there were but two colors, two entities: the blue gulf of the sky and the green of the spreading forest. These two alone—and between them, in the far distance where blue and green met, a band of white shining clouds.

We waited. Forest and sky and clouds waited.

Then the sun rose.

We did not see it rise, because our faces were turned to the west, but we saw its rays, sudden and warm, sweep like a wave over the miles of the treetops. The sky glittered. The jungle glowed with green fire. And in the distance now the clouds seemed suddenly to be weaving, shifting, thinning; there seemed to be a darkness behind them, a shadow, a substance; and no, it was not imagination—it was real, it existed, *it was there:* a long low range of wooded hills notching the horizon.

For a few moments the image held, unchanging. Then a bright filament of light struck down across the hills into the forest below. Was it a river shining in the sunlight? I couldn't tell. I didn't know. And then suddenly, in the next instant, I did know. For in that instant I was no longer on a knob of earth above the treetops, but in the cockpit of a plane soaring over the forest—and Joan was in the cockpit beside me—and Joan was pointing. And yes, there it was beneath us: the clouds parting, the earth emerging, the gleam of a golden river; and the plane was roaring now, the sun was wheeling, and we were rushing toward it, closer and closer, across the green miles of the jungle-ocean. . . .

As abruptly as it had risen, the roaring sank into stillness. The plane became a knob of earth again. It was no longer Joan who was pointing, but Nils Barna. For a few seconds more the apparition stood out clear and shining in the horizontal beams of the sun, like a lightning-streak impaled on the hillside. Then its brilliance began to fade. It dwindled and receded. Drawn by the sun's heat, a film of vapor rose slowly upward out of the intervening miles of the forest, paling the blue of the sky and the green of the treetops, catching the sun's rays and diffusing them into the blinding glare of full day. Looking around, I saw that the sun was already clear of the horizon, a yellow eye in the sky to the east. And when I turned again the shining thread was gone—even the hills were gone—and there was only heat and glare and a cauldron of slowly rising vapor, and beyond them, on the far horizon, a bank of white low-lying clouds between the earth and sky.

"Well, gentlemen," said Nils Barna quietly, "was it your river—or an illusion?"

For a moment no one answered. I saw that McHugh and Cobb were watching me.

"It was the river," I said.

The heat, on the unsheltered knob, was already becoming oppressive, and presently we turned and began the descent. Reaching the main path below, we followed it back toward Graça de Deus, again in single file and in the same order in which we had gone before. We didn't talk; for a while, as we skirted the cachoeira, the roar of water was too loud for talking. But even after its sound was gone, we walked in silence.

I was scarcely aware of the others moving on before me; or of the sounds and colors of the awakening forest. Before my eyes were still a bank of mist, a range of hills, a flash of golden brightness. I had almost forgotten them. After two years they had blurred and receded, until they had become only a fragment of dream and memory. But now here they were again: clear on the horizon, clear in my mind and heart. It was for these that I had come here: the first time—and this. And now, for the first time in two years, they were no longer in the past, but in the future; no longer behind me, but ahead. . . .

I had stopped. The forest closed in again. It was whirring and flickering around me: with the sharp cries of macaws and monkeys, the snapping of branches and stirring of fronds, the hovering of butterflies and the darting of birds and slow billion-footed march of the ants. I looked at the emerald filigree of the ferns, and at the dark boles beyond the ferns, and then up the boles at the green tracery of boughs and leaves above me and at the window of sky that shone down through the treetops. And when I moved on again the others had disappeared ahead, and I was alone.

I don't know how far I had gone when I came upon the opening of a path which forked off to the right of the main trail and which I had not noticed while going in the other direction in the darkness. All I know is that I followed it, and that it twisted for perhaps a hundred yards through bright galleries of ferns and lianas and then debouched into a small glade.

And in the center of the glade was a gleaming pool.

Actually, as I was to discover later, it was not a pool, but part of a deep twisting backwater of the Malaguay. I did not know that then, however. Nor did it matter then. All that mattered, all I was aware of, was that somehow, whether by chance or obscure design, I had come at last to a place I had been searching for. The knob above the treetops had been the high dome of the forest. This was its secret chamber, its sanctuary, its enchanted heart.

I stood still at the pool's edge, and the forest stood still around me.

The boles of great trees circled the pond like the columns of a temple, and between them and behind them, in rank upon rank, tall screens of greenery rose rigid into the windless air. From a branch overhanging the water two small ringtailed monkeys stared down at me with bright inquisitive eyes. They were in shadow. The trees and the fronds and almost all the tiny glade were also in shadow, but a single thin beam of sunlight, arrowing down through the foliage, struck the dark mirror of the pool and splintered its surface into a hundred glinting discs.

I closed my eyes. It is Eden, I thought. It is Eden and Arcady and the lost bower of the Green Mansions, and in a moment now Adam and Eve will walk naked from the forest, Diana will kneel to drink at the pool's rim, and the bird-cry of Rima will ring through the treetops. It is Paradise. And when you open your eyes again it will be gone.

But when I opened them it was not gone. The glade was still there. The trees and the fronds and the two watching monkeys were still there. The shining pool was still there. And now I moved forward a little and bent and touched the water, and it was not warm and silted like the jungle rivers, but clear and cool and fresh as morning against my hands. Lying prone, I drank from it; I plunged my arms and face into it; and then, on sudden impulse, I rose and was stripping off my clothes . . . when a voice behind me said quietly: "I would not recommend this, Mr. Allison, as a place for bathing."

Wheeling, I saw Nils Barna and just behind him the young Indian, Cambar, tall and brown-skinned, with his bamboo blowgun in his hand. The spell that had held me was too strong to be broken instantly, and for a long moment, I think, I merely stared at them.

Then—"Why?" I asked dully.

Barna came closer. I looked past him at the opening of the path from which he and the Indian had come; but no one else appeared. Then I looked back at the pool, and Barna stood looking at it too. Presently he raised his eyes to the two monkeys, who were still watching us from their perch above the far side of the water.

"I shall show you why, Mr. Allison," he said.

Turning, he spoke a few words to Cambar, and with what seemed a single lightning motion the Indian swung his blowgun to his lips and snatched a dart from a quiver at his waist. Simultaneously there was a commotion on the branch, as the monkeys scampered for the shelter of the foliage behind them. But one of them was not quick enough. There was a thin whistling sound, a screech, stillness; and then, through the stillness, a crackling of broken twigs and a grotesque brown body falling with a soft splash into the water. Slow glinting ripples spread out across the pool in widening circles. At their center the monkey turned over once and began to sink. Soon monkey and ripples alike had disappeared, and the surface of the water was still again, except for the gently weaving patterns of shadow and sun.

Then there was a flash. It was not a flash of sunlight, but quicker, brighter, sharper than sunlight. It was not gold, but silver; not a single flash, but ten, twenty, fifty flashes—a shining nimbus of whirling converging fire. In the next instant the quiet pool was a churning frenzy of glinting fins and snapping jaws. A red froth rose to its surface, and for a moment it seemed almost as if the whole pool would overflow its banks, like boiling water from a cauldron, and spill its turmoil out onto the earth before us. Then, as suddenly as it had begun, it was all over. The flashing silver faded. The wild churning subsided into gentle wavelets, and the wavelets into the same smooth, sun-dappled mirror at which I had gazed, enchanted, perhaps five minutes before. At a word from Barna, Cambar broke a branch from a tree, dredged with it for a few minutes along the pool's bottom, and presently scooped out a small round object that lay motionless at our feet and seemed to stare up at us with hollow eyes. It was the skull of the monkey, as white and fleshless as if it had been buried in the earth for a hundred years.

"You are acquainted with the piranha, Mr. Allison?" Barna inquired.

I nodded.

"They are rather dreadful little creatures, you know. But also most interesting, I find. Most instructive. There is so much in the world that is ambiguous, dreamlike, illusory, and the piranha is one of the true enemies of illusion."

I looked neither at the pool nor at the small round white thing that stared up at me from its edge. Picking up the clothes I had discarded, I began putting them on again.

"Of course, it is the odor of blood that attracts the piranha," Barna went on. "They are reputed to attack only a wounded man, and you, I am sure, Mr. Allison, are quite sound and whole. Still one cannot be certain. Sometimes the merest scratch, the tiniest lesion . . . ."

He and Cambar waited, watching me while I dressed. Around the pool the forest rose green and utterly still toward the shining sky.

"It is peaceful in our Eden, is it not?" said Barna, as we turned to go.

15

We HAD SEEN the hills. We had seen the upper river flowing down from them. But between Graça de Deus and the upper river were the four miles of rapids.

"Maybe your black river would have been better, after all," McHugh said musingly.

There was, of course, no way of telling. For the time being, at least, we had made our choice; and if there had been disappointment, there was also encouragement, for we had found Nils Barna and glimpsed our goal ahead. Also, as far as we could see, there were no further obstructions beyond the cachoeira and the upper river flowed straight down out of the hills. In any case, McHugh's concern was not with might-have-beens but with the situation as it confronted us. If we found oil, he pointed out, a road or railway track would eventually have to be laid around the obstructed stretch. Meanwhile, at least there was the old trail, and the next step was to portage our three outboard-motored canoes to the upper river and get on about our business of reaching the Serra Aurora.

Nils Barna had taken us to the "high point." He had shown us the way. At the time we had accepted this as an indication that he had decided to cooperate with us; but, once back in Graça de Deus, he had again withdrawn behind a screen of guardedness and evasion. Each time, during the next few days, when we brought up the matter of practical plans, he either changed the subject or recalled that he had "work to do" at his cabin.

What work, we didn't know. What designs and purposes were concealed behind his ambiguous facade, we could only vaguely surmise.

Or, at least, McHugh and I could only surmise; for Mordecai Cobb had his own opinions. "Chrissake," he told us, "it's plain as your nose what he's up to. He's been in to them hills, and don't fool yourself about it. He's been there and knows what the score is, and he don't want us to find out. So he plays dumb. He tells the Indios to play dumb. And pretty soon whatever outfit he's tied up with comes moseying up-river, and they're in—and we're out."

"If that's it," said McHugh, "why did he show us the way?"

"On account of he knows we'd find it anyhow. He can't come right out and say he's against us. He's got to play cagey. And he figures that with us not knowing the country it'll take us so long that. . . ."

He went on with his theories, but McHugh seemed occupied with his own thoughts. And presently he called in O Touro. What had Barna been like back at Esperança? he asked him. What had he done there? How had he spent his time? Had he given any indication of his personal interests and plans?

The big Negro, however, had little to add to what he had already told us.

"Did he seem in any way—well—peculiar?" asked McHugh.

"Peculiar?"

"Uncommunicative. Secretive. Hard to put your finger on."

"He was a man who liked to be left alone, if that's what you mean."

"Didn't it strike you as rather strange?"

"Strange? No, I don't think so." Touro paused and his eyes went from McHugh to Cobb and then back again. "There are a lot of people who like to be let alone, sir," he added.

McHugh let it pass. After a while he let the Negro go.

215

"How about *you?*" he asked me later, when we were alone together. "What do you know about Barna?"

"I don't know any more than you do," I said.

I saw that McHugh's eyes were watching me curiously. "It had occurred to me that perhaps—"

"Yes?"

"—that perhaps Christine had told you something."

"No," I said evenly, "Christine hasn't told me anything."

He didn't pursue the subject farther, and for the next two days he seemed almost to forget about Barna, as he busied himself supervising the last of the construction work in the clearing.

"Holy cow, Mac," Cobb pleaded on the third morning. "You *are* going to get after that perfessor, aren't you?"

McHugh nodded. "Yes, we'll have to get after him," he said.

"It's like I been telling you. Wait and see. He knows the whole story, but he's hooked up with another outfit."

"Maybe," said McHugh.

"Meaning you don't think so?"

"It's possible, of course. But the longer I'm here—the more I get, well, the smell of things—the less I think it's the answer."

"If it ain't, what is?"

"That's what we don't know yet." McHugh paused and his lips tightened. "But what I do know," he added, "is that it's damn well time we found out."

That night Barna and Christine had supper with us in the staff shack. When the meal was over Christine excused herself, but McHugh asked Barna to stay. The two of them sat at opposite ends of the rough table, with Cobb and myself between. A cloud of insects hummed and clicked around the oil lamp in the center.

"We've been here three weeks now, Doctor," said McHugh. "Our construction work is about finished, and we're ready to move on up-river."

Barna nodded, without speaking.

"We would appreciate any advice you can give us."

"I am afraid I have none," said Barna.

McHugh spread his hands on the table and went on patiently: "It's obviously impossible for us to get our launch and barges around the rapids. We plan to portage three canoes with outboard motors and then work our way upstream in them. Since you say you can't help us, we want the services of a few Indians as guides."

"Have you asked them?"

"We've asked them a lot of things. But we got nowhere." McHugh paused, his eyes fixed on Barna's face. "Perhaps you'd speak to them for us," he said.

"I?" Barna asked. "Why I, Mr. McHugh?"

"They know you better. You seem to have influence with them."

"Influence? No." He smiled a little. "I am a man who exerts influence over no one."

"At least they like you, then. They accept you."

"Perhaps it is simply that they are not afraid of me."

"Meaning that they are afraid of us?"

"Naturally."

"Why?"

"Perhaps I should explain to you a few things about the Tupari, Mr. McHugh. They are a very unfortunate people, you see—and a very unhappy people—neither civilized on the one hand, nor, on the other, truly savage. As I have told you, they no longer build or use canoes. They have forgotten how to make curaré. They do not roam far afield, as their ancestors did for generations. Has it occurred to you why their village is located where it is, so close to the river and yet not on its banks? It is because of fear, Mr. McHugh. They are afraid of the deep forest from which they once came, because it is now unknown to them. And they are afraid of the river which was once their highway, because it has become the highway of the white men who enslave them."

"I thought there'd been no other white men in here for years," said McHugh.

"In recent years, perhaps not. But in the rubber-boom days there were many. And I imagine it does not seem so very long ago to old Pombal, for instance, that he was a young man with two eyes, two ears and two hands."

"You mean—"

"I understand that Mr. Cobb here was on the Putumayo in his younger days. I am sure he can explain the origin of Pombal's mutilations."

"He sure as hell didn't get 'em shaving," said Cobb.

There was another pause. McHugh was leaning forward a little, his jaw set, his lips tight, but Barna, across the table, seemed self-possessed and relaxed. Now and then, as he spoke, his mouth had smiled slightly, but whether or not his eyes were smiling, I could not tell. In fact, he appeared now to have no eyes at all, but only two opaque glinting discs, where the lenses of his glasses refracted the yellow lamplight.

McHugh got to his feet and paced up and down across the little room. Then he came back to the table. "Look, Dr. Barna," he said, "suppose we stop playing cat and mouse with each other."

"Cat and mouse, Mr. McHugh?"

"Or whatever you choose to call it. As you know, we've come here looking for oil."

"I recall your mentioning oil—yes," said Barna.

"We're looking for oil, and it so happens we're very much in earnest about it. The company we represent is putting a great deal of money and effort into this venture. A large boat will be arriving here shortly, bringing men and machinery for the job."

"I see."

"As the advance party," McHugh continued, "our job is to do the preliminary organizing and exploration; to find the best route in to where our geologists believe the oil to be. At the beginning, frankly, I didn't believe an advance party would be of much use. But when we learned at Esperança that you had gone up-river, I changed my mind. Naturally I had heard of you and your work—both with the Rubber Development Corporation and before. And I assumed you'd come up here for somewhat the same reason we were coming and would be in a position to help us."

"I am sorry if I have proved a disappointment," said Barna.

"Let's dispense with the courtesies, Doctor. What I'm trying to find out is: first, why you disclaim any interest in oil, and second, why you're so obviously hostile toward us."

"To take your questions in order, Mr. McHugh: I disclaim any interest in oil because I have none."

"You're a geologist, aren't you?"

"I have worked in geology at various times—yes. I have also worked in chemistry, agronomy, metallurgy and various other fields. At the moment, however, as I believe I have mentioned, my only scientific work is concerned with the Indians and their curaré. I suppose that would classify me as a pharmacist."

Was there irony in his voice? I wasn't sure. There was no hint of expression in the eyes behind those glittering lenses. "In any case," he went on, "my investigations in other fields are at an end. Does that answer your first question? As to your second—what you refer to as my 'hostility': why, if I were hostile, would I have taken you the other day to show you the hills you are looking for?"

Cobb couldn't control himself any longer. "On account of you know damn well," he began—

But McHugh interrupted him quietly. "That's what I'm unable to understand," he said. "One minute you seem willing to work with us, and in the next you refuse."

"Suppose we say that I am willing to work with you," said Barna "—up to a point. Specifically the high point above the rapids. Does that seem so unreasonable to you, Mr. McHugh?"

The latter didn't answer at once, but sat rubbing his jaw

and studying Barna across the yellow-lit table. Then he said, "No, there's no way we can force you to cooperate, any more than you choose to. But let me point out, Doctor, that there are a few things that must be clearly understood between us."

"Such as?"

"Such as the fact that the Southern Cross Corporation has the exploration—*and* exploitation—rights to this area, under contract to the Brazilian Government. If you're working for another organization, it will make matters simpler if you tell me so now."

"I had thought that perhaps that was disturbing you," said Barna. "But there is no cause for it. I am working for no one."

"I have your word for that?"

"Let us not be childish, Mr. McHugh. If I chose to lie to you, I would not change my mind because you rephrased the question."

"And you still maintain that you know nothing about the existence of oil in this region?"

"That is correct."

"And that you are not looking for oil?"

"Also correct."

"May I ask then why you came here?"

"I came to live here."

"Why specifically to this place?"

"Sometimes I have wondered a bit about that myself. One reason, of course, was that the Reverend Mr. Lassiter was coming here. Another was that I liked the name."

"The name?"

"Yes, Graça de Deus. A place abounding in the Grace of God rather intrigued me. I felt that perhaps I was in need of a little." A thin smile touched Barna's lips. And then he added, "Perhaps we all are, you know."

"In other words, you ask us to believe that, in coming here, you were looking for nothing."

"No," said Barna after a moment's reflection. "I would not say that it was nothing, Mr. McHugh."

"What then?"

"Suppose we call it a lost world."

"A lost—?" McHugh stared at him uncomprehendingly, and again Barna half smiled.

"You are thinking of Conan Doyle's sort of world?" he asked. "Or Colonel Fawcett's perhaps? . . . No, Mr. McHugh, I mean nothing so romantic or archaeological. Other things have been lost on the earth besides Inca ruins and duck-billed dinosaurs."

McHugh didn't say anything. For a moment no one said anything. Then for the second time Cobb lost control, and he jumped to his feet, his hands thumping the table. "What is this, anyhow?" he rasped. "What sort of game are you playing?"

"Stop it!" McHugh told him sharply.

"Like hell I'll stop it. Maybe you don't mind sitting around being made a monkey of, but, by God, I'm not going to—"

"That's enough, Cobb. Be quiet."

Cobb's mouth worked for another moment, but no more words came. In the silence that followed Barna showed no reaction whatever, and McHugh, at the far end of the table, sat watching him steadily. Then he leaned forward and said in his usual quiet voice: "You say, Dr. Barna, that you're neither employed by any other organization nor engaged in any special project of your own; and I'm willing to take your word for it. Your private life and motives are your own affair. But it so happens that you're a trained scientist. You've been in this country a long time, and I believe you can be of help to us. To come to the point, I'm offering you a position with the Southern Cross Corporation."

There was another silence. The lamplight danced and glittered on Barna's lenses.

Then he said: "That is most flattering of you, I am sure."

"Do you accept?" McHugh asked.

"I am afraid I cannot."

"Why?"

"Because I prefer to remain—shall we say—unattached."

"We would pay you well."

Barna shook his head. "I am sorry."

"Perhaps even some form of participation in profits could be arranged."

"I am truly sorry."

McHugh abruptly pushed back his chair. "All right," he said, "if that's the way it's to be—"

"What way, Mr. McHugh?" asked Barna.

"Your way. Suspicion—antagonism—refusal to cooperate."

"My only refusal has been to accept employment with your company; and that, you must surely concede, is a decision I am entitled to make myself. As for suspicion and antagonism, it appears to me that it is you who feel them, not I."

"Why won't you help us, then?"

"Help you? How? In what way?"

"In any number of ways, which you know as well as I. Right now, specifically, by persuading the Indians to act as guides."

"Ah, we are back to that," said Barna.

"Yes, we're back to that. Will you speak to them?"

"As I have already indicated I would prefer not to. However—"

"Yes?"

"However, Mr. McHugh, allow me to ask you a question in return. If the Indians refuse to supply you with guides, what do you propose to do?"

McHugh did not answer at once. Cobb started to speak, stopped, and sat drumming softly on the table.

Then McHugh said quietly: "In that case I'm afraid we'd have to requisition them."

Was he bluffing? I didn't know. I rather doubt if he knew himself. But his voice was firm and his eyes steady and cold, as he stared across the table at Nils Barna.

"I see," said the latter, nodding slowly. "Yes, of course. That would be the only practical step, would it not? And in the very best tradition of the march of progress. . . . Under the circumstances, then, I will speak to them for you."

"Good," said McHugh.

"No, not good exactly. But rather 'better.' Better than the other alternative."

"In any case, we'll be grateful." Now at last it was McHugh's turn to smile. "Particularly since it's against your principles to exert influence."

"I am afraid you have misunderstood me, Mr. McHugh," said Barna. For an instant his lips seemed to return the other's smile, but his eyes were still two flashing prisms of light. "I do not concern myself with principles any longer. Merely with expediencies."

There was no moon that night. The stars were faint and remote. Nils Barna, walking across the clearing with me a little later, was no more than a thickening of shadow in the darkness at my side.

For a few paces we walked in silence. Then Barna said: "He reminds me much of the Reverend Lassiter, your Mr. McHugh."

I waited for him to go on.

"So full of purpose," he said. "What they call in German *gewidmet*. Devoted. Only the Reverend Lassiter was devoted to God and Mr. McHugh to oil."

"That's what he's here for," I said.

"Yes, of course. Exactly. What he is here for. When such men go somewhere it must be *for* something. On to the Kingdom of God—to the Kingdom of Oil—to the Kingdom of Zion—to the Kingdom of Marx. It is interesting for me to observe, you see, because once I had such a kingdom myself. The Kingdom of Science. . . ."

He seemed about to continue, but didn't; and presently the hut where I slept loomed out of the darkness ahead.

"Well, goodnight," I said.

"It is still early," said Barna. "Perhaps you would like to come to my place for a while?"

Taken by surprise, I hesitated.

"It is scarcely a mansion, as you know, but I can offer one or two amenities. Also, I am sure that Mrs. Barna would be pleased to have company."

"Thank you," I murmured. "But—"

"It is hard for her here," he went on. "Hard and lonely. She is used to a very different sort of life."

I didn't say anything.

"It was a courageous thing of her to come here as she did, and I am deeply touched by it. But it was a foolish thing, too."

"She's your wife, after all."

"Yes, my wife." For a moment he seemed lost in meditation. Then he said: "She is my wife; she needs and wants so much; and I have so little to give her. It is an unhappy thing, Mr. Allison, when one wants so little oneself and is yet unable to give to another."

His voice was as cool and urbane as ever, but his figure, standing beside me in the darkness, seemed suddenly even thinner and more stooped than before. "Well," he went on, "it will not be for long, fortunately. Soon your company boat will be here, and then she can go back to the world in which she belongs."

I started to speak, stopped, and there was a silence. "You are sure that you won't change your mind about coming to my place?" Barna asked. "I am sure my wife would be happy to see you."

"Not tonight, thanks. Some other time, perhaps—"

"As you say."

"Goodnight," I said again.

"Goodnight, Mr. Allison. . . . And by the way, there is no need for you gentlemen to worry."

"Worry?"

"About the Indian guides. You may rest assured that you can set out for your Kingdom of Oil without the necessity of cutting off any ears or hands."

As the days went by, that remained the extent of my contact with Nils Barna. And with Christine I had even less. We said: "Good morning. Good night. It is hotter today. It may rain tomorrow." She sewed buttons on my shirts, along with those of McHugh, Cobb and her husband. I painted a sign that read ENFIRMARIO—DISPENSARIO and nailed it beside the doorway of the shack which she had converted into a makeshift hospital. But that, during those first days at Graça de Deus, was the sum-total of our relationship.

As at Esperança, she made nursing her function in the community. In the beginning, happily, she had nothing genuinely serious to cope with, but there was a steady procession of patients suffering from minor wounds and ailments: some with ax and machete cuts, some with mild fever and diarrhoea, almost everyone with some form of heat rash, insect bite or infection. O Touro's wife, the plump Tereza Carolina, helped her in her work. Young Tourinho raced in and out on eager, if obscure, missions, and Frei Ambrosio, his round face glistening with good will and perspiration, shuttled back and forth between chapel and infirmary and in a moment of eloquent inspiration cajoled Serafima Batista into serving as assistant-assistant. There was no report of her performing any major medical cures; but her presence promptly doubled the sick-call attendance among the younger caboclos, who previously had been in the habit of treating their cuts and bruises with generous applications of spittle and mud.

I went to the infirmary to put up the sign I had painted. I went there once again to get some calamine lotion for my itching skin. And those were the only times I went there during those first few weeks at Graça de Deus. To Barna's cabin I did not go at all—nor did he repeat the invitation of that one evening. Sometimes I could not help trying to visualize the life which he and Christine lived there together, but there was no reality to my imaginings. There was not even pain or resentment, but only blankness. Christine

Barna was a woman glimpsed through a doorway, across a clearing, at the far end of a lamp-lit trestle table. She was an acquaintance, a stranger.

Until the darkness came and I lay alone in my hammock. . . .

Then late one afternoon, coming along the trail, I was passing through the clearing where Barna's cabin stood, when I heard a voice, soft but clear behind me, speak my name. And turning, I saw Christine standing at the door of the cabin.

"Mark—" she repeated.

"Yes?"

"I want to talk with you."

I hesitated.

"Please," she said.

Another second passed. Then I walked back until I was standing beside her.

"Come in," she said.

I followed her in and found myself confronted only by the plump Indian girl whom McHugh and I had seen on our first visit to the cabin. "This is Omina," Christine said. "Nils brought her from the Tupari village to help me with my housekeeping."

As before, the girl simply stared at me. Then she darted out the door, and I stood looking around me again at the little room. It was substantially as I remembered it, with the addition of a few embellishments—a bowl of wild-flowers, gauze curtains at the windows, a cloth on the chest—that had obviously been supplied by Christine.

Then, when there was nothing else left to look at, I looked at her. It was the first time I had really looked at her since that night on the deck of the *Cantora*.

She was dressed in the same boy's shirt and rolled-up linen trousers that she had worn much of the time on the trip up-river; but her bare arms and legs were darker now and her gray-green eyes seemed lighter in her deeply sun-browned face. Chic? Hardly. Cool and groomed and untouched by the jungle? Not by a damn sight. I saw her cracked and roughened nails, the welts of insect bites on her wrists and ankles, the sweat-stains on her shirt at throat and armpits, the strand of hair straying damply over her forehead. She looked exactly what she was: a civilized and fastidious woman strayed out of her accustomed domain of hot tubs, cold cream and Kleenex and gallantly struggling to make the best of it.

"Mark—" she said.

"Yes?"

"What's the matter? Why have you been acting this way?"

"What way?"

"Avoiding me. Ignoring me."

"What do you expect me to do?"

She started to speak, stopped, and passed her hand slowly over her eyes. "I don't know," she murmured.

I could hear the humming of insects in the foliage beyond the windows.

"Is it all right, Chris?" I asked.

She didn't answer.

"Is it what you expected it would be?"

"Expected? . . . Yes, in a way, I suppose. . . . And in another way"—she hesitated—"I'm not even sure that I know myself. It's been like seeing something plain and clear before you, and then reaching out and touching—nothing."

"Does he resent your coming?"

She shook her head slowly. "No. That's what I was afraid of, of course, but it hasn't been that at all. He's been deeply touched by it." She paused again, groping for words. "It's simply that—well, as I said—that I haven't been able to get at him. That he doesn't seem really to be *there.*"

"What does he do with himself?"

"He walks in the forest. Visits with the Tupari."

"What does he talk about?"

"He doesn't much. When he does it's usually about little day-to-day things. The plants and animals in the forest.

How the Indians live. How he's experimenting with poisons for their hunting darts."

"He spends a lot of time with the Indians, doesn't he?"

"Yes."

"Do you know why?"

"He says that they need his help. And that he needs theirs."

There was another silence.

"And you?" I asked. "What has he said about you and himself?"

She walked to one of the windows and stood looking out. It was getting on toward evening now; the glare of the sky had softened, and the shadow of the forest lay long and dark across the clearing. I went over and stood beside her and said, "He wants to stay here, doesn't he, Chris?"

"Yes," she murmured.

"And you to go."

"Yes."

"Then—"

"Then I'm going?" Christine looked up at me, and then away again. "No, Mark—I'm not. I can't. Unless he comes too."

"But if he no longer wants you—"

"That's just the point. He does want me—terribly. He needs me so terribly." I stood looking at her without speaking, and presently she went on: "Until a few days ago I didn't know. I wasn't sure. It seemed to me that I simply would never get through to Nils; that there was nothing left of him; that I might as well get on the *Fortaleza* when it came—and it would be all over. And then—"

She paused.

"Are you sure you want to tell me, Chris?"

"Yes, I want to tell you. I have to tell you. . . . Then, just a night or two ago, I awoke in my hammock, and Nils was standing beside it, looking down at me. I was lying in shadow, and he couldn't see that my eyes were open; but a bar of moonlight was streaming through the screen behind me, and I could see his face. Oh, Mark, I have never seen such a face. He had his glasses off, and it was—naked. Naked and terrible. More terrible even than the face of old Pombal, the Indian. Terrible with grief and loneliness and hunger. For a few minutes I simply lay there, not moving, while he stood there above me in the moonlight. And then—then I put out my hand to him—and for another moment *he* didn't move; then he took my hand in his and pressed it so tightly that I thought the bones would crack; and then he let it go and turned away and walked out the door."

She was silent. She seemed to be waiting for me to speak.

"I understand, Chris," I said.

"Do you—truly? I want you to so much, because—because—" Her voice caught. "Maybe I shouldn't have tried to tell you. But I had to tell you. I couldn't just pretend that you didn't exist."

"Good luck, Chris," I said.

"Don't go," she pleaded. "Not yet. Not like this."

"I have to go."

"Where? Why?"

I smiled at her. "To look for an oil well," I said, and went out and closed the door.

16

THE THREE CANOES we had brought from Esperança were narrow but long. On the straightaways the old trail around the rapids was just wide enough for portage, but at its turnings, which comprised about half its four-mile length, bow and stern promptly became entangled in a welter of greenery, and all progress stopped. The trail had to be widened. Again the sound of axes, saws and machetes was heard in the forest.

The caboclos went about the work with sullen reluctance. The first day they cleared perhaps half a mile, the second day about a quarter, the third a mere three hundred yards. They lounged and slept on the job. They thronged to sick call. Even the usually patient and reliable João Batista was aggrieved, and on the evening of the third day he came with two other men to speak to McHugh.

"This is not the work for which we have come here, senhor," he said.

"It will take only a few days," McHugh told him.

"You have said we come to work with the oil."

"Yes, oil—that's correct. But to reach the oil we must first get the canoes around the cachoeira and on into the hills."

João Batista looked at his two companions.

"In Esperança," said one, "we are seringueros. All day we go from one rubber tree to the next, tapping for the borracho, and it is a hard life and no good. You say to us, up the river it will be no more with the rubber but with the oil, and it will be a better life. But it is not a better life."

"In Esperança," added the other, "it is only tapping the trees. Here it is chopping them, sawing them, tearing them. It is being devoured by insects and ripped by thorns."

"Yes, senhor," said Batista. "We are men of the rivers and fazendas—not of the forest."

"Damned if I think you're men at all," Mordecai Cobb put in disgustedly. "Know where you fellers should have been? Back on the old Madeira-Mamoré, that's where. Whacking your way through two hundred miles of bush, instead of a lousy four."

"It is four miles around this cachoeira," the caboclos argued. "But what if there are more cachoeiras beyond?"

"By that time," said McHugh, "the Company's big ship will be here. With many men—many machines."

"And we will work only with the oil?"

"Only with the oil."

In the end they agreed to go on with the trail-clearing, and McHugh appeared reasonably satisfied. But Cobb spat out the doorway after them and shook his grizzled head. "Yep, that's where them lilywhite jokers should of been," he snorted. "Back in the devil's green acre of hell on that old Mad Mary. . . ."

"I'll lay you five contos that nigger's behind it," he declared that night.

"Touro?" said McHugh doubtfully.

"When the spiks get stirred up it's always him."

"I don't know," said McHugh. "There was that trouble at Esperança, of course, but he's been right on the job ever since."

"And besides," I added, "the rest of them wouldn't even be here if it weren't for him."

Cobb grinned, showing the brown stumps of his teeth. "Neither would he, laddie boy, if it weren't for yours truly. Remember?"

I remembered all right. I could still see that neat bright room in the cottage on the rubber plantation, and Cobb, like an old gray spider, weaving his web of blackmail. I could still see the giant Negro sitting opposite him, hands closed over knees, feet flat on the floor, not speaking, not moving. I could still see the glinting whites of his eyes.

"Don't get me wrong," Cobb went on. "I got nothing against that old Touro. Like you say, he's a good foreman. One of the best niggers I've seen. All I'm saying to you, amigos, is don't forget what he is and what got him here in the first place. There's more to that Touro boy than meets the eye."

Yes, much more: I didn't need Mordecai Cobb to tell me that. For from the very beginning the big Negro had aroused an interest in me that amounted almost to fascination. At first it had been simply the huge blue-black bulk of him; then his manner, his voice, his choice of words. But as the days and weeks went on, as we lived and journeyed and worked together, I began to realize that it was far more than stature, color or origin that differentiated him, not only from the caboclos among whom he lived but from us other outlanders as well. His outstanding characteristic was—how shall I put it?—a diffidence, perhaps, a deep and reserved apartness; and this, combined with his size and strength, gave him a remote impenetrable quality that was partly animal and partly almost godlike. What went on inside of him I didn't know. But whatever it was, it seemed in no way to interfere with his effectiveness as a worker. Each day now, while the caboclos grumbled and soldiered, he stayed out on the cachoeira trail from sunrise to sunset and, as far as I could see, did more work than any other four men combined.

Yet something of Cobb's suspicion apparently communicated itself to McHugh, for on the second day after the "strike" he asked me to go out on the trail to keep an eye on the situation. I didn't like spying on Touro. I also didn't think there was any need for it and said so to McHugh. But there was now little for me to do in the office shack. I welcomed the chance to get away from the dust and boredom and hot lethargy of the clearing. Above all, I welcomed the chance to get away from the sight of Christine, as she made her rounds of the huts of sick caboclos or appeared and reappeared behind the screen windows of her dispensary-infirmary. It was with relief that I put the clearing behind me and followed the trail into the forest.

Along its first mile the trail was much wider and clearer than it had been before—no longer a tunnel, but almost an avenue between the great walls of foliage. This stretch was deserted. But presently the path narrowed; I passed groups of men chopping and hacking at its margins; and finally, at perhaps the two-mile mark, I came to the main body of workers and what was apparently the head of the line. If Touro was engaged in any politicking or agitating among the caboclos, there was no evidence of it here; for there he was out in front of the others, advancing step by step, machete flailing.

I remember his arm rising and falling, and the flash of the great blade, and his almost naked sweat-streaked body looming huge and black against the green foliage, like a legendary figure from some African mythology. I remember watching him for a while, and then on impulse taking a machete myself and advancing beside him, hacking and swinging. At first he acknowledged my presence only by a nod, and for perhaps half an hour we moved together in silence. Then, turning, he smiled a little. "We're getting there now," he said. "Gradual but sure."

I was already too tired to do more than grunt my answer.

"Always feels good to be getting somewhere," he added. "Even if somewhere turns out to be nowhere."

I nodded.

And yes, he was right: it felt good. My arms ached, my body sweated, thorn and pium fly bit searingly into my flesh —and still it felt good; it felt better than anything I had done or experienced for almost as long as I could remember.

There was the sound of the cachoeira off to the left of us, very close now and deep and pervading. There was the sunlight and shadow on the still, tiered forest. There was the flash and bite of steel, and the green veils parting, and the path slowly widening around us at each turn and then plunging ahead to the next turn and the next. . . . And that was all there was. . . . And everything else, yesterday and tomorrow, hope and fear, dream and reality, Nils Barna and Christine, were blessedly remote and inconsequential. And when night came—for the first time for me at that place—there was only darkness and a swaying hammock and deep sleep.

I went out on the trail for a second day. And a third. Touro accepted me without question, and through the long hours we moved forward, side by side. Occasionally he would sing softly in his deep rich-timbered voice—a few bars of a familiar spiritual, perhaps, or a plangent Portuguese chant. More often we worked in silence. And yet I was aware that a point of contact was slowly being formed between us. It may have been the influence of the forest, or simply the bond of shared work. I don't know. But it was there; it was growing. And I knew that soon now I would have a glimpse behind the ambiguous facade of the O Touro "who met the eye."

It happened on the evening of the third day, while the two of us were returning along the trail through the quickly darkening forest. The last group of caboclos was moving along ahead of us; we were alone together; and for a while we walked, as usual, without speaking. Then quite suddenly and without looking at me the Negro said: "Well, are you still worried, Mr. Allison?"

"Worried?"

"That there's something dangerous about me."

"I don't know what you mean," I said.

"Yes, Mr. Allison, I think you do. I think that's why Mr. McHugh asked you to come out on the trail to watch me."

A few moments passed before Touro spoke again. When

234

he did, however, his voice was as courteous as ever, soft and a little sad. "It's too bad that Mr. Cobb had to be at Esperança when you and Mr. McHugh arrived," he said. "And that the things that happened—did happen. Not that I blame you and Mr. McHugh for anything. I don't even blame Mr. Cobb. It was simply unfortunate that things worked out the way they did."

We walked in silence again. Then he said: "You know that I'm a fugitive, Mr. Allison."

"All I know is what Cobb said that day in your cottage."

"What he said was true. I'm a fugitive and a murderer."

"All that's in the past," I said. "There's no use thinking about it now."

"It's not a question of 'use,' but of fact. Mr. Cobb's facts. My facts. And there's not much past or future about killing, I'm afraid, but only a present. You kill a man, and he's dead, and he stays dead."

"Why did you kill this man?"

"Because I hated him."

"Why did you hate him?"

"Because—" Touro paused. "Because there was hate in my heart."

"You were a ship's stoker then?"

"Yes."

"What were you before?"

"A longshoreman. A laborer."

"And before *that?*"

The big Negro looked at me curiously. "What makes you think I was anything before that?" he asked.

"I'm not blind, Touro," I said. "I'm not deaf."

He didn't say anything. The light had grown fainter as we walked along, and the rumbling of the cachoeira was fainter too. The caboclos were out of sight beyond a turning of the trail.

"What did you start out as?" I asked him.

"I started out as a law-student," he said.

Before O Touro there had been Bull Jackson. Before Bull Jackson, I now learned, there had been Herbert McKinley Jackson. And Herbert McKinley Jackson had grown up in Memphis, Tennessee, the son of a pastor in the African Methodist Church.

"My father wanted me to be a preacher too," he said, "but right from the beginning I knew that wasn't for me. I didn't want to save souls. I wanted to save men. Men as they were all around me in those Memphis slums: poor men, exploited men, black men. I decided the best way to do it was to be a lawyer. Eventually a politician. A leader. From the time I was twelve I did hardly anything else but study, and when the time came for law school one of the run-of-the-mill Negro colleges wouldn't do. It had to be a real school—a white man's school—up north. I think I was the proudest man on earth when I got into Midland University, in Chicago—the first Negro ever accepted."

He had stayed there almost two years, he said. In professional training they were all he'd hoped for. In everything else they were terrible. Blow by blow, humiliation by humiliation, he learned what it meant to have a black skin in a white man's world.

"I tried to shut all that out," he went on. "All I wanted to think about was my work, the life ahead of me, the things I was going to do for my people. Maybe I'd have done better to think a little of the frustration and hate that were spreading like poison inside me.

"Anyhow—it all ended, crazily enough, because a few white boys wanted to be kind to me. We'd just finished a series of examinations; some of my classmates were planning to celebrate with an evening at a bar and grill; and they invited me along. At first I said no, but they knew what I was afraid of and told me they'd spoken to the manager and it was all right. So I went, and at first it *was* all right. It was better than I'd ever thought a thing like that could be, and after four or five beers we were all singing together and joking, almost as if we were simply six human beings instead of five white men and a black. But then the party started growing. Other students came in and joined us, and some of them were pretty drunk. And suddenly, like a rifle shot, I heard somebody saying, 'I'm damned if I'm going to drink with a nigger.'

"I didn't say anything. I just got up and started to leave. A couple of the men I'd come in with tried to stop me, but before they could do anything somebody threw a glass, and then somebody else gave me a push, and then I turned around on them and everything went red and black and wild. I don't know how many men I hit, or how often, or with what.

"The next morning I woke up in jail. And two days later I had a notice telling me to report to the dean's office at the university, but whether they were going to expel me or not I didn't find out, because I never went back. I went out and walked the streets of Chicago all of one night, and when I got back home there was a hardbitten-looking white man in a derby hat waiting for me.

"Another cop, I thought. But he wasn't. He was the owner of a poolroom over on South Division Street, and he said he'd seen the fight in the bar and that I'd looked pretty good to him. . . . And that's how Herbert Jackson, the student, turned into Bull Jackson, the prize fighter."

Touro paused in his story. We walked side by side along the darkening trail.

How long had he fought? I asked him. About three years, he said. First in the crummy little clubs around Chicago's South Side, then in bigger ones up in the Loop, finally around the country, in Detroit, Pittsburgh, Philadelphia, New York. "And I guess Bull was the right name for me," he went on, "because that was the way I fought—head down, wild and charging, as if someone were waving a red flag in front of my eyes. I wasn't fast or ringwise enough ever to become a first-rater, and besides, I never seemed able to win against another colored man. I didn't want to fight colored men. I wanted to fight white men. And I didn't just want to beat them on points; I wanted the knockout, the kill. That was the only thing that made me a fighter: hate."

But he had quit?

Yes, he had quit. Even though he was just beginning to make real money. He had known that if he went on he would sooner or later kill a man. And he had quit.

And then?

Then came trucking, stevedoring, roadbuilding; a stretch on W.P.A.; a stretch on relief. "No use going into all that," Touro said. "It was no worse than the life that millions of Negroes were living, but finally I just couldn't go on with it any longer. If it was the last thing I did on earth, I had to get away from Jim Crow and lynch law and niggertown—and from the hate that was still eating into me. For the first time since I'd left school I'd begun reading again: not just law books this time, but history, geography, politics, economics —everything I could lay my hands on. And one day I began reading a book about Brazil, and it said that this was the one country in the civilized world where the color of a man's skin didn't matter, and where white and Negro and Indian lived side by side and had an equal chance for a decent life. From then on that was all I thought about—Brazil. I read more about it, talked about it, dreamed about it, and pretty soon I decided that, come hell or high water, that was where I was going. For six months I knocked around from one East Coast and Gulf port to another, looking for a berth on a ship that would take me there. And at last I found it: fireman third class on the freighter *Alcazar*, bound south out of Norfolk for Belem, Bahía and Rio."

Touro paused again. Then he said: "Maybe it all would have worked out all right, if it hadn't been for a man named Mr. Albert Spendrow. . . .

"I don't know how to tell you about Mr. Spendrow," he went on. "He was no worse than plenty of other men, I suppose; he just happened to be the wrong man in the wrong place, which was Second Engineer in charge of the stokehole crew. As a matter of fact, with most of the other men he wasn't too bad—hard and driving, yes, but not unfair—but he had it in for me right from the start. Partly, of course, it was my color, for I happened to be the only Negro in that particular crew. And partly it was my size, I think, because Mr. Spendrow was a small man, and my bigness and blackness were an insult to him. Then, to make things worse, he soon began to suspect me. I don't mean he knew I was planning to jump ship; nobody aboard knew that; but there must have been something in my manner that made me stand out in his mind from the others. Anyhow, he watched me and rode me—and hated me."

When the *Alcazar* docked in Belem, which was its first port in Brazil, Touro (he had still been Jackson then, of course) had been the only man in the stokehole who was not given shore leave. But he had taken it anyway. He had packed his few things and sneaked ashore and, going to the immigration bureau, asked what he had to do to be allowed to live there.

"To stay in Brazil?" they asked.

"Yes, to stay in Brazil."

"You cannot stay in Brazil," they said.

"I had my sea-bag with me," said Touro, "and I guess that made them suspicious of what I'd do, because they had the police take me back to the *Alcazar*. And there was Mr. Spendrow standing at the rail, waiting for me. He didn't say anything then—just sort of grinned a little and had me locked in the brig—but later that evening he came in and started letting me have it. I tried not to listen, but every time I turned away he swung me around by the arm and stuck his face up to mine like some kind of white hissing snake.

" 'Go away, Mr. Spendrow,' I asked him.

" 'You black bastard,' he said. 'You thought you were putting something over on me, didn't you? Well I guess they showed you.'

" 'Please go away, Mr. Spendrow,' I asked.

"But he wouldn't go away. 'You don't think Brazil wants niggers, do you?' he said '—any more than any place else.'

"And that's when it happened. To this day I don't know what I used: a wrench, I suppose, or something else that was lying around handy. I brought it up once and I brought it down once, and that was all there was to it. Well, almost all. Because now that he was lying there in front of me I suddenly did something even more full of hate than hitting him. There was a can of black paint standing in a corner that they'd had me using on the iron-work in the brig, and I picked it up and emptied it on his face.

" 'How do you like it, Mr. Spendrow,' I asked him, 'now you're a nigger too?'

"Then I got out of there. I didn't even stop to get my sea-bag. I went up on deck and down the ladder and across the wharf and into Brazil.

"That was twelve years ago last April," he said.

We walked on again in silence. Darkness had all but closed in, and the path showed merely as a thread of twilight between black towering walls.

"And you've been here ever since?" I asked.

Touro nodded.

"At Esperança?"

"No," he said. "Esperança didn't come until later. At first I kept moving around, up and down the river, from one village and fazenda and jungle camp to another, because I was afraid they'd catch me. Once they almost did, but a girl who lived at the fazenda where I was working hid me under a pile of wash in her hut. Her name was Tereza Carolina Gonçalvez, and I married her."

"Then finally they stopped looking?"

"Yes, finally they stopped. Tereza and I moved on to another place. There are many Negroes along the Amazon, and by now I spoke good Portuguese. My name became O Touro. I had a son. I became a Catholic."

"Haven't you ever wanted to go home?" I asked.

"Home?"

"To the States."

240

He shook his head. "No, I don't want to go back to the States. Not even if I could. Not even if I could take my family. Can you imagine what sort of life my wife would have there? And my boy—half Negro, a quarter Portuguese, a quarter Indian?"

"Has it been a good life here?"

"Better than there, at least. Better than anywhere where men hate other men because of the color of their skin."

"You've found what you wanted, then?"

"I've found part of it," said Touro. "I've learned, of course, that in some things the world is the same world, wherever you go. But here—yes—it's been better. Esperança, most of all, was better. It was a poor place, a small insignificant place. But at least men lived there together without hating one another. All kinds and tongues and colors of men, living and working and trying to build together. It was a good place; a decent place."

"And you didn't want to leave it?"

"No, I didn't want to leave it."

"This place we've come to—" I said. "Can't this be made into a good and decent place too?"

"Perhaps," he answered.

17

Roughly a month after our arrival at Graça de Deus the work on the cachoeira trail was finished. The three out-board-motored canoes were ready to be carried up and launched in the upper river. Then, two days before the scheduled departure of the reconnaissance party, McHugh called the "staff" together for a discussion of plans—and I discovered that I was not to go along.

McHugh himself would be in command of one canoe (plus, of course, the whole expedition), Cobb of the second, and O Touro of the third; and with them they were taking nine of the younger caboclos, two Indian guides, and enough food and supplies for a maximum of four weeks. As for my-self—I was to be in charge at Graça de Deus, either until their return or until the prior arrival of the *Fortaleza*, in which event I would turn the reins over to Wooderson. Ac-cording to McHugh's reckoning the latter would more likely be the case, for it was now already the last week in July and the boat should be arriving no later than the middle of August, if it were to have time to unload and get back down-stream before the worst of the dry season. Even now the level of the water along the mudbank was more than a foot lower than when we came.

"Until the boat arrives," said McHugh, "it will be simply a matter of marking time. Keep the caboclos busy. Keep an eye on the Indians. As for Barna—" He shrugged. "Well, with Barna use your own judgment."

My first impulse was to protest. Throughout that whole

month in Graça de Deus I had waited for the day when I could break away from the frustration that hemmed me in like the very walls of the clearing; when I could set off at last for the hills, for the River of the Sun. But I didn't protest. The day had come—and there was to be no breaking away—and still I sat silently while John McHugh spoke. For one thing, of course, there was no use arguing, for he had clearly made up his mind. Compared to Cobb or Touro, I would be of little use on the trip, and, since someone in authority had to stay behind, I was the logical choice. . . . Also —when now at last I faced the issue squarely—also I knew that in my heart I wanted to stay. River and hills would still be there next month, next year, next century. But when the *Fortaleza* came—and left—what would become of Nils and Christine Barna?

Yes, I told McHugh, when he had finished his instructions: I would keep the caboclos busy; I would get along with the Tupari; I would see that the *Fortaleza* crowd got well established, if they arrived before the others returned. . . .

The next day Barna kept his promise about the Indian guides, bringing two of them to the clearing and leaving them in the care of Touro and João Batista. It was apparent, however, that he had not bothered to pick any outstanding members of the tribe. Both McHugh and Cobb, I think, had been expecting that young Cambar, the chief's son, would be one of those to go along. But the two who came were old lethargic-looking men, obviously among those who could best be spared from the Tupari's own activities.

McHugh looked at them with disappointment and Cobb with unconcealed disgust. "How's to our going over to the village and doing a little selecting of our own?" the latter suggested.

As before, though, McHugh vetoed any ideas of force and decided to make the best of what was offered. For one thing, he pointed out, we could speak with none of the Tupari except the chief, Pombal, and, whoever went along, their use would be limited to the simplest indicating of routes. Of course, if Barna were telling the truth about the Tupari and their unfamiliarity with the country beyond the circumscribed range, these two men would be of no use to us in any case. But McHugh and particularly Cobb were inclined to discount Barna's word on this as on other matters. And I suspect McHugh was nursing the hope that at the last minute Barna himself would change his mind and go along. Nothing of the sort happened, however. Later that day, when the canoes were being carried along the cachoeira trail to the upper river, Barna was not even physically in evidence. According to Christine, he had gone off to the Indian village "to work on his curaré."

The following morning I watched the canoes chug out into the smooth waters of the upper Malaguay, turn their prows upstream and disappear behind a green elbow of the forest. Then I walked the four miles back along the cachoeira trail to Graça de Deus. No sound of ax or machete now broke the murmurous silence, and the clearing, when I reached it, lay in flyblown sun-scorched torpor. For perhaps an hour I went through the motions of keeping busy in the office shack and then took to my hammock for the rest of the morning. Once I heard the shrill sound of Serafima Batista's laughter. A while later Tourinho Jackson and two other boys raced past, shouting, in pursuit of a scurrying marmoset. Then there was no sound or movement at all, except the slow heavy-winged flapping of the vultures as they flew their endless patrol back and forth over the clearing.

Have I mentioned the vultures?

When we first reached Graça de Deus there were none there. "Never are around these Indio settlements," Cobb had explained. "Reckon the pickings are so thin they just can't be bothered." And apparently Nils Barna alone had failed to produce enough superior offal to interest them.

"Don't worry, though, we'll be having visitors soon enough," Cobb added. And we did.

They didn't seem to fly in from any place, but simply one

244

morning to be *there*. They perched on the thatch roofs and in the branches of the trees, squatted in obscene ranks around the cook-house and latrines, and circled with slow patient watchfulness in the sky above the riverbank. In the beginning I hadn't paid much attention to them, but simply accepted them as part of the place, like the river, the forest, the heat, the insects. Now that the reconnaissance party had left, however, and the early activity in the clearing was supplanted by changeless lassitude, they began more and more to intrude into my consciousness, until they were affecting me in an emotional, almost irrational manner. One morning I awoke to find a knot of them congregated next to my hammock, scratching and squawling over the putrid entrails of some long-dead animal; and, getting a gun, I banged away at them in a cold frenzy of loathing. For every one I killed, however, three new ones seemed to materialize out of nowhere. "As well try to catch all the fish in the river, senhor," said João Batista, watching me, "or to cut down all the trees of the forest."

And he was right, of course. I put the gun away. And the urubus went on squatting and circling, watching and waiting.

Except for the vultures, the pattern of life at Graça de Deus had reverted pretty much to what it must have been when only the Tupari and Nils Barna were there. True, there were two communities where before there had been one. There were the new shacks, the widened trail, the piles of equipment, the moored launch and barges. There were syringes and gasoline drums and privies and guns and a chapel, plus roughly twice the population there had been before. But all this now seemed to be simply a matter of so-and-so-many "things," so-and-so-many numbers, and to have no connection with the actual routine of living. The exploration party, no less than the almost mythical *Fortaleza*, existed only as a vague irrelevant abstraction. Oil was no more than a three letter word. What was real, and all that was real, was heat, insects, river, forest, sky. And of course the hammocks. When I think back on Graça de Deus during those days and weeks of waiting I can still hear the creaking of the hammock cords as the caboclos dozed away the eventless hours.

"Keep them busy," McHugh had said. And I did what I could. I ordered a thorough restacking and cleaning in the storage sheds, assigned a crew to keeping the trails clear, and set another to work removing the mold and river-slime that had formed like a pustulous skin over the idle launch and barges. They went through the motions, but nothing seemed to come of it. At the end of two weeks the sheds were still dark evil-smelling dens of litter and roaches, sections of the cachoeira trail were again half overgrown with vines, and the deck-boards of the two barges lay warped and rotting in the sunlight. Apathy lay like a suffocating blanket over the parched clearing, and when occasionally it lifted slightly, it was never for more than an hour or two at a time. Then, again, the only movement would be the circling of the vultures, the only sound the creaking of hammocks.

In my own hammock, which I had slung in the shade of a jacaranda tree behind the staff shack, I lay under a shroud of mosquito netting through the sweltering noons and endless nights. I counted off the days. I tried to visualize the progress of the three canoes moving slowly upstream toward the hidden hills. I thought of Christine. And of the enigma of Nils Barna. . . .

There had been no real communication between Barna and myself since that night we had walked together across the clearing. For the first week after the up-river party had left I saw him scarcely at all. But finally, one day when I was in the infirmary on some matter or other, Christine asked if I would come that night to their cabin for supper.

As when Barna had asked me there before, I was taken by surprise and hesitated. Would her husband want me? I asked.

"It was Nils who suggested it," she said.

The conversation at supper was casual and desultory:

about the weather, the insects, the habits of the urubus, the Tupari's technique of fishing (mandioca poison) as against the caboclos' (dynamite). And when the meal was finished Barna said, "My wife tells me you are a card-player, Mr. Allison. Do you know any of the European games? Halma, bezique, piquet . . . ?"

Thereafter we ate or played cards together every second or third night, sometimes in Barna's cabin, sometimes in the staff shack in the big clearing. Or rather, Barna and I played cards, silently and concentratedly, while Christine sat in a far corner of the room, reading or mending. It was a rather dull threesome, for we were now the only outlanders in Graça de Deus, and the patterns of our lives crossed and recrossed daily. Yet we continued the meals together. We continued the cards. And each evening was the same as the one before and the one that followed.

Until on the sixth or seventh evening. . . .

I remember it had been a day of more than usual heat— not bright and burning, as were most of the days, but close, glazed, almost without sun; and when darkness came the sky shimmered with lightning and dull rumblings of thunder rose and fell in the distance. If it comes closer it will rain, I thought hopefully, as we sat at supper in the staff shack. But it didn't come closer. It diminished into stillness. And then suddenly, out of the stillness, came a new sound, far louder and closer than the thunder, a hollow ululating reverberating sound that seemed to fill the whole of the night beyond the circumference of the clearing. For a few minutes the din, even in the shack, was too loud to speak through. Then, like the thunder before it, it began to fade.

I looked at Barna. "Howlers?" I asked him.

"Yes," he said. "The howler monkeys."

"I've never heard them so loud."

"The threat of a storm sometimes stirs them up."

We listened while the wave of sound receded into the distance. Presently it was only a murmur, and then out of the murmur, with sudden clarity, rose a single high-pitched scream.

I felt the hairs rising on the back of my neck, and, looking at Christine, I saw that she was sitting motionless as a carved figure. The scream was gone now, and the murmuring too. The only sound was the whir and click of insects around the yellow chimney of the oil lamp.

"It sounded—human," Christine said.

"Perhaps it was," said Barna, smiling a little. "Perhaps it was Preisinger."

Christine merely looked at him, and so did I.

"You have not heard of Preisinger, Mr. Allison?" he asked me.

"No," I said.

"Then I shall tell you about him—with your permission, of course—for he is really a rather interesting fellow." Barna paused, and the gray eyes behind the glasses looked at me coolly and steadily. "Well, this Preisinger, according to the story they tell, was a German who came to the Amazon a long time ago. What he was looking for I do not know, nor does it matter. Let us call it gold, or rubber. In any case, he spent many years here, sailing the rivers, threading the trails, pursuing whatever variety of Fata Morgana it was that lured him on. Outwardly, I gather, he was an altogether conventional type, with nothing to distinguish him from the usual run of jungle adventurers.

"Inwardly, however, Preisinger seems to have been a man of imagination; and an imagination, as you will discover if you live here long enough, is not always a good thing in this part of the earth. He lived alone a great deal. Some say he drank a great deal. And as the years went by, the forest, instead of becoming more and more familiar to him, as it should have, seemed instead to become increasingly alien. In his lonely camps he would sit awake through the nights, listening to a thousand sounds of which he could not see or even imagine the source. On the trails he felt himself no longer the hunter, but the hunted. I have heard it told that

248

he gradually worked out a theory of his own whereby the whole world of the jungle was divided into two parts: the *inside,* where dwelt everything that truly belonged in it, and the *outside,* where man, the interloper, lived alone.

"The forest became a place of terror for him; of shadows and whisperings and watching eyes. But along with terror there was also fascination—fixation—and instead of withdrawing from it he found himself plunging always farther, always deeper into the wilderness. Finally he relinquished his status as a white man altogether and went to live with a tribe of primitive Indians; but even they, he discovered, were still men, still *outsiders,* barely suffered to exist in a world in which they did not belong, perpetually ringed in by darkness and fear. Worst of all for him was the fact that the particular tribe he had selected lived in a region infested with howler monkeys. They are quick and elusive, the howlers, and he never saw one; or at most a flickering shadow in the forest maze. But every night—night after night, week after week, month after month—he would sit in the darkness and listen to the sound of them in the black jungle beyond the Indians' clearing. You have heard the sound. You know how unearthly, how compelling, it can be. And gradually, in Preisinger's haunted mind, it grew to the proportions of an obsession. The howlers became for him the symbol of the forest itself. Of the Unknown; of The Mystery. . . .

"How long all this went on I do not know. Some say a year. Some say more. But inevitably the time came when he could stand it no longer, and then, being a singular man, he did a singular thing. He went out into the jungle one night and howled himself. That first time, to be sure, he howled very briefly and amateurishly, and nothing happened. Even the Indians paid no attention to the strange new noises, thinking they were merely the squawkings of some injured macaw or parakeet. But Preisinger was now caught up in the momentum of a great enterprise, and each night thereafter he went back into the jungle, and stayed longer, and howled louder. And at last the night came when he had his reward. The black darkness around him dissolved into moving shadows, and then the shadows became hundreds of monkeys, and the monkeys squatted in a great dim circle on the surrounding branches, and they and Preisinger howled together."

Barna paused and cleared his throat. "In the morning," he went on, "the Indians searched for him all over their clearing and even a little way into the forest beyond. They could not find him, nor did they ever see him again; and at first, of course, they believed him dead. But when night came again, and then other nights, and they lay in the darkness listening to the howlers, the evidence of their own ears told them that this was not so. Certain travelers in the deep forest who have subsequently visited this particular tribe claim to have seen a most interesting sight. In the hut of their witch-doctor, they say, in a place of honor among their godlings and fetishes, is a crude little wooden carving of a white man with a wide-open mouth and a fine long tail.

"The tail, of course"—Barna smiled a little—"is the Indians' artistic embellishment. But all the stories agree that Preisinger did go to live with the monkeys, and, in all respects except the anatomical, he has apparently made a remarkable adjustment to their way of life. Take his howling, for example, which you have perhaps just heard. All authorities agree that he had perfected it to a point where it far excels that of his instructors. Indeed, the howlers themselves are now reputed to stand in awe of him—as, of course, do all the other jungle creatures—whereas he, once a poor terror-ridden specter of a man, is no longer afraid of anything. For he has finally penetrated The Mystery, you see. He is *inside* at last. He *belongs*.

"And they say he is very happy."

Another pause; another little cough; then Barna was silent. Christine said nothing. I said nothing. And in the stillness, fantastically, I found myself straining my ears to the night outside. The shriek, however, was not repeated. The howling was not repeated. Even the distant thunder was gone now, and beyond the windows the heat-lightning pulsed soundlessly across the blackness of the sky.

"I did not know you were a Catholic, Mr. Allison," said Barna, a few days later.

"I'm not," I told him.

"I have noticed that you have been attending the padre's masses."

"A few times, yes."

"And have you found them—helpful?"

"No," I said.

"That is unfortunate," said Barna. "But only to be expected, I am afraid. Frankly, I have never been able to understand what a thinking man can hope to find in the rituals of formal religion."

"Perhaps he realizes that he has lost something—and is trying to get it back."

"Yes, of course. To get back what we have lost. To begin over again. That might almost be said to be the primary need of mankind, might it not? But why Catholicism? Why go back only to the Middle Ages? To begin again, it appears to me, one must go back much farther than that. One must go back all the way."

"To where?"

"To our origins, Mr. Allison. To where we began—and where, quite possibly, we are going to end." Barna paused and smiled faintly. "To where Herr Preisinger has gone, perhaps. . . ."

He held in his fingers a great black-and-gold butterfly, bent over it carefully and then released it. "I thought it might be a rare variety of *Pyraustinae*," he explained, "but it was only a common *siga liris*."

"Are you an entomologist too," I asked him.

"Oh yes," he said, "after a fashion. Entomology, biology, chemistry, geology, agronomy—I've dabbled in them all, I'm afraid. In my younger days my friends used to accuse me of

251

harboring a Faust complex. All science, that was to be my province, no less. All knowledge. And, of course, all wisdom." Barna made a sound deep in his throat that might or might not have been a cough. "Yes, Faust," he went on. "He was my beau ideal once. And even more than Faust, Goethe. Do you perhaps remember what Goethe said as he lay dying? *Mehr licht,* he said. More light. That is what I too once wanted: more light. So that I might see life steadily and see it whole."

He paused and regarded me with a curious abstracted expression. "But I have since discovered that it is not easy to see life whole," he went on. "It is not easy to see the truth, even when it seems to lie plain before you; for truth, as you may have observed, Mr. Allison, can be possessed of a terrible ambiguity. Which is the truth, for example, about the butterfly which I just showed you: its exquisite and delicate loveliness or the fact that I found it feeding on the putrid carcass of a bird? Which is the truth: the bright earth we see by day or the black universe we see by night? The quiet pool in the heart of the forest or the rending death in the heart of the pool?

"In my own life I have known only one man who saw life steadily and whole. He was a Dyak tribesman, in Borneo, who had been caught spying by the Japanese; and his captors, with a rather overdeveloped sense of irony, had very skillfully removed his eyelids. Unfortunately, however, I never learned much about his unique preceptive powers, because by the time I encountered him he was both blind and mad."

"Science," he murmured. "Ah, science. . . . You were a scientist of sorts yourself, I understand, Mr. Allison. A master of technics and dynamics, of propulsion and concussion. My own work has never been in so spectacular a field, of course, but still we were workers in the same vineyard. I as the scientist-thinker, you as the scientist-doer: together, we have been the great team of the twentieth century. The prime movers. The earth shakers."

Barna paused and riffled the deck of cards that he held in his thin long-boned hands. "Yes, science was my Kingdom," he said, "and my Faith. To search and find, build and grow —patiently, objectively, devotedly: that, I was convinced, was man's destiny and his glory. Of all that he had achieved, all of which he boasted, I believed that it was science, and science alone, which could truly set him free.

"Need I tell you that it was an illusion, Mr. Allison? If you have not yet discovered it, I suggest merely that you look carefully around you at the world into which you have come; for the world of science and the world of the jungle operate, I assure you, on almost identical principles. Natural selection—the struggle to live—the survival of the fittest: what could be more objective, more impersonal, more purely scientific? Here, as in the laboratory, one has passed beyond the realm of wishful thinking and value judgments into the realm of truth. There is no moral responsibility, no ethos, no choice, but only Immutable Law. One does not blame a jaguar for clawing or a snake for striking or a pirhana for rending, any more than one blames a scientist for creating a formula that will corrupt a civilization or an equation that will destroy it. For they are not free and independent entities, you see. As you and I have been, they are cogs in a machine; technicians fulfilling an appointed function; means to an end which is beyond their power to foresee."

"And politics—" he said. "Are you interested in seeing communism at work? Let me show you the ants. Or fascism? The piranhas will do. As for democracy, I suppose we shall have to go to the howler monkeys. Perhaps that is another aspect of our friend Preisinger: the Strayed Democrat. I imagine that his superior howling has by now won him a premiership or a presidency."

"Yes—politics, science, art, philosophy, faith," he said. "There are many trails through the forest, Mr. Allison, and I am afraid that all of them are devious. . . . But I am sorry," he added, picking up the cards. "I have been talking too much and boring you. It seems that my long solitude has made me garrulous."

He dealt out the hand.

"Well, your friends should be back soon," he said, "and then instead of talk there will be action. On to the hills—to the high country—to the River of the Sun!"

I picked up my cards.

"You are the fortunate men," Barna went on. "The Men of Purpose. No need for you to get lost in the forest of uncertainty and doubt, for yours is the one path that cuts straight through it to the goal. Perhaps that is the answer to everything, Mr. Allison. To have one goal: plain, simple, palpable. The Kingdom of Progress. The Kingdom of Power. The Kingdom of Oil. . . ." He paused in arranging his hand and looked at me across the lamplit table. "Oil *is* your kingdom, is it not?" he asked.

"That's right," I told him. "I'm looking for oil."

"Yes, of course. Of course." He looked down at his cards again. "Your play, I believe. . . ."

This, as nearly as I can transcribe, was how Nils Barna talked. His conversations were brief, elliptic, beginning nowhere and ending nowhere. His words flickered, ambiguous and evanescent, like the lamplight on his glasses and the faint bitter smile on his lips.

And what was behind the words? Was there a conscious and subtle probing? Or simply a fortuitous echo of my own inner conflict and doubt? Time and again it seemed that Barna was about to raise the screen he held before him. But he never did. He remained what he had been from the beginning: a face and a voice in the darkness of a jungle; a figure waiting at the turning of a trail.

Then finally the evening came, the moment came, when the figure began to emerge a little more clearly. It was an evening on which Barna and Christine were to have supper at the staff shack, and on my arrival I found that Christine was already there—alone.

"Isn't your husband coming?" I asked.

"Yes, Nils is coming," she said. "But I came on ahead. I came to talk to you, Mark."

I could see at once that she was tense and overwrought. "Easy, Chris," I said. "What is it?"

"It's something I've found out. Or rather, that Nils has told me. It happened yesterday—last night—and ever since I've been trying to decide what I should do. Now I have decided. I have to tell you. . . ." She paused, and went on with an obvious effort. "The exploration party—John and the others—they've gone the wrong way."

"The wrong way?"

She nodded. "The upper river beyond the rapids—after ten or fifteen miles it bears away to the south. It doesn't lead to the hills at all."

For a long moment I simply stared at her. Then—"Your husband said that?" I asked.

"Yes, Nils said it."

"How does he know? When did he find out?"

"He's known all along," she said.

"Before they left?"

"Yes, before they left."

"And he never—" Again I stopped, trying to find a way through the confusion of my thoughts. "He never told you until yesterday?" I said.

"No, not until yesterday."

"Why did he tell you then?"

"I don't know."

"And why had he done it? What explanation did he give?"

"He didn't give any. He simply told me that. . . ."

". . . I simply told my wife, Mr. Allison," said Barna, appearing in the doorway, "that I love and respect her too much to tell her anything but the truth."

Christine and I turned and faced him. "I'm sorry, Nils," she said. "I've told him. I had to tell him."

"That's all right, my dear. There is no harm in it," he reassured her. "Mr. Allison would know in a few days anyhow—when his friends return."

"Then it's the truth?" I said.

"That the upper river does not lead to the hills? Yes, that is the truth,"

"How do you know? You told us that you hadn't been to the hills."

"That is correct."

"Or beyond the upper end of the rapids."

"That is not correct."

"You mean you lied to us?"

"Yes," said Barna blandly. "In that I am afraid I lied to you, by a matter of a few miles."

"Why?"

"For reasons of my own. One of which was that I was anxious to see you gentlemen on your way."

"The wrong way—"

"That frankly was immaterial to me."

"If it was immaterial, why did you send them the wrong way?"

"Send them, Mr. Allison? I did not send anyone anywhere. I showed you the upper river; I showed you the hills; and you reached your own conclusions. What did you expect me to do: lead you by the hand to your destination?"

"How about the guides?" I asked. "The two Indians. Where do they come in?"

Barna smiled a little. "They came in, as I recall, at Mr. McHugh's request. In fact, at his insistence. If they were of no help, I at least told you as much. . . . And now, if the catechism is over—" he said, turning as if to leave.

But I stepped quickly between him and the door. "No, Barna," I said quietly, "it isn't over."

For an instant I thought he was going to try to shove past me. But he didn't. He stopped. His eyes fixed on mine, cold and questioning. "Well?" he asked.

"What are you up to anyhow?"

"Up to?"

"What are you doing here?"

"I seem to remember having been asked that before. And having answered it. I am living here."

"Why?"

"Because I choose to. Being no longer a scientist and not quite a jungle beast, you see, I am able, to a degree at least, to exercise choice."

"And one of your choices is to get rid of us, is that right?"

"Putting it bluntly, yes—that is quite right."

"So you can—"

"So I can go on living the life I have chosen."

"Never mind your life. I'm talking about those hills. About the River of the Sun." I took a step toward him. "If the upper river is the wrong way to the hills," I said evenly, *"what is the right way?"*

Barna didn't answer.

"It's another river, isn't it? It's the river that joins this one at the next Indian village below here."

"I am afraid I cannot go into all these geographical matters with you."

"I'm afraid you're going to have to."

There was another silence. I had almost forgotten that Christine was there, but now suddenly she spoke for the first time since Barna's entrance. "Nils, please—" she said. "Listen to him. Talk to him—"

"There is nothing to talk about," he said in a flat toneless voice.

"No, Nils—no, you're wrong." Going to him quickly, she looked up into his face. "There *is* something to talk about. There's everything. . . . That's what I've been trying to show you for all these weeks now. And that's why I came to Mark and told him what you told me. You know that, don't you? You understand that? It was for your sake, Nils. Only for you."

Barna looked down at her without speaking and then started to turn away. But she put her hand on his arm and

257

stopped him. "You say you love and respect me, Nils. Then listen to me—please! It isn't just rivers and hills I'm talking about. It's yourself—ourselves—everything. You can't go on turning your back like this; shutting yourself away; living in the past. Whatever dreadful things happened—they're what you must shut away. What you must forget. You have to live again, Nils. In the world. With other men. . . ."

Nils Barna looked down at her: tall and stooped, motionless and silent. It was like that, I thought, that he must have looked at her on the night when Christine had wakened and found him standing in the darkness beside her hammock. But this time he didn't take her hand. Instead, he turned away again, and then he said, "This is the world. The Tupari are men."

"I mean the world you've left, Nils. Your own kind of—"

"No, not my kind," said Barna, his voice suddenly harsh. "Once my kind—yes. But no longer. Nor ever again." He looked past Christine at me, and the eyes behind the glinting lenses seemed to be made of gray stone. "If it is oil you want, Mr. Allison, go find it. If it is rivers or hills or El Dorado, go find them too. I cannot stop you. But do not expect me to help you. Or to become one of you."

"They're expecting nothing of you," said Christine. "All they want is—"

"All they want is the earth," said Barna. "You see, I happen to know, Mr. Allison, because I too once wanted it. I too was once a conquistador, an El Dorado seeker, a soldier of the Kingdom of Progress. And one day, a few years ago, in another jungle on the other side of the world, I learned what it meant to be these things."

Christine had put her hand on his arm again and was looking up into his face. "Is that what it is, Nils?" she asked gently. "Even now? After so long?"

Barna said nothing.

"Yes, it's that, isn't it? What happened in Borneo. What happened to Jakob Koppel—"

Still Barna was silent.

And now, suddenly, Christine was holding him tightly, her face raised to his, her voice filled with a quiet but almost desperate pleading. "Nils, Nils—you can't go on thinking about it for the rest of your life. Letting it torture and poison you. Jakob is dead, yes—and it was a terrible thing, I know that. But it's done, Nils. It was the war, and it happened and it's done, and you have to forget it. You have to come back to the world, accept it, be part of it. . . ."

Barna was no longer looking at her. Gently he released himself from her hold.

"Jakob himself—" said Christine. "—he'd have wanted you to, don't you see that? Yes, Jakob most of all. He looked up to you so; believed in you so. If you won't do it for me, Nils, or for yourself, then do it for him—please—I beg you. . . ."

"Stop, Christine," he murmured, almost gently. "I do not want to hear about it, or to speak about it. Why do you think I have come to this place, if not to get away from such things?" Then suddenly the softness was gone. The gentleness was gone. The cold eyes seemed to blaze out at us, and the voice, though still quiet, was harsh and strangled, as if wrenched up from the depths of his body. "All I ask is to be let alone, do you understand? For the love of God—all of you—*leave me alone!*"

Brushing past us, he seemed half to walk, half to run to the door. This time I didn't stop him. He went out and disappeared in the darkness; and Christine and I stood for a moment looking after him; and then she too quickly crossed to the door and went out.

"Nils!" her voice came back to me, calling. "Nils—Nils—"

18

THERE WAS NO way of going after the reconnaissance party. Nor would there have been any use in it, for they would long since have discovered for themselves that they were on a goose chase and were probably well on the way back to Graça de Deus. Furthermore, the *Fortaleza* was due any day now, and it was obvious that no more action could be taken until all our forces were marshalled in one place.

Driven both by impatience and by an almost overwhelming need to get away from the clearing, I went up along the rapids to the "high point" and through binoculars peered long and carefully along the river in both directions. But there was no sign of smoke from below, no flicker of movement from above. The tiny world of Graça de Deus lay lost and alone, insulated from everything beyond by a vast arc of empty miles.

There had now been no rain to speak of for almost two months, and each day the level of the river was an inch or two lower against its bank. Shunning the office shack, where there was nothing to do anyhow, I took to spending long hours on the moored *Cantora*, where it was a degree or two cooler and an occasional wisp of breeze eddied in across the water. I slapped, now indolently, now viciously, at the multiplying gnats and pium flies. I watched the slow circling of our guardian vultures. I forced down the endlessly repeated meals of beans and rice and farinha and stringy fowl and bloated my stomach with gallons of warm river-water. I watched the river. I waited.

As the days passed, too, I found it increasingly hard to get the caboclos to do any work whatever, and when I remonstrated with them, the only effect was to turn their apathy into smoldering resentment. Finally I called in João Batista, who was the only even remotely reliable one of the lot. He listened silently while I spoke, his brown pock-marked face solemn and impassive, and when I had finished said: "When the men are unhappy, senhor, they alas do not work so good."

"What are they unhappy about?" I asked.

"About the oil, senhor. They wish to know about the oil."

I decided there was no use getting into *that* just now. "We'll know about the oil when the canoes come back," I told him.

"And about the ship, too. They wish to know why the big ship does not come."

"It will come," I said.

"When, senhor?"

"Soon," I said. (And saying it, I thought with a grim inward smile of the old commandante of the *Dom Pedro*.) "Cedo, Batista. Very soon."

He left, saying that he would speak to the men. But I doubt if he did, and if he did they couldn't have listened. Two days later I called them all together and spoke to them myself, and this time I knew they weren't listening.

"Where are those in the canoes?" one asked.

"They're coming back," I told him.

"And the ones in the ship?"

"They're coming, too."

"Quando, senhor? When?"

"Cedo," I said. "Soon."

If O Touro had been there, with his prestige and his understanding of their natures. . . . Or McHugh, with his sureness and drive. . . . In their absence I was a weak substitute as a chefé. "Yes, senhor. That is true, senhor. Tomorrow, senhor," the caboclos replied to my orders and

261

arguments, and then proceeded to do what they would have done anyhow—which was usually nothing. They paid as much attention to me as to a macaw squawking from a forest branch.

Once or twice I tried to discuss the situation with Frei Ambrosio, but the round and amiable little padre was having troubles of his own. Most of them stemmed from the ridiculous circumstance that we had somehow lost track of the days of the week; and while this was a matter of no great importance to anyone else, it was highly upsetting to Ambrosio, because he no longer knew Sunday from any other day, and the conduct of a religion without a recognized and unimpeachable sabbath is a precarious business. He did his best to cover up, of course. But his flock knew that he was unsure of himself; and if a man is unsure of himself he is fallible; and if a priest is known to be fallible he loses face with disconcerting rapidity. A few of the less devout caboclos were already openly contemptuous of him. Others simply stopped attending mass. And even the women, who had always been his true dependables, were becoming querulous and questioning, fuller of anxieties and harder to comfort.

Especially was this so of the women whose men were away in the canoes, and Frei Ambrosio's voice, as he assured and reassured them, was like an echo of my own. . . . Yes, they would return soon. The big ship would arrive soon. "In the Lord's good time, my daughters, and by the grace of Mary. . . ."

The only person on whom he, or anyone, could wholly depend was O Touro's wife, Tereza Carolina. Placid and cheerful as when her husband had been at her side, she went about her daily duties: helping Christine in the infirmary, keeping her cabin neat and spotless, sitting for hours at the still-gleaming sewing machine that stood in the place of honor in the center of her cabin. Not only did she sew for herself and her own family, but for almost everyone else in the community as well. I hadn't known her long before I realized that she belonged no more than did Christine in that desolate jungle outpost, and it was easy to understand why Touro had been reluctant to uproot her from the at least partly civilized existence of Esperança. But not once did I hear her complain or grumble, as did all the others. Not once did I see her other than calm and absorbed as she sat at her sewing. The satisfaction and pride which she derived from the machine seemed, alone, to compensate her for all the hardship and rough gracelessness of the new life into which she had been thrust.

Cheerful, too, though scarcely calm or placid, was her son, young Tourinho. The boy's bright eyes took in everything; his brown button of a nose was into everything; and each day the torpid stillness of Graça de Deus was shattered by his scampering and chattering. Among his other enterprises he had laid out the clearing as an imaginary baseball field, on which he waged an interminable World Series between his all-star heroes. Could o grande José DiMaggio, he asked me, hit a beisbol over the trees in left field? Did Roberto Feller throw his pitches as fast as the blow-darts of the Tupari? I had been an aviador in the war, yes? Well then, if a bomba atomica were dropped on the Yanqui Stadium, would the . . .

No, Graça de Deus would not have been a listless place if there had been more Tourinho Jacksons around. Nor would it have been one of complaint and fear, had there been more Tereza Carolinas. But there were not more; and though the latter, together with Christine, tried to help Frei Ambrosio with his many problems, the morale of his flock continued, day by day, to deteriorate.

"My mission in coming here," said the padre unhappily, "was to bring the word of God to the heathen. But my own people have been so troubled in their souls that there has been no time for me to give to Indians."

As far as the Indians' part of it was concerned, I was a long way from sharing his disappointment; for, in spite of the caboclos' fears and suspicions, actual trouble with the Tupari was the one thing that had thus far been successfully avoided. I commiserated with Ambrosio and changed the subject. And when he left me it was with the assurance that he would make every effort toward getting a firmer hold on his wayward parishioners.

The very next day, however, he was back with more trouble. And this time the subject of his agitated discourse was Serafima Batista.

"She is wearing an *olho de boto*," he told me.

"A what?"

"An *olho de boto*. The eye of a porpoise. It is a heathenish abomination, a sort of voodoo love charm that godless women wear to attract a lover."

"Wear?" I repeated. "How?"

"In a little pouch that hangs from a necklace or throatband. First the eye is dried and preserved, then unholy incantations are said over it to give it its powers, and then it is put in the pouch. Oh, I have seen it many times up and down the rivers—on the evil ones, the unbelievers, the prostitutas. But never before among my own people." Frei Ambrosio shook his head in anguished incomprehension.

"Have you talked to her?" I asked.

"Yes, of course I have talked to her. I have told her she must desist from this thing for the good of her soul."

"What did she say?"

"She said it did not concern her soul, but only her—" The padre stopped and closed his eyes. "Here she used a word, Senhor Allison, that I cannot bring myself to repeat."

I managed to bite off my smile. "How about her parents?" I said.

"They too have reasoned with her, pleaded with her. João Batista has once even beaten her. But to no avail. When they are near she hides the abomination. And as soon as they are gone she has it out again, flaunting God and the Virgin."

Having no suggestion to offer, I was silent.

"I think it is necessary that you speak to her," said Ambrosio.

"I?"

"Yes, you. You are a chefé, a senhor. Perhaps she will listen to you when she will not to us others."

I shook my head. "I can't get into a thing like this," I told him. "It's a religious matter. A personal matter."

"No," he said, "it is not only personal. You do not know these people as I do. They are simple, easily influenced, like children. A thing like this can spread like a disease among them, corrupting and demoralizing. Particularly—" He hesitated.

"Yes," I said.

"Particularly because the abomination has worked."

"What do you mean—worked?"

"She has found a lover."

This time I couldn't hold back the smile. "Maybe it is all for the best then," I told him. "If she has someone, maybe that will keep her quiet."

"I am afraid, Senhor Allison," the padre said solemnly, "that there is nothing to smile about in this thing. Nor is there any quietness to look forward to. For unfortunately it is not a single man she has taken, but the caboclo Pedro Alveiros, who has a wife and three children."

Trust Serafima, I thought.

"How do you know about this?" I asked.

"They have been seen at night, entering and leaving the forest together."

"Does everyone know?"

"Fortunately not. The person who saw them was discreet and so far has spoken only to me. But soon, if it is not stopped, it will come out, and then I am afraid there will be great trouble. The wife of this Alveiros is a proud woman, and João Batista is a strict father. There would be anger, threats, perhaps even violence." Frei Ambrosio shook his round head slowly. "It is not a good thing, Senhor."

"No," I agreed, "it's not good."

"You see then why I have come to you, and that it is not only a matter of this poor child herself. With Senhor Mc-

265

Hugh gone, you are the chefé here—the leader—and she must listen to you. As for the *olho de boto,* I could perhaps manage myself. But with this other, no, it is too much, too dangerous—you understand?"

"Yes," I said. "I understand."

"And you will speak with her?"

"I'll have to think about it," I told him.

. . . And yes, I thought about it all right. Sitting alone in the office shack after the padre had left, I thought about Serafima Batista, Pedro Alveiros and the eyes of porpoises. I thought of the sullen restless caboclos, and of the unseen Indians whom they feared, and of the ship we were waiting for, and of Nils Barna watching me across a lamplit table and saying quietly: "There are many trails through the forest, Mr. Allison, and I am afraid that all of them are devious." I thought of the almost too-perfect irony that I, whose whole existence for the past two years had been a flight from entanglement and responsibility, had come to this uttermost end of the earth only to find myself more entangled and responsible than perhaps ever before in my life.

I had seen little of either of the Barnas since that night of his revelation. Indeed, I had deliberately avoided them. As far as Barna was concerned, there was no point in further recriminations. What had been done was done, and no amount of talk would undo it, or bring back the reconnaissance party a minute earlier. . . . But what of all that still remained to be done? . . . We had learned which was the wrong route, but still we had to find the right one. Had I been correct, after all, in my original belief that it was the righthand fork of the Malaguay, which we had passed at the mudbank village five days below Graça de Deus? If so, did Barna know it? What in God's name did the man know? And what, if anything, did it all have to do with Borneo and Japs and a dead friend called Jakob Koppel?

A dozen times during those days I was on the point of going back to Barna; of quizzing him, hammering at him, even threatening him. But— Well there were too many buts. There was the situation with the caboclos. There were the Indians, who would obviously side with Barna in the event of trouble. There was McHugh returning, the *Fortaleza* coming, and the knowledge that in a few days the Southern Cross Corporation would be taking over in force. And also. . . .

Also, there was Christine. And I know that whatever conflict of aims and wills developed between Barna and myself, Christine would be as deeply involved as the two of us. It was she who had brought the whole thing into the open, broken her husband's confidence, tried to help the rest of us by telling me the truth. But she had done so—as she had said—not so much for our sake as for his; and I knew that, however hard it might be for her, if a showdown came she would be on his side. She would have to be on his side.

Sitting there in the stifling office shack, I tried to wrench my mind away from Christine. I tried to think about Serafima Batista. I went out and walked around the clearing and looked into the infirmary and the Batistas' cabin, but Serafima was nowhere to be found; and leaving word that I wanted to see her, I went to the *Cantora* and lay down on the bunk in the cabin.

This afternoon it was as hot on the launch as in the office, and sweat poured from me until my clothing and the bunk were soaked, and every inch of my body seemed to crawl and burn. A drink will make you sleep, I told myself. But I didn't move. Just a single drink would do the trick, I thought. Or at most two. And presently I got up and took a bottle from Cobb's locker and drank and fell asleep. When I awakened it was almost dark, and I got up again and started across toward the staff shack for supper; but as I approached the open door I saw Christine alone at the table, and, feeling the rum inside me, I turned and went back to the launch. I opened the locker and took out the bottle again. And after a while there was the sound of light footsteps on the deck outside, and Serafima Batista appeared.

"Hallo, Senhor," she said.

"Come in and sit down," I told her.

I had not seen much of Serafima since her outbursts when we first reached Graça de Deus, and now that she was in the spotlight again I looked at her with curiosity. She was quite a piece of baggage, all right, with a smooth tawny skin, glinting black hair and eyes, and a ripe young body that seemed about to burst from her bright cotton dress. Her legs, arms and throat were bare, and around the latter she wore a multi-colored bead necklace from which hung a small velveteen pouch. She sat down on the side of the bunk, pulled her skirt well up to accommodate her crossed legs, and then noticed the rum bottle at her feet.

"I would like a little drink—yes, please?" she asked.

I shook my head. "I want to talk to you, Serafima," I told her. "I was trying to find you this afternoon, to talk to you."

"I was in the forest this afternoon," she said, still looking poutingly at the bottle.

"Yes, that's what I thought. You were with a man, weren't you?"

She looked up at me, but said nothing.

"With a married man. With Pedro Alveiros. Isn't that right?"

"Perhaps," she said.

"That's what I must talk to you about, Serafima," I went on. "I must ask you not to—well—go with this Pedro any more."

Silence again. And two dark eyes fixed on my face.

"Do you understand?" I asked.

She shook her head.

"This Pedro is a married man."

"I cannot help it, senhor," she said demurely.

"What do you mean, you can't help it?"

"It is not I who have done something wicked, senhor." She tapped the pouch at her throat. "It is my *olho de boto*. My little porpoise, he looks at a man one day. I do not pick the man. He picks the man. He picks Pedro Alveiros. And

268

I can do nothing about it. I am powerless. Even though he has three children and black hairs in his nose, I must go to Pedro Alveiros."

There were no two ways about it: the eyes were mocking me. "Listen, Serafima," I said severely, "this is a serious matter. What you've been doing with this man isn't right. And this Evil Eye thing you've been wearing," I added, indicating the pouch at her throat "—that isn't right either, and you know it."

"It is not an Evil Eye," she answered. "It is an *olho de boto.*"

"Whatever you call it, it's not a thing a young girl should be wearing. It's against the teachings of your religion."

"There is nothing in my religion that says all women should be nuns."

"Also it makes Frei Ambrosio very unhappy."

"Frei Ambrosio is an old fool."

I rose to my feet, staring down at her in indecision, and suddenly I was again conscious of the sweltering heat in the cabin. I could feel the rum I had drunk throbbing dully in my head. The little pouch swung gently against the girl's brown skin.

She smiled up at me. "If the senhor is not only a senhor but also a man," she said, "perhaps my little porpoise-eye can look in another direction."

"Look, Serafima—"

"It is a very sharp little eyes, my *olho de boto,*" she went on. "It has been watching the senhor for a long time and knows how much he has been wanting a woman." With a quick snakelike motion she was off the bunk and standing close against me. "Put your arms around me—yes?" she murmured.

For a moment I stood where I was. I could feel the rum again. I could feel the heat and the darkness and the warm scented smell of the girl, mingling and pounding in my blood. In the next instant, I think, I would have pulled her to me. . . .

And then she said: "If the senhor holds me close and shuts his eyes, perhaps he will think it is the Senhora Barna."

I stepped back. Serafima was still smiling, but I didn't smile back at her.

"Please go," I told her quietly.

"Go?"

"Yes. Now."

She shook her head. "No, I will not go. You do not want me to go." She came close to me again. "It is a woman you want. It is the senhora you want. But if you cannot have the senhora—"

I pushed her away. Roughly. Almost savagely.

"Get out," I said.

She stood motionless, looking at me. Then her eyes went black with sudden anger. "So it is this kind you are," she spat at me.

"Yes, I'm that kind. Now get out."

"I am not good enough for you, hey? No one is good enough for the great senhor except the cold-fish senhora."

"For God's sake, stop talking about—"

"About the Senhora Barna? Why should I stop talking about the Senhora Barna? Everyone in Graça de Deus talks about you and the Senhora Barna. They laugh at you. I laugh at you. See—" she threw back her head—"I laugh."

And she did. Quick as a child, she veered from anger to mirth, and the sound of her laughter filled the tiny cabin.

"And you know why I laugh at you?" she said at last, her voice soft and mocking. "Because you are afraid."

"Please go, Serafima," I said.

"You make a speech like a priest that I should not want a man who is married. You, who want a woman who is married. The only difference is that you are a coward, and I am not. I want Pedro Alveiros and I have him. But the great chefé Norteamericano, he is afraid. He wants the Senhora Norteamericana, but he is afraid. He is afraid of her, of her husband, of me, of everybody. And most of all he is afraid of himself."

She flicked a finger at the velveteen pouch that hung from her neck. "Poor little *olho de boto*," she said. "Sometimes he sees—how you call it?—cockeyed."

This started her laughing again. She walked past me out the doorway and leapt lightly from the launch to the shore. I stood in the stifling heat of the cabin while the sound of her footsteps faded away along the mudbank. And then at last her laughter faded too.

19

It was on the following day that I realized the *Fortaleza* was not coming.

I was standing alone on the deck of the *Cantora,* idly staring at the striations in the mudbank that marked the successive levels of the falling river; and presently, looking downstream, I was conscious that the vista—the same which I had now seen every day for almost two months past—was in reality no longer the same at all, but seemed overnight to have utterly changed. The trees of the forest's edge towered far higher above the water, and their boles no longer rose out of its surface, but from the red mud of the shore. The center of the river, formerly a smooth unbroken stream, was now a patchwork of swirls, eddies and cross-currents. Freshly uncovered sandbanks glittered white and bare in the sunlight. Near the shore, perhaps a hundred yards down from me, the current split sharply upon the protruding black trunk of an enormous sunken tree.

It was not, to be sure, something that had happened overnight. But my awareness of it—or rather my awareness of what it meant—was as sharp and sudden as if it were. I remember listening to the sound of the cachoeira. It was softer than before. Much softer. I remember standing for a long while, searching the sky to the north and east. But there was no smoke, no cloud, nothing. . . . And, yes, then and there I was sure. *I knew.* No boat the size of the *Fortaleza* was going to get up that maze of snagged and tortuous waterways until well on into the next rainy season, some four or five months hence.

There it was now—the fact. But a fact with so many ramifications that one scarcely knew which to consider first. Sitting in the staff shack through the long hours of the afternoon, I struggled to add up the possibilities and counter-possibilities. As it would affect our existence at Graça de Deus, our search for oil, our going on or staying or returning. As it would affect McHugh and Cobb, the caboclos and Indians, our hopes, our fears, our welfare, the very sustenance of life. As it would affect Nils and Christine Barna. . . . And then at last I stopped the struggle, because there was no end to it; and in any case, as with the whole Barna affair, no decision could be reached, or action taken, until McHugh and the up-river party returned.

There was nothing to do but wait.

And I waited. . . .

But the caboclos didn't. What had suddenly become obvious to me was obvious to them too, and the next morning a delegation again appeared in the office shack.

"The big ship it is not coming, senhor," said João Batista.

"No, I'm afraid not," I said. "At least not until after the next rains."

"The next rains will not be for months."

"That's right."

"Then what will we do, senhor?"

"That will be decided when Senhor McHugh comes back."

"But he is not coming either," said one of the other men. "Those in the canoes are lost."

"Nonsense," I told him. "They'll be back any day now."

"It is many days ago they should have been back. Three weeks the Senhor McHugh told us they would be gone. It is now four weeks—perhaps five—"

"No, it's just over three."

"Three, four, five—it does not matter. They are not coming."

"They are lost," said João Batista.

"Or drowned in a cachoeira."

"Or killed by Indians."

"And we too will be killed by these Tupari if we stay here. We will starve. We will be eaten by insects and consumed by fevers."

"We must leave this accursed place."

"And return to Esperança."

"How could you do that?" I asked.

"The way we came. With the launch and barges."

On this last matter, however, I soon learned that the caboclos were divided. Some were unequivocally and vociferously for leaving at once. But there were many others—particularly the women whose men were members of the exploration party—who, though hating Graça de Deus and fearing the worst, were not yet ready to abandon hope. And it was they, more than anything I did, or could do, that kept the community from disintegrating into outright hysteria and violence.

At least nothing further happened that day. Nor the next day. Nor the next. But in the darkness of the third night I was suddenly awakened by the touch of a hand on my shoulder, and even before I was up and out of my hammock I knew that the explosion had come.

It was the boy Tourinho who had waked me, and he whispered quickly: "It is my mother who has sent me, senhor. She says to tell you that some of the men are trying to leave."

"On the launch?" I said.

"Yes, senhor, on the launch and barges."

I pulled on my mosquito boots and seized a shotgun and flashlight. It was a black night, without moon, and at first the clearing seemed, as usual, to be silent and deserted. After a moment, however, I made out the shadows of human figures along the riverfront. There was a sudden shout, and then a second; the gleam of lanterns pricked the darkness; and running to the point where the boats were moored, I found a crowd of what must have been every caboclo in the place above the age of six. Only some fifteen or twenty of them, including several women, were actually aboard the launch and barges; the rest stood quietly along the bank, watching them. But if the latter were not actively aiding in the getaway, they were also doing nothing to hinder it. I could see the figures below swarming over decks and gunwales. I could hear the swish and thud of loosened ropes, and above it, a low coughing whine, as someone primed the *Cantora*'s engine.

Pushing my way through the crowd, I reached the best vantage point I could find. "Stop it!" I shouted. "Stop!"

I felt fifty pairs of eyes turned toward me in the darkness. But no one spoke. And the men on the launch and barges continued their activity.

João Batista was standing near me in the watching crowd. "Tell them to stop," I ordered him.

But Batista merely shrugged and then shook his head. "They will not stop, senhor," he answered.

My eyes moved quickly over the crowd, searching for Frei Ambrosio; but if he was there I did not see him. I raised my gun to fire a warning blast over the fugitives' heads. Before I could get it to my shoulder, however, what seemed like twenty hands reached out of the darkness and wrested it from my grasp. No blow was struck. No hand actually touched me. It was simply that one moment I was holding the gun, raising it, and the next moment it was gone. I looked around me, hesitated briefly, and then scrambled down the mudbank.

What happened during the next few minutes was so quick, so shrouded in darkness and confusion, that I can do little more than guess at the actual sequence of events. I remember grasping the gunwale of the nearer barge and starting to pull myself aboard, and then a wooden-sandalled foot kicking at my hand until I had to let go. I remember a sharp report that I first thought was a shot, but then realized was a snapping rope, and then myself falling back onto the mud as the barge seemed suddenly to lurch away from the bank. As I got to my feet, I saw that both barges, and the *Cantora* as well, had begun moving downstream and away from the shore. But apparently they were no longer lashed together in a unit, for each appeared to be following a course of its own in the darkness, scraping and thudding against the others, drifting and revolving in the currents and eddies of the river. Beaming my flashlight, I first picked up three gesticulating figures on one of the barges; then the second barge, which seemed to be empty; finally the *Cantora*, which was already fifty yards downstream, close in to our own bank and moving almost broadside to the river's flow. Then I lost it. A moment later there was a ripping, tearing sound, followed by a series of diminishing shouts, but whether they came from the launch or one of the barges I couldn't tell. Then even the swirling shadows were gone and there was only darkness and stillness.

When I climbed back up the bank I found the crowd of caboclos milling about, shouting and pointing, but none of them seemed to have any clearer idea than I as to exactly what had happened.

"We'll get one of the fishing rafts," I said to João Batista.

But he shook his head. "We could see nothing in the night, senhor," he murmured. "In the morning we will look."

And when I turned to the others they seemed of one accord to melt away into the darkness. In a matter of seconds I was alone on the bank, except for a solitary figure—a woman, it seemed to be—who had been standing a little apart from the others and now approached me. It was Christine.

"What are you doing here?" I asked her, almost harshly.

"I heard the noise. I thought maybe—" she paused, looking up at me. "Are you all right, Mark?" she asked.

I ignored her question. "You shouldn't have come out," I told her. "There might have been even worse trouble." Thinking of Barna, I looked around; but he wasn't there. No one was there. "Where's your husband?" I asked.

"He went over to the Tupari village. He was afraid they might think they were being attacked."

"Didn't he tell you to stay in your cabin?"

"Yes."

"Why didn't you, then?"

But even as I spoke I knew why she hadn't. For a moment I stood looking down at her in the darkness. Then I said, "I'll take you back, Chris."

I snapped on my flashlight, and we walked without speaking along the black trail to Barna's clearing.

In the morning I took stock:

The *Cantora* was spitted on the half-sunken tree a little way downstream, slewed over on her side and with her cabin and engine awash. One of the barges, close by, was wholly submerged except for a protruding gunwale. The other barge was gone. And eighteen caboclos—ten men, five women and three children—were also gone. Whether some had drowned or all had got safely off there was no way of telling.

To my considerable disappointment, Serafima Batista was not among the missing.

Her father and several of the other men helped me in my survey, and neither they nor, indeed, any of the remaining caboclos seemed at all different in manner or action from what they had been before. Like a tropical thunderstorm, the tempest of the previous night had risen, raged briefly and blown away, leaving scarcely a mark behind it. A few faces were missing. There were some arguments as to who would take over the vacated huts and various odds and ends of possessions that had been left behind. And that was all. The routine of life quickly reverted to its familiar pattern, and the hammocks creaked in the shade. God was a Brazilian, and missing a siesta wouldn't change what He had ordained.

With considerable effort I stirred them to the accomplishment of a few things that obviously needed doing. One was to salvage what we could from the *Cantora;* and another was to take precautions against the mosquitoes, which were now rising by the million from the freshly uncovered levels of the mudbank. I set a gang to work digging ditches, in an attempt to drain out at least the worst of the swamps on the immediate margins of the clearing. Summoning everyone to the dispensary, I helped Christine issue atabrine tablets and bolts of netting. And subsequently we went the round of the caboclos' huts in a more or less hopeless attempt to cajole them into using them.

By this time, of course, Christine knew that I had given up hope for the *Fortaleza;* but she had accepted the situation without visible emotion. Even more than before, we had, since that last evening in the staff shack, raised a screen of impersonality between us, and our conversations were limited to discussions of daily events and the work at hand. As for Barna, almost a week went by without my seeing him at all. From occasional remarks of Christine I gathered that he was, as usual, spending much of his time at the Tupari village; but what he was doing there—what he was thinking or planning—what effect these new developments had had on his relationship with Christine—I could only vaguely surmise.

And then one afternoon when I was sitting alone in the staff shack, dealing myself hands of solitaire, I heard the sounds of footsteps outside, and a moment later there he was in the doorway.

"I see you are keeping in practice, Mr. Allison," he said, indicating the cards. "Perhaps we could resume our own game sometime."

For that first instant, I think, I simply stared at him. Then I asked him to come in.

"However, it wasn't about cards that I came to speak to you," he went on. "It was rather about future plans."

As he spoke, he came into the shack and seated himself across from me at the table. Both in voice and manner he was his usual quiet controlled self, and it was hard to believe that he was the same man who had been so possessed by anguish and anger the last time I saw him.

"Plans?" I repeated. "What plans?"

"Yours, Mr. Allison," he said. "And mine. . . . It appears

now that you and your people will be staying on here for a while. And that involves several new considerations."

"Such as?"

"Such as the situation of the Tupari, for one thing. As I have mentioned before, they are an unfortunate and unhappy tribe. Their past contacts with civilization have not, to put it mildly, been very pleasant ones, and since your arrival here they have been fearful about the possible consequences. In fact, they too—like your people who went off the other night—would like to leave Graça de Deus as soon as possible."

"What reason have they to be afraid?" I asked. "We haven't harmed them."

"No," said Barna, "you haven't harmed them. But they were not at all happy about the two of their men whom I requisitioned for you as guides; and they are worried that when your exploratory party returns, without having found what they were after, things will go badly for them. Throughout all their history, you see, the white man has meant only one thing to them. And it has not been a good thing."

"Where do they want to go?"

"Back into the forest."

"Where in the forest?"

"That is what they have been speaking to me about. And what I have found quite interesting." Barna paused and studied me across the width of the table. "Perhaps you recall my having once spoken about a 'lost world'?" he continued with a faint smile. "Well, it seems that the Tupari have one, no less than the rest of us. How much is fact and how much legend is hard to say, but according to their tradition the small group which you find here was once part of a much larger tribe that inhabited this region for centuries past. With the coming of white men—conquistadores, rubber-hunters and the rest—part of the tribe was enslaved, and the Tupari who are here now are their descendants. But the rest of their people, according to their story, moved back so far and so deep into the forest that no invaders could find

279

them, and there they live to this day, wild and free, without ever having been touched by civilization. It is this—well, lost tribe I suppose you might call it—that the Tupari here want to join. But they do not know where to find it. And also, pathetically enough, they are afraid. As afraid of the forest as of the river; as afraid of their own wild brothers as of the white man. For that reason they have asked me to help them."

"How can you help them?" I said. "What do they expect you to do?"

"As I have said before, it is all quite ironic. First I find myself trying to help them rediscover their curaré poison. And now they want me to become their guide through their own country."

"Their guide?"

"Yes. It is interesting isn't it? In fact, so interesting that I have decided to try it. Whether I can find their 'lost tribe' for them I very much doubt; but what I can do, perhaps, is to help them overcome their fear of the unknown. In any case, I have told their chief, Pombal, that I would be willing to take a reconnaissance party for a few days into the forest to the west of here. As a sort of reverse Moses, you might say—a leader *into* the wilderness. Young Cambar and a few of the other men have volunteered to go along, and we are planning to set out tomorrow morning."

Barna paused again, and the pale opaque eyes searched my face. "I was wondering if you would care to come too?" he said.

"I?"

"Yes, you, Mr. Allison. It should not be a hard trip, as jungle journeys go. And even if we find no lost tribes, we might come upon—well—another river, perhaps—"

For a long moment I looked back at him without speaking. Then I said, "You've decided at last to help us. Is that it?"

"I have decided to help the Tupari. And if, in helping them, I can also be of some aid to you, I am willing to do it."

"To find the other river?"

280

"I said that we *might* find another river. The Tupari speak of one—but very vaguely and not from their own knowledge. According to their story, the lost part of their tribe, when they vanished many years ago, traveled first overland through the forest to the west and then up a river in the direction of the Serra Aurora. That is all they have to say; and even that, of course, may be only a story. But it had occurred to me that you might be interested in finding out."

There was another silence. My eyes went from Barna to the cards that still lay spread out on the table, and I began picking them up, slowly, one by one.

"You are skeptical, Mr. Allison?" Barna asked.

"Yes," I said.

"You do not believe that there is another river?"

"Yes, I believe there's another river. A black-water river. I've believed from the beginning that that was the right one and this was the wrong one."

"Of what *are* you skeptical, then?"

"Of you. Of your motive." I had the last of the cards in my hand, and now I was looking at Barna again. "What *is* your motive?" I asked him. "Why, suddenly, after all this time, are you willing to work with us?"

"It is scarcely a question of 'suddenly.' On the contrary, it is a decision I have reached only after much thought."

"All right then, it isn't sudden. But still—what's the reason?"

"The reason," said Barna, "is my wife."

I waited for him to go on, but he didn't go on.

"You mean it's she who has asked you to do this?" I said.

"You know very well that she has asked me," he answered. "You were present once when she asked me."

"But—"

"But until now I have refused? Yes, that is correct. As I think you also know, Mr. Allison, my own desire was to have no part of your enterprise. Frankly, that is still my desire. But I find that I am no longer able to withstand the

281

appeals of my wife. She has repeatedly begged me to come to you. Now at last I am doing so. And if anything comes of it for you, you have only her to thank."

I watched him for a moment; then I said, "*You* have her to thank too, Dr. Barna. You know that, don't you?"

"Yes, I am aware of that," he answered. "I assure you that if I was not aware of it I would not be here." He paused, rose from the table and walked to the far side of the cabin. "Let me explain one or two things to you, Mr. Allison," he went on, "simply so that there will be no misunderstandings, either now or later. I came to this place of my own choice, because of certain things that had happened in the past. To be blunt about it, that is none of your business. No more than it is my business to inquire—well, for example—what there might be in *your* past that causes you to look so often and so intently at that small scar on the back of your hand." He paused briefly. "In any case—here I am. And here you are. The latter circumstance happens to be one of my two miscalculations, for I had thought it would be many years before any white men found their way to this place.

"My second miscalculation had to do with my wife. Our marriage, because of various happenings, has been a rather sketchy affair, and I am afraid that I did not know her very well. Certainly I did not know that she would follow me here, or that she was the sort of woman she has shown herself to be since she came.

"Anyhow—she is here. You are here. And whatever our various desires, it appears that we shall all, for a while at least, continue to be here. In the circumstances, then, I am willing to enter into, shall we say, a limited partnership with you. But when I say 'limited,' Mr. Allison, I mean exactly that. I am not interested in your corporation. I am not interested in your oil. And I am promising you nothing. Whatever comes of our relationship, it will, for my part, be entirely incidental to my relationship to the Tupari—and to my wife.

"If that is clear to you," he concluded, "and if you are

agreeable to such an arrangement, I am willing for you—and you alone—to go with me tomorrow into the forest."

Barna crossed to the door and then turned and glanced back at me. "Will you go?" he asked.

I looked at him, and then past him, out the doorway, at the glare of the clearing and the black-winged vultures circling slowly through the sky. The way things now stood, I reflected, there could be no harm in leaving camp for a few days. And this offer of Barna's seemed to offer the key to all our hopes. . . .

"Yes, I'll go," I said.

Barna nodded. "There is just one further thing," he added, "and this, again, has to do with the Tupari. From now on, it appears likely, you will be in closer contact with them than heretofore; and I must have your assurance that under no circumstances, either here in Graça de Deus or farther on in the forest, will you or your people attempt to coerce them or interfere with them in any way."

"I assure you of that," I said.

"You promise it?"

"Yes, I promise it."

Barna nodded again, and then he smiled a little. "Well, it will be interesting to see what we find," he said. "Oil for you? A lost tribe for the Tupari? Or, perhaps, merely old Preisinger, up a tree. . . . Meanwhile, I suggest you meet me at my cabin at, say eight tomorrow morning."

"I'll be there," I said.

And he went out.

But it was to be a good deal later than the next morning before I went to Nils Barna's cabin. For on that same day, toward dusk, there was a sudden shouting from the direction of the cachoeira trail, and when I emerged from the staff shack it was to see the exploration party filing out into the clearing.

20

THEY WERE ALL there. McHugh, Cobb, Touro, the nine caboclos, the two Indians—they had all returned alive. But that was about the best you could say of them, for they were a battered and dispirited crew. Their faces were bearded and hollow-cheeked, their flesh torn and raw, their clothing in tatters. One caboclo had a hugely swollen leg and was being half-carried, half-dragged by two companions. Three others were running high fevers. Even Touro's great body appeared stooped and drained with fatigue, and McHugh and Cobb, though still able to move under their own power, were obviously close to exhaustion.

McHugh stopped and looked slowly around: at the river; at the empty inlet in which he had expected the *Fortaleza* to be safely moored; at the forlorn and lifeless clearing which should by now have been swarming with men and machines. But his eyes remained dull. He showed no emotion. In those first moments he didn't even comment or ask questions, but merely walked on to the staff shack, dropped his pack and said, "Well, let's get the sick ones to the infirmary."

We put them to bed, cleaned them and did what else we could. Christine had appeared almost immediately and taken charge. Soon Frei Ambrosio and Serafima Batista arrived to help us, and McHugh, too, insisted on staying to do his part.

"Get some rest yourself, Mac," I told him.

"I'm all right," he said. "I'll rest later."

But within half an hour he was sprawled on one of the cots, still fully dressed, but fast asleep.

In the morning I sent a message to Barna, saying that I would be delayed in joining him. I had breakfast in the staff shack, where I was presently joined by McHugh and Cobb. I told them about the night the eighteen caboclos had made their break; and then we went down to the riverbank, and I showed them the *Cantora*, spitted and awash on its sunken tree, and the almost submerged barge nearby. McHugh still showed neither anger nor indignation, but merely put in a brief question here, a curt comment there; and even Cobb, from whom I'd expected God-knows-what when he saw the cadaver of his launch, contented himself with a few sotto voce selections from the bottom drawer of his vocabulary. (It didn't occur to me until later that he had already figured out that the Southern Cross Corporation owed him a fine new boat in place of the old one.)

McHugh stared meditatively off down the river at the high dry banks, the eddies and cross-currents, and the long sandbars glinting in the sunlight. "Not a chance for the *Fortaleza*," he said quietly.

"No," I agreed, "not a chance."

On the way back to the staff shack they told me what had happened on the up-river expedition. They had, of course, not reached the hills. In fact they had had only one glimpse of them, in the early morning of the third day, and then the river had curved away sharply to the south. Thereafter, they had spent a fruitless two weeks trying to follow various of the small feeder streams that flowed into the river from the west, and finally even made the attempt to beat a way overland. That too, however, had been hopeless; and after several days, with almost no progress made, their food supply dwindling and the caboclos near open rebellion, they had had to turn back.

I listened closely as they spoke. And watched them closely too. After a night's sleep Cobb seemed little different than before. A bit seedier, perhaps, if that were possible; looking even more as if he were strung together with old wire and adhesive tape. But still the same Cobb. Still alternately bright- and watery-eyed; still veering unpredictably back and forth from lethargy to vehemence; still scrawny, loose-lipped and indestructible. With McHugh, however—yes, there was a difference. Now that he had washed and shaved, he was, of course, nothing like the apparition of the previous night; yet he was, somehow, not the same as he had been before he went away. Part of it, I knew, was simply tiredness, part of it discouragement at all that had gone wrong. But the change, I felt, went deeper than this. It was elusive—but it was there. In the slow, toneless deliberation of his speech. In his eyes, which he kept fixed abstractedly on the ground. In his heaviness of movement, as we again entered the staff shack and sat down at the table.

"What about the Indian guides?" I asked him. "They were no help, were they?"

McHugh shook his head. "They were useless."

"They were ten times worse than useless; they weren't even trying to guide us," Cobb put in. "And do you know *why* they weren't trying?"

"Yes, I know why," I said.

And then I told them about Barna. . . .

McHugh sat silently throughout my recital. At the beginning Cobb tried to interrupt, and when he heard that Barna had known all along that the up-river route would lead nowhere, he almost exploded out of his chair. But as I went on with the story, he too fell quiet, and when I had finished my account of Barna's coming to me the previous day, the only sound, for a few minutes, was the rasping breath in his long, lopsided nose.

Then he said, very softly: "Well, the son of a bitch. So he's decided to come around at last."

McHugh got up, went to the door, and stood squinting out across the clearing.

"Looks like friend Marco here was right, after all," Cobb
286

said to him. "About that other river of his. The black river. If there's another branch of the Malaguay out in the bush to the west of here, that sure as hell was it." He went on talking, theorizing, asking and answering his own questions, getting more and more excited as he did so, and finally jumping up and prowling around the cabin like a caged anteater.

McHugh turned back from the door and said, "Maybe that was the right river and maybe it wasn't. It doesn't matter now, anyhow, because we can't get back there."

"Okay, so we can't get back," said Cobb. "But we can damn well—"

"Find out about Barna's river—yes."

"You were starting off with him today, is that it?" Cobb asked me.

"That's right," I said.

"Good enough. So now we're all starting off with him." He banged on the table with a bony fist. "What are we waiting for? Let's go!"

McHugh thought it over. Then he said, "First I think there are a few more questions in order. And maybe even a few answers. Go over to Barna's cabin, will you?" he asked Cobb, "and tell him I want to see him."

Cobb seemed on the point of arguing, but then changed his mind and went out. McHugh came back to the table. Pulling out a handkerchief, he mopped his face and throat, and then sat silently looking at the floor. I began telling him a few more details of my last conversation with Barna, but he answered only with an occasional nod, and then even the nodding stopped, and presently I saw that his eyes were closed.

"Mac," I said.

But he didn't answer.

"Mac—"

"Yes?" he asked, looking up at me.

I went over and stood beside him. "Look, Mac," I told

him, "you've had a rough trip and you're still short of sleep. Talking to Barna can wait a day."

He shook his head. "No," he said, "I'm all right. You've got to expect this kind of thing in a war, and I'm—" He paused and passed a hand over his eyes. "Got mixed up for a minute." He pulled out his handkerchief again. "Christ, it's hot here, isn't it? Hotter even than Guadal—"

"Look, Mac. Take it easy. Get into your hammock for a while."

But he only shook his head again, and a moment later Cobb reappeared in the doorway. Barna was not with him, but he carried a folded note in his hand.

"The perfessor wasn't there," he announced. "But here—this is for you." He handed me the note. "That Indian gal of his gave it to me."

I unfolded it and read:

Dear Mr. Allison:
With the return of your exploration party I can well imagine that you are busy with other matters. The Tupari, however, are most anxious to begin their own explorations, and I am therefore setting out with Cambar and a small party at the hour agreed upon. I am confident that during my absence you will honor your promise about your relationship with the remaining Tupari; and you, for your part, may rest assured that, upon my return, I shall report to you on any matters that may be of interest.
                                                        N. B.

I read it again, aloud.

For a moment neither of the others spoke. McHugh took the note from my hand and re-read it himself, silently. Cobb looked from me to McHugh and then back to me again, and his usually pale watering eyes were now, suddenly, as bright and hard as blue glass. "So the perfessor's going to help us?" he said. "That's the hottest one I've heard in twenty years—"

There was an instant when I thought he was going to laugh. But, instead, he began prowling the room again, his

288

clawlike hands opening and closing and his nose twitching
like a rabbit's. "Sure," he spat out with savage mockery,
"he asked you to go along with him. Sent you an engraved
invitation mebbe?"

McHugh paid no attention to him. He had been staring
at the floor again, but now he looked up and asked quietly:
"What do you make of it? Why should he come to you just
yesterday, and then—"

"Why?" Cobb exploded. "Jesus H. Christ, the man asks
why! . . . Because he's putting one over on us, that's why.
Because he's been making fools of us all along—and still
is. . . . A lost tribe! For God's sweet sake: a lost tribe! You
believe that, hey? The perfessor's just gone off to look for
some naked Indios." He stopped at the table and banged
it with his fist. "I been telling you right from the start we
had to watch him. He knows what's up in them hills. And
he knows how to get there."

I looked past Cobb at McHugh. Ordinarily he would
have long since shut the old man up, but he still seemed
scarcely to have heard him. And when now, finally, he
spoke again, it was very slowly and softly, and not to Cobb
but to me.

"Barna said definitely that he'd take you," he said. "Is
that right?"

"That's right," I answered.

"Who cares what he talked about?" Cobb broke in. "It's
what he's up to that matters. And I'm telling you what he's
up to."

My patience was wearing thin. "You have it all figured
out, haven't you?" I snapped at him.

"You're damn right I have. A halfwit could figure it.
Only with me and Mac gone—"

"Only what?"

"And you too busy making eyes at the senhoro—"

"That's enough, Cobb," I said.

But at that instant McHugh interrupted with startling
suddenness. "Yes, that's enough," he almost shouted. "Enough

out of both of you. . . . Barna's gone: all right. And the boat's not coming, and the launch and barges are gone, and we haven't found a way to the hills. All right, too. Or if it's not all right at least it's the way it is, and there's no use fighting about it."

His abstraction and listlessness were wholly gone now. His eyes were no longer dull but bright and hard, and his voice was edged. Suddenly he got to his feet with so abrupt a movement that his chair pitched to the floor. "Do you two understand me?" he said. "This damned quarreling has to stop!"

"I ain't quarreling with nobody," Cobb told him. "I'm just asking some questions."

"All right, now you've asked them."

"No I ain't. I still got the big one."

"Well?"

"What are we going to do now?"

For a moment I thought McHugh was going to flare up even more violently. But, instead, he stood quite still and closed his eyes briefly, and when he spoke again his angry, almost wild intensity seemed to have drained away as quickly as it had risen.

"You were to meet Barna at eight?" he asked me quietly.

"Yes."

"And it's now—?"

"Ten-thirty."

"If we get on over to the Indio village," Cobb began—

But McHugh was following his own train of thought. "That can wait," he interrupted. Then, without further explanation, he went to the door and called to one of the caboclos in the clearing. "Go to the infirmary," he told him, "and ask the Senhora Barna to come here."

When the man had gone he came back to the table and sat down again. Cobb resumed talking, but McHugh merely nodded occasionally and didn't reply. Presently he pulled out his handkerchief once more and wiped his forehead.

"Yes, it's hot today," he said, his voice soft and a little thick. "Hotter even than—"

He stopped and stood up, as Christine came in. She was dressed as usual in a shirt and lopped-off slacks, but with a white hospital apron over them and a white cloth bound around her hair; and her sunbrowned face was streaked with sweat.

"How are your patients?" McHugh asked her, his voice crisp again, but courteous.

"The three with fever seem a little better," she said, "but I'm worried about the one with the infected foot. As a matter of fact, I was about to change the dressing, and—"

"Yes, of course, I'll keep you only a moment." McHugh paused. "We wanted to ask you about your husband," he said.

"My husband?"

"Yes. Where has he gone?"

"Into the forest."

"Why?"

"Because the Indians asked him to." Christine looked at me questioningly. "Nils told me he'd spoken to you," she said, "and that you were going with him."

"He went without me," I said.

"And that's what we're trying to find out," said McHugh. "*Why* did he go without Allison?"

Her glance went from one to the other of us. "I—I don't know," she answered. "I didn't know he had."

McHugh handed her Barna's note, and she read it silently. I could see that she was greatly upset but doing her best to hold it back.

"You know nothing about it?" McHugh persisted.

Christine shook her head. "He says here," she began—

"He says there that he doesn't want to keep the Indians waiting. Do you expect us to believe that *that* was the reason?"

Christine looked at him, and the concern in her face

tightened suddenly into anger. "You think he was lying?" she said. "Is that what you mean?"

"Yes," McHugh answered.

"We know damn well he was lying," said Cobb.

She stared at them; then at me. "Is that what you think, too?" she asked.

I hesitated. "I don't know," I said.

"Look, Christine," McHugh said quietly, "we don't mean this as a personal thing. But it so happens that we're here on serious business. We're looking for oil. And we have good reason to believe that your husband knows a lot more than he's been willing to tell us."

"Nils doesn't know anything about oil in this place—he's told you that. And I don't know anything about it either." Suddenly Christine's voice became sharp and strained. "What do you want of him anyhow? What do you want of me? Why can't you leave us alone?"

"All we want—"

"All you want is for me to be a spy for you," she flared back at him. "Ever since we left Manaos you've been questioning me as if my husband were some sort of criminal. . . . Where did he go? Why did he go? What is he doing? . . . He's living his own life: that's what he's doing." Her voice broke, and I thought she was going to burst into tears. But instead of tears it was anger that rose again, and behind the anger, defiance and a deep fierce loyalty. "You may own this mudbank," she said, "but you don't own my husband, and you don't own me. And it's none of your damn business what he's doing!"

"Look lady," said Cobb, stepping forward with eyes narrowed—

But I decided the badgering had gone far enough. "Leave her alone," I told him sharply. Then I wheeled on McHugh. "What do you expect of her anyhow?" I said. "She's told us all she knows. For Christ's sake, man, she's been trying to help us all along. If it weren't for her, Barna wouldn't have come to me. We wouldn't know *anything*."

From the corner of my eye I saw Christine turn and run from the cabin. I took a step after her. And then a startling thing happened. A powerful hand seized my arm from behind and swung me around, and I found myself staring into McHugh's suddenly livid face. "No you don't, Mr. Allison," he rasped at me. "You're not running this man's navy yet."

I tried to jerk away, but his grip only tightened. "And I'll tell you something else," he stormed on. "Your friend Barna isn't running it either. The Pacific is full of your kind—everything fouled up, loused up, snafu. But do you think I'm lying down and taking it? Hell, no. What I'm saying to you, Mister, is what a Seabee always says: *Can do*. And by God, neither you nor—"

Suddenly his face swayed in front of me. The eyes seemed to be all whites. Then the eyes were hidden as he put his hand to his face, and it was no longer he who was holding me, but I who was holding him.

"Get a chair—quick," I told Cobb.

"No, I don't want a chair," McHugh muttered. "Come on, let's go. . . . Can do. . . ."

I tried to force him into the chair that Cobb brought up. "Mac, sit down—listen—" I said.

But he wrenched away from me, his eyes blazing again. "No, you listen to me," he snapped. "Come on, you men, get cracking! Call the duty officer—the shore detail—the bo'sun. . . ." He started for the door, but stopped halfway and looked vacantly around him. "Christ, it's hot here. Hotter than hell. Hotter than Guadal . . ."

Then he took another step, lurched sideways, and collapsed in a heap on the floor.

When Christine took his temperature in the infirmary, it was 103. That night it was 104.5, and the next night it reached 105 and we thought he was going to die. But he didn't die. Hour after hour and then day after day he lay helpless on his cot, now burning-dry, tossing and moaning, now soaked in sweat and so rigidly still that one had to put one's ear to his mouth to catch the faint flutter of his breathing. At various times we thought he had dengue, cholera, enteric fever, blackwater fever, and a particularly virulent form of malaria; and then at last we simply admitted that we didn't know. We watched over him. We did what little we could for him. We waited.

But if McHugh didn't die he also didn't get well. His illness developed a pattern of alternate fever and normal temperature, the former usually striking along about noon, lasting for a few hours, receding, and then returning again toward the middle of the night. During those fevered periods he was often delirious, but never violently so. For the most part he would simply mutter, over and over, the names Edna, Frances and Helen (who I assumed to be his wife and daughters); and then suddenly, switching to his command-voice, he would call out "Let's go" or "Can do" and issue brief orders to imaginary Seabees. But, after his collapse in the staff shack, there were no wild hallucinations or seizures; merely a quiet, almost orderly transference of time and place. It was remarkable—in other circumstances it might have even been comic—that his delirium was scarcely less disciplined and controlled than his usual conscious life.

Each time the fever ebbed we watched hopefully for a sign of rallying strength. But it didn't come. He lay in a heavy torpor, his eyes closed or staring vacantly at the thatch ceiling, too weak even to stir or speak. The color of his face turned from pink-red to gray and from gray to a blotched muddy yellow. Each day the bones of his hands, shoulders and face stood out more prominently under the once solid flesh.

We talked of trying to take him down-river in one of the canoes, but we knew that the idea was hopeless. He couldn't have survived for three days, much less the necessary two or three weeks, in the pitiless heat and glare of those endless waterways.

"You're positive the *Fortaleza* can't reach us?" asked Christine.

Yes, we were positive.

"Perhaps they might send up a small boat?"

Yes, perhaps they might.

But all that appeared along the glazed vista of the river were new sandbars, new mudshelves and the dark shapes of alligators and turtles lying torpid in the sun. The tree-trunk on which the *Cantora* was spitted emerged higher and higher above the river level, until one day, with a tearing sound, the launch detached itself from it and fell keel up into the water. Mosquitoes and pium flies rose in black clouds from the newly emerged riverbanks and marginal swamps.

During those days Christine and I were more together than at any time since we had come to Graça de Deus; but, with five seriously ill men now in the infirmary, our talk was almost entirely about temperatures and pulse rates, dosages and hypodermics. Then, one night as we left Mc-Hugh's bedside, she said: "If I'd only known how sick he was that day I flared up at him—"

"But you didn't," I told her. "You can't blame yourself, any more than you can him."

We came out of the infirmary into the darkness of the clearing. "I'm sorry I flared at you too, Mark," she said. "I suppose I was just—upset."

"Forget it," I said.

"No, I've been thinking about it and wanting to talk to you. You see, I do know a little more than I told you then about why Nils went off without you."

"You mean you knew then that he'd gone alone?"

"No, I didn't actually know it until I saw you were still here. But I wasn't surprised. He'd talked to me a bit the night before, and I think I know what was in his mind."

"What, Chris?"

"The exploration party had come back that evening. And he was worried about it."

"Because he'd let them go on a false trail?"

"No, I don't think he cared much about that. It was that he was afraid the others would come along with you."

"The others?"

"John—Cobb—maybe some of the caboclos. He was willing to take you along, but if there were more of you, he didn't think the thing would work out right for the Tupari." I didn't answer, and in the darkness I could see her looking up into my face. "You don't believe that, do you?" she went on. "That that's why he was going—for the Tupari. . . . But it's true, Mark. I promise you, it's true. . . . Oh, I know it sounds incredible—that a civilized white man should be leading a tribe of Indians through a jungle. But Nils isn't an ordinary man. You know that by now. And in some strange way he's become terribly attached to these Tupari. I think it goes back somehow to those two years in Borneo, after I left—to his friend Jakob and some tribe of natives there—and what happened to them. Nils won't talk about it, but I know that's what it is. And I know that's the only reason he has gone now. For the Tupari. . . ."

She paused and we stood silently for a moment.

"Please believe that, Mark," she said. "I'm not lying to you. And Nils isn't lying to me. At first he might have— yes. But not any more. Because he's begun to change, truly he has. All that terrible bitterness and loneliness is slowly going. It can't happen all at once, of course, but at least he's trying now. He's willing to help you now; to live in the world again; to be a man among other men. . . . Please believe me—please," she murmured. "If not for his sake, then for mine."

"I believe you, Chris," I said.

And I think I did.

But in any case, of course, the final answer would not be forthcoming until Barna's return. And meanwhile Graça de Deus was so full of immediate problems that there was scarcely time even to think of him.

For McHugh still didn't improve; the sick caboclos didn't improve; and the rest drifted, day by day, deeper and more hopelessly into despair. Since the return of the exploratory party the only work to which the men had really bestirred themselves was the building of a cane-press and still, and for hours each day now they lay in their hammocks, stupefied with cachaça, or squatted listless and dull-eyed on the river-bank, watching for the ship they knew was not coming. Reprimands and pay-docking had no effect. Even confiscating the cachaça did little good; for the trouble went deeper than that. Just as the hookworms crept through their flesh into their blood and organs—just as the pium flies stung and the vultures clawed and the dry mold devoured—so had poverty and futility and endless disappointment eaten their way into the very fabric of their lives. Left to their own devices, I think that most of them would have been content simply to rot away in that hellish clearing like so much driftwood on a mudbank.

The most important thing that needed doing—now that we knew the *Fortaleza* would not appear—was the planting of some sort of food crop to tide us over the months ahead. Touro and I had already discussed the matter, and he had called out a gang of men to work at clearing additional ground. But the response was feeble and the result negligible, and the more Touro urged and exhorted, the less seemed to happen. The fact of the matter, I soon discovered, was that, since our arrival in Graça de Deus—and particularly since the fiasco of the up-river trip—Touro's prestige and authority had greatly diminished. He had been the caboclos' leader, their counsellor, the one who had been responsible for their leaving Esperança. And now that everything had gone wrong, they held him responsible for that too. It was he who had brought them to this place of privation, disease and fear, of lurking savages and oil that was nowhere and ships that did not come. It was he whom they blamed even more than the chefés.

Touro knew it, of course. And he knew that their resentment was, in part at least, justified. But what was worst of all for him, I'm sure, was his own private knowledge of *why*

297

he had come here—and thereby caused them to come. He himself did not complain or slacken his efforts. He remained patient, soft-spoken and conscientious. But it was obvious that, neither in outward effectiveness nor in his inner self, was he the same man who had once been the undisputed leader at Esperança.

Meanwhile, Mordecai Cobb was having—and causing—problems of his own. From the very beginning, of course, he had wanted to follow Barna into the forest; and now, as the days passed and no Barna reappeared, he became increasingly impatient—and surer than ever that his suspicions were correct. Time and again he urged that we go to the Indian village, quiz the Tupari, and, if necessary, do "a little persuading." But I managed—just about—to restrain him. Then, for a few days, he contented himself with investigating, on his own, the various trails that led back into the forest to the west. Here too, however, he met only with frustration, for, as Barna had said, they were apparently designed not to lead from one specific point to another, but merely as hunting circuits, twisting aimlessly through a green labyrinth. One, according to Cobb, swept around in a great, almost imperceptible arc and came out on the Malaguay a scant three miles below Graça de Deus. A second wound on like a snake for the distance of a two hours' journey and stopped dead at a dried-up water hole. Most either doubled back on themselves after a few miles or petered out into trackless jungle.

"So what are we going to do?" he asked one evening, when he, Touro and I were together in the staff shack. "Sit here and rot?"

"We're going to wait until Barna comes back," I told him.

"And if he don't come?"

"He'll come," I said.

But Cobb wasn't satisfied. He veered back to the Tupari again. Just let him go to their village and he'd show them "who's running the show around here." When I still said no, he began arguing again. And in the end I had to point out to him—firmly and not too gently—that I, not he, was "running the show" during McHugh's illness, and that, as long as I was, there were not going to be any strongarm tactics with the Tupari.

Cobb eyed me and shook his head. Then he said sarcastically: "Just a couple of pacifists, you two—aren't you? Wouldn't as much as look crosseyed at a jaguar. . . . How do you like to handle things, Touro boy: bash people over the head nice and gentle, like you did that feller on the banana boat? . . . And you, Mister Aviator—I suppose you just go for something real cultured and edicational, hey? Like a blockbuster or a buzz-bomb." He made a noise in his nose that was half snort and half cackle. "Yeah, I sure get a laugh out of you sweetness-and-light boys," he added.

Presently he was off on another tack.

"What about the caboclos, then?" he asked.

"What do you mean, what about them?"

"As long as the Indios are too holy to touch, how's to rounding up our own spiks and seeing if we can get somewhere?"

I shook my head. "They're fazenda men—river men," I said. "You've already seen they're no good in the forest."

"And besides, there's the clearing and planting," Touro put in. "These people have had a hard time, and we have to consider their welfare too. Raising some food for them is a lot more important than wandering around in the jungle."

"We can leave the old ones and the women to piddle around with your crops. And anyhow," Cobb taunted him, "I ain't noticed you getting much work out of them with this food business of yours."

Touro said nothing, but I could see that the barb had struck home.

"Couldn't be that you're losing your hold on them, Touro boy?" Cobb went on. "Or that you're getting a little jittery, mebbe?"

For a few moments the big Negro still didn't answer, but merely sat looking at his tormentor with dark expressionless eyes. Then he said quietly: "No, not jittery, Mr. Cobb. Just a little discouraged, perhaps. Just a little ashamed of my-self—"

And when, soon after, he rose and left the cabin, his huge shoulders were stooped and his step was heavy and slow.

21

Two days later Cobb raided the Tupari.

The first inkling I had of it was when the boy Tourinho came running into the infirmary, where I was sitting by Mc-Hugh's cot, and began jabbering about guns and Indios.

"What are you talking about?" I interrupted him sharply.

"About Senhor Cobb," he said.

"What about Senhor Cobb?"

"He has gone to the Tupari village. He has shot them and conquered them. He has taken them off into the forest."

I glanced at McHugh, but he was lying motionless, with eyes closed. Then I ran out into the clearing.

During the next half hour, from various of the caboclos, I pieced together at least a general idea of what had happened. Cobb had for the past several days, apparently, been trying to induce some of the younger men to go with him on a search for Barna. He had promised them oil, gold, El Dorado on a platter—*plus* Indian guides to show the way—and finally he had persuaded a dozen-odd to join him. They had secretly assembled supplies, Cobb had got guns from the storage shed, and during the morning just past they had left the clearing and gone to the Tupari village. As to what had happened from then on, the stories varied greatly. João Batista said only one shot had been fired. Another said there had been dozens. The Indians had been disarmed; they had fled with their arms; they had all been taken as guides; only three or four had been taken as guides. On just two points were they all agreed: that Cobb and his followers had raided the village; and that now they were gone into the forest.

After the first moment, as I recall it, I felt neither anger nor even surprise, but only a sense of inevitability. Yes, of course, that's what's happened, I found myself thinking. You've known all along something like this was going to happen. Avoidance of real trouble with the Indians had been our single successful achievement in all the weeks we had been at Graça de Deus. And now that too was finished. Cobb and his guns had been the one thing needed to cap the climax of the whole miserable mess.

I called in Touro and Frei Ambrosio, but they knew no more than I did. Obviously there was only one thing to do, and that was to find out the facts. At first I considered organizing a whole party to go to the village, but then decided that in this case there would be neither safety nor usefulness in numbers. Going to the storage shed, I took two of the rifles that still remained there. I gave one to Touro and kept one for myself. And a few minutes later the two of us were following the trail to the Indians' clearing.

For most of the way we moved as quickly as we could, but as we neared the village we slowed our pace and peered warily ahead. What we would find, I hadn't the remotest idea. A shambles, perhaps? Or a mustering war-party? The Tupari all gathered together? Or no Tupari at all? . . . But when finally we came to the edge of the forest, it was none of these things that we found. Indeed, the clearing seemed exactly the same as when I had seen it the first time—the small stream, the circle of huts, the scattering of women and children, all the same—except, I saw presently, that a group of Tupari men were seated in a rough semicircle on the ground in front of the largest of the huts.

We stopped briefly. Then we stepped out into the open. Carrying our guns slung on our shoulders, as on our first visit, we walked slowly toward the circle of huts; and, as before, the women and children stared at us, but made no sound or movement. We approached the group in front of the big hut, and I saw that it was apparently composed of all the men remaining in the village. Cambar and several others, of course, were off with Barna; and now Cobb, I guessed, had taken the rest of the younger men as guides. What was left were the elders of the tribe: a pathetic collection of half-naked scarecrows, with gnarled bodies, rickety limbs, and seamed toothless faces beneath the matted bangs of their hair. . . . And, at their center, hunched and mutilated, their chief Pombal. . . . As we came up to them, he seemed to be staring at us not with his one good eye, but from the dark cavern of his eyeless socket.

He didn't answer when first I spoke. No one answered. No one moved. For a moment my glance moved to the hut behind them, and I saw that the javelins and blowguns that had formerly been ranged along the wall were now no longer there.

"Tell us what has happened," I said. "We have come as friends."

But there was still no answer; and presently I unslung my rifle, and Touro did likewise, and we laid them on the ground at our feet. "As friends," I said again.

Then at last Pombal spoke, in a slow guttural monotone. His account of what had occurred was far briefer than that of the caboclos, but in essence it was the same.

How many men had Cobb taken? . . . Fifteen.

And their weapons, too? . . . Yes.

Had there been shooting? . . . Yes.

Anyone killed? . . . No.

Wounded? . . . Yes, three.

"We will take the wounded to our village," I said. "We have a hospital there and medicines."

Pombal shook his head.

"We will make them well."

But Pombal didn't answer.

"And the others—" I said. "We want to find them. Give us some of your men to help us find them."

"We do not know where Barnanda is," said Pombal.

303

"I don't mean Barnanda's men. I mean the men that have just been taken."

"No, it is Barnanda you look for. Like the others with their guns."

"If you help us find the others, we shall bring them back here. We shall set them free."

"No," said the chief, "you are lying. This much we have learned—that when white men speak to us they are lying. Even Barnanda himself has lied to us, for he said that you would not harm us while he was gone."

There was a silence. Then I tried again. I explained, argued, all but pleaded. But there was only a ring of dark impassive faces and, behind the faces, an impenetrable wall of distrust and fear. If a white man with a pointed gun was an evil, at least it was a comprehensible evil. But a white man, talking, promising, with his gun lying on the ground. . . .

Pombal shook his mutilated head. He sat silently, sifting grains of dust between the fingers of his one huge hand, and his men sat around him in their tight semicircle—silent too, and motionless. At last Touro and I stooped and picked up our guns. And when we turned and left I could feel the fear and hatred in their eyes following us, long after we had entered the forest trail.

The knowledge that something was wrong had in some way filtered through to McHugh's consciousness. When I returned to the bedside, shortly afterward, he began mumbling questions and orders in a garbled voice; and then suddenly his eyes went wide open and he struggled to get up from his cot. But within a few minutes his mind was back again in Guadalcanal. And when presently I left him again he was lying with his eyes half shut and scarcely enough strength left to move his lips.

Meanwhile there had been no improvement, either, in the four sick caboclos; and the day before they had been joined in the infirmary by still another two, who had come down with fever and diarrhoea. By now there were no more cots left, and we had had to sling them up in hammocks along the walls. Christine and Frei Ambrosio moved tirelessly back and forth, seeing to their needs and comfort. With the increase in patients, Touro's wife, Tereza Carolina had volunteered to help with them, and now she too was spending many hours a day on duty, her husband, her son, her home and even her beloved sewing machine for once neglected, if not forgotten. The tiny hospital was filled with groans and retchings and the intermittent babble of delirium. And in the clearing outside a huddled knot of caboclo women fingered their *figa* charms and murmured chanting prayers, as they gazed toward the screened door with dark frightened eyes.

With the sick we were at least doing what we could. But now, too, there were Cobb and the Tupari—and I knew that it was a thing that could have no less dire end-results than fever and dysentery. I called in Touro again. Then I called the available men together. It was necessary to go after Cobb, I told them. It was necessary to bring back the caboclos and Indians who were with him. They were a large unwieldy group, I pointed out, and it should not be hard to follow their trail and catch up with him. Touro and I were going, and we needed ten men besides. We would leave at once. Who would volunteer?

As I had expected, there was a sullen silence; then arguments and protests. Cobb himself, I knew, had taken the most venturesome of the caboclos, and these who were left wanted no part of either Cobb, the Tupari, or any other hazards—known or unknown—of the jungle.

"We, too, are sick, senhor," they said.

"We are weak."

"And ignorant of the forest."

"This Cobb, he will not come back. He will shoot at us."

"The Indians will ambush us."

"We shall be lost."

"We shall be killed."

305

But, ironically, it was not until Touro appealed to them that their reluctance flared into resentment and hostility. Had he not done enough to them already, they asked, in bringing them to *this* place? No, now he wanted them to go on to even worse places. To all manner of horrors. To their death.

"It will be for only a day or two," the Negro told them patiently. "No harm will come to you. And it is a thing that must be done."

"No," said one of the men, "we will not do it."

"You have to do it."

"Why do we have to?"

"Because you are working for the Companhia Cruzeiro do Sul, and the Companhia requires it."

"No, the Companhia does not require it. The chefé of the Companhia lies with the fever and gives no orders. It is you who gives them, and from you we do not take orders any more."

For a moment O Touro stood silently, his head and shoulders towering above the group of little brown men; and I don't think I had ever felt sorrier for a man than I did now, watching him, and knowing the conflict tearing his mind and heart. I was on the point of stepping forward, of taking over again. But I realized that if Touro was to retain any vestige of respect and authority, this was a thing he must handle himself.

Presently, he said, in the same soft voice as before: "An injustice has been done to the Tupari, and we must help them."

"No, it is we who need help," said a caboclo. "Why should we worry ourselves about some savage Indians?"

"If we don't help, they will be our enemies. If we do, they will be our friends and help us."

"How can they help us?" asked another.

"In getting food. In finding the way to the oil."

"We do not believe you."

"In Esperança we believed you, and look what has happened to us."

"What the white chefés want—that is all you think of."

"You are the white men's servant."

"The white men's nigger."

There was a silence again—almost palpable—and then, through the silence, the sound of Touro's breathing. I am not certain if the ring of caboclos actually moved. But it seemed to. As if an invisible wave had passed over them, the men appeared to sway and withdraw a little, their eyes fixed on the huge black man who stood in their midst. The black man took a step forward and stopped. He looked slowly around the circle, as if searching for the one who had last spoken. But when finally he spoke again it was only to say quietly: "Very well, I shall pick the ten to go. And they will be at the storage shed in fifteen minutes. . . ."

The ten were there. We issued them rifles and rations. Then we started off. Circling the Tupari village, we investigated the hunting trails that veined out beyond it and presently found one trail that had unmistakably been used by a fair-sized party not long before. Following it, we moved on through the hours of the afternoon along a dim changeless tunnel across the floor of the forest. And apparently it was a trail that Cobb had missed in his recent reconnoitering, for it neither ended nor curved back on itself, but bore on, twisting but still true, toward the west.

We walked in single file and in silence, with myself leading and Touro bringing up the rear to make certain there would be no deserters. But, once underway, the caboclos moved on with the dumb patient resignation of pack animals. Tree trunks and foliage flowed past. The hours and the miles flowed past. And still we saw no Indians, no other caboclos, no Cobb, no sign of life at all—except only the continuing blurred pattern of footprints on the trail before us. In all the veiled forest-world nothing seemed to move, or even to live, except ourselves, gliding on like shadows through the deep greenness of the earth. Twelve shadows, I thought sardonically, searching for Mordecai Cobb, who was searching for Nils Barna, who was searching for . . . . what?

When night came we stopped, cooked a meager meal, slung our hammocks and slept. And at first light we moved on again. Either we would have to find Cobb and his men on that second day, or turn back without them, for our food supply wouldn't permit us to go on farther. Again hour followed hour, without change or sign of our quarry, and toward noon I had almost begun to lose hope, when presently I saw that something at last *had* changed in the trail before us. For, whereas formerly it had been a fairly well-beaten path, marked only by footprints, it was now thickly carpeted with undergrowth, and its margins were littered with lopped branches and leaves. From this point on, obviously, Cobb's party had no longer been following an old route, but cutting its own way; and this should mean that their progress was now slow enough for us to catch up with them.

I don't know how much later it was that I became suddenly aware that it had grown darker. My first thought was that evening had already come, but looking up, I saw a tiny patch of bright sky beyond the treetops, and then I realized that we had come to an area of forest even denser than that through which we had been passing before. It was almost inconceivable that the labyrinth of surging growth could become still more tangled and impenetrable. Yet it was so. The boles of the trees that lined the path were no longer spaced like columns but rose close and tight against each other, as if they were the pilings of a solid wall. Every chink and interstice between them was choked with an almost solid mass of vine and frond. And the tiers of greenery overhead were so thickly interwoven that the bright sunlight far above penetrated only as a thin distillation of dusk. As we walked on now the illusion possessed me that I was no longer walking on the earth's surface at all, but along the floor of a subterranean cavern leading ever farther, ever deeper down into its core.

. . . . Except that in the earth's core there would not have been the sudden cloud of pium flies needling like tiny flamepoints into our flesh. Nor the brown-and-yellow-striped snake that darted, quick as sight, across the path ahead. Nor the sound—I stopped, listening—no, nor the sound of axes, that now, as I advanced again, grew louder and clearer, until I came to the next turn of the path, and the next, and there all at once in the gloom before me were the dull flashing of steel, the moving figures of men, and, a little apart from the others, seated on the root of a huge ceiba tree, a familiar scrawny figure with a gun across his knees.

Turning, Cobb watched silently as our column approached. "All right," I said to him in a quiet voice, "you can tell them to stop now."

Cobb rose and faced me. His eyes were bloodshot, his flesh torn and bitten, his clothing in tatters; but, far from playing the culprit, his air was one of confident, almost jaunty defiance. Beyond him, a bit farther along the trail, were the ten or twelve caboclos he had taken with him, perhaps half of them with guns and the other half with machetes. And beyond them, in turn, was a slightly larger group of all-but-naked Indians, with machetes and axes. At our first appearance, all except those with the guns had been chopping and hacking at the forest wall, with their backs turned to us; but now at the sound of my voice they turned and stared, and suddenly they seemed no longer human beings at all but merely images frozen motionless on a screen. They made no sound or movement. In the dim light that filtered down from the treetops their faces were like greenish masks peering from the shadows.

"Tell them to stop," I said again to Cobb.

"Looks like they have already," he commented.

"Tell the Indians they can go."

"Go? Where?"

"Back to their village."

Cobb drew his tongue across his lips and said nothing.

"Tell them, Mr. Cobb," said Touro in his soft, almost gentle voice.

But Cobb neither moved nor spoke. Touro looked at me, and I nodded, and, quick as a striking snake, his great black arm reached out and took the rifle from Cobb's hand. Then he ordered the armed caboclos to lower their guns, and after a moment's hesitation they obeyed. "Go now," we told the Tupari. But they merely stared at us dumbly.

Touro and I stepped forward and took the machetes from their hands. I pointed back along the trail. "Go," I said again.

This time they understood. They moved. Swift and silent as forest animals, they darted past us, past Cobb, past the ranks of watching caboclos, and in a matter of seconds had vanished along the twisting path. Touro and I put down the machetes. The caboclos who had been with Cobb squatted wearily among the stumps and roots. Some of them, I could see, were in the grip of fever. Two or three had great festering sores. All of them looked less like human beings than limp understuffed scarecrows, and it was obvious that whatever light of El Dorado Cobb had briefly kindled in their eyes had long since flickered out into disillusionment and apathy.

"Do you still have food?" I asked them.

Yes, they said, they still had a little food.

"Eat, then," I told them. "And rest."

Bit by bit we learned what had happened since they left Graça de Deus. The overpowering of the Tupari had apparently been ridiculously easy, guns having accomplished most of it and surprise the rest. Cobb had picked the guides in short order. They had taken all the tribal weapons and hidden them in the forest. And then they had started out. For the first day and a half they had followed an already beaten trail—presumably Barna's—but then the Indians had either lost it or strayed from it willfully, and for the past several hours they had been hacking and clawing their way through almost impenetrable virgin forest.

"We are lost, senhor," they said to me.

"It is an evil place we have come to."

"Even at noon we move in darkness."

"Our machetes break in our hands."

"And the wood demons stalk us."

"The accursed *curupiri.* . . ."

Soon they were all asleep, lying sprawled where they had stood in the muck and undergrowth of the trail. They were obviously too worn out to begin the return journey that afternoon. And also, in a few hours it would be dark. We would start off in the morning, I decided, and with luck could make it back to Graça de Deus in one day. I conferred briefly with Touro and we gave our orders to the caboclos who had come with us. They set about slinging hammocks and building fires.

Through all of this Cobb had sat silently, watching. And I, for my part, had ignored him. But now, presently, he was standing before me again, his grizzled head still cocked defiantly and his pale eyes squinting up into my face. "Sort of taking over in a big way, ain't you?" he asked.

"That's right," I told him. "I'm taking over."

I started to turn away, for I had long since decided that whatever arguments and recriminations there were to be with Cobb could better wait until we were all back at Graça de Deus. But he didn't let me turn. His bony hand reached out for my arm. "Look, amigo," he said. "I'll make a deal with you."

"A deal?"

"Yeah. You rescued your precious Indios. Okay. You and your spiks are going back now. Okay. But leave me my spiks. You be the chefé at Graça de Deus, and I'll be the chefé out here."

I shook my head.

"Leave me half of them then," he pleaded. "Leave me six spiks, that's all. With six I can get along fine."

My eyes moved over the figures of the exhausted sleeping men and then past them to the dense walls that rose around us. "Fine?" I repeated.

"So we lose the trail for a while. So there's a few more trees and some rough going. Chrissake, man, don't you know what this kind of trees mean? They mean we're on lower ground again—that we're getting near to a *river.*"

"Good enough," I said. "When we've got things straightened out with the Indians and at our own place, then we'll come back and reach it."

"Maybe you'll be coming back, amigo," said Cobb. "But not me. And the reason I won't be coming back is I'm staying right here. Spiks or no spiks, Indios or no Indios, I'm staying, see?—and going on until I find Barna."

"Alone?"

"Sure, alone if I have to. I been worse places than this alone. What do you think I am, anyhow? Another yellow spik mebbe? Or a dude explorer?"

He spat on the ground at my feet. Then he turned, slung on a pack and rifle, took a machete in his hand, and walked on past the sleeping caboclos to the final dead-end of the trailhead. "Me and Barna'll send you a wire," he called back, "when we got a nice paved road running straight to the Rio do Sol."

Raising the machete, he began chopping and slashing at the jungle wall before him. At first I thought that it was a bluff; that he would keep at it for only a few strokes and then stop. But as time went by he was still hacking away, and through the remaining hours of daylight—or what passed for daylight in that deep labyrinth—he proceeded to stage an astonishing one-man performance. The sweat poured from him. His bare back and shoulders bled from a hundred thorn scratches and insect bites. It was incredible that his rickety old body could stand the strain to which he keyed it. But still he drove himself on, never pausing, never resting, attacking the green walls ahead not as if they were a mere inanimate obstacle but an active resisting enemy whom he was battling for his life. In the first half hour he advanced perhaps fifty yards, and, going up the trail, I told him to stop being a fool and come back. But he paid no attention to me, and presently I returned to the others. Touro and I sat on a fallen tree trunk, watching him. The caboclos—or at least those of them who were awake—squatted around us, watching too. And out there ahead of us was Mordecai Cobb, looking less like a flesh-and-blood man than some improbable apparition—a scrawny graybearded old goat frenziedly lunging and butting his way into ever-thickening darkness.

It was macabre, lurid, a flickering image from a nightmare. Yet at the same time it was grotesquely magnificent. In the world in which we live men have learned to cover the nakedness of their souls no less than that of their bodies. In almost every act, and even thought, of our lives we are so clothed in rationalization and dissemblance that we can recognize but dimly the deep primal impulses that motivate us. But with Cobb now there was no dissemblance. Here was Greed, plain and simple, bare and burning; and terrible though it was, obscene though it was, it yet possessed a directness and savage animal honesty of which I could not but stand in awe. What place was there here, I thought, for McHugh's cool objectivity or O Touro's pangs of conscience or my own complex self-questionings? None—that was the answer. Cobb's passion, and that alone, had validity and meaning in this primordial world beyond the world of men. He alone, in his stark singleness of purpose, was equipped to match his own strength to the strength of the wilderness, fighting the jungle with the weapons of the jungle.

By the time he had cut his way out of sight it was almost totally dark. All but a few of the caboclos were stirring again, and, huddling about the small fires, we ate a meager meal of jerked beef, tea and mandioca paste. But still Cobb did not reappear; nor had he done so when, an hour later, I lay down in my hammock to sleep. Presently the fires faded into embers and the embers into nothingness. The forest loomed around our tiny lost pocket in the night.

In the morning, as the others made ready for the return trip, Touro and I followed Cobb's trail out from the campsite, but after a few hundred yards it became so sketchy that it was impossible to follow. Stopping, we called out; but there was no answer. And after a few moments we retraced our steps. If Cobb was serious in his determination go on alone, I was certainly not going to any great lengths to stop him. He would get back well enough, I knew, in his own good time. And, meanwhile, the problems that lay in wait at Graça de Deus would have a better chance of solution without him than with him.

Perhaps ten minutes later our long column was moving along the trail to the east. Again I walked in the lead, with Touro in the rear, and the hours and miles slipped past with scarcely a word spoken along the twisting length of the file. Judging from their appearance, half the caboclos could scarcely have walked the width of a room. But now that they were on their way out of the dreaded forest their assorted infirmities seemed to vanish as if by magic; we traveled swiftly and steadily, with only one brief stop for rest; and by midafternoon we had come into the network of trails that threaded the jungle behind the Tupari clearing. As on the way out, I avoided the village. We encountered no Indians on the encircling paths. And then, presently, the tunnel of the trail opened up before us, the sun struck down like a hammer against our skulls, and we emerged at last into the yellow furnace of Graça de Deus.

The boy Tourinho was there, as always, to greet his father with a shout and a flying leap. But no one else was there. No one else was in sight. There was no movement anywhere except the watchful circling of the vultures, no sound except the distant rumble of the cachoeira.

"Where is everyone?" we asked.

"Everyone sick," the boy replied. He was obviously more

314

excited than depressed at being the dispenser of such important news.

"What do you mean, everyone?"

"Yes, yes—almost everyone. The old ones and the young ones and the big ones and the little ones. The Yanqui senhor, he is with the fever again. And this morning, mother, she was helping with the others and—"

O Touro grasped his son's arm. "What about your mother?" he said sharply. "What's happened to her?"

"She is with the fever too. She lies with her eyes open, counting the saints on her fingers, and—"

Touro didn't wait for more. He strode quickly across the clearing toward the infirmary, and I followed him. . . . What of Christine? By the time we reached the infirmary my heart was pounding and I was drenched with sweat. . . . But Christine was all right. Drawn, worn, close to exhaustion—but all right. She met us in front of the little shack, opened the door and took us inside.

It may not have been quite as bad as Tourinho had said, but it certainly was not much better. Not only were all the cots still occupied, but most of them now held two patients each. Other sick men lay on the floor and in hammocks. Two, said Christine, had already died and been quickly buried. Two or three others were so far gone that it seemed impossible that they could live much longer. Only the most serious cases, she explained, had been brought to the infirmary. There were many others with varying degrees of fever who had had to be left in their huts.

What was it? Neither she nor any of us knew. The catalogue of fevers that a man can acquire in that country ranges even beyond the knowledge of most physicians. Presumably it was the same illness that had stricken McHugh, but even this was mere supposition. All that was certain was that during the past thirty-six hours fever had run like a bushfire through the little community, until, by the last count, it had struck down almost a third of its population.

McHugh lay in his cot in a corner of the infirmary, his

eyes closed, his face like yellow wax and beaded with sweat. During the previous night, said Christine, his temperature had soared again to almost 105, and, though it was lower now, he was still very weak and had had only a few fully conscious moments since morning. On the next cot to his was Touro's wife, Tereza Carolina, obviously in the grip of raging fever. Her eyes were open but unseeing, and the flesh of her usually plump brown face was mottled red and drawn tight as parchment across her cheekbones. Hers, according to Christine, had been the most sudden seizure of all. One moment she had been bending over a cot taking the pulse of a delirious patient, and in the next she had slipped soundlessly to the floor. That had been a little before sunrise that morning, and she had not regained consciousness since.

As we looked at her she began to speak in a strained rasping whisper. It was not a list of saints that she murmured, however, but the single word, *"Maquina—maquina. . . ."*

"It's her sewing machine," said Christine. "All day she's been asking for it; worrying about it."

Touro was crouched beside his wife, holding her hand. "Your machine is all right, little pigeon," he told her. "I have oiled and covered it and there is no dust on it anywhere."

Tereza turned her eyes toward him, but they were glazed and sightless, and presently she began mumbling again: *"Maquina—maquina . . ."* Leaving Touro beside her, I turned away and stood looking out through the screened doorway. It was almost dusk now, the hour at which the clearing was usually most crowded, but there was still not a soul in sight.

"Where are the others?" I asked Christine. "The well ones?"

She told me that a few were scattered among the various dwelling-huts, nursing the sick who lay there. Frei Ambrosio had taken the others to a temporary camp about a mile down the riverbank, in the hope that this might cut down the spreading of the fever and the almost equally dangerous spreading of panic. "They think the Indians have put the evil eye on them," said Christine, "and that the sick ones are possessed by some sort of forest-demon."

Standing beside me now, she suddenly closed her eyes and swayed, and I had to put my arm around her to keep her from falling. Then I picked her up and carried her out of the infirmary and across the clearing to the staff shack and laid her gently in the hammock that had formerly been McHugh's.

"Sleep now," I told her. "All night. Do you understand me? All night."

"No, I can't," she protested feebly. "There's too much to do. There are too many—"

But the words trailed away, blurring; and by the time I had taken off her shoes and adjusted the mosquito netting around her she was already deep in sleep.

Two more patients died in the infirmary that night, bringing the total thus far to four. One was an old, worn-out caboclo called Miguel Deoceira. And the other was Tereza Carolina Jackson.

22

WE BURIED THEM at the edge of the forest, not far from the grave of the Reverend Lassiter. Frei Ambrosio consecrated the ground and commended their souls to God. Some of the caboclos carved and set up four ceiba-wood crosses, which soon became the favorite roosts of our guardian vultures.

For a few days no one knew how many others might be joining them. But as it turned out, there were no others, for the scourge passed as quickly and inexplicably as it had struck. The sick caboclos, most of whom seemed not to care whether they lived or died, got well. Only McHugh, struggling against his illness with every ounce of his strength, remained spent and helpless in its grip. Day after day he lay on his cot in the infirmary, alternating between attacks of fever and drained sweat-soaked exhaustion. And without him our little community, though spared from extinction, had neither head nor heart, purpose nor function.

McHugh or no McHugh, however, there were certain immediate steps that had to be taken. One, of course, was to do everything possible to avoid a recurrence of the epidemic, and for the better part of a week Christine and I did little else but cajole and browbeat the caboclos into observing at least rudimentary precautions. Another was to get on with the interrupted crop-planting; and for this I made João Batista foreman, assigned him every able-bodied man in camp, and offered bonuses for the best daily jobs of clearing and seeding.

Then, too, there was the matter of the Tupari. On the

day after our return from the forest a group of the caboclos who had been with Cobb went out in the forest to where they had hidden the Indians' weapons, brought them back to our clearing, and deposited them in the storage shed. This meant that, for the time being at least, we were free from any danger of all-out attack. But we were cautious nevertheless, and strict orders were issued against entering the forest except in large well-armed parties. For a time I considered going once again to the Tupari village, in an effort to explain what had happened and make peace with them; but I soon abandoned the notion. For one thing, any such overtures would stand a far better chance of success after Barna's return. And for another—to be honest about it—I had certain recollections of what had befallen one Reverend Lassiter.

So I remained in Graça de Deus. I waited for Nils Barna. I did what I could to instil the breath of life into the little clearing on the riverbank, and for a day or two even the deep lethargy of the caboclos was broken by an occasional glimmer of energy and purposeful work. Partly, I think, this was because of the comforting knowledge that the neighboring Indians were now even worse off than they; partly because the epidemic and deaths had frightened them. In any case, most of them, for the first time since we had come up-river, actually used their atabrine and mosquito netting, and a few even went so far as to work without supervision at the clearing and planting.

But, like the fever before it, the spark flared and burned itself out. The weaponless Tupari did not present themselves for massacre. There were no further corpses to bury. They had been promised oil, and there was no oil; a ship, and there was no ship; a new life, and there was only a drearier harder life. Soon the caboclos sank back into an even deeper apathy than before. Within a week after they had been planted the vegetable patches were sprouting with weeds. The hammocks creaked again, and the netting hung from them in ragged shreds. "Deus e Brasiliero," they said, shrugging, when I called them to task. "The earth is made for weeds and the flesh of man for the mosquito, and nothing we can do, senhor, will change His inscrutable purpose."

Not only at night now, but during the day as well, many of the men were sodden with cachaça. The thick sweet reek of it filled their huts; its dark glaze was in their eyes. But far from stirring them to action, or even to disorder, its only effect was to increase the empty hours through which they lay, limp and feckless, in their hammocks. Drunk or sober, there seemed to be no more life in them than in the river below the mudbank, creeping brown and sluggish among the sandbars and rotting logs.

I did what I could, but it was not enough. And of the two men in Graça de Deus who might have been able to accomplish what I could not, one lay like a yellow ghost on a cot in the infirmary, and the other, though untouched by fever, was even sicker than McHugh—even more hopelessly lost and defeated. . . . This was O Touro. . . . And to the day I die I shall remember his figure, huge, black and motionless, standing by the graveside while the shovelfuls of earth slowly hid from his view the dead woman who had been his wife. He spoke to no one; he looked at no one; and when the grave had been filled and the cross raised he walked alone across the clearing and closed himself in the solitary darkness of his hut. There he stayed for three days, never emerging. The boy Tourinho ate and slept with a family in a neighboring hut. Twice each day (for the caboclos ate only two meals) he went in to his father carrying a plate of dried fish and farinha, but each time he appeared again after a few minutes, with the plate untouched.

On the evening of the second day Frei Ambrosio went into the hut, but when he came later to the office shack his plump face was clouded with anxiety.

"Wouldn't he eat?" I asked.

"No, he would not eat," said the padre. "And worse than that, he would not pray."

The next morning I went over to O Touro's myself, and,

receiving no answer to my call, walked in and found him lying in his hammock, apparently asleep. But he was not asleep. His eyes were open, watching me; and the whites glinted.

"You've got to get up, Touro," I told him. "You've got to get out of here—get something to eat."

"And get to work," he said. "Isn't that what you mean, Mr. Allison?"

No, I explained, that was not what I meant. . . .

I don't know how long I talked to him, or even what I said. For what, after all, *was* there to say to him—except words?—and Touro had long since passed the point where words held any meaning. While I spoke, he lay motionless in his hammock, his eyes closed. He may or may not have been listening. And when I finished all he said, very quietly, was, "All right, Mr. Allison, I'm ready to go to work again."

A few hours later he came out of the hut. He went about his work. He picked up the threads of living. But they were, I knew merely the outward and visible threads, for deep within him now there was despair even blacker than that of his own personal bereavement. His wife was dead—and it was his doing. Three others were dead—and that was his doing too. A whole community of human beings had put their fate in his hands, and he had betrayed them, and now he moved as a pariah among those of whom he had once been leader. Touro the Judas, the caboclos called him. Touro the killer. Touro, the white man's nigger. Stolidly, sullenly, they still obeyed him, but only from fear. And he, for his part, retreated ever more broodingly behind the walls of his grief and guilt.

His son Tourinho became his only companion, and few others so much as spoke to him, other than in the line of work. One of the few exceptions occurred when a group of women came to him to ask about Tereza Carolina's sewing machine. They all wanted it. They bid for it loudly and importunately. One offered to cook for him in exchange; another to wash his clothes; a third to care for Tourinho. If there had not been so many competing witnesses I'm sure that half of them would have offered him the comforts of their sleeping-mats. Touro stood among them, his face impassive, scarcely seeming to listen. Then he went into his hut and emerged a moment later carrying the heavy machine in his hands.

"Oh, it is beautiful!" they cried. "It is a maquina maravilhosa! See how it shines in the sun!"

"It is for me," one pleaded.

"No, for me," begged another.

For me. . . . For me. . . . For me. . . .

"It is for all of you," said O Touro. "To make yourselves your shrouds—"

He set the instrument down, went back into the hut, and came out with an ax. Raising his great arms, he swung the ax down upon the bright nickel and black-enamelled steel: just once; straight and true.

And now the fragments of Tereza Carolina's machine were merely another anonymous item among the litter and refuse of the clearing. The vultures and then the ants investigated the debris, found it of no interest, and turned their attention elsewhere. Rust and mold devoured it. Presently the sifting dust hid it from sight.

For the dust was everywhere: a veil, a blanket, a pall. It hung like a noxious gas in the air, permeated our food, our clothing, our very skins, transformed everything it touched —which was everything there was—into a parched sulphurous yellow. It was no longer a jungle in which we were living, but a desert, and even the Malaguay, coiling thick and ochrish beneath the desolate bank, seemed to have become a river of dust. Through the film above us the sun burned down like a bloodshot eye. Around it, the sky, spreading to the horizon, was hard and glittering as polished brass.

Then one morning João Batista appeared in the doorway of the staff shack and announced that Cobb was back.

"Back? Where?" I demanded.

"In the hut next to mine, senhor."

"What's he doing there?"

"He is sleeping, senhor."

Crossing the clearing, I entered the hut, and there, sure enough, was Mordecai Cobb, sprawled in a corner on the earthen floor. According to the occupants, he had appeared late the previous night, called for a gourd of cachaça, and spent several hours draining it. Now the empty gourd was lying beside him on the floor, and the stale fumes of rum enveloped him like a cloud.

When I spoke his name he neither answered nor stirred. But as I bent over him, to see if there were anything wrong with him besides drink, he grunted slightly, and one pale red-rimmed eye opened and fixed on my face.

"Are you all right?" I asked sharply. Cobb's reply was another grunt, and I shook him. "Are you all right?" I repeated.

"Million bucks," he muttered.

"Where have you been?"

"Million bucks."

I shook him again—harder. "Barna," I said. "Did you find Barna?"

"Sure," he said.

"Where is he?"

"Million—"

"Last night when he comes," said the caboclo who lived in the hut, "he says that the Senhor Barna he is here too."

"Here?"

"Yes, senhor—that they came back together."

I looked down at Cobb, but he was asleep again. Then I left the hut and crossed the clearing. I walked along the trail that led to Barna's cabin, and as I approached it the door opened and Barna came out. "Ah, Allison," he said. "I was about to pay a visit to your place."

He closed the door of his cabin and came toward me, and I saw that two weeks in the jungle had left scarcely a mark of hardship or fatigue. His flesh was unbitten and untorn, his face as pale and smooth as ever beneath the star-tling crest of reddish hair. Behind the lenses of his glasses his eyes were colorless and cool.

"My wife has told me about Mr. McHugh," he said, "and asked if I would try to help him."

"Yes, he's damned sick," I said.

Barna nodded. "I have been rather afraid something of the sort would happen. Of course I am not a physician, and my opinions are merely a layman's; but I have often had occasion to observe that men of his type do not flourish in this country."

"What do you mean—his type?"

"Sound men, Allison. Strong and purposeful men. I have found it rather fascinating to see how similar the pattern here is to that in—well—certain other jungles I have known. How, inevitably, the strong become weak and the weak become strong." He paused and cleared his throat. "This must have been an active time for you," he added. "Even more active than if you had come into the forest with me. In any case, I am happy to see you looking quite fit yourself."

He made as if to walk on, but I forestalled him. "You were gone longer than you'd planned," I said.

"Yes, I know. There were a few unforeseen delays."

"We were concerned about you."

"So I gather." Barna smiled a little. "And apparently Mr. Cobb in particular."

"Where did he find you?" I asked.

"Find us? I am afraid you have received a wrong impression. Mr. Cobb did not find us, but rather we found him. To be quite frank about it, he was lost."

"And you brought him back?"

"Yes, we brought him back. Considerably against his will, I might add." Barna permitted himself another smile. "In his own peculiar fashion, you know, Mr. Cobb is quite a determined man. It is rather a pity his great effort could not have been crowned with success."

324

There was a moment's silence. Then I said: "And what about *your* effort, Doctor? Was that successful?"

"My effort?"

"Did you find what you were looking for?"

"What the Tupari were looking for, you mean? The lost branch of their tribe? . . . No, I regret to say we did not find them. But we scarcely expected to this first time, of course. And meanwhile—"

"Meanwhile you found a route. Didn't you?"

"We found many routes."

"Including another river?"

"I am afraid that—"

"Did you find the other river?" I demanded.

"As I was about to say when you interrupted me, Mr. Allison, I regret that I cannot go into all the details with you." Barna cleared his throat again. "And now if you will excuse me," he said, "I really must get on to seeing Mr. Mc-Hugh. Otherwise my wife will be quite upset."

He gave me no answer then. He gave me no answer later. His eyes, cold and hostile, watched me from behind their glinting lenses, and nothing I was able to say or do drew from him so much as one word as to where he had been or what he had found.

"But you promised—" I argued.

"And so did you," he said; "but you did not keep your promise. Suppose we say that the two broken promises cancel out."

"As I've told you, it was only Cobb who—"

"Yes, of course: it was only Cobb. It is always 'only Cobb,' is it not, Mr. Allison? Always the force beyond control, and the rest of us merely 'work here.' "

"The Indians are all free now. No harm has come to them."

"No harm? Is violence no harm? Are the distrust and fear which they now feel no harm? Perhaps you are not aware

that the Tupari now distrust not only you and your people
—but me as well."

"Surely they can understand that you had nothing to do
with it."

"They understand that I am a white man. And that you
are white men. That, unfortunately, is a clearer thing in
their minds than the six months during which I tried to be
their friend."

"But if now you've shown them the way—"

"Yes, that is my hope: now that I have shown them the
way, they may come to trust me again. . . . But not if I show
you the way, too, Mr. Allison. They know what will happen
if I show you the way. As well as I do. As well as *you*
do. . . ."

"So we're back where we started," I said. "Is that it?"

"Roughly," Barna agreed.

"And with your wife?"

"My wife?"

"Are you back where you started with her, too?"

"I am not sure that I follow you."

"I seem to remember your telling me that you would help
us, not for our own sake, but for hers."

Barna didn't answer at once. His pale eyes rested on my
face for a few moments and then moved past me—through
me—and when he spoke again it was not so much to me as to
his own self. "Yes," he said quietly, "I have tried to do what
my wife wanted of me. I have tried to believe that because
she wanted it it was possible. But it is not possible, of course.
One is either part of the world or outside it; a dweller in one
jungle or the other; a seeker after your Kingdom, Mr. Allison
—or after mine."

He paused and then went on quietly: "My wife is a wonderful woman, and I shall do all I can for her. But there
are certain things that I cannot do, and one of them is to
break my trust with these Indians."

"Better to break it with your own kind, is that it?" I said.
"Better even with your wife?"

"Yes," said Barna.

"Your first allegiance is to the Tupari?"

"Yes."

"Because—"

"Because I owe them a debt, Mr. Allison. Because I owe a debt I can never repay to every innocent trusting defenseless human being who ever lived."

There was only one further conversation between us, and this time it was again the Tupari who were on Barna's mind. "You have not yet given them back their weapons," he said to me.

"No," I answered.

"Will you, now?"

I turned the thing over in my mind. "No," I said at last, "I can't give them back now."

"Why can't you?"

"It would be asking for trouble. Both from the Indians themselves and from our own people."

"I would undertake to promise you that the Indians will do nothing."

I shook my head.

"Meaning that you don't trust me either?" he said.

"I can't take the chance."

"Perhaps you do not quite understand the situation. As I have told you, the Tupari are planning to move inland, to try to rejoin the rest of their tribe. Since the unfortunate incident during my absence they are particularly anxious to be off as soon as possible, and their preparations are now almost complete. But they cannot, of course, move without their weapons. Give them back to them, and I assure you that in a few days they will be gone."

Again I thought it over. Then I said, "Maybe this is the time to strike a bargain, Dr. Barna."

"A bargain?"

"I'll give the Indians their weapons. You'll get their consent for you to show us the way to the other river."

Barna shook his head. "I am afraid they would not agree to that."

"You could get them to agree."

Barna didn't answer.

"You won't do it?"

"No," he said. . . . "Shall we call it an impasse?" he added a moment later, as he turned to go.

And I suppose that was as good a word for it as any.

The next morning when I went into the infirmary, Christine was boiling up a syringe for one of McHugh's injections. The few times I had seen her in the past two days had also been in the infirmary, and we had not even mentioned the fact of Barna's return. Nor did we now. For a while I sat by McHugh's cot, watching the slow rise and fall of his breathing.

And then it was no longer he whom I was watching, but she. . . .

The heat and dust of Graça de Deus had impelled her, a few days before, to cut her hair, but I hadn't realized previously how thorough a job she had made of it. It was almost cropped, I saw now; as short as a boy's, with the ears and the nape of her neck uncovered, and the nape was a soft creamy-white where the sun had not yet had a chance to burn it. It provided a startling contrast to the rest of the exposed flesh, which was as brown as the khaki of her shirt and trousers and which I had come to accept as her natural coloring. I found myself looking at her face, throat and arms, trying to visualize them as white as that strip beneath her hair, trying to see her as she must have been only a few months before, clothed like a woman, powdered and scented like a woman, soft and white as a woman. I was looking at her hands, lifting the instruments from the sterilizing pan, and they were roughened and welted but still slender and light and fine-boned, and it occurred to me that I had scarcely ever seen her use them for any other purpose than to wield a broom or take a pulse or hold a syringe.

I sat watching McHugh again, while she filled the syringe and gave him his injection; and then we walked out of the infirmary into the clearing.

"He's no better, is he?" I said.

Christine shook her head.

"Will he ever get better?"

"I don't know. If he were in the right sort of place I think he would. But he needs real care, doctors, medicine."

"What does your husband say?"

"He says there's nothing he can do either."

"Nothing?"

"Except to try to keep him from dying before the *Fortaleza* comes."

We walked on for a few paces.

"Perhaps he wants him to die, Chris," I said.

"No," she said. "That isn't so."

"He hates us."

"No, that isn't so either. At least not as people." She paused again. "If he feels hatred, it's only for what you represent to him."

"Civilization?"

"Yes, that's part of it, I think. Civilization—progress—conquest: all the things he's tried to put behind him. But, most of all, he sees in you what he used to be himself."

"Three weeks ago he seemed almost willing to be friendly."

Christine nodded.

"But now he's turned against us again."

"I know," she said.

"Is it only this thing with the Indians?"

"I'm not sure. Oh, Mark, I've tried so hard to understand him, to get at him. But—" She broke off, and when she spoke again it was quietly and with tight control. "But it isn't easy," she said. "It all goes back so far and so deep: to the war, and his scientific work, and what happened in Borneo, and this Jakob Koppel. . . . For a while I thought he was really changing; that I'd accomplished it just by coming to him, just by being with him. But I see now I was wrong. It isn't that simple. It can't happen that quickly."

She seemed about to go on, but didn't; and a moment later she left me and disappeared down the trail that led toward Barna's cabin.

No, I thought, as I walked alone back to the staff shack—there was nothing to do. About Barna. About McHugh. About Touro or Cobb or the caboclos or the Indians. About oil. About anything. Least of all was there anything to do about Christine and myself.

We could only wait for the *Fortaleza*.

And wait. . . .

Incredibly, it rained.

During the night there was again the rumbling of thunder in the distance, and in the morning the sun hung pale and shrunken behind a pall of mist. Toward noon the first drops fell, slapping like buckshot on the brittle thatch of the huts; then an hour later came a deluge, sharp and vicious, that whipped the river to a frenzy and churned the dust of the clearing into a sea of yellow paste. By mid-afternoon, however, it was all over. The sun emerged again, and later the stars, brilliant and enormous. And by the following morning even the mud had been transformed back into bone-dry powdery dust.

Sitting hours on end in the staff shack, I listened to the drone of the flies and cicadas and then took out the cards and played hundred-point matches of solitaire casino. I left the shack and sat on the mudbank above the river, looking down at the brown slow-coiling water and at the eddies and sandbars and the black half-sunken tree on which the *Cantora* had once been spitted. When darkness came I went to my hammock and tried to sleep, but couldn't, and in the middle of the night I went back to the staff shack and played solitaire again.

Looking back on it now, I think I had never felt so alone in my life as during those days of blank nothingness at

Graça de Deus. Fifty-odd human beings lived in a radius of a hundred yards around me. McHugh was there. Cobb and O Touro were there. Nils and Christine Barna were there. And at the same time, they were not there. For all there was of contact or companionship, no one was there.

Cobb celebrated his return by staying drunk for two days. Then for another three he lay in his hammock with what seemed to be half delirium tremens and half a recurrence of his old malaria. Sometimes he babbled about gold, sometimes about his ballet dancer from Manaos. And, at intervals, something even darker in his past would take form in his fevered brain and he would start up with a quavering shriek that could be heard across the length and breadth of the clearing.

As for Touro, he was little more than a black shadow, moving silently across the clearing or sitting at the edge of the forest beside the cross that marked his wife's grave. Now and then he worked with the caboclos in the vegetable patches, but left all supervision to João Batista, speaking to no one and approached by no one except his son Tourinho. He ate alone. At night he closed himself alone in his hut. And then one morning he appeared in the staff shack and said simply and without preamble, "I would like to leave, Mr. Allison."

"Leave?" I said. "What do you mean, leave?"

"I am of no more use to you, or to the company. The people here will be better off if I am gone."

"But there's no way of—"

"I don't mean down-river. I've spoken to Dr. Barna, and he said I could help him around his cabin and in his work with the Indians." His voice was toneless, his face wooden. "I'll take my boy with me," he said. "We can't stay here any longer."

I didn't argue with him. I rose and stood looking out the doorway, and then I turned back to him and said, "Do what you think best, Touro."

"Thank you, Mr. Allison," he said.

331

"Later, if you want to come back—"

"No, I won't be coming back."

That same morning he and Tourinho shouldered their possessions and headed up the trail toward Barna's cabin. Passing through the smaller clearing, a few days later, I saw that he had built a small thatch hut on its margin. The boy sometimes reappeared in the big clearing, either on errands or simply because his restless feet carried him there. But Touro himself never returned.

In the black stifling night I lay in my hammock and looked at the forest wall. . . . "Beyond the Alps lies Italy—" (That was Napoleon. Or was it Hannibal?). . . . Beyond the desert lies Canaan; beyond the ocean lies Cathay; beyond the forest lies the River of the Sun. . . . Yes, of course, I thought: it was the old story all over again. Behind the here lies the nowhere. Beyond reality lies the dream. But in the dream now, as I closed my eyes, there was only more forest, more shadow, more depths of trackless darkness. . . .

Then there was only the clearing again. Only the steep darkness of the forest wall. Each night the wall seemed a little higher, a little nearer; it seemed to be slowly and relentlessly closing in about me; until the night when I could stand it no longer, and I jumped from the hammock, trembling and sweating, resolved that I must break out of it at last, away from it at last—somehow, anyhow—downstream in a canoe, or on into the forest—but if it was the last thing I ever did I must break out of the nightmare that held me, out of the heat and dust and nothingness of that prison in which I was trapped. . . .

But I didn't break out of it. I didn't go down the river, or into the forest. The next day and the next and the next I lay in my hammock, I sat with my cards in the staff shack, I watched the dust-clouds rising and listened to the insects humming in the lifeless yellow-burning oven of the clearing. And then one day toward noon it seemed to me that the hum was growing louder. It rose to a drone, and from a drone to a roar, as it had so often in my dreams. Except that this time it was not a dream—it did not fade—but grew and swelled until the little shack almost trembled to its familiar but half-forgotten sound. In the same instant I heard a caboclo shout, and, pushing away the cards, I ran outside.

And looking up, I saw the plane.

23

THERE IT WAS; high, shining and incredible.

It was coming in from the northeast, following the river, and as it passed over I saw the familiar blue lettering on its side and a white sleeve waving from the cabin window. It roared off upstream, banked, turned and came back again, much lower now, and this time I could see the face of the pilot peering down through the windscreen at the shallow water below. Then it was past, banking and turning again. Three more times it came in, skimming even closer to the surface of the river, and three times it roared up and away. But on the fourth, just as I was expecting it to pull out again, the pilot cut the engine. The plane dipped, wobbled, seemed to hang motionless above a long sandbar. Then it cleared the bar, struck the water, bounced and struck again. It slowed, turned and moved in toward the shore.

Eustasio Moranda stepped up onto the bank and put both his arms around me in a Brazilian *abraço*. He walked gingerly across the clearing, and his black shoes glistened in the yellow dust. He followed me into the infirmary and stood shaking his head as he looked down at McHugh, lying strengthless and wasted on his cot.

"He has been this way long?" he asked me.

I told him about it.

"There has been much trouble, then?"

I told him about that, too.

From the infirmary we went to the staff shack. Moranda

sat patting his face with a silk handkerchief and at intervals popping tablets into his mouth from a vial in his pocket. The pilot who had brought him, a slender young Brazilian whom I had not met before, stood in the doorway and gazed watchfully toward the riverbank and the moored plane. And I sat looking from one to the other, as if they had been visitors from interstellar space.

"There have been certain difficulties down-river as well," Moranda conceded.

The *Fortaleza,* he told me, had reached Esperança late in August—roughly a month after we had left. Within a week it had unloaded its cargo for the plantation and was ready to move on again, but, with ample time available, it had been decided to wait for the second ship, which was already on its way up-river with the colonists from Europe.

So the D.P.'s had arrived at last?

Yes, said Moranda, they had arrived. First in Belem, and two weeks later in Manaos. But in Manaos there had been trouble. Many of the refugees had taken sick. A few had died. There had been difficulties with the health and immigration authorities. He—Moranda—and Senhor Wooderson had flown back and forth three times between Esperança and Manaos, but each time there had been new problems with the D.P.'s, and finally the *Fortaleza* had had to leave without them. This had been during the third week in August, in plenty of time, according to all calculations, to get up to Graça de Deus and back well before the height of the dry season.

Moranda spread his hands. "In any other dry season, yes," he said. "But in this one, no. When I get back to Manaos later they tell me it is the earliest dryness there has been in upper Amazonas for thirty years. Anyhow, the *Fortaleza* it goes up the main river to the Juruá, and then up the Juruá to near the mouth of the Yurima, and then it stops. There are the sandbanks, the mud, the shoals, the trees sticking up from the water. Three times we go aground and we are almost wrecked; and then the commandante says no, we cannot do it; and we go back. The Unplaced Ones they are now at Esperança—ha! But they cannot go up the river. For three months no one can go up the river. So Senhor Wooderson and the others, they all sit at the fazenda, and I go down again to Manaos to find a pilot who knows the Amazonas, and now I fly up with him to bring you out."

"To bring us out?" I repeated dully.

"Yes, of course. Why do you think we have come here? And for the poor Senhor McHugh at least, I can see it is not too soon." Moranda took another pill. "Do you know something, Marco amigo?" he added. "It is a most lucky thing that we found you at all. For an hour before we came here we are following the wrong river."

Up to this point I had been only half listening to him. But there was no halfway about it now. I was staring at him.

"Yes," he went on, "we came up the Juruá, the Yurima, the Malaguay. Then we came to a fork in the Malaguay, and one side is brown and one side is black, and I remember of course what you have told me from your own flying, and I tell da Silva here"—he indicated the pilot—"to follow the black. So we follow it, but it is no good. We fly on for fifty, sixty miles, but you are not there. Nothing is there. So we fly back. We go once again to the fork and then up the brown river, and da Silva he is saying we must turn, there is not enough gasolina, when then at last we see this place, and it is a lucky thing."

"This other river—" I said, "it's to the west of here?"

"To the west, yes."

"How far?"

"You have seen yourself where it joins—"

"I don't mean where it joins. I mean from here. Across-country."

"We did not fly across-country."

"How far would you guess?"

Moranda looked at the pilot, and the latter shrugged. "Perhaps thirty, forty miles," he said.

"Was there a range of hills?"

336

"Hills?"

"Up the other river. Beyond where you turned back."

Moranda shook his head. "No, we saw no hills."

"There was only mist," said da Silva.

Now it was they who were only half listening to me. Da Silva kept looking at Moranda, and the latter stood up. "But black rivers, brown rivers, hills—we can speak of such things later," he said. "The important thing now is to make ready and leave."

"Leave?" I repeated. "Today?"

"Yes, today; now; as soon as possible. Senhor McHugh, he is very sick, no? And also you have seen how it is with the river and the plane."

Da Silva nodded. "The landing was a dangerous matter," he said.

"You handled it well," I told him.

"Thank you, senhor. But it is not a thing I would like to try many times."

"And the river it is still falling, is it not?" asked Moranda.

"Yes," I said.

"If it falls a few more inches," said the pilot, "it will be impossible to take off."

"You see, we must hurry," Moranda declared. "Come—da Silva and I will get Senhor McHugh ready, and you, Marco, will go get the others."

"The others?" I said.

"Doutor Barna—the senhora. They are here, are they not?"

"Yes, they're here."

"And the doutor, he is working now for the Companhia?"

"No."

Moranda was obviously surprised. But even more, he was in a hurry. "So, it does not matter," he said. "He is here, he is an important man, and Senhor Wooderson wants that we should help him."

"Wooderson?"

Moranda drew an envelope from his pocket. "It is all here—from Senhor Wooderson to Senhor McHugh. That the *Fortaleza* cannot come. That nothing more can be done until the rains. That he should come back to Esperança; and also you, the senhora and Doutor Barna."

"What about the rest?" I asked.

"The rest?"

"Cobb. O Touro. Frei Ambrosio. The caboclos."

"We shall call them together. We shall tell them that they should carry on the work as well as they can and that we shall be back when the rains come."

"And then simply leave them here?"

Moranda shrugged. "The plane it can carry six at the most. Besides da Silva and myself, then, there is room for only those whom I have said."

He looked at da Silva for confirmation, and the pilot nodded. "Even with six," he said, "it will be difficult to take off from this river."

"And about the others," Moranda went on, with a reassuring gesture, "there is, I promise you, no need for concern. This Cobb—if I know him aright, he would not go back anyhow. And for the rest, it does not matter. For them one riverbank and one thatched hut is the same as another."

"It wasn't the same for some of them," I said. And I told him of the caboclos who had made off down-river. . . . Had they reached Esperança? I asked.

He shook his head: he knew nothing about it. Nor, obviously, was he interested. "Forgive me that I am insistent," he said, peering anxiously at his watch, "but if we not leave within the hour it will be necessary to wait until tomorrow; for one cannot fly over such country in darkness. So if we may now please begin the preparations—"

As he spoke, my glance moved out through the doorway to the clearing beyond. A group of caboclos was gathered nearby, brown and motionless as the stumps of trees. But there was no sign of Cobb or Touro. Of Barna or Christine.

"There is something wrong, Marco?" asked Moranda.

For a long moment I didn't answer. Then I said, "I'll have to think about this, Eustasio."

"Think about it? Mother of God, amigo, what is there to think about?"

"I have to talk to the others."

"Yes, of course—that is what I say. Talk to them. Tell them. But quickly, please. Now. The time is passing, and soon it will be too late for the plane to go any more today."

"Then it will go tomorrow," I said.

"No, tomorrow it is too late. Too dangerous. And for the Senhor McHugh, too, who is so sick—"

"McHugh's been sick a long time. Another day won't kill him."

Moranda continued arguing, but I got up, crossed to the door and went out. I felt him and da Silva staring after me with puzzled angry eyes.

First I checked on Cobb's whereabouts, and, to my relief, found him drunk again in his hammock, obviously unaware of planes, visitors, or anything else. Turning away, I walked down to the riverbank. A group of caboclos was assembled there, as in front of the staff shack, looking out at the moored plane with dark impassive faces. And for a while I stood staring too: at the broad silver wings, the frozen props, the power-bulging nacelles, the whole sleek functional image, at once so familiar and so strange. I looked away and then back again, half expecting it to be gone. But it was still there. Metallic and glittering, tangible and real, an amphibious airplane was floating on the muddy waters of the jungle river.

The eyes of the caboclos were no longer fixed on the plane, but on me. And presently one of them spoke.

"The aeroplano will leave soon, senhor?" he asked.

"Tomorrow," I said.

"With the sick chefé?"

"Yes, with the sick chefé."

"And with the other chefés too?"

I didn't answer him.

"Yes, of course with the other chefés," said a second caboclo. "They will all go. Only we will stay."

"They will leave us here alone with the savages."

"To starve."

"To die."

"In three months now the big ship will be here," I told them. "As soon as the rains begin the ship will come."

"And then the new chefés can cut more crosses from the ceiba trees and put them on our graves."

I walked away, and across the clearing again; but everywhere now there were groups of caboclos standing in front of the huts and staring sullenly out at the river and the plane.

"When the Senhor Chefé is sick," they said, "a silver aeroplano comes and takes him away. But when we are sick all that comes are the urubu, waiting on the roofs and crosses."

I moved on, left the clearing, and walked slowly along the forest trail. Well, here it is, I thought. What you've been waiting and praying for. The way out—escape—salvation. Yes, of course, that was it. A plane called Salvation. . . .

I walked on to Barna's clearing. First I looked into Touro's new hut, but neither he nor his son was there. Then I crossed to the larger cabin and knocked on the door, and after a moment it was opened by Nils Barna.

"Come in, Allison," he said. "I have been expecting you."

Entering, I found myself once again in the neat, sparsely furnished little room. Christine was not there.

"Then you know about the plane?" I said.

"Yes, I am aware that a plane has come. It has brought some of your associates, I assume."

"Only one. And a pilot. It's come to take us down-river."

"Ah, I see. A rescue plane."

"Of sorts, yes. Among those it's prepared to take are you and your wife."

"I see," said Barna again.

"It will take off tomorrow morning as soon as it's light. I've come to tell you so that you can be ready."

"That is kind of you, I am sure." Barna studied me briefly and passed a hand slowly over the reddish crest of his hair. "But what makes you think that I wish to be—rescued?"

"I'm afraid that's beside the point," I told him.

"Meaning that you are ordering me to leave?"

"Yes."

"And if I refuse?"

"Then I shall have to force you to leave."

Barna was silent again. The gray eyes behind the glasses seemed to be smiling at me. Then he said, "I see that among your other talents you have a flair for drama."

"This has nothing to do with drama. It simply has to do with the fact that this place is the property of the Southern Cross Corporation; that due to McHugh's illness I'm in charge, and that I think it advisable that you go."

"And may I ask why you think it advisable?"

"Because it will be best for all concerned."

"All?"

"Yes, all."

"I appreciate your interest in my welfare," said Barna, "but it so happens that I myself am more interested in the welfare of certain others. The Tupari, for instance. What do you propose to do about the Tupari?"

I had known, of course, that this was coming. And I was ready for it. "I propose once again to suggest a bargain," I said.

"Yes?"

"That I give them back their weapons. And that they take me with them when they start off for the Rio do Sol."

For the first time since I had known him, Barna's face showed surprise. Or, if not his face, his eyes. Again he stared at me in silence, and then he said, "You are not going in the plane, then?"

"No."

"You are still resolved to go on?"

"Yes."

"And you want me to—"

"I want you to go now to the Tupari village. I want you to tell them my offer and advise them to accept it."

"And if they do?"

"Then you'll bring Pombal and his son Cambar to the office shack tonight. And if I'm convinced that they're sincere and willing to be friendly, I'll give them their weapons."

"Have you considered, Mr. Allison, that without my assistance the Tupari may be unable or unwilling to seek this mythical homeland of theirs, which you persist in identifying with the oil you are hoping to find?"

"Yes, I've considered that. It seems worth a try at least, and there will be little enough to do here after you and the rest are gone."

Barna crossed the room and stood, tall and stooped, looking out the doorway. "I am receiving my orders, is that it, Mr. Allison?" he said.

"You're receiving my suggestion on how to help the Tupari."

"And, incidentally, on how to help you?"

"Incidentally, yes."

Barna turned back into the room. "If I arrange this thing for you," he said, "will you be prepared to leave with the Tupari immediately?"

"Yes," I said.

"What about Mr. Cobb?"

"Cobb will stay here."

"How can you be sure? He disobeyed you once before."

"If we leave at once, he will be in no state to follow."

"I can assure the Indians of that?"

"Yes."

"How many men will you take?"

"I shan't take any."

"You mean you will go alone with the Tupari?"

"Yes, alone."

Barna seemed to be examining me as if I were some sort of new and interesting specimen under a glass. "Would that not be taking a great risk, Mr. Allison?" he asked, "—to trust yourself to these savages in this way?"

"You've trusted yourself to them."

"Yes. But I am their friend."

"I intend to be their friend, too," I said.

Silence again. . . .

"Will you speak to them?" I asked.

"I seem to have no choice," said Barna.

I nodded and went to the door. "I'll expect you, with Pombal and Cambar, tonight."

"If they agree—yes."

"They'll agree, if you want them to."

I went out, and Barna came to the doorway after me. "You are a more determined man than I had thought, Mr. Allison," he said. "Perhaps one day you will reach your El Dorado after all."

Next: O Touro. . . .

Crossing Barna's clearing, I saw that the big Negro was now in his hut, and as I approached it he came to the door.

"You know about the plane, Touro?" I asked him.

He nodded.

"It will leave early tomorrow, with Mr. McHugh and the Barnas. I think you should go too."

Touro said nothing.

"With your boy, of course," I added. "The plane's designed for only six, but I'm sure a point can be stretched for a child."

Still Touro said nothing.

"You should get away from here, Touro," I said.

"And go where?" he asked.

"Back to Esperança. That's where you'd want to go, isn't it?"

"It makes no difference to me where I go."

"It will make a difference to your son. You still care about your son, don't you?"

"Yes."

"In Esperança he'll have a better life. And so will you. You'll be among different people and have work to do. Mr. Wooderson probably needs a foreman badly."

The Negro looked at me for a moment. Then he said: "You are ordering me to go—is that it, Mr. Allison?"

"Yes, I'm ordering you, Touro. For your own sake."

"Very well, Mr. Allison."

He said nothing more. I stood there, wanting to say more, but not finding the words. And then Touro turned back into the darkness of his hut.

Next: Christine. . . .

She might be at the infirmary. Or at the staff shack with Moranda. I walked back along the trail toward the big clearing, reached its edge—and stopped. From the instant when I had first seen the plane it seemed to me that I had known exactly what I must do, and I had gone coolly and surely about the business at hand. But now all sureness was gone. All coolness and clearness were gone, and where they had been was a cold blank emptiness. Next: Christine. . . . Yes, of course. Go to her. Speak to her. . . . "Goodbye, Christine."

The clearing spread before me, bare and blazing, like a scab on earth's living flesh. Above it, a single urubu circled, and at its far side, along the riverbank, a row of caboclos still stood staring at the moored plane. A shaft of sunlight, striking off the plane's wings, stabbed into my eyes.

Turning, I re-entered the trail. I walked slowly through the cool gloom—away from the clearing—deeper into the forest; not toward any destination, so far as I knew, but first along one path and then another, farther and deeper, with the clearing and the river and the plane behind me, and, before me, only a still green vault of lacquered fronds. There was only the next turning of the path, the quick glints of plumage, the sudden cries, the rustling silences . . . and then a fork in the path, a deep twisting gallery of ferns and lianas . . . and in front of me now, exactly as they had been before, exactly as I remembered them, a circle of trees, a glade, a dark gleaming pool.

I stood watching it, but there was no hint of movement

in its depths. Then I followed its bank around to the far side; and there, sitting on a slope of moss at the foot of one of the great ceiba trees, was Christine. . . .

She sat bent forward a little, with one hand extended, and as I came closer I saw a small ringtailed monkey crouched on the bank perhaps a yard away from her. Its brown body was motionless, its bright gaze fixed on a piece of fruit in Christine's palm. And now, with a sudden bounding motion, it leapt forward, snatched the fruit, and in another bounding leap disappeared among the trees. "It was the first time he would come to me," said Christine, smiling.

"You've been here before, then?" I asked.

"Yes, many times. It's such a lovely place."

"Yes," I said, "it's a lovely place."

I sat beside her and looked down at the pool. It was utterly still, utterly black, and beneath its surface the reflected image of a great ceiba tree plunged down into the cool darkness. Only at one point, near the far bank, an irregular patch of water shone gleaming and silvered in a shaft of sunlight.

Or was it only the sunlight?

"This is the one place here," said Christine, "that I'll always remember. And want to remember. I had to come once again before I left."

"Then you know—" I began.

"Yes, I know that we're going. I saw Moranda a little while ago in the infirmary. And then, later, Nils."

"It's the only thing to do, Chris."

"Yes, of course." She paused. "It's the one hope for Nils— I know that. To get away from this place. To live among men again."

"What did he say about it?"

"I saw him for only a few minutes. Then he went off to the Indian village—and I came here."

"How do you think he feels?"

"I think he feels it's inevitable. That he has to go."

"And he's willing to try?"

"I—I think so."

There was a silence between us. Then—"Where will you go?" I asked.

"I don't know," she said.

"The States? Europe?"

"I don't know. It doesn't matter, really, so long as it's back into the world. Where Nils can work again and be a useful man. Perhaps, eventually, even a happy man."

Another silence.

Christine was watching me. "Isn't there something else you have to say to me, Mark?" she asked quietly.

"Say to you?"

"You told Nils that he and I must leave tomorrow. But there was something else you told him, wasn't there?"

I didn't answer her.

"That *you* are staying here," she said.

I looked away. "I have to stay, Chris."

"Have to?"

"There are all these people we've brought here. And also —also, for myself. . . ." I paused. "That's the strange part of it," I went on. "For weeks all I've wanted in the world was to get out of this place. Anyhow. Anywhere. Now the plane's here—it's possible to get out—and I can't. I have to stay here. I have to go on with it until—"

"Until what?" she asked.

I smiled thinly. "Until I find oil, I suppose."

Yes, of course, I thought: oil. That's what you're here for —have you forgotten? For the Kingdom of Oil. . . .

I sat watching the pool again. Then Christine spoke my name.

"Yes?" I said.

"Here we are, Mark."

I nodded.

"Do you remember when you said that?" she went on. "One evening at Esperança when we were playing cards; when we were just beginning to—to know each other. And do you remember what you said next? You said, 'And pretty soon, on we go.'"

346

"Yes," I said. "I remember."

"We can't say that any longer, can we, Mark?"

No, I thought, we couldn't say that any longer. There was nothing we could say any longer. . . .

She stood up.

"I should be getting back—" she said.

"Yes, of course." I rose too.

"Goodbye," she said.

"Goodbye."

She raised her head and kissed me on the lips. Then she turned, walked quickly around the pool, and disappeared into the forest path.

24

Moranda was still sitting in the staff shack, a study in exasperation and sweat-soaked linen. "Well, I hope you are satisfied," he greeted me. "Now it is too late to leave today."

"You can leave in the morning," I told him.

"In the morning we will probably hit an abomination of a sandbar or sunken tree, and that will be the end of all of us. What is the matter with you people, hey? You are crazy maybe? You do not want to be saved from this place?"

My first impulse was to snap back at him, but I held it in. After all, Moranda had taken a not inconsiderable risk in flying up to get us, and one could scarcely blame him for taking a lively interest in his own survival.

"I'm sorry, Eustasio," I said.

"Sorry—hah! So you will be sorrier tomorrow, perhaps, when we cannot go at all." Moranda paused, and his sharp eyes studied me curiously. "This delay is because of the Barnas, is it not?" he asked. "Yes, I am sure—it has to do with these Barnas."

"It has to do with everything," I said. "The Barnas partly —but all the others too. And all we came here for."

"What you have come for is oil."

"That's right."

"And you have not found it."

"No."

"And you will not find it until the *Fortaleza* comes—and the scientistas—and the machines. Is that not right too?"

"I suppose so," I said. "But still—" This palavering would

get us nowhere. "Still, it's too late to fly now, Eustasio. Suppose we let it go at that."

Moranda obviously had more to say, but before the words came I was out the door. By this time the shadows of late afternoon were lying long and slender across the yellow dust. Down on the river the pilot da Silva was clambering about on his plane, examining and tinkering, while a row of caboclos watched him silently from the bank. Nearby, in his hammock, lay Cobb, still stupefied with cachaça, and at intervals the stillness was broken by his moving or a thick jumble of unintelligible words. That was what *I* wanted, I thought: to be drunk, too. To be stupefied. To lie there like Cobb, not even knowing that a plane had come; not knowing anything or feeling anything; not having to think, to decide, to act.

I went to my own hammock and lay watching the dusk spread swiftly over the river and clearing. I lay watching Christine, as she walked around a dark pool and disappeared into a forest trail. . . .

Now it was almost night. The pium flies withdrew. The mosquitoes advanced. Raising myself in the hammock, I pulled down the white shroud of the netting; but presently the inevitable single mosquito was inside it with me, circling and darting, a maddening invisible whine in the darkness. Within ten minutes I was bathed in sweat, and my flesh itched and burned with a hundred tiny pricks of fire. I got up and walked across the clearing. Coming to the staff shack, I saw Moranda and the pilot inside, eating their supper at the lamplit table. But I wanted neither food nor talk, and I didn't go in. I walked on past and down to the riverbank and stood staring at the improbable shape of the moored plane, now no longer gleaming silver, but rigid and black against the softer weaving blackness of the water. The caboclos who had been watching it were gone. There was no one in sight; no light except the single yellow glow that came through the door of the staff shack.

Then I heard the drum. . . .

It was very soft, barely audible; less an actual, distinguishable sound than a deep muffled pulse in the darkness. But as I stood now, listening, I knew that it was no illusion. . . . It was there. . . . My first thought, of course, was that it came from the Indian village. As I turned, however, and again moved across the clearing, I became aware that its source was not inland, but downstream along the riverbank.

Ahead of me a figure materialized out of the darkness. It was Frei Ambrosio.

"Is it our own people?" I asked him.

"Yes, senhor," he said. "It is our people."

"Where are they?"

"At the clearing where I took the well ones during the sickness."

"It's that damn cachaça again."

"Yes, it is the cachaça. Only tonight it is different from the other nights. It is more. It is worse." The little padre's voice was strained. His hands, clasped together in front of his cassock, were opening and closing spasmodically. "The drum that you hear, senhor—" he went on—"it is a macumba drum. A voodoo drum. Where they have got it from, or how they have made it, I do not know. But I know that it means a new ungodliness, and a wildness in the blood. . . ."

We were silent. Again I heard the thumping in the darkness. And presently, through the thumping, still another sound—the sound of voices. There was a hoarse cry, then only the drumbeat; a shrill cry and again the drumbeat. Then voices and drumbeats rose together in a reverberating din, held a moment on a pitch of savage frenzy, and died away into a restless murmuring.

"Before tonight it was only fear they felt," said Frei Ambrosio. "But now it is anger too."

"About the plane?"

"Yes, partly about the plane. They say it has come to fly away with the chefés and leave them here alone. But even more it is about the Indians. They say you are giving the

Indians back their weapons, and that tomorrow when you are gone the Indians will come and kill them all."

"How in hell did they find out?" I murmured, more to myself than to the Padre.

"I do not know, senhor," he said. "I do not know anything about it. But that is what they say. And that is what they are angry about."

"What do you think they'll do?"

"It is hard to say. Perhaps it will be no more than the drum and the shouting. Or perhaps it will get wilder and wilder, until—"

"Let's go and put a stop to it," I said, starting off along the bank.

But Ambrosio came quickly after me and held my arm. "No, senhor," he said agitatedly, "you must not go. You are a chefé and it is no good that a chefé goes, for with the drunkenness the macumba it will only make them wilder."

I stopped, hesitating.

"It is I who shall go," said the little priest. "To you they would not listen, but they are my own people and perhaps they will listen to me. . . . Yes, it is the only way. I shall go now," he added. And before I could speak again he had vanished into the darkness.

I took a few steps after him, changed my mind, and stopped. Ambrosio had undoubtedly been right: if he couldn't control the caboclos, surely I couldn't. And besides—I looked at my watch—it was now eight forty-five, and Barna and the two Indians would soon be arriving in the clearing. Again I stood still, listening, and there was another single hoarse shout and then only the thump of the drum. At least it was no louder than before, no nearer than before.

There was one precaution, however, that I knew must be taken, and, going to the staff shack, I confronted Moranda and da Silva. "It's not likely that anything will happen," I told them, "but it's best to play safe." And I suggested that

351

they take the plane from its mooring on the shore and move out into mid-river for the night.

"This is not a jungle we have come to, but a madhouse," Moranda muttered; but his muttering did not interfere with the alacrity of his preparations. I think he would have preferred a year of nights in the cramped cabin of a plane to another hour on that godforsaken mudbank of Graça de Deus.

I walked with them down to the shoreline and stood watching while da Silva started up the amphibian's engines and taxied slowly out to midstream. Presently I heard the engines go off and the plop of an anchor in the water. Looking along the bank, I saw the faint glow of a fire in the down-river clearing. The drum still throbbed in the night, but I heard no chanting or shouting.

I went back and sat on the steps of the staff shack. Off to the east, beyond the river, the moon rose, round and yellow. The dust of the clearing around me gleamed like phosphorus, and flecks of silver winked along the wings of the anchored plane. Turning, I sat and watched the entrance of the trail that showed faintly in the black forest wall. I waited. I looked at my watch, and it was nine-fifteen; and when I looked again it was almost nine-thirty. . . . Perhaps the Tupari had refused to come, I thought. Perhaps Barna hadn't gone for them. Perhaps he had changed his mind and. . . .

Then I saw a movement against the darkness of the forest wall, a shadow emerging from the deeper shadows of the trail's mouth. . . . Here they are, I thought. . . . But there was only one shadow. Barna alone? . . . No. The shadow moved closer and became a person, and the person was Christine.

Her face seemed white and bloodless in the moonlight.

"They're not here, Mark?" she asked.

"No," I said.

"They've not been here?"

"No."

"Where are they, then? What are they doing?"

Instead of answering, I took her by the arm and led her into the staff shack. "You shouldn't have come here," I told her. "The caboclos are worked up tonight. There may be trouble."

"I had to come, Mark. I'm afraid."

"They have nothing against you. They won't harm you. But you should have stayed—"

"I don't mean about the caboclos," she said. "I mean about Nils."

She was struggling for control. She was more agitated than I had ever seen her before.

I made her sit down. "What is it, Chris?" I asked. "What's happened?"

"I don't know if anything has happened. That's just it, I don't—" She broke off. When she went on again it was quietly and evenly. "Nils and I had supper together. He spoke very little, but that wasn't unusual, and I scarcely gave it a second thought. When we'd finished I began packing our things for tomorrow, and he got up to go over to the Indian village. In fact, I thought he'd already left; but then a few minutes later I looked up from my packing and saw that he was standing in the doorway, watching me. Do you remember, I once told you about the night, soon after we came here, when I woke up and found him standing beside my hammock? Well, it was like that. That was how Nils was watching me."

She paused and then continued: "As soon as I looked up, he turned and went out. And I went on with my work. For a while I don't think I even thought about it. . . . But then I began thinking about it. I couldn't stop thinking about it. . . . I knew that he and the Indians would have to pass the cabin on their way here, and I kept watching the door to see them when they went by. But a half hour went by—and then an hour—and they didn't come. And then—I don't know why—I couldn't stand it another minute, waiting there alone; and I went over to Touro's hut; but it was dark and he wasn't there—not even Tourinho was there. I put on my flashlight and looked inside. Their hammocks were gone, and their cooking things and their clothes. . . .

"Then I came here," she said.

I felt the sweat suddenly cool and glazed along my back and shoulders. I went to the door and watched and listened. But the drumbeats had not resumed. Across the moonlit clearing there was no faintest stirring, even of water or leaf. The stillness was absolute.

And yet—(I, too, was perfectly still now)—yet it was not, I knew, the stillness of sleep but of wakefulness, not of peace but of slow, germinating tension. Deeper than movement, deeper than sound, I was aware all around me of a dark rhythm of emptiness—a tremor, a palpitation—as if silence itself were being stretched out in an immense skein to the last pitch of trembling tautness.

I went back into the hut. "Look, Chris," I said. "You stay here. I'm going to—"

But that was all I said. For at that instant came the sound of a shot.

I remember the silence that closed in again after it. I remember the scuffing of my boots as I ran for the rifle in the corner. Then, all together, there were more shots, running footsteps, a muffled shout, a chorus of shouts. Across the clearing a lantern flickered, and behind it I could see a dark confusion of shadows moving swiftly along the riverbank. Seizing the rifle, a flashlight and a few clips of cartridges, I made for the door again; and by the time I emerged the place was in pandemonium, with yelling, gesticulating figures racing among the huts and sheds. My first thought was that they were going for the plane, and I ran toward the shore. But halfway there I was all but bowled over by a swarm of caboclos coming in the opposite direction. I called out to them to stop, but they ran on, unheeding. A man darted by, close beside me, and lunging out, I seized him and beamed the flashlight in his face. It was one of the younger çaboclos —a fellow called Moniz—and at first he made as if to swing at me with the machete in his hand. Then, recognizing me, he held still. But his eyes, staring at me, were dark and wild, and his mouth twitched and jerked with excitement.

"What is this?" I demanded. "What are you doing?"

"The Tupari—" he muttered.

"What do you mean, the Tupari?"

"They have been here. They have taken their weapons."

Before I could speak again he broke away and raced across the clearing. The whole open space between forest and mud-bank was now alive with shadows—darting, shouting, brandishing machetes and axes. But I saw no Indians; and there were no further shots. Threading my way through the confusion, I reached the storage shed where we had kept the Tupari weapons and saw that Moniz had been right. The door hung limp on broken hinges. The javelins and blow-guns were gone. And now the shed was filled with milling yelling caboclos, some already with guns and others in the act of snatching them from the racks. None of them offered me any violence, but neither did they pay the slightest attention as I ordered them to stop. Following them out again, I found what must have been virtually the entire population of Graça de Deus congregated in front of the shed. A few were carrying flaming torches, and their light flickered eerily on the metal of knives and gun-barrels. Many were jumping about with jerky convulsive movements. And the sound that came from them, now that they were all banded together, was no longer a diffused shouting, but a low long-drawn concerted howl.

I raised my arms and tried to speak, and Frei Ambrosio, materializing from the darkness, did likewise; but it was obvious that we were not going to be able to control them.

"Who saw the Indians?" I asked.

"I did," someone yelled. . . . "And I". . . . "And I". . . . "We all saw them."

"How many were there?"

"There were ten". . . . "There were twenty". . . . "Fifty" . . . . "All of them."

They were all yelling at once now, jumping and jerking

355

and swaying in the torchlit darkness. Some of the voices were thick and hoarse, some so high-pitched that they were almost a scream. Off in the background the drum was thumping again. The heavy reek of cachaça filled the air. And then, suddenly, an apparition appeared among them, even weirder than the rest. It was Mordecai Cobb, weaving through the turmoil with a machete in one hand and a cachaça gourd in the other. He was dressed in filthy pajamas. His eyes were glazed and bloodshot. When I called to him he seemed neither to see nor hear me, but wandered aimlessly about among the caboclos and shouted as loud as any of them.

"They have their blowguns," someone yelled.

"They have their darts and their poison."

"When the plane is gone they will come back."

"To kill us."

"To kill our wives and children."

"To kill us all."

Their feet were pounding. Their guns and machetes waved. Their bodies and voices alike seemed to be losing their separate identities and mingling together in a rhythmic, almost liturgical chorus.

"We must kill them first. . . ."

"Yes, yes."

"Kill the savages. . . ."

"Yes, yes."

"Kill them all. . . ."

"Yes, yes."

A dark figure with a torch leapt into the doorway of the shed beside Frei Ambrosio and myself and began swinging his brand in a wild hissing circle.

"Attack, attack, attack," he chanted.

"Attack, attack, attack," came back the answer.

The many voices were like one voice—deep and wild. The drumbeats were louder, and through them, suddenly, came the high piercing sound of a woman's scream. I too was shouting, but I couldn't hear my own voice. I tried to seize the torch from the man beside me, but he twisted away and vanished, howling, in the crowd. I raised my gun and fired over their heads, but the only response was a scattering of other shots. And now, abruptly, with one great concerted roar, the crowd broke and turned and in the next instant was racing in wild confusion across the clearing toward the entrance of the forest trail. Hopelessly and ridiculously, I was still shouting after them. I was firing again into the air. I was standing with Frei Ambrosio in the midst of a shrieking knot of women and children while the last of the men disappeared behind the black wall of the trees.

Then I was running after them.

I reached the edge of the clearing, entered the forest, plunged and stumbled along the dark tunnel of the trail. Ahead, I could hear the voices of the caboclos and see the occasional gleam of a torch through the foliage. I came to Barna's clearing, passed the empty cabin, and then that too was behind me, and I was in the forest again, moving as quickly as I could along the trail to the Tupari village. I was running and stumbling again, falling, picking myself up, bursting out of the forest at last. . . .

And then I stopped.

Before me lay the bare earth of the Indians' clearing, gleaming faintly in the moonlight, and a little way ahead rose the black shapes of the conical huts. I could hear the shouts of the caboclos and see their darting figures, and here and there was a sudden comet-like streak of light as the flames of a torch streamed out behind a running man. But there were no shots, no sounds of fighting. Nor did any of the shadowy figures seem to be Indians. Running forward again, I reached the nearest hut and beamed my flashlight through the doorway. There were only thatch walls, earthen floor and emptiness. Then I moved on to a second hut and a third and a fourth, and these were empty too—not only of inhabitants but of food, implements, possessions, everything.

I ran to Pombal's hut. . . . Empty.

A group of men raced by me, shouting, "They are gone—they are gone," and I tried to stop them but they plunged away into the darkness. I circled the clearing and came back again to its center, but there was still no sign of an Indian.

Nor of Barna, Touro or Tourinho. . . .

There was a crackling roaring sound, and a burst of flame shot upward. Someone had put a torch to the tinder-dry thatch of one of the huts. A moment later there was a second burst, and then another and another, until all the huts in the village were blazing like a great circle of bonfires in the night. Against the orange glare were silhouetted the black figures of the caboclos, leaping like so many devils in hell; brandishing their guns and machetes, yelling at the top of their voices; more savage than the savage Indians whose home they were destroying, as they exorcised their dark long-pent-up fear and hatred in the bright ferocity of fire.

There was no way of stopping it. I crossed toward the inland side of the clearing, and a moment later a group of caboclos rushed after me in a ragged tide. We reached the entrance of the trail that led on from the clearing into the jungle to the west. And there we stopped and stood still. No torch or flashlight was needed now, for the flames behind us lighted the forest wall and the mouth of the path with a lurid brilliance. And that was all there was—forest and path —and in the dusty earth of the path the jumbled tracery of hundreds of footprints. A low howl, less human than animal, rose from the caboclos; then it faded away, and the only sound was the crackling and roaring of the flames. Three or four of the men advanced a few yards along the path and then stopped again, afraid to go farther. Beyond them, and beyond the last flicker of the glowing fires, the trail led on into darkness.

Perhaps an hour later I circled the heap of ashes that had been the Tupari village and walked back toward our own clearing through a night grown strangely empty and still.

Christine had returned to Barna's cabin and was waiting for me at the door.

I told her briefly what had happened. And then, taking me inside, she showed me the note she had found lying in the folds of her hammock.

PART THREE

THE FOREST

25

This time Barna's note consisted of only one line:

Goodbye, Christine. Forget me and be happy. Nils.

From Touro there was no note. But in the morning I saw, lying on the grave of Tereza Carolina, a sprig of blue jacaranda blossom that had not been there before.

The big clearing lay still as death in the dawnlight, as the caboclos slept off their orgy of the previous night. But soon after I reached it the sound of an engine came from the river, the amphibian moved in again from midstream, and Eustasio Moranda, linen rumpled and face drawn, stepped warily up onto the shore. "What in the name of the Ten Thousand Virgins has happened?" he demanded.

But he wasn't interested in the details. "So at last it is morning," he interrupted, almost immediately; "and by God's grace the plane is all right and we are all right. Now we go—yes. At once." While he spoke, he kept glancing around him as if he momentarily expected a hundred howling savages to burst out of the forest. "Da Silva and I will go get Senhor McHugh. Meanwhile you call the senhora and her husband and—" He broke off and looked toward the staff shack. "They are not ready?" he asked. "The Doutor and Senhora Barna—where are they?"

"Dr. Barna is gone," I said.

"Gone?"

I began telling him what had happened. But again he seemed scarcely to be listening, and before I finished he had turned to da Silva, who was standing on the plane's pontoon, and was jabbering at him in many-sainted Portuguese. This was an accursed place, he informed him—a place of evil and abomination—and we would leave in five minutes. Come—he and da Silva would fetch Senhor McHugh.

The pilot climbed up the bank, and Moranda turned back to me. "This is a sad thing," he said. "A most terrible thing; and when we arrive in Esperança we will have the consultations and decide what must be done. But first we must get to Esperança. We must get into the plane. . . ." He motioned to da Silva to follow him to the infirmary. "You Marco, you bring the Senhora and—"

He half turned to go, but the expression of my face must have stopped him. "There is something more wrong?" he asked apprehensively. "Why do you stand there? There is something the matter?"

"We're not going, Eustasio," I told him.

Moranda stared at me.

"Mrs. Barna refuses to go," I said.

"Refuses—?"

"Yes."

"You mean—" Moranda's bewilderment was complete. "You mean she will stay *here?*"

"Yes."

"And you?"

"I'm staying too," I said. "I have to stay."

"Have to?"

"I can't walk out now."

For a moment, again, Moranda simply stared. Then his astonishment turned to anger. "Who speaks of walking out?" he said. "It is on the order of Senhor Wooderson that you will go. For the reports. For the arrangements. So that everything will be better for everyone."

I shook my head. "I can't do it," I told him.

"What do you mean, you cannot? Mother of God, you *want* to stay in this filth of a place? It is an insanity!" Moranda's sharp eyes fixed on my face. "It is these Barnas—yes, is it not?" he demanded. "They are crazy, and now you are crazy too. . . ."

He broke off and looked at da Silva, who was standing by impatiently. Then he shrugged, turned abruptly, and the two men headed across the clearing toward the infirmary. After a moment I followed them.

Christine met us at the door. Her face was bloodless, her eyes tired and red-rimmed; but she was a nurse now, not a woman.

"He's ready," she told us.

Moranda seemed about to resume his arguing; then changed his mind and followed her in silently. McHugh lay on his cot, with a windbreaker over his pajamas and sneakers on his feet. Obviously he heard us come in, for he opened his eyes and kept them open; but he didn't say a word as we picked him up and carried him out. His body seemed almost weightless, and it took only a few minutes to get him down to the shore and into the plane. Whether or not he knew what was happening, I couldn't tell; for he showed no emotion, nor even interest. After we had propped him into a seat in the cabin he spoke for the first time, but only to ask for water. Then, before we could bring it to him, he seemed to fall asleep.

Da Silva clambered back and forth on the plane, making last-minute adjustments. Then I walked with him along the river-bank, while he studied the maze of sandbars, snagged logs and brown eddying water.

"Over toward the far bank is the best," I told him.

When we returned to the improvised gangplank that connected plane and shore, Moranda was talking pleadingly with Christine. "You will not allow this, Marco," he said to me. "No, you cannot allow it. You will tell her she must go."

I shook my head. "I can't make her go, Eustasio," I told him. "She has to do what she thinks best."

"What she thinks best? God and the Virgin, how can such a thing as this be best?" He turned back to Christine. "You are concerned for your husband—yes, of course. But believe me, senhora, there is nothing you can do by staying here. It is by leaving now that you can help him. By coming to Esperança and talking to Senhor Wooderson and . . ."

He went on talking, but I only half heard him. The grayness of the dawnlight was brightening swiftly over the clearing and the river. A faint mist drifted upward, and behind the encircling wall of trees the hidden forest-world burst into a din of yawping and screeching. In almost the same instant, the sun rose. Its level beams struck against the wings of the plane and kindled them into bright silver fire. . . . The Plane called Salvation, I thought. No—the Plane called Illusion. Illusion for Christine and me, no less than for Nils Barna.

Clambering back into the cabin, I put a hand on McHugh's shoulder. "Happy landings, Mac," I said.

At first he didn't answer. Then, without opening his eyes, he murmured, "No, I'm not going. Take me ashore."

"You'll be coming back soon," I told him.

"No, I'm going ashore. Now." Suddenly his eyes opened, and he said quietly, but with perfect clarity. "Do you understand, lieutenant? You are to take me ashore."

He tried to lift his wasted body from the seat, but I held him back gently. "Goodbye, Mac," I said.

"That is a direct order, lieutenant."

"Good luck, Mac."

Da Silva had cilmbed into the pilot's seat and was revving up the engine. As I descended from the cabin, Moranda came along the gangplank, but this time it was not to argue. There was only one thought left in his mind now, and that was to be up and off.

"So, Marco—go with God," he said. "By February, no later, the *Fortaleza* will come; and even before that, with the first rains, I shall come again in the plane. Meanwhile I shall tell Senhor Wooderson how it is with you."

"Goodbye, Eustasio."

He looked at me for another moment and then said, "It

is really crazy that you are, hey, amigo? Crazy with the fever of the Amazonas." His eyes went past me to the shore; to Christine. "Or is it maybe with the fever of—"

A roar from the engine drowned out his words. He made a gesture that was half shrug, half salute. Then he turned and climbed into the plane, and I rejoined Christine on the bank. On either side of her now were a dozen-odd caboclos, ranged in a ragged watching row. Off to one side a little stood Frei Ambrosio. Behind him, his bloodshot eyes squinting into the sunlight, was Mordecai Cobb.

No one spoke. No one moved. When I turned, the plane was already moving out toward the center of the river, and for a while it maneuvered slowly about among the channels and sandbars. It taxied upstream and returned, downstream and returned. It squatted motionless on the muddy water, and for a moment I thought da Silva had given up; but in the next instant the engine roared and the plane leapt forward. As in the landing of the day before, it was a close thing. But as before, the plane made it. A scant twenty yards or so from an onrushing sandbar its pontoons lifted from the water. It climbed, banked, swooped low over the clearing and arrowed away into the east.

Soon its roar became a drone and its drone became stillness. Its wings left a final winking gleam in the distance, and then the gleam too was gone. The caboclos stood in their silent row on the mudbank, and the vultures rose from their perches on the crosses by the forest wall.

The plane was gone. McHugh and Moranda were gone. Touro, Tourinho and Nils Barna were gone. There was nothing left on the riverbank but brown water and yellow dust; nothing inside me but tiredness and numbness. Through the numbness I felt Christine beside me, as we walked across the clearing. But we didn't look at each other; and we didn't speak.

Whatever there was to say had already been said. During the long hours of the night we had sat together and talked together, groping our way through shock, disbelief, acceptance—and guilt. . . . *Goodbye,* he had written her. *Forget me.* . . . But, with what had happened now, she could never forget him. More than ever before, his image would remain with her—following, haunting—as long as she lived.

That much we knew from the beginning: that we couldn't go. Even before we spoke of it, each of us had reached his own decision, and I could no more have ordered, or even urged, her to leave than I could have left myself.

We came to the staff shack and went in. Christine set about brewing a pot of coffee, and I sat down at the table. Lying on the table was Wooderson's note to McHugh, and under it, I now noticed, a second envelope that had obviously also been left by Moranda. In the corner of the envelope was written

Projecto de Colonização, 1
Companhia Cruzeiro do Sul
Esperança, Amazonas

And it was addressed to Dr. Nils Barna.

Christine came to the table, and I handed it to her, and for what seemed a long while she held it motionless, looking down at the neat angular script. At last she opened the envelope and took out two sheets of paper; but instead of reading from the beginning, she merely glanced at the first page and went on to the bottom of the second. There was another pause. Her face was expressionless, her body as unmoving as the table. Then she put the page down in front of me, and I saw that the letter was in a language I couldn't read.

. . . Except—(my eyes went down the page)—except the last line. I could read that all right. The last line was

Jakob Koppel

I looked at Christine. I looked back at the letter. My eyes moved slowly over the undecipherable lines of Dutch script. "Can you read it?" I asked.

Christine shook her head. "Only a few words."

I, too, could make out a word here and there: *Borneo.* . . .

368

wonderbaarlijk. . . . *Europa.* But they didn't greatly matter. What mattered was *Jakob Koppel.* And two words on the envelope: *Esperança, Amazonas.*

I put the letter down. Christine sat beside me at the table.

"But I thought—" I began.

"That he was dead?" she said. "So did I. So did Nils."

"And instead—"

"—he's at Esperança."

Christine took the letter again. She began going through it slowly, word by word. "He came with the D.P.'s," she said presently. "Yes, that's what this says, I'm sure: he's one of the refugees." . . . She read on. . . . "Here's something about 1945. . . . And the Japanese. . . . *Ik werd*—yes: 'in 1945 I was released by the Japanese.' . . . And then *Nederland*: Holland. He went to Holland. . . ."

"But how in God's name did he get *here?*"

Christine puzzled on through the second page of the letter. "He writes about that too. . . . Yes: *Brasil.* . . . I think he's saying, 'At last I heard you were in Brazil. . . . I—something, something—the Refugee Organization.—I would rather—something—a new life—with my dearest friend. . . .' "

She put the letter down again, and for a long time we sat without speaking.

"Oh, God, Mark," she murmured at last. "If Nils had only seen this. If he only knew—"

"Would it make a great difference?"

"It would make all the difference. For years that's what's been deep inside him: torturing him, poisoning him. Not the war. Not anything that happened to himself. But Jakob —and what happened to Jakob. That's all that mattered, Mark. Nothing else. Not even I. Not even you and I. . . . No, none of it would matter. Not if he knew that Jakob was alive—was *here.* . . ."

She paused and then went on with an almost desperate quietness. "He has to know, Mark. We have to find him and tell him. We have to!" Suddenly she was on her feet, her face drawn and white, and I saw that the strained fusion of tiredness and emotion had brought her to the edge of hysteria. "Please, please—" she begged, gripping my arm. "We can't let him go like—"

She began to cry, but the crying made no sound. I put my arms around her and held her gently.

Toward evening I awoke from restless sweat-soaked sleep. Most of the caboclo families were now in evidence about their huts, preparing their evening meal. Their eyes were dull, their movements slow and lethargic, and it was hard to believe they were the same people who only the night before had goaded themselves on cachaça and voodoo to a pitch of homicidal frenzy. It was like the ash after flame, the exhaustion after fever. Wrapped in her own exhaustion, Christine lay asleep on the infirmary cot.

Going to the staff shack, I foraged myself something to eat. Then I went back to my hammock and slept again, and when I awoke it was past midnight. . . . Was it a sound that had wakened me? . . . I listened, but could hear nothing. Then, turning, I saw a gleam of light showing through the thatch walls of the storage shed.

For a wild moment I thought it was the Tupari again. Then I lay still, watching, and saw that the glow was from a moving flashlight. Rising, I got my own torch and a rifle, and walked over to the shed. And inside I found Mordecai Cobb.

"Looking for something?" I asked.

He didn't answer me. Beaming my light down, I saw at his feet a pile of tools, utensils and tinned food.

"Planning a trip?"

"Yeah," he said guardedly. "I'm going on a trip."

"Anywhere in particular?"

"Away from here. That's where."

"I can see your point," I told him. "It's a long trip down-river, though—without a boat."

"I ain't—" He stopped abruptly.

"Oh, I see. You're not going down-river?"

He didn't answer.

"You're going into the jungle, is that it?"

Cobb decided to brazen it out. "All right, so I'm going into the jungle," he said. "What's it to you?"

"It's very interesting to me," I said. "You think you can find them, then?"

"You're damn right I can find them."

"How?"

"By following their trail, that's how. By heading straight off west like I was doing two weeks ago, before you stopped me."

He began furiously sorting the pile of tins and equipment on the floor. "Gold, oil, million-dollar-bills—whatever that perfessor's got in there," he almost shouted; "he's leading me to it, and nobody's stopping me. Not him. Not you." He paused at his scrabbling and eyed at me defiantly.

"Take it easy," I told him. "I'm not stopping you. I'm going with you."

That was the mistake, of course. Cobb. . . . In the light of all that had happened—and, even more, of what was still to happen—it is hard for me to understand my agreeing to join forces with him. By this time I should have learned my lesson. And, in not having learned it, I shall always hold myself as responsible as he for the bitter events that were to follow.

Yet, if I were to go at all, it had to be with someone; and Cobb was the only person left in Graça de Deus even remotely capable of pulling his weight. Then, too, he had another trump up his sleeve, for I presently discovered that he had already persuaded two caboclos to accompany him. One was named Luiz, the other Garcia, and when Cobb called them in I recognized them as two of the group who had gone with him on his earlier foray. Apparently he had used the same blandishments as before: gold, the Big Bonanza, a first mortgage on El Dorado. But I soon gathered that it was neither Cobb's promises—nor certainly Barna—

that really impelled them. . . . It was O Touro. . . . They were convinced that the big Negro had gone off to stake some fabulous claim of his own, and they were resolved to follow him and demand their share.

Anyhow, they were willing to go with us.

Working through the morning, we selected our food and equipment and packed them into four loads of some thirty pounds each. We took rifles for Cobb and myself and shotguns for Luiz and Garcia. How long we could stay in the jungle depended largely, of course, on what we found in the way of game and fruits. But I, at least, scarcely even thought of the journey before us in terms of time or distance. We would go as far as we could. We would return when we had to.

Toward noon I went to the staff shack to get Jakob Koppel's letter. And there was Christine. She was wearing long khaki trousers and heavy boots, and a half-packed canvas bag lay before her on the table.

"No, Chris," I said. "You can't come."

"I have to come, Mark."

"It's impossible."

"No, it's staying here that's impossible."

"You'll be all right here. There'll be Frei Ambrosio and Batista and—".

"It isn't that. You know it isn't that."

"It will be a hard trip, Chris," I said. "The roughest sort of trip."

"Not rougher for me than for you."

"If we find him," I said, "there'll be the Tupari, too. They won't like being followed. They'll be hostile."

"Less hostile with me along," she pointed out quickly. "The Tupari love and respect Nils—you know that. They'll do what he tells them. If there were only the rest of you, he might let them have their way. But not if I were there. Don't you see, Mark? He wouldn't let them harm me."

That was true, of course. I had thought of it myself. But still—

She was standing close beside me, looking up into my face, and her voice held a deep pleading urgency. But at the same time it was quiet; it was controlled; and there was no trace of the exhaustion or near-hysteria of the day before.

"Please, Mark. Please," she said.

I took Jakob Koppel's letter from the table, put it in my pocket, and watched her silently while she finished her packing. Then Cobb appeared in the door and said, "Hey, amigo, where'd you put the bug-powder?"

It was early afternoon when we slung on our packs and crossed the clearing. Frei Ambrosio, João Batista and a handful of others were on hand to receive last-minute instructions and bid us goodbye; but most of the caboclos paid no more attention than if we had been going up to the cachoeira for a swim.

"Have no worry, though," the padre assured me. "With the Indians gone, there will be no further trouble here in your absence."

Amen, I thought.

"And now may God and the Virgin go with you."

Amen to that, too.

Entering the trail, we went in single file: Cobb first, the caboclo Luiz second, Christine next, myself next, the caboclo Garcia last. We passed Barna's cabin, followed the inland trail, and threaded our way through the ruins of the Tupari village. Before re-entering the forest on the far side I turned briefly and looked back, and the last I saw of Graça de Deus were the black shapes of its guardian vultures, wheeling slow and heavy through the sky.

26

Before us, around us, above us, were the emerald screens. The sun was gone, the sky no more than a hint of brightness beyond the treetops. The path led on before us, seeming almost a living thing as it twined through enveloping shadow.

During the first few hours there were a few forks in the trail, for we were still in the area of the Tupari hunting circuits. But the marks of the Indians' recent passing were still plainly in evidence, and there was never any doubt as to which was the route to follow. Then there were no more side-paths, but only a single one, boring on between unbroken walls. Up at the head of the column, Cobb turned. "Well, here we are again," he called back. For it was the same trail on which he had followed Barna before, and along which, in turn, I had followed him.

Our progress was slower than on that first occasion. We walked with a measured plodding stride that carried us at perhaps two miles an hour along the path, but little more than half that in a direct line toward the west. And ten minutes out of each hour we rested. At first the dim greenness of the forest seemed pleasantly cool, but by degrees its dank airless twilight became even more oppressive than the glaring sunbeat of the clearing. Though there had been no more rain here than at Graça de Deus, the web of vegetation that surrounded us seemed to be sweating and oozing as if with an inner self-generated moisture of its own. Soon my clothes were clinging to me like saturated rags and my breathing was as labored as if I had been running along the trail.

Ahead of us, beyond Cobb's moving figure, the ribbon of the path unrolled out of tangled obscurity. Huge blue-and-white morphos butterflies pirouetted through the foliage beside us, and at intervals the stillness was broken by a screech high above us and a bright flash of plumage in the upper tiers of the trees. But on the path itself there was no sound or movement. I stared ahead at it until its changeless monotony began to exert an almost hypnotic spell, and suddenly I stumbled on a root and almost fell. Then I lowered my eyes, so that all I could see was a strip of earth directly before me and the back of Christine's boots moving in and out of my field of vision. Even after several hours her step was steady and firm.

Nevertheless I was resolved that we shouldn't wear ourselves out that first day, and shortly after five I called a halt. We built a small fire, ate our evening meal, slung our hammocks and crawled in under the netting. Twilight became night, and night became blackness. High above the treetops, I knew, the moon and stars were blazing, but we were no more able to see them than if we had been lying ten thousand feet down on an ocean floor.

For once, in spite of sweating and itching, I was tired enough to sleep soundly, and when I opened my eyes it was again to gray twilight. In less than an hour we had eaten breakfast, packed our gear, and were on our way.

We were still on the trail that had been blazed by Cobb and the caboclos, but I knew that by midday or thereabouts we would reach its end—and what would happen then? As it turned out, however, we didn't have to reach the end to find out; for we had been on the march no more than two hours when, up ahead, Cobb stopped, and on joining him I saw that we had reached a fork in the path. Or if not a proper fork, at least a parting of two ways. For while Cobb's trail bore on straight ahead, there was here, in its lefthand wall, a gaping rent in the foliage; and it took only a moment's inspection to see that the rent was freshly made and that a large party had passed through it into the forest beyond.

Gradually I became aware that we were coming up onto slightly higher ground. The slope of the earth was certainly not steep enough to be called a hill, nor even to be noticeable from one step to the next; but a slight thinning of the mass of vegetation around us was all the evidence that was needed. Unless all our theories were wrong, we were crossing the low watershed that separated the drainage system of the Malaguay from that of the "other river" to the west. Then, toward midday, probability became proven fact. Through the first day-and-a-half of our journey the dozens of creeks and feeder-streams we had passed had all been flowing in a roughly easterly direction, but now at last we came to one whose course was in the same direction as our own.

Out in front Cobb plodded on steadily, rifle in hand. Under the tattered pajama-top his scrawny frame was bent to the weight of his pack; but his old bowed bony legs moved as if they could carry him on forever, and it was hard to believe that this was the same man who, for days past, had lain senseless and delirious in his hammock. Not once during the march did he so much as trip or stumble; and when at intervals the path ahead became so obscure that he had to stop to get his bearings, it was never more than a moment before he was again on his way. Here, I recognized, was the true Mordecai Cobb performing his natural life-function: the pilgrim on his pilgrimage, the hunter on the trail. His long nose positively quivered as it sniffed out the scent of our quarry. His eyes, peering out from under the tattered brim of his straw hat, were no longer pale and rheumy but as bright and quick as a predatory bird's.

The two caboclos, Luiz and Garcia, were, like Cobb, slight, stooped and scrawny to the point of emaciation, but there the resemblance ended. They walked with their eyes fixed dully on the ground before them. Their feet, in the unaccustomed heavy boots with which we had supplied them, dragged heavily among the roots and creepers. So far they had done all that was required of them and not complained; but their very faces and bodies were in themselves complaints—against lifelong drudgery, against lifelong hunger, against a world in which their only destiny was to carry a load and swing a machete. If they still had faith either in Cobb's promises or in their own theories about Touro, they showed no slightest sign of it. They trudged on, stopped, ate, slept, trudged on again. And that, they themselves seemed to know, was all they would ever do, their life long, until they slung their hammocks for the last time, crept into them, and died.

Most of the time, however, it was neither Cobb nor the two caboclos whom I was watching. . . . It was Christine. . . . Her step, as she moved along before me, seemed as steady and firm as on the first day. Her face, when occasionally she turned to look back at me, was composed and without strain. Several times, during our hourly halts, I asked her if she would not like to rest longer, and each time she said no, she was ready to go on. Yet I knew, as well as if she had been faltering and failing, how great a strain each hour of sweating progress was putting on her physical strength. And even more, how heavy a burden of uncertainty and fear she was carrying with her in her mind and heart.

We plodded on. The straps of my pack bit deeper into my sweating shoulders. My rifle hung from my arm like a bar of lead.

Toward midafternoon the foliage became denser again. The streams we encountered—all flowing to the west—were broader and more sluggish. We were obviously coming down off the watershed onto lower ground, and for a while our spirits lifted in the anticipation that at least the first stage of our journey would soon be over. But it was not to be as easy as that. For presently now the forest seemed to rise up against us in an almost solid wave; the great boles of the trees closed in until often there was not even space to squeeze between them; and the trail became merely the faintest trace of broken greenery boring through an inextricable tangle of

377

roots and branches, lianas, vines and ferns. Luiz and Garcia moved up ahead of Cobb and tried to hack out the way with their machetes, but our progress was still no more than a weaving stumbling crawl. Creepers twined themselves like snakes around our feet, and thorns ripped our clothing and plucked with spiny fingers at our packs and guns.

We had hoped to come out of the worst of the labyrinth before stopping; but by five-thirty it was already too dark to follow the vestigial trail, and soon we were building our fire and slinging our hammocks in still another tiny pocket of the night. By full daylight we had already breakfasted and were on our way again. Christine's step was perhaps a shade slower than on the previous day, and her face and hands were blotched with insect bites. But otherwise she seemed all right. Cobb and the two caboclos seemed all right. The machetes swung again; the roots and vines and creepers slid past; the trail twisted on. . . .

After perhaps an hour the forest began to thin perceptibly. The trees and fronds were no longer pressed quite so tightly together, and the trail before us was actually a trail again and not merely a spoor of broken foliage. We came to a stream broader than any we had seen before. We moved along warily, our eyes fixed on each vista before us, our ears straining for any sound that might come to us out of the stillness ahead.

But it was not sound that came. It was a flaring of the path, a sudden brightness of sky. Cobb stopped; the rest of us came up to him; and he was pointing, but there was no need to point. Before us was the edge of the forest, a mudbank, a river. . . .

A blackwater river.

There it was: broad, slow-coiling, gleaming darkly in the sun. At intervals its surface was broken by long sandbars that shone in contrast with an almost intolerable whiteness. But that was all there was—river and sandbars—and beyond them the farther shore. In either direction, as far as the eye could see, the shore stretched into the distance in rigid green stillness.

We stepped out into the mudbank, and our eyes moved searchingly over the empty miles. Then, presently, they were fixed on the bank to the left of us, and Cobb was pointing again. On the reddish earth was a cluster of black circles and within each circle the ashes of a dead fire. Roundabout them was a maze of footprints and, scattered among the prints, vestiges of discarded equipment, broken implements and refuse. The facade of the forest, close at hand, was notched by a series of ragged gashes, and in the open space before them was a litter of branches, bark, vines and fronds.

"They've built canoes," I said.

Cobb looked at me sideways. "How'd you guess it, amigo?" he inquired. "I was thinking mebbe it was a railroad."

"How could they build them that quickly?"

"These Indios move fast when they got a mind to. And besides—" Cobb rubbed the stubble of his chin. "Besides, I got an idea it wasn't so quick. My guess is that's what the perfessor and his boys were up to when they were out here the last time. Mebbe took a short course in canoe-building."

He walked down to the water's edge and then back again. "Well, sightseeing won't get us nowhere," he said. "If they can build a fleet of canoes, we can damn well build *one*."

This much was obvious: either we built a canoe or we turned back. And a few hours later, after we had eaten, slung our hammocks and rested a little, we set about the job at hand.

Luiz and Garcia, wielding ax and machete, assembled the raw material that was needed, and Cobb sorted through it, selecting and rejecting. Then, with such tools as we had, we went to work on the actual construction of our craft and by evening had hewn out something resembling a rough keel and frame. We of course had no nails, which meant that the various parts had to be lashed together by vines; and in this phase of the job Christine worked with us, spending hour after hour patiently cleaning and braiding the tough fibres and cutting them to the required lengths. By the time we stopped work for the day her fingers were raw and swollen. But that evening she seemed calmer and more at peace with herself than at any time since Barna's disappearance, and she fell asleep almost as soon as she lay down in her hammock.

It was the next morning, as I recall, that I became aware of a slight and subtle change in the weather. At first I thought it was simply a matter of being out on a riverbank again after three days in the forest, but then I realized that the change was not only from the forest but from Graça de Deus as well. Though the sun burned as hotly as before, it was with a less naked brilliance. The sky was as cloudless as before, yet not so blue, as if the void between were filled with a weaving invisible vapor. There was no glare of yellow dust, to be sure, and that was a welcome blessing. But the air was as heavy and lifeless as in the deepest recesses of the jungle, and no faintest wisp of breeze touched either the trees or the surface of the river.

The hours crept past in a glaze of heat, as we laboriously applied a skin of bark and fronds to the skeleton of our canoe. By mid-afternoon the job was virtually done, and we carried the craft the few yards to the water's edge and tested it for leaks. To my surprise, there were only a few minor ones, and these we succeeded in caulking with large applications of clayey mud. Later we hacked out two thwarts, four paddles and a rough back-rest for Christine. And finally, as evening came again, we sat silently on our mudbank, numb with fatigue, and stared at the crude but finished craft that lay before us on the black water.

Then the blackness spread quickly from the river to the sky, blotting out everything except the dying embers of our fire. The time of the full moon had passed. The stars were faint and remote. For a while, after the others had gone to sleep, Christine and I sat on the bank, silently watching them.

Then I said, "All right, Chris?"

She nodded.

"You still want to go on?"

"Yes."

"Cobb and I could go on, and you could—"

"No, Mark. I'm all right," she said.

Soon we too went to our hammocks. During the night I awakened once to the rumble of distant thunder.

Luiz and Garcia paddled, Amazon fashion, in the bow of the canoe. Christine sat amidships, and Cobb and I rode astern, where we alternated at paddling and steering. The leaks in the canoe were now negligible. The river's current, though slightly stronger than that of the Malaguay, was not enough to be a serious obstacle to our progress.

I was as convinced as one could be, without actually knowing, that the Tupari had headed upstream; but first we paddled over to the far bank to make wholly certain that they had not merely ferried across and entered the forest beyond. There was no evidence of a landing or of any break in the screen of trees. And after an hour of watchful cruising we pointed our prow into the current and began the slow ascent of the river.

"The river," I have called it so far. "The other river." "The blackwater river." . . . But what river *was* it? For all we knew of it, it was nameless, directionless, sourceless. Was it the stream that flowed into the Yurima at the Indian village below Graça de Deus? The stream that Joan and I had followed in the plane? . . . Was this actually, at last, the River of the Sun? . . . As I gazed out along its twisting course, dark and heavy between the jungle walls, it seemed to me that it might better be called the River of the Night.

We paddled on. Occasionally we nosed in to an open place on the shore for a meal or a snatch of rest. Then we paddled on again. Each bend in the channel was the same as the last, each new reach the same as the last—an endless unchanging vista of black water flowing down through the stillness of forest and sky. In retrospect there remains in my mind almost nothing to distinguish one hour from the next, one day from the next. Time flowed like the river, and the river like the dark tide of eternity.

The sky seemed lower now—a lid of pale glazed enamel clamped over the rim of the earth. During our first night's halt we built a rough thatch canopy for the canoe, to shield us from the sun, but the shade brought no coolness. The heat seemed no longer to come from the sun itself but to be a damp enveloping emanation of the earth and air. Trailing my hand in the river, I experienced no feeling of wetness. Our bodies were as saturated as if we had been actually swimming in the black waters that coiled around us.

There was the heat. There was the dull ache of straining muscles, the soft gurgling of the paddles. And that was all there was. We spoke infrequently and moved about in the canoe no more than was absolutely necessary. We bore on through the miles—shadows in quest of shadows on a river without a name.

During the first day we kept scanning the shores for further campsites or other signs of the Tupari's passing. But we found nothing and when evening came made our own bivouac on a desolate mudbank. Toward noon of the second day, however, Luiz, up in the bow, pointed toward the left bank, and, nosing into it, we found another jumbled pattern of blackened fires and footprints. An air of indescribable loneliness pervaded the place. And, as presently we moved on again, the stillness seemed even more oppressive, the river more disquietingly empty, than before.

Cobb, during those days, was keeping his own counsel—for which I was properly grateful. At first I had been worried that he would try to push on too quickly for the rest of us, but so far there had been no trouble on that score. In the canoe, as on the trail, he was quiet, patient, deliberate, persevering; and he was a more effective pilot, fisherman and hunter than the rest of us put together.

"Take it easy, amigo," he would tell me, in a conscious

parroting of what I had said to him in the storage shed back at Graça de Deus. "We're getting there, slow but sure."

And to Christine: "Don't fret, senhora. Don't worry. We'll be flushing out that husband of yours any minute now."

Sometimes I wondered if our journey would ever have an end. By evening of the third day we had covered some forty miles on the river, but how far in a direct line I could not even guess. The stream had become no narrower. There had been no change in the country on either side. Yet, in spite of innumerable turnings and meanderings, our course held generally to the southwest, and each day I was more certain that we were on the black river I had seen from the plane. A dozen times an hour I strained my eyes into the distance for a glimpse of hills. . . . Where *were* they? Did the river really flow through them? Had Barna and the Tupari already reached them and passed through onto the highlands beyond? . . . With a dogged effort of will I tried to close my mind to tantalizing and futile speculation. I concentrated on the next twist of the channel, the next stroke of the paddle.

Occasionally there was a slight movement in the stillness around us: a fish breaking water, a bird arrowing from the treetops, a quick glint of silver in the dark shallows near the shore, which I recognized as the mark of foraging piranhas. And occasionally, too, there were sounds. At intervals, from behind the forest wall, came the yawp of an unseen macaw or monkey. Once we passed a long belt of weeds which resounded to the deep honking of bullfrogs. And during the third night on the river I again woke to the distant intermittent rumbling of thunder.

It was now roughly the middle of November and the beginning of the rainy season was still officially almost a month away. "Never can tell, though," said Cobb, squinting up at the sky and sniffing the saturated air. "Sometimes it just goes on building up like this for weeks, and nothing happens. And sometimes, bang, it's on top of you before you know it."

As it turned out, no rain fell; but the next morning river and sky were muffled in fog, and even later in the day, when the veil lifted a little, the sun showed only as a shrunken disc in the remote depths of the sky. The shores, looming on either side of us, were no longer brilliant green, but a pale miasmic gray, and the river was as sluggish and heavy as black treacle. I was now convinced that we had penetrated the belt of mist that habitually shrouded the slopes of the Serra Aurora. But if the range was there before us, no sign or hint of it met our eyes.

We saw no hills. We saw no further campsites of the Tupari. But neither did we see any of the signs which must inevitably have been left on the riverbank if so large a party had landed and headed off again into the forest; and if anything at all was certain in that shrouded jungle-world, it was that we were still on the trail of those we sought. The premonition of their imminent appearance became so strong that Cobb and I were presently as tensely watchful as the two caboclos in the bow. At each turning of the river we paused and peered ahead before moving on into the next open reach.

But reach followed reach and turn followed turn, and when the grayness of day became the deeper grayness of evening and we made camp for the fourth night in the shelter of a small wooded promontory, it was as ringed by stillness and emptiness as any before it. Once again we slung our hammocks, built our cook-fire, ate, and lay silently in the blackness. And once again, when morning came, we squatted on the mud of the bank, downing a meagre breakfast, while the sun rose, red and malignant, behind the mists of the farther shore. When we had finished, Cobb and Garcia got into the canoe and paddled out toward the tip of our sheltering promontory, from which they would be able to see the reach beyond. Meanwhile Christine, Luiz and I unslung the hammocks, collected the equipment and guns, and stacked them at the water's edge. The only sounds were the buzzing of flies and the faint lapping of the river against the shore.

Then, quiet but distinct across the water, there came a voice. . . . Not Cobb's. Not Garcia's. . . . "Turn your canoe around, Mr. Cobb," the voice said in English.

Looking up, I saw that a second canoe had appeared from behind the screen of the promontory, a scant few yards from our own. There were four men in it, of whom three were Tupari—two in the bow and one in the stern. And between them, squatting amidships, was Touro Jackson.

27

"TURN THE CANOE around, Mr. Cobb," the Negro repeated, "and take it into shore."

Cobb had wheeled, his body tensed for action, but now he sat with his paddle frozen in his hands, eying the rifle which O Touro held across his knees. Luiz took a step toward our own guns, which were stacked at the water's edge a few yards away; but I quickly gestured to him, and he stopped. Christine had risen and was standing beside me. As we watched, Cobb and Garcia paddled in to the mudbank, and the Tupari canoe followed close behind them.

"Now get out," Touro said. "And keep away from those guns."

The two men got out, and Touro and the Indians also came up onto the shore. One of the latter, I now saw, was young Cambar, the chief's son, and in his hand he held a machete, while his two companions carried long bamboo javelins. Touro was still holding his rifle, which in his huge grasp seemed as light and inconsequential as a sliver of wood. He was wearing only sandals and a pair of ragged lopped-off trousers.

Seeing Christine and me, the Indians paused, stared, and then advanced toward us, but stopped again at a command from Touro. Then, for a long silent moment, it was the Negro's turn to stare. Whether he had not seen us at all from the canoe, or assumed that we were simply more caboclos, I don't know. But whatever the case, there was no mistaking his utter surprise as he stood motionless, confronting us.

"What are you doing here?" he asked.

"What are *you?*" I said.

"We thought you left on the plane."

"You thought wrong."

There was another silence, and then Christine spoke in a low strained voice. "Where's my husband?" she asked.

Touro didn't answer.

"Where is he?" I said. "Where's your son?"

"They are safe," he said.

"Where?"

"With the Tupari."

"How far from here?"

Again Touro didn't answer.

"Take us to them," Christine said. "Take us to my husband."

He shook his head. "No, I can't, Mrs. Barna."

"What do you mean—you can't?" I demanded.

"When Dr. Barna left Esperança," the Negro said quietly, "I promised that I wouldn't help anyone to follow him. That time I broke my word—but not again."

"Touro, please—" Christine took a half-step toward him. "After all, he doesn't know that *I'm* still here, or that I'm looking for him."

The big Negro met her eyes for only a second. An encounter with Christine Barna was obviously the last thing he had bargained for, and I could see that it was deeply upsetting not only to whatever plans he had, but to his peace of mind as well.

"We have news for him, Touro," she said. "News that will make all the difference."

"Nothing will make any difference, Mrs. Barna," he answered. "Your husband isn't coming back—for anyone or anything."

"He told you that?" I said.

"Yes."

"When you asked him to come back with you?"

"I didn't ask him to come back with me."

"Why not?"

"Because I'm not coming back either, Mr. Allison."

For a few moments the only sound was the buzzing of flies. My eyes went to Touro's rifle—to the weapons of the Tupari—then back to the Negro, standing huge and silent before us.

"What are you doing here then?" I asked him.

"We thought we might be followed," said Touro. "Since we believed that you and Mrs. Barna had gone, we assumed it could be only Mr. Cobb, with perhaps a few caboclos; and yesterday it was decided that some of us would stay behind and wait."

"To do what?"

"To tell him to go back."

"And if he wouldn't?"

"I think he would."

Up to this point Cobb had stood a little to one side, between Luiz and Garcia, watching the Negro from beneath half-closed hooded lids. But now suddenly he said, "Real king of the jungle, ain't you, Touro boy?"

"Keep quiet, Mr. Cobb," said Touro.

"Yessir, a big man with a gun—that's Touro."

"Keep quiet, Mr. Cobb."

Touro didn't raise his voice. It was still low and even. But it had a new note in it—of tautness, of threat—that had been lacking before. Even the three Indians, ranged beside him, were obviously conscious of the change, for, whereas, until now, they had simply stood by, waiting, with wooden faces, their eyes now became fixed on Cobb, black and hate-filled, and Cambar took a step forward. The sun's rays glinted on the steel of his long machete and on the red streaks of achiote paint on his cheeks and forehead.

Cobb hawked and spat with insolent deliberation. But he didn't speak again. Luiz and Garcia stared at the Tupari like two rabbits at a poised snake.

Keep talking, I thought. Keep control. . . .

"And now that it isn't only Cobb that's following you," I said to Touro "—what are you going to do now?"

The Negro's eyes returned to me slowly. "I must tell you all to go back, Mr. Allison," he said.

I shook my head. "We're not going, Touro."

He wet his lips. His glance went from me to Christine and from Christine to the Indians. I could see that he was no less uncertain than the rest of us as to when they might suddenly decide to handle things in their own way.

"Listen, Touro," I said. "You can't make us go back now, and you know it. We're not trying to interfere with you, or these Indians either. You can do anything you want, go anywhere you want. But first you're going to take us to Barna."

Touro said nothing. The knuckles of his hand were grayish-white against the black steel of his gun.

"Tell the Tupari to get in their canoe," I said. "Tell them we're going upstream with them."

Christine put her hand on his arm. "Please, Touro," she begged. "I know how you feel, after all that's happened. I know you hate us, and I don't blame you—"

"I don't hate you, Mrs. Barna. But I'm not coming back with you—and neither is your husband."

"Yes, he's coming back. And so are you, Touro." Her eyes were fixed on his in quiet pleading desperation. "You have to—don't you see that? You as much as he. You can't run away from the world, any more than he can. Because you're part of the world. Because you're not a savage, but a civilized man."

"I *was* a civilized man," he said. "I'm through being a civilized man."

"And you think you can turn yourself into a jungle Indian?"

"No, not an Indian. I'll still be a black man. But at least I won't be ashamed and afraid because I'm black."

I thought of the boy Tourinho. "What about your son?" I put in. "What will he be? Have you thought of him?"

"I've thought of him most of all," said Touro.

"And you want him to grow up as a savage in the jungle?"

"Better in this jungle than in that other."

"No, Touro," I said, "you can't do that to him. He has a life of his own; rights of his own—"

"Yes, the right to be a nigger in a white man's world."

There was another silence. Christine started to speak again—and stopped. No one moved.

Then Cobb moved . . . .

One moment he was standing motionless, like all the rest of us, and in the next he was lunging toward where our guns were stacked at the water's edge. Touro was turning, and the Indians were turning, and one of the Indians was drawing back his arm. Then a javelin sped through the air, there was a single hoarse cry, and Cobb sprawled in the mud.

What followed was like the wild flickering of a nightmare. Pushing Christine behind me, I jumped forward; but before I had taken two steps the Tupari had wheeled again and were facing me. Touro called out to them, but they paid no attention. Then they charged us—Cambar with his machete in the center, his companions and their javelins on either side. I shouted to Christine to run. I looked about for a stick, a stone, anything I could use as a weapon. But there was nothing, and in the next instant I, too, was running. I was stumbling, falling, picking myself up, turning and facing the swift silent rush of the Tupari. I saw a brown arm drawing back again. I saw the javelin hang poised. . . .

But this time the javelin never left the arm. A great black hand reached out, snatched at it, wrenched it. A great black shape flashed in front of me, and there was Touro charging like a bull into the Tupari, his body plunging and twisting, his gun-butt flailing. For a moment they were all tangled together. Another javelin was drawn back—thrust forward—but apparently it missed its mark, for Touro remained upright. Yelling at Luiz and Garcia, I made a break for our guns. Even as I started, though, I saw that one of the Indians—Cambar—had broken away from Touro and was coming on again; not at me, this time, but at Christine, who had stopped and was standing near the forest's edge, perhaps ten yards away. There was just time to turn and fling myself upon him from the rear. I grasped the arm that held the upraised machete, pulled back on it, struggled to hold it—and lost my grip. I saw the steel go up again, flashing, and beyond the flash the face of Christine. . . .

And then there was only Christine. The raised arm was gone. The bright steel was gone. There was a single dry sharp sound, like the crack of a limb, and Cambar's body jerked, swayed and fell. Swinging about, I saw Touro standing a few yards off, his rifle still raised and the smoke drifting from its muzzle. Beyond him, Luiz and Garcia had reached the other guns and, even as I looked, began firing at the two other Indians. But these had already turned and were running swiftly along the mudbank; and in another moment they had disappeared into the forest.

Now, with incredible suddenness, the flickering and flashing stopped. Where nightmare had been there was utter stillness. In the stillness Touro took a few slow steps forward and stood looking down at the naked painted body that lay sprawled in the mud. He didn't stoop to examine the body. There was no need to. He simply stood there beside Cambar, and then at last he raised his eyes and looked at me.

"Satisfied, Mr. Allison?" he asked quietly.

I didn't answer. I was staring at the great bare chest and torso that was now turned toward me—and at the broad red stain that glinted darkly against the smooth blackness of the flesh. At the same instant Christine, standing beside me, took a quick step toward him. "You're wounded, Touro," she said. "You're hurt—"

The Negro looked down at her. He was standing very tall and straight, but his eyes were clouded, and when he

391

spoke his voice was low and muffled. "Yes—hurt," he repeated. "The savage is dead and the civilized man is hurt." His lips parted in a slow smile. "You were right, you see, Mrs. Barna," he added. "I'm a civilized man after all."

Suddenly and horribly, he began to laugh. The laugh became a deep convulsive tremor. His lips tightened and his teeth locked together. "Help him, Mark. Spread out a hammock," Christine told me. "I'll get the bandages and—"

Before she had finished she was running toward the pile of equipment at the water's edge. Going to Touro, I braced my shoulder under his armpit and tried to support him, and in an instant my shirt and forearm were crimson with his blood. But he wouldn't let me hold him. Quietly but powerfully he released himself and turned away. He turned and stood motionless again, staring out past me toward the river, and, following his gaze, I saw that what he was staring at was Mordecai Cobb.

I had forgotten about Cobb; for all I knew he might have been as dead as Cambar. But now I saw that he was half sitting, half crouching at the spot where the Indian's javelin had brought him down, and one of his hands was clasped over a red stain on the right shoulder of his pajama top. The two caboclos, Luiz and Garcia, were standing nearby staring down at him, as if uncertain what to do.

Cobb raised his eyes and looked at Touro. And Touro stood looking back at him.

"Satisfied, Mr. Cobb?" he asked.

Cobb didn't answer. Again an absolute silence lay over the narrow strip of riverbank, and through the silence Touro moved forward. He still held his head high and his body erect, but his feet moved very slowly, without leaving the ground.

"Touro!" I called sharply. But he paid no attention.

Christine came back with bandages and a medical kit and ran quickly to his side. But he pushed her gently away as if she had been a child blocking his path.

"Touro!" I said. "Put down that gun!"

This time he stopped. He glanced down at the rifle in his hand, as if in surprise that it was still there. But then he shook his head. "No, Mr. Allison," he said. "Mr. Cobb and I have some unfinished business to take care of, and if I put it down I'm afraid you might interfere."

He moved forward again. I stepped toward him and found myself looking into the bore of the rifle. "I am serious, Mr. Allison," he said quietly. "I don't want to harm you, but I will if I have to."

I stood still. Christine and the caboclos stood still. Cobb, crouched on the mudbank, was as motionless as if hypnotized, staring up at the Negro with pale slitted eyes.

"Don't be afraid of the gun," Touro said to him. "I'm not going to shoot you. I don't need a gun for you, Mr. Cobb—any more than I did for Mr. Spendrow."

He took another step forward.

"You know why I killed Mr. Spendrow, don't you, Mr. Cobb?" he asked. "I killed him because I hated him. But I didn't kill the Indian Cambar because I hated him, Mr. Cobb. I killed him because you made me kill him."

Another step. Another pause. And now, when Touro spoke again, it was softly and rhythmically—almost in a singsong. "Do you know why I killed him?" he said. "I killed him because I am civilized. Cambar was a savage, but I am civilized, God help me; and when the test came I was not on his side, but on yours. . . ."

The words ran together, blurred, stopped. His whole body was seized by a retching spasm, and for the first time he put a hand to the gaping bloodiness of his wound. He pressed back against the life that was flowing out of him. He braced his legs wide against the earth. Then with a shuddering effort he moved forward again. His eyes gleamed, fixed and white-rimmed, in the black mask of his face.

He was now very close to Cobb. His arm stretched out toward him, and suddenly Cobb began to shuttle away sidewise, like a crab. "No, don't run away," said Touro, almost gently. "Don't hide. . . . I can still find you, Mr. Cobb, wherever you hide. I can still see you, because your face is so white."

His hand opened and his gun fell to the ground. Both arms were out now—groping. The great body lurched forward, caught itself, stopped, drew erect again. For another instant it stood poised and terrible, no longer moving but rooted like a tree to the earth. Then it shuddered—swayed—and toppled broken to the mud of the riverbank.

Christine and I ran forward. She pillowed Touro's head on her lap. Together we pressed the bandages down against the thick red stream that welled up over the black flesh. Once, for an instant, his eyes opened, the whites shone faintly, and then the lids closed over them again. His breath rasped, faded, fluttered. His lips moved a little, and bending close, I could hear, deep behind them, the faint sound of his voice. "Tereza, little wife—" he whispered. "Tourinho, little son. . . ."

I spoke his name, but he didn't hear me.

"Little son—" the whisper came again.

Christine was fumbling for something in the medical kit, but by the time she had it out there was nothing to do with it except put it back again.

The sun slowly climbed the sky above the black river. The pium flies buzzed. A bird cawed and was silent. The wilderness around us lay in a glaze of sodden heat.

I had covered the two bodies with fronds from a nearby malanga shrub and posted Luiz and Garcia as guards against the possible, though unlikely, reappearance of the two escaped Tupari. And now I turned my attention to Cobb. The Indian's javelin had struck him in the back of the right shoulder, and though the wound was deep and obviously painful, it didn't seem likely that it would prove serious—unless, of course, infection set in. Even after I covered Touro's body Christine had remained sitting beside it, as motionless as if stunned; but now she arose and joined me, and together we cleaned and bandaged the wound as best

394

we could. Once Cobb started to speak to us, but I cut him off before the words were out of his mouth.

"Keep quiet," I ordered him.

"I was only going to say—"

"You're not going to say anything."

He didn't try to speak again. Christine and I didn't speak. When we had finished with the bandaging Christine walked slowly across the bank to the edge of the forest and sat down on a patch of moss among the trees. Presently Cobb, too, got up and moved off into the shade. Luiz and Garcia squatted with their guns at either end of the open bank.

I went to where Touro lay under his shield of fronds, lifted it, and looked down at him. His face was so thickly covered with ants that the black flesh itself appeared to be crawling over the bones beneath; and another dark tide flowed like a river across the red rent in his chest. The maggots had not yet appeared. Nor had the stench begun. But neither would be long in coming. Even now, lying in the fetid mud, the thing before me seemed less the body of a man just dead than a nameless featureless cadaver.

My eyes went along the mudbank; then to our pile of equipment which still lay on the shore. There was no pick, no shovel, no digging tool of any kind. Beyond the shore the river flowed by, black and viscous. I gestured to the caboclos to come and help me.

First we picked up Touro, half-carried and half-dragged him to the water's edge, and laid him in our canoe. Then we went back and did the same with Cambar. Covering them again with the malanga fronds, we clambered in ourselves, pushed off, and, with Luiz and Garcia in the bow and myself astern, paddled out toward midstream. As I was about to give the order to stop, I realized that we had nothing with which to weight the bodies. But in the same instant a sharp silver glinting in the dark water told me that nothing was necessary. There was a moment then, I think, in which I hesitated; but only a moment. . . . It was terrible. . . . But it was quick.

I gave the order to stop.

We hoisted Touro's body to the gunwale.

"What does one say for a Catholic?" I asked the caboclos. But they only stared at me dully.

"Our Father Who art in Heaven—" I said.

We let Touro go.

Then we hoisted up Cambar's body, and I noticed how much lighter it was.

"Hallowed be Thy name—" I said.

We let Cambar go.

And now we were paddling across the black waters, back to the shore. Away from the floating bodies and the floating malanga fronds. Away from the bodies that were no longer floating but being pulled down into the water by an incalculable force from below. Away from the silver churning and red foaming that suddenly stirred a small patch of the river into a frenzy and then slowly subsided again into the smoothness of its opaque tide.

Morning had passed into midday, and midday into afternoon; but the two canoes still rested motionless on the slope of mud. Cobb and the two caboclos, stretched on the ground nearby, seemed to have fallen asleep. Christine was sitting, as before, on a patch of moss at the forest's edge.

I brewed a pot of maté and brought her a cupful, and she sat sipping it slowly, holding the cup in both hands.

"I'll get some supper ready," she said.

"No, rest," I told her. "I'll get it."

But instead of going I sat down beside her. For a while we were silent, and then she said, "Will we stay here tonight, Mark?"

"I suppose it's best to."

"And then—"

"Then in the morning we'll get an early start."

"You mean—go back?"

I nodded.

Through the long hours of that day I had struggled to

find an alternative. But there was no alternative. Luiz and Garcia, I knew, would as soon throw themselves bodily to the piranhas as to go on another yard. As for Cobb—he obviously couldn't go on. And if he could, I wouldn't have let him; for if there was one thing I was sure of, it was that I wasn't going on again—anywhere, ever—with Mordecai Cobb.

Christine had set down her cup, and I put my hand lightly over hers; but it lay slack and unmoving under my touch. She seemed drained of strength, of blood—even of tears. Her eyes, as she sat staring now out at the river, were dry and dull. Her voice, when she spoke again, was low and toneless.

"It's been our fault, Mark," she said.

"Don't, Chris—you mustn't think that."

"It's the truth."

"We couldn't help the way things worked out. We couldn't forsee it."

"Yes, we could have. We should have. . . . Because this is the way it's been—almost—from the very beginning. Touro was happy before we came. The people at Esperança were happy. The Indians were happy. Even Nils, I think, was happy, in his own strange way. . . . All we've brought with us is unhappiness. All we've brought with us is—death."

"Chris, stop—" I said.

But after a moment she went on again, her voice now no more than a whisper: "Maybe it's best we can't go on, Mark. Better this way. Better for Nils." She turned her face away from me. "Oh God, I've wanted so much to help him. And instead—"

"He'll be all right, Chris. He knows the jungle, and the Tupari worship him. Then in a couple of months, when the ship comes—" I stopped, hearing the old familiar echo.

Yes, of course: *when the ship comes.* . . .

But Christine had obviously not been listening. Her eyes were closed. She seemed suddenly almost asleep. Throughout that long bitter journey—through forest and river, through doubt and fear—she had kept her strength and hope

397

alive. But now at last, I realized, they were gone—extinguished by the horror of this day just past. Even if the others would, and could, have gone on, she, Christine, could not. . . .

So that was it. In the morning we would go back. There was nowhere to go but back.

A while later Luiz and Garcia began to stir. We opened a few tins, built a fire, and the five of us sat together around the orange glow. Cobb's wounded shoulder had stiffened and he was apparently in considerable pain; but he didn't complain, nor indeed speak at all. Christine ate a few mouthfuls and went back to her place at the forest's edge. After the caboclos and I had slung the hammocks I went over to her and said, "Try to sleep now," and without a word she arose, went to her hammock and lay down under the netting. Soon the others followed suit. The fire sank to embers and the embers went out. Night closed in, black and heavy.

And now, far into the night, I sat alone on the riverbank. A monstrous weight of tiredness lay upon me, but I couldn't sleep. I stared out at the dark flowing water, and presently it seemed to me that, deep beneath it, I could see two sunken shapes, round and gleaming white. As white as the skull of the ringtailed monkey in the pool at Graça de Deus. . . .

Getting up, I crossed to the trees where the hammocks were slung. Cobb and the caboclos were asleep. Christine was asleep. As I stood beside her she stirred slightly, her hand reached up in a vague groping gesture, and her lips moved. But she didn't awaken, and after a moment she lay still.

I went back to the shore. I sat again watching the black water. And that was all there was now: black water—and, above it, mist. The rest was gone. The hope that had dreamed it, the strength that had struggled for it, the illusion that had lighted it—they were all gone—as lost and irretrievable as that quick vision of splendor seen once from a plane through a rent in the clouds. It was no River of Oil by which I sat. It was not the River of Quest, the River of Fulfillment, the River of the Sun. It was the River of Night, of Defeat, of Emptiness, of Nothingness, and at its source was not El Dorado, but only more nothingness, more darkness. At its source was a jungle of darkness and, deep within it, a receding shadow. . . .

I dozed and wakened again. The river and the darkness were the same, but the mist had lifted. And looking up, I saw the hills.

28

THEY WERE NO more than a rim of blackness against the softer starlit blackness of the sky. But they were no illusion. They were there. As nearly as I could judge, the nearest ridges were perhaps five miles away, but how much closer the base was I couldn't tell, for the trees of the promontory hid the lower slopes.

A charge of life—almost of excitement—flowed through the numbness of my body and brain. Here it was at last: the goal long sought and long despaired of. Or, if not the goal itself, at least the clue to it—the key to the riddle. Did the river flow out of the hills? Did it flow *through* them? That had been the prime question through all the past months of speculation, search and struggle; and now the answer was at hand, at almost the instant of our turning back. Touro was dead, and we could not bring him back to life. Nils Barna was gone, and now we could not bring him back either. But this much, at least, might be salvaged from the wreck. This at least might give a shred of meaning to the long idiot's tale of frustration and defeat.

It was a little past five by my watch. By five-thirty it would begin to grow light and the hills would be at their clearest. Then, by six, it would be full day; the mist would close in and they would be gone. I looked out at the point of the bend that shut off the up-river view. It would take no more than a few minutes to paddle out past the point, see the base of the hills, and return. There was no stirring at the forest's edge, where the others lay in their hammocks. Quickly I stepped into one of the canoes and pushed off.

The black waters glided past. The black shore glided past. I counted fifty strokes of the paddle—then a second fifty—and when I looked ahead again I saw that the tip of the bend was much nearer. Also, it appeared even blacker than before, and then I realized that this was because the sky above it was paling. Off beyond the treetops the crest of the hills seemed to be moving slowly and majestically into focus.

Another fifty strokes. Another. A final fifty. The point was very close now. I was abreast of it, swinging round it, beyond it. Ahead of me now was gray dawnlight, the next reach of the river, the base of the hills. . . .

And, beside me, three canoes filled with Tupari.

One of the canoes nudged against my own. I rose, grappled, fell. Water sloshed in over the gunwale, and something crashed against the back of my skull.

There was darkness, and, through the darkness, white darts of pain. Then the darkness faded; beyond the pain was thin twilight; and I realized that my eyes were open.

I was lying on my back in the bottom of a canoe. I was not bound, but one Indian was squatting at my head and a second at my feet, both with machetes. In the bow and astern were four others, paddling. Raising my head a little, I could see the other canoes on either side of us, and beyond them the gliding shores. It was now full daylight, but there was no sun. Above the treetops there were only gray banks of mist.

There was the pain again, stabbing and blinding. I lay with eyes closed until it receded slightly, but then, suddenly, in its place, was a thing deeper and sharper than pain. For the first time I realized clearly what had happened—and what the consequences might be.

From that moment on I lay in an agony of apprehension and self-accusation. Not over what I had brought upon myself. The hell with that. But over what I had brought upon Christine. . . . I looked at my watch, and it was almost seven. She would be awake by now. She and Cobb and the two caboclos would be standing on the mudbank, staring incredulously at the keel-marks of the missing canoe. . . . And then what? Would they too head upstream? No, that was impossible. Cobb couldn't. Luiz and Garcia wouldn't. . . . What then? They would wait. They were waiting now. . . .

For a wild instant I considered trying to leap from the canoe. No—steady, I thought. Getting myself killed wouldn't do anyone any good. . . . Then what *could* I do? . . . Suddenly I thought of Barna. Yes, of course: Barna was the answer. That's where I was being taken—to Barna. And he couldn't leave Christine abandoned on a jungle mudbank, any more than could I.

(Except, of course, that I had. . . .)

Raising my head again, I spoke to the Tupari. "Barna?" I said. "Dr. Barna?"

There was no answer.

I pointed up-river. "Barnanda?"

Still no answer. The Indian squatting at my head prodded my chest with his machete.

Barna *had* to be up ahead, I told myself. And it couldn't be far. Very soon now I would be seeing him—speaking with him. In an hour we would be on our way back downstream to the mudbank.

I looked ahead, but there was only black water and mist. The hills were gone. Even the forest walls were barely visible. The mist flowed in out of gray distance and seemed to mingle with the throbbing ache in my head. I lay back and closed my eyes again. . . . and the next thing I was aware of was the canoe's scraping against the shore.

It was another clearing. The Tupari's clearing. Rows of dark faces stared down at me from the bank. My two guards pulled me to my feet and out of the canoe, and for a moment I thought my knees would buckle—but they didn't. We came up onto the bank, and I looked for Barna, but didn't see him. There were only the brown watching faces—the motionless figures—and then, moving swiftly out from among them, a single small figure; and I found myself looking down at a young Indian boy: naked, dark-skinned, with daubs of red achiote paint on his face, arms and chest. Except. . . . (he was close beside me now) . . . . except that it wasn't an Indian boy. It was Tourinho Jackson.

"Senhor Marco—it is you, yes—you have come—"

I had stopped, and now he seized my hand.

"It is not true, is it, senhor? You will tell me—it is not true about my father?"

"Yes, it's true, Tourinho," I said.

"No, no—it is not—it cannot be. My father he was too strong, too great, too—" The words stumbled over one another. Tears filled his eyes. Then suddenly his small hand was gripping mine fiercely. "Who has done it?" he demanded. "You will tell me. Who has done it?"

"It was an accident, Tourinho."

"No, it was not an accident. You will tell me who it was, and I will kill him. I am big and strong, like my father. I will kill—kill for him—"

The tears swelled into sobs. He clung to me. Then the Indians pulled him away, and I was prodded from behind by a machete. I was led across the bank, along a rough trail through the forest, to a small clearing, where stood a single crude hut. My captors pushed me into the hut, and two of them, with javelins, mounted guard outside.

All movement stopped. Time stopped. . . .

My prison was absolutely bare: a mere circle of thatch walls and a roof of malanga leaves. There was one narrow doorless opening. I sat on the earthen floor, facing the opening, and waited. But nothing happened. No one came. For the first time since I had been brought ashore I was conscious of the ache in my head, and, putting my hand to it, I felt a large swelling and clotted blood. I pulled my handkerchief from a pocket and dabbed at it. Then I felt in my other pockets, looking for I don't know what. But there was only a crumbled pack of cigarettes, some matches, and a stub of pencil. And in an oilskin case, my few maps—and Jakob Koppel's letter.

I went to the doorway and peered out at my guards. "Barna?" I said. "Barnanda?"

They didn't answer.

Then I called out at the top of my voice: "Barna! Barna!"

But there was no answer to that, either.

I looked at my watch. Ten-thirty. And again panic ran through me, sharp and wild. I had to get out of there. No matter what, I had to get back to Christine. . . . My eyes returned to the doorway. Beyond it were the two Tupari, the cleared space, and then the forest. The nearest trees were no more than fifteen yards away, and a sudden dash would probably bring me to their shelter before the Indians realized what was happening. . . . But when then? Where then? . . . I would have even less chance of getting away than if I had leapt from the canoe into the river.

Sitting down again, I tried to visualize what was happening beyond the dim confines of my prison. Where was Barna? Where was the chief Pombal? What were they waiting for?

An hour passed, and still no one came. Occasionally I could hear the sound of voices or footsteps outside, but when I peered through the woven wall all I could see were the two guards. I tried speaking to them again, but again with no result; and once I took a tentative step from the doorway, only to be confronted by two raised javelins. Back inside, I sat down with my back to the wall. My head ached. My bones ached. Presently I closed my eyes. And when I opened them again a figure was standing above me.

I stood up and faced Nils Barna.

"Well, Allison—" he said.

In the moment of wakening he had been no more than a blur. But now he was plain to me—and in no way different from when I had last seen him back in Graça de Deus. The faded khaki of his clothing was the same. The thin pale face was the same; the thatch of reddish hair; the cool eyes behind the lenses of his glasses. . . .

"Where have you been?" I demanded. "What have you been doing?"

"To be quite honest about it," he said, "I have been saving your life."

"Then the Tupari—"

"Yes, the Tupari wanted to kill you. Under the circumstances I cannot say I greatly blame them. But I have pointed out that it would serve no purpose, and I believe I have dissuaded them." I started to speak, but he stopped me. "There is no need to thank me," he added. "Both their and my considerations were purely practical."

A current of excitement ran through me. "We can go, then?" I said.

"Go?"

"Back downstream. To Christine. To Graça de Deus."

Barna shook his head slowly. "No," he said, "I am afraid there is no possibility of that."

I stared at him. "What do you mean?"

"I mean that the Tupari would not let us. That we shall have to remain with them."

"But—"

"And I also mean," he went on quietly, "that I did not even suggest such a thought to them. I have never considered going back."

"But good God, man—Christine. Your wife. You know what's happened—and where she is. A few miles downriver on a mudbank. Waiting there—helpless—"

"I have thought of my wife, Allison. With Mr. Cobb and two caboclos, I scarcely think she will be helpless. And also—"

Anger flared up in me. "Also, you don't give a damn, is that it? She gives up everything for you, comes five thousand miles, follows you through jungles—and you don't give a damn." Barna started to speak, but this time it was I who shut *him* off. "All right, she means nothing to you. . . .

Here—" I was fumbling in my pocket. "Maybe this will mean something—"

I brought out my map-fold and took Koppel's letter from it. "It's for you," I said. "Read it."

I held it out to him, and Barna looked at me for a moment and then took it. He turned the envelope slowly in his hands. Then he opened it. He read the first page, then the second, and then stood staring at the bottom of the second, where was written *Jakob Koppel.* In my life I have seen men undergo quick and terrible changes. I have seen them laughing one instant, weeping the next; alive one instant, dead the next. But I have never seen anything more terrible than the change that took place in Nils Barna from the moment he looked down at that letter to the moment he looked up from it. It was as if the naked essence of the man had stepped out from behind a screen. His face had been pale before, but now it was deathly white. His eyes had been pale, but now they were dark and deep. The hand holding the letter was trembling—his whole body was trembling—and his lips were twitching, but no sound came from them. . . .

Then, with a supreme effort, he held himself still.

"Where did you get this?" he asked.

His voice was toneless.

"It was brought up on the plane from Esperança," I said.

"Have you seen this man?"

"No. But—"

"But he is here," said Barna. "He is coming. . . ." He was no longer looking at me, but at the wall behind me. And beyond the wall, at time and distance. . . . "Jakob—Jakob—" he murmured, as if the name were wrenched up out of the core of his body.

I took a step toward him. "Barna!" I said. "Barna—what is it? . . . He's alive, do you understand? Alive and all right."

Barna's eyes returned to my face. A long moment passed before he spoke again. Then he said, slowly and quietly, "Yes—alive. He is alive. That is very interesting, is it not, Allison? I killed Jakob Koppel, but he is alive. . . ."

He was silent. In the dim light his face seemed less that of a man than of a ghost. He looked down at the letter he held, opened his hand, and let it fall to the ground. Then he turned toward the doorway.

"Barna!" I said.

But he didn't stop.

"Barna—wait!" I took a quick step after him, grasped his arm, swung him around. "For God's sake, what is it? What are you doing?"

"I am going—with your permission."

"Going? Where?"

"Does it matter?" he asked.

"You're damn right it matters." My astonishment and confusion were gone. Hot anger seized me again, and I was holding him with both hands—almost shaking him. "You're going—yes. But we're *both* going. Now—do you understand? Down-river. . . ."

Barna stood quietly in my grasp. "If you will please let me go—" he said.

"No," I told him. And then, suddenly, there was desperation—almost pleading—in my voice. "Listen to me, Barna. I don't know what happened between you and this Koppel. I don't know what's happened between you and your wife. But one thing I do know: you can't go on like this. . . . Jesus Christ, man, what are you doing with your life? What are you hiding from—running from? From your wife? Your friend? From being a human being?"

"In a world of fugitives, Allison, a man taking the opposite direction will seem to be running away."

"The opposite direction. . . . But which direction? Toward what? . . . You've hidden yourself up these rivers. Now you've gone off with these Indians. Why? Because you can't stand being a human being—is that it? Because you want to play God, and they're the only ones who'll let you? All right, it's a world of fugitives. It's a jungle-world. God knows I've learned that. But it's the only world we've got, Barna. We've got to face it—live in it. . . ."

Now it was I who was almost trembling. Sweat covered my body. And still I talked on—arguing, pleading—scarcely conscious of my words, or of myself, but only of the tall stooped man before me; only of the eyes watching me; only that I was struggling, face to face, hand to hand, with the hidden core of a man's soul.

For an instant it almost seemed as if I was winning. I released Barna, but he didn't move. I paused, but he didn't speak.

"We're going," I said. "You and I together. Your friend's alive—waiting for you. Your wife's waiting for you. You're going back to them, Barna. Back to the world—to life. . . ."

I stopped. I waited. . . . And then I saw that I had *not* won. . . . Suddenly it was no longer a man who stood before me, but an image—a shadow. Where the soul of Nils Barna had been was an opaque impenetrable wall. Where the darkening deepening eyes had been were two cold discs of glass.

"Have you finished, Allison?" he asked quietly.

"What I've told you is the truth," I said, "and you know it. It's your one hope, man—to go back."

Barna regarded me for a moment without speaking. No trace remained of the terrible emotion that had shaken him a few short moments before.

"Yes," he said, "what you have told me is the truth. One truth. But there happens also to be a second, which you do not seem to understand: that I am not interested in your 'one hope'—or any other."

I made a last try. "Look, Barna—I owe you my life, and I know it. But that doesn't mean I'm going to let you turn around and throw both our lives away."

"I see. And what do you propose to do?"

"Will you come with me?"

"No."

"Not for your wife?"

"No."

"Not for your friend?"

"No."

"All right then—the hell with you!"

I crossed to the doorway . . . and faced the raised javelins of the two guards. When I turned back into the hut Barna was smiling a little.

"Yes, there are certain difficulties," he said. "I am afraid that our conversation has been purely theoretical."

"Tell them to let me go."

Barna shook his head. "No, I cannot do that."

"They'll obey you."

"Perhaps. But still I cannot."

"Why not?"

"Because it has been agreed that you will stay."

"Agreed? By whom?"

"By the Tupari and myself," said Barna. "As I told you, they at first wanted to kill you. When I spoke to them, they reconsidered; but, as I told you too, for a practical reason."

"Why should they want me to stay? What do they want of me?"

"They want you as a hostage, Mr. Allison."

I stared at him.

"A hostage—?"

"Yes," said Barna quietly. "I pointed out to them that killing you would be simply useless revenge—and on the wrong person at that. What the Tupari are most concerned about is escape from the white man. They do not want to be followed again. And, with you in their custody, they will not be followed."

"What sense does that make? If no one knows—"

"They will know. Perhaps they already know. Luckily there was someone here whom the Tupari *did* want to send back, and an hour ago the boy Tourinho was put into a canoe and dispatched downstream. He will joint the others; go back with them to Graça de Deus. And he will tell them that, if they value your life, they will not come after us."

There was a silence in the hut. A long shred of mist

drifted slowly in through the entrance and hung like a white ectoplasm in the stale gray air.

"So you see," said Barna "—we shall be going on. Both of us."

"Going on where? To what?"

"To the River of the Sun. *Your* River of the Sun". . . . He was half smiling again. . . . "After all, that should not distress you too much: to go on toward your goal. That is why you are here. Why you followed me."

"I followed you to—"

"Yes, I know—to bring me back. That may have been a secondary motive; but unsuccessful, I am afraid—and already in the past. That is a strange and salutary thing about the forest: it strips away the non-essential. It brings one back to original motives. To first causes. . . ."

"Barna, listen—for God's sake think what you're—"

But he went on speaking: a quiet, all-but-disembodied voice in the dim light of the hut. "Well," he said, "it will be interesting to see where our various motives and causes bring us. Will it be the Tupari's lost tribe that we find? Your oil? My sanctuary? . . . Or will it, perhaps, be only our friend Preisinger, up a tree?"

He paused and looked upward, and in the stillness I could hear a soft pattering on the thatch of the roof. "You should be pleased, Allison," he said. "The rains you have waited so long for are coming at last."

29

THE NEXT MORNING the guards were gone from in front of the hut. A bowl of food and another of water had been placed in the doorway. When I had eaten and drunk I stepped outside.

Following a rough path, I came to a second, much larger clearing, that was obviously the center of the Tupari encampment. There were a few makeshift shelters, slung hammocks, a circle of cook-fires, and, moving about among them, a number of Indians, mostly women and children. The far side of the clearing fronted on the river, and I moved on until I stood on the bank. The air was heavy with mist, and I couldn't make out the river's course, either above or below me. But, a little way upstream, I could see the outline of a wooded hill, slanting away into gray distance.

Close by, pulled high up on the bank, were perhaps twenty canoes, guarded by armed Tupari. They paid no attention to me as I moved past; nor did the other Indians who were moving about in the clearing when I retraced my steps across it. I was free. Free to drown in the river, starve in the forest—or stay where I was.

The hours passed. I sat alone at the edge of the clearing, watching the Tupari come and go. Apparently they were busy replenishing their supplies for the journey ahead; for most of the men were off in the forest, hunting, and the women and children were collecting shoots and berries in the nearby brush. From these activities and what I could judge from the white-flecked water, I gathered that the river above this point was too swift for canoeing, and that the next stage of the journey would be overland.

Once, the old chief Pombal appeared, and I went over and spoke to him. His one eye fixed on me for a moment, dark and unwavering; but he moved on without answering.

Of Barna I saw no sign at all.

Toward evening it rained again. Returning to my hut, I found another bowl of food in the doorway. I ate; then sat alone in the gathering darkness.

For the hundredth time that day I thought of Christine. Of Cobb and the caboclos. Some thirty-six hours had now passed since I had paddled off from that lonely mudbank, and they were as lost to me as if they had vanished into another world. I tried to imagine how they had spent those hours. Christine would have wanted to come after me, but the others were unable or unwilling. If by some miracle she and Cobb had persuaded the caboclos to paddle them, they would long since have come this far and, like myself, been captured by the Tupari.

No, they had waited. And then—then Tourinho had appeared. The boy had come and told them what had happened and what the Indians had told him to say. (Or was it what Barna had told him to say?) Anyhow, they knew now. Christine knew. There had been nothing for them to do except turn back down the river. . . . How far had they got, I wondered. . . . The trip downstream would be quick and easy, and they might already have reached the entrance of the forest trail. Wounded or not, Cobb would still know the way. Terrified or not, the caboclos would still have their strength. Yes, I comforted myself— they'd make it back all right. Christine would be all right. . . .

Well, at least she'd be alive.

I sat alone in the hut, waiting. . . . For what? . . . The letter from Jakob Koppel still lay on the earthen floor where Barna had dropped it, and presently I picked it up and looked again at the angular, all-but-indecipherable script.

There was one thing I could read, though. . . . *Jakob Koppel.* . . . There it was: plain and clear.

There was a voice, too, that was plain and clear. . . . *That is very interesting, is it not, Allison? I killed Jakob Koppel, but he is alive.*

I got up, left the hut and followed the path to the main clearing. It was almost night now, and the encampment glowed with the light of many fires. One of the fires, larger than the others, was in the center of the clearing, and around it sat a group of men. In the circle of dark faces there was one white face.

"Barna!" I called.

There was no answer.

I approached closer. "Barna!"

He still gave no indication of hearing, but two of the Indians arose and came toward me, and one of them indicated by a gesture that I should go away.

"Barna," I said again. "Barnanda—"

But they shook their heads. And when I still didn't go, they moved up on either side of me and led me back to my hut.

The next day, at dawn, we broke camp.

I was summoned to the big clearing, given a rolled hammock and a sack of food, and told where I should wait while the final preparations were being made. Within an hour they were finished. The scattered groups of Indians became a column, and we started off along the riverbank.

First in the line of march was an advance guard of younger tribesmen, some armed with machetes for trail-clearing and some with javelins for protection against possible attack. Then came what I suppose could be called "headquarters," consisting of Barna, Pombal and several of the tribal elders. Behind them the rest of the tribe was strung out in more or less haphazard fashion: women with enormous loads supported by straps over their foreheads; children with loads varying according to their sizes; men with both loads and

413

weapons; a few, very old or very young, with nothing at all. Finally there was another group of men, with javelins, bringing up the rear, and it was among these that I was placed. I was well aware it was no accident that I was almost at the other end of the column from Nils Barna.

How long a journey was anticipated was impossible to tell. On my flight over the Serra Aurora two years before I had estimated that the distance across the hills to the open plateau was perhaps twenty miles; but that had been straight on through the air, and it was hard even to guess how much greater it might be along the course of a twisting river. Then, too, the plateau might not even be the Indians' objective. It was not, after all, a specific place that they were seeking, but the "lost" branch of their tribe; and this, of course, might be anywhere, or nowhere, in the wilderness ahead. On that first morning of our march the future was as shrouded as the hills themselves, rising before us into gray veils of mist.

As it developed, we were able to follow the river for less than a mile. Once the hills began, its banks rose precipitously into bluffs, and the tangled growth along their margins made progress almost impossible. Accordingly, we bore away from the bank, to the south, with the intention, I assumed, of cutting back to the river later on, and meanwhile finding somewhat easier going on higher ground. There was, however, no quick change in terrain. After a rise of a few hundred feet during the first hour, the ground leveled off, and for the rest of the day we moved on through typical low-lying rain-forest, almost indistinguishable from that which surrounded Graça de Deus.

After many days on the open river and riverbanks the forest seemed to press in with almost suffocating closeness. We moved through depth beyond depth, through shadow within shadow. Once, toward midafternoon, we heard the pelting of rain on the treetops high above us, but scarcely a drop penetrated down through the thick tiers of greenery. And when darkness came, and we stopped and slung our hammocks, the world around us was as black and airless as if we had been in a cave deep under the earth.

That night I found myself under guard again, for the Tupari were taking no chances of my slipping away and following the trail back to the river and the canoes. As for Barna—he was as inaccessible as if he had not been there. Throughout the day's march he had remained near the head of the column, where I had not had so much as a glimpse of him. And now the forward end of the camp, which he occupied, was forbidden ground to me.

There was a second day the same as the first; a third the same as the second. Or, rather, almost the same, for during the afternoon our route traversed the steep side of a valley and we could catch occasional glimpses of the river far below. On the fourth morning, however, it was gone again, and we twisted on, hour after hour, through deep folds in the hills. When occasionally the screens of foliage parted slightly, all we could see beyond them were more foliage, more valleys, more hills. And beyond and above them, mist.

Indeed, the mist was now even heavier and more continuous than it had been on the river—billowing, suffusing, hanging like great curtains in the still vistas before us and paling the green of the forest into ghostly gray. Through it, at intervals, rain fell: sometimes with a moaning of wind and a stirring of trees, more often in straight vertical streams from an invisible sky. But, unlike most tropical downpours, these were not followed by quick clearing and bright sunlight. The mist remained and thickened. We moved on through a labyrinth that was devoid of color, sound or movement of any kind.

Once again we had passed beyond hours and miles. As, on the river, time and distance had been the swing of a paddle, here they were the tread of feet. And the tread was soundless. The sodden leaves and twigs made no crackling underfoot, and the dripping branches yielded limply as we pushed them aside. We moved on, camped, moved on again.

For twelve hours there was twilight and for twelve hours dark.

Once—only once—during those days did I have a chance to exchange a word with Nils Barna. We had been struggling through a particularly dense stretch of forest, and presently there was a dead stop and the head of the column doubled back past us.

"Are we lost?" I asked Barna, as he appeared.

"Of course we are lost," he answered. Then the familiar faint smile touched his lips. "In a lost world, Allison, what should one be but lost?"

But apparently he still knew what he was about, for a few hours later we came out on a hillside above the river; and for the rest of that day it remained in sight below.

The next morning we came up over the rim of a long incline, and the growth around us began to thin. Then there was a flicker of daylight among the trees ahead, and a hundred yards farther on the trees ended. We stood looking out across a sea of grass.

Flying across Amazonia over a period of many years, I had, of course, often looked down on the jungle-girt savannahs—called *campos* by the Brazilians—which dot the remote upland wilderness; but this was the first time I had ever stood at one's margin, and the effect, in emerging from the seemingly endless forest, was strange and startling. The Tupari, I could see at once, were startled too. Slowly they moved up to the forest's edge—but no farther. Their bodies were tense and their eyes wary as they gazed out over the mist-shrouded grassland.

Nothing stirred on the grassland, and the Indians did not stir either. A little way off, I saw Barna speaking to Pombal. Pombal, in turn, spoke to a group of his men. But still no one moved. Bred to the forests and riverbanks, the Indians were obviously afraid of the open land ahead.

Barna stepped forward. He advanced for perhaps twenty

yards through the coarse knee-high grass, stopped, and gestured for the rest of us to follow. A minute passed. Another. Then Barna turned his back and moved on again. It was not until he was a scarcely visible speck in the distance that the column of Indians emerged from the forest and followed him like a slow brown centipede across the empty plain.

We journeyed on. For a day we lost altitude and our way ran tortuously through a deep choked valley. Then we again toiled up along the flanks of hills. On one side the dim outlines of crests and ridges appeared and reappeared out of the mist, and on the other we had occasional glimpses of the river far below. An enveloping dampness lay over the earth like a shroud, through which the sun glinted, weak and watery, even at midday. The rain beat down for an hour, stopped for an hour, and beat down again. It had grown perceptibly cooler, and at night the all-but-naked Tupari huddled closely around their moist sputtering fires.

After the fashion of their kind, they had thus far done little complaining. They trudged on, made camp, broke camp, and trudged on again in stolid silence; but I could see their hope fading and their fear increasing, hour by hour and day by day. Then came a morning on which several of them reported ill, and for the whole of the day we did not move on at all. Through most of it Barna sat in conference with Pombal and his circle of elders. And that night there was a new sound in the darkness: the monotonous rhythmic chanting of the tribal medicine man.

When we set off again, it was with three Tupari lying on improvised litters. Our progress was much slower than before. Increasingly, now, our way lay over open grass-covered *campos,* and at the margin of each there was a long wait and much cautious scouting before the column crept out from the forest into the rain and mist. Every step of the way, of course, a close watch was kept for any sign of the "lost tribe" for whom the Tupari were searching; but thus far there was no slightest indication that anyone other than

417

ourselves had ever penetrated into this world beyónd the world. Indeed, even animal life had all but disappeared. We saw no monkeys, no birds, no butterflies. On the open grasslands there was not so much as an insect's droning to break the stillness that enveloped us.

My clothes were in tatters; my bones ached; my flesh itched and burned. Raising my hand to my face, I felt the scratches and welts, the stubble of beard, the rank matted hair. You must be as pretty a sight as Mordecai Cobb, I thought.

... Cobb ... the caboclos. ... Christine. They would be— where? Back in Graça de Deus by now. Back with the boy Tourinho. With the message he had brought them. . . . They were doing—what? . . . Waiting? Planning? . . . During the first days of the journey they had been in my thoughts every hour—every moment; but then they had begun to recede, until now they were no more than haunting shadows. My mind, like the outward world, had become shrouded and blurred, and I think that for much of the time I was mildly feverish. Indeed, as I look back on that remote fantastic pilgrimage, I find it hard to recall either thought or emotion of any kind. I remember only the sodden forests, the gray savannahs, the mist—and the hunched, silent column moving on through the mist. I remember the growing sensation that we had come not merely to the end of the earth but to the end of reality as well; that we had passed beyond reality into dream; that I would move eternally through that dream, even farther, even deeper, while a slow file of Indians moved on before me.

And at the head of the file, the figure of Nils Barna. . . .

It was on the fifth or sixth day, I think, that we came to a region of no life at all: a scorched desolate upland, half forest and half plain, that had obviously once been swept by fire. The earth was a waste of gritty cinders, crisscrossed by a wild confusion of charred stumps, out of which, here and there, rose the still-upright trunks of black blasted trees. It was the first time, I am certain, that the Tupari had ever looked on a landscape utterly devoid of greenness; and now, for the first time too, their apprehension swelled into unconcealed and fullblown terror. For every hour of progress there were two of hesitation and protest, and a dozen times they seemed at the point of turning in their tracks and fleeing in panic.

That night our campsite offered no foliage for shelter. The rain beat down for hours, and when at last it stopped it was only to be replaced by a pall of thick bone-chilling fog. Toward midnight one of the sick Indians became much worse, and a few hours later he died. The medicine man began another interminable chant. The women added a low toneless moaning. And in the morning, after the funeral rites, there was still another tribal council.

This time, however, there was a difference. In the beginning the Tupari sat alone, with Barna excluded; and when at last he was summoned to join them, it was not to take his usual place beside Pombal, but to stand before them—a witness facing his inquisitors.

In the deathly stillness of the waste I could hear the words that were spoken.

"This is a cursed place we have come to," said Pombal.

"We shall soon be past it," said Barna.

"Past it—and then where?"

"In the forest again."

"And beyond the forest: what will be there?"

"The river."

"The same river? The black river? The river that has no end—"

"It will end," said Barna.

"When? Where?"

"In a few more days' journeying. Where it rises in the uplands and meets the River of the Sun. That is how I have understood your tribal legends."

The old chief was silent, studying Barna with his one dark eye.

"How do we know you are telling the truth?" he asked.

"I have always told you the truth," said Barna.

"This time we are not sure. Many of my people do not believe you. They do not want to go on."

"What do they want? To stay here?"

"No, not to stay here."

"What, then?"

"To go back."

"Back where?" asked Barna. "Back to the white men? Back to the drunken one and his gun?"

Pombal didn't answer. He and his men spoke together and then sat regarding Barna from their motionless semi-circle. Distrust and fear were in their faces. But even stronger than their distrust, I knew, was their dependence on Barna; and even deeper than their fear of going on was their fear of going back or remaining where they were.

Then finally Pombal said:

"You say to me that you are taking us where you have promised?"

"Yes," said Barna.

"To our lost people?"

"Yes."

"To the high bright place? To the River of the Sun?"

"Yes."

"Very well, we shall go on with you. But if we do not reach them in a few more days—"

"We shall reach them," said Barna.

The council dispersed, and we broke camp again.

We moved on across the scorched upland, emerged from it, crossed a belt of savannah, and re-entered the forest. Its web closed in about us, tight and hermetic, and the rain beat down on the treetops high above. But even though the waste was behind them, the Tupari remained sullen and fearful. Their medicine man walked among them with arms raised above his head, holding a charmed rod to ward off evil spirits. The warriors moved warily, their javelins at the ready. And when night came and we stopped, there was little of the usual activity of camp-making, but only heavy silence and groups of dark figures huddled motionless under the trees.

Another day. . . .

Through the gray hours we moved on through the forest; and then, at last, toward late afternoon, the country once more began to change. The ground rose and fell. The trees thinned. The steep shoulders of hills nudged in out of the mist. Soon they were pressing in on both sides of us, higher and higher, and I realized that we were approaching the apex of a deep valley. Dim walls loomed to right and left— and then another wall ahead. We came down into the trough of the valley, out of the last of the trees, onto the bank of the river. . . .

It was as wide as when we had last seen it. It was still a large stream—broad, dark and flooding—pouring down out of a great gash in the hills ahead. Then, raising my eyes, I saw that what I had taken to be hills, like those on either side of us, was actually not any such thing at all, but rather one hill—an escarpment—a single monolithic barrier of rock, rising gray and monstrous out of the depths of the valley. . . . Were we cut off? . . . At first it seemed so, for the river cut through the cliff face in a canyon that was obviously impassable. But then I saw something else. That there was a way up and out. A short distance back from the river, and on our side of it, a long ridge slanted up from the valley floor; and though its base was half-obscured by mist, its upper reaches rose bare and clear into the evening light, and I could see plainly the point at which it joined the summit of the escarpment. It might not be easy. But it was climbable. It was a way.

The valley was almost in darkness. Ridge and summit loomed sombre against the sky. But from behind them— crimson and gleaming—streamed the last shafted light of the dying day.

Barna pointed. "It is there beyond," he said. "The bright country. The River of the Sun. . . ."

But the Tupari stared silently, frozen with awe and fear.

Night fell. Rain fell. Other than the beat of rain, the only sounds were the occasional moaning of a woman or the whimpering of a child.

I was lying in my hammock under the trees, when a figure appeared out of the darkness.

"Allison?"

"Yes."

Barna came closer. "I think it would be better if you came with me," he said.

I got out of the hammock. "Is there trouble?"

"There may be."

"They won't go on?"

"No, they are afraid of the ridge."

"What will they do?"

"It is hard to tell yet. But it will be safer for you if you are with me."

He turned and I followed him through the trees. At intervals we passed small fires, with groups of Indians huddled around them; and the Indians watched us silently as we went by. Then we came to a fire and a hammock that were apparently Barna's. No one else was there. Barna sat down near the fire and beckoned me to do the same.

For a while he was silent. I listened, but the only sound was the patter of raindrops. If Pombal and his men were holding another council, it was off somewhere where we couldn't hear them. . . . What were the Tupari planning? To kill us? . . . And if so, what could we do about it? I had no gun, of course—nor, indeed, a weapon of any kind. As far as I could see, Barna had none.

"Can we get away?" I said.

Barna didn't seem to hear me.

"If we cut up the side of the valley—"

He shook his head. "I would not try it if I were you," he said. "They have posted guards all around."

I started to speak, stopped, and we were silent again.

Then Barna said: "It is ironical for you, isn't it, Allison?"

"Ironical?"

"To have struggled so hard to reach a place. To be almost in sight of it. And then—" He paused and laid a branch on the fire. "Yes," he went on. "I find myself feeling genuinely sorry about it. You are a tenacious man. I have developed rather an admiration for you."

I scarcely heard him. My mind was groping through ways and means, plans and counterplans.

"There must be some way—" I said.

"Of persuading the Tupari to go on? . . . I shall try. . . . But they are very wrought up, I am afraid. Very fearful."

"Then of escape—"

"Yes, of course—escape," said Barna meditatively. "We talk about our purposes, our goals, our motives, but what does it all come down to in the end? . . . Escape. . . . These poor Indians, for instance. All they wanted was to escape from the white man; now they must escape from their fear of the unknown. And you, Allison: you wanted to escape from the world; from the past. All right, you have. But now you want to escape from the Indians."

"I want to live," I said.

"Yes, of course—to live—"

I half rose to my feet. "Come on," I said. "Will you try it with me?"

Barna shook his head slowly. "No, I shall not try," he answered.

"But if this is the end—if it's hopeless—"

"I am afraid ends do not greatly concern me any longer. Nor hope, either. . . . No, if there is to be any escape, it will be yours—not mine. . . . My own escape, Allison, was made a long time ago. . . ."

He seemed about to go on. But he didn't. He fell silent again. His face, in the firelight, was a dead masklike white.

His eyes were hidden behind the glinting discs of his glasses.

The beat of rain slackened—then stopped. Off in the darkness I could now hear the low chanting of the medicine man. A while later two Tupari appeared and gestured to Barna; and he rose and went off with them. When I tried to follow, I was stopped by two other Indians who stood in the shadows nearby.

I sat down again and waited.

I tried to think; desperately willed myself to think.

I struggled against the tiredness and numbness within me. A cool glaze of mist covered my body, and I knew that I was feverish.

I was awakened by a hand on my shoulder.

"Come with me," said Barna.

I rose to my feet. The fire had gone out, and there was only darkness around me. But the darkness was thinner than before, and I knew that it was almost morning.

"What's happened?" I asked. "Where are we going?"

"We are going on," Barna said.

"The Tupari are willing?"

"No, they are not willing. They refuse to go. But you and I are going."

I looked at him, uncomprehending.

"I have been most of the night at their council," said Barna. "What they would like most, I think, is to kill us. But they are afraid to kill us, because they are afraid to be left alone. . . . However, they are also afraid to go farther. They are terrified of the escarpment and the ridge, and are convinced they are haunted by demons."

"Then—?"

"Then I told them that they could do as they wished. That you and I would go on alone." Barna paused. "Unless I am very much mistaken, they will presently follow us."

"Up the ridge?"

"Yes—up the ridge." He picked up a pack which he had set on the ground beside him. "Come," he said.

I still didn't move.

"I advise against hesitation, Allison. Perhaps you have not noticed, but the Indians are all around us, watching. If they get the impression that we are unsure of ourselves—"

He slung the pack on his shoulders and started off through the trees. I followed him.

And, as we walked on, I became aware that we too were being followed. Fanned out in a wide semicircle, the Tupari moved after us through the forest. Half-turning, I could catch glimpses, in the graying darkness, of gliding figures and watching faces. "They are making certain," said Barna, "that we go forward—not back."

For a few hundred yards our course paralleled the river. Then we bore off diagonally to the left. Presently the ground began to rise under our feet—at first gradually, then more and more steeply—and I knew that we had reached the base of the ridge. The jungle growth thinned. We crossed an almost open treeless space. A tide of cool air moved gently down the slope from the heights above.

Barna paused, looking back, and I looked back too. At the edge of the open space the Tupari had stopped. There were perhaps twenty of them—all men—with their javelins and blowguns; and at their center was the dark gnarled figure of Pombal.

Barna gestured to them, but they didn't move.

"Come," he called.

But they didn't answer.

Then we climbed on, and when I turned again they were out of sight below.

We came to more trees and threaded through a maze of vines and creepers. But we were now on the hump of the ridge, and there was no longer any question of direction. Behind and on both sides of us the earth sloped downward to the valley floor. Ahead, it climbed upward. The night was fading quickly, and the black boles around us emerged, one by one, from obscurity. Overhead, the branches and leaves assumed form and pattern, and beyond them, where

425

had been only darkness, were deep graying gulfs of sky. There was no wisp or shred of mist. There was no clamor of awakening life. Day, on this soaring spur above the forest-ocean was being born in utter stillness and clarity.

We climbed on. . . .

Gradually the growth on the ridge was thinning again. The trees were smaller and more widely spaced. Looking back between them, I saw the valley and river, far below, emerging from the night as if from beneath the waters of a dark withdrawing sea. Above and to the right, the wall of the escarpment gleamed cold and crystalline in the windless air. Straight ahead, the ridge climbed on through gray space until it joined the rim of the escarpment, high above.

We were crossing a patch of almost level ground—when Barna stopped. "There is no need to hurry," he said. "We may as well enjoy the morning."

He unslung his pack and sat down; and, after glancing at him curiously, I sat beside him. For a while we were silent, our eyes ranging through distance. Then he said:

"Even last night, in the darkness, this place seemed some-how familiar to me. Now I know why. It is like Kinibalu."

"Kinibalu?"

"The great mountain of Borneo. It is far larger than this, of course—a huge massif, actually—but some of its lower flanks are very similar in contour and coloring."

He paused and looked at me. "You do not know Borneo?" he asked.

"No," I said.

"It is a fascinating country: almost as wild and untouched as Amazonia. I was there for almost two years—during the war mostly, while the Japanese held it—and it was really rather a miracle that I ever got out." He paused again. The pale eyes behind the glasses were full on my face. "Last night you were speaking of escape, Allison," he said. "Let me tell you about my escape from Borneo. I think you might be interested. . . ."

Once more he looked away, over the valleys and the tree-tops.

"I imagine my wife has told you of our going there," he went on, presently; "and of her taking sick and having to leave. After her departure I went on with my work, which was the investigation of possible new oil fields. I heard of the outbreak of the Pacific war, of course, but, like everyone else, never dreamed that the Japanese could advance so quickly. The result was that a few months later I was trapped. Borneo was invaded and taken. And to make matters worse, I knew that I was a marked man. The Japanese had a thorough espionage system of long standing; most of the white men on the island were known to them by name and occupation; and I was well aware that my knowledge of oil and other natural resources made me a highly desirable prize for them. They almost captured me at the very outset. And it was a certainty that they would have captured me sooner or later, if it had not been for Jakob Koppel—the man whose letter you have been kind enough to bring me.

"Koppel was an old friend of mine—a dear friend—who had lived in Borneo for several years. I had made my headquarters at his plantation, and he became virtually my assistant. He knew the country well. He was resourceful, courageous, and devoted to me. And when both his plantation and our oil camp were overrun by the Japanese, it was he who made possible our successful flight into the bush."

Barna paused again. "I hope you are not finding all this too dull," he said.

"Go on," I told him.

"Well, of the next eighteen months or so there is really not much to tell. We lived in the bush. We hid. We moved from one native village to another. It was during this period that we several times had occasion to cross the lower slopes of Kinibalu. Our general plan was to work our way clear across the interior of the island to the southern coast, and there try to get ourselves aboard some sort of native craft that would take us down toward Australia or New Guinea.

It was a wildly ambitious scheme, of course, and we had our difficulties from the beginning; but gradually we made our way across the length of Borneo, until we were actually in sight of the south coast. I should explain that for the most of this journey we were not alone, but with a small group of Dyak tribesmen. They took a great risk in helping us, and they knew it; for it was common knowledge that the Japanese took terrible reprisals on natives who were caught helping the enemy. Why they did it, I was never certain. More than anything else, I think, it was because of Jakob's wonderful way with them. In any case, they helped us. And they got us through. We were camped within two miles of the south coast, when we were found by the Japanese. . . ."

Another pause. Then Barna continued. His voice was low and toneless, his face like chalk in the gray dawnlight.

"There is a thing I have not yet mentioned," he said. "The most important thing. . . . This escape of mine was not simply a matter of an individual's fleeing from an enemy. At least not as I saw it. . . . I must go back a way. . . . As I have told you, I have worked in many fields of science, both theoretical and applied. I had gone to Borneo for oil. I came to the Amazon for rubber. But primarily I have always been a research chemist, and my interest is in the nature and properties of all organic matter.

"Anyhow—during my months with this Dyak tribe I had become involved, fantastically enough, in the most momentous project of my life. It had its beginning, soon after Jakob and I joined them, when one of the men returned from a hunting trip with a frightful festering wound on his foot. I offered to do what I could, though amputation seemed the only possible way of saving the fellow's life. But the tribal medicine man would not let me touch him. Instead, he simply plastered what looked like a handful of mud onto the wound, and a day or two later—I could scarcely believe my eyes when I saw it—every trace of infection was gone.

"It is well known, of course, that various primitive people

have made remarkable scientific discoveries—witness, for instance, the Amazon tribes and their curaré. But the thing I had seen was beyond one's wildest imaginings. I was astounded, enthralled. And during the months that followed, while we remained with the Dyaks, I struggled to discover the secret of this incredible cure. I saw it attempted many times. It did not always work. But in most cases it did. In enough cases to convince me that I had stumbled upon something of incalculable importance.

"The medicine man himself was of little help. He believed—or at least claimed—that most of his powers came from his mystic incantations, rather than from the muddy substance he applied on the wounds. But presently I discovered that the principal ingredient of this 'mud' was an unusual type of soil mold that grew on the roots of certain jungle trees and shrubs. I collected specimens of this mold and analyzed them. Naturally I had only the crudest facilities, but nevertheless I finally succeeded in extracting its essential components and getting at least an idea of its chemical structure. One day Jakob cut himself, and the wound infected. I tried my extract on him—and it worked. A few weeks later I had the chance to try it on myself. And it worked again.

"You are not a medical man, Allison. Neither am I. But it does not take a physician to see the possibilities that this thing presented. As far as I could see, it was more effective, even in its crudest form, than all the then-known anti-biotics put together. I thought of its immense usefulness in the war. And beyond war, too—in fighting disease, suffering and death, everywhere. You see, I felt sure that from my precious sample it would be possible for laboratories in the States to synthesize the drug and distribute it widely and cheaply. Oh, I tell you I was a possessed man in those days! A fugitive Ehrlich. A jungle Pasteur. If it was the last thing I did in my life, I had to get off that island—to reach my own people —to give what I had found to the world.

"The point I am making is that all this was not incidental

to my escape. It was the essence of it. All I thought of during that long struggle across Borneo were those few ounces of crystals that I carried in a pouch against my chest. I no longer conceived of myself as an individual, but as a messenger, a torch-bearer, a part of a whole infinitely greater and more important than myself. In the best scientific sense, the best patriotic sense, the best Christian sense—I was selfless. Bear that in mind, Allison. In it lies the whole meaning of what I did."

Barna's eyes moved out from the ridge to the gulfs of air and the brightening valley below.

"What finally happened," he said, "was very quick—very simple. As I said, we had crossed the island and were bivouacked within a few miles of the south coast. I had gone off to a nearby rise of ground, to see the lie of the land. Jakob and the Dyaks remained in the camp. All at once a Japanese patrol burst out of the bush around me, and apparently it was I, specifically, whom they were looking for. 'Barna?' said their leader. I shook my head and pointed to the camp. I could see Koppel looking toward me, startled by the commotion. Someone knocked me down with a rifle butt, and then they all rushed on. I picked myself up, darted into the jungle, and, as I ran, I heard the sound of their sub-machine-guns. . . .

"Three days later I was on a native trading-boat, bound south across the Java Sea."

Barna was silent, and I was silent too. In another few moments, I saw, the sun would rise. From below the eastern horizon long beams flowed up into the pure blue depths of the sky.

"Koppel is alive, Barna," I said.

He didn't answer.

"Think of that—not the other. *He is alive. . . .*"

No answer.

But Barna was watching me. And presently he said:

"You are the only person, Allison, to whom I have ever told this. Just why I have told you I am not sure. But I

430

think perhaps you are one of a very few who might understand."

"Koppel would understand. Christine would understand."

He shook his head. "No. They would be kind; they
would forgive. But they would not understand. They would
think that what I did was from weakness. But it was not, of
course. It was from strength."

He paused and then continued: "That is the core of it all,
you see: that I acted neither from selfishness nor cowardice,
but from what the world holds to be the loftiest of motives.
Devotion to science—to human welfare—to concepts above
and beyond one's own personal self. Why did I do what I
did? For my own sake? No. For my loyalties; my alle-
giances; my ideals. The end justified the means, I thought.
Very well; I attained my end. And in doing it I renounced
my humanity."

The sun rose. The earth gleamed. A shaft of light struck
fire in the crest of Barna's hair and glittered on the lenses
of his glasses.

"You've tried to renounce it," I said. "But that's the one
thing a man can't do. . . . Go back and face it, Barna. Go
back and face Koppel."

He shook his head slowly. "No," he murmured, "I cannot
go back. Jakob is alive—and I am glad, of course—but none
the less I killed him. And, with him, everything else. . . ."
The pale eyes looked through me—beyond me. "It is not a
question of facing the world, or Jakob Koppel—but of facing
the truth. And the truth is that my life was a lie. What I
cherished and believed in was a lie. The world whose standards I accepted was a lie. Now I have withdrawn from those
lies—and I shall not return to them."

"That's all you have to say of life? . . . Nothing is left?"

"Yes, one thing at least is left for me. Not to betray these
Tupari, as I did the Dyaks who befriended me."

"And nothing else?"

"The jungle is left." Barna gazed over the still, green

miles. "The jungle where we began, Allison . . . and where some day, perhaps, we may begin again. . . ."

"What about your discovery?" I asked. "The mold? This great thing you had to give to the world?"

Barna's eyes came back to me. The old faint smile touched his lips. "Ah, yes," he said "—the great thing I had to give—"

"Did you get it out?"

"Yes, I got it out. I brought it back with me. My extract was a crude form of penicilin. By 1944 the laboratories knew all about it. . . ."

He stood up and looked down the ridge.

"I see that I was right," he said. "The Tupari have decided to follow us."

Peering down, I could make out a column of tiny figures moving across an open space far below.

Barna unslung his pack.

"Here," he said. "There is enough food in it for ten days."

I stared at him, unmoving.

"You have heard the story of one escape, Allison. I wish you better luck with yours. . . ." He pointed down the flank of the ridge, to the right. "Climb straight down. Cut through the forest and across the hills into the next valley, and follow that valley to the east. In a day you will pick up our trail, and it will be easy. At the river camp you will find the canoes."

Still I stood rooted—wordless. The pack dangled from my hand.

"I would not delay too long," said Barna. "In ten minutes the Tupari will be here."

I looked down toward the valley, but the moving figures had disappeared.

Then I turned back to him.

"Barna—for God's sake: come with me—"

He shook his head again. "No, Allison, this will be your journey—not mine." He looked up the ridge. "My journey is in the other direction."

432

"Barna—"

But he moved away up the slope.

"There is not much time, Allison," he said, turning.

He was standing a few feet above me on the ridge, and the sun was full on him. Behind and above him, it shone full on the vast walls and tiered buttresses of the escarpment. On the rim of the escarpment there was a flash of light, golden and dazzling. . . .

"Tell my friend—tell my wife—" said Barna, "that I am sorry I cannot come to them. Give them my greetings, please. . . . Give them my love."

I slung on the pack and plunged down the slope.

The jungle enveloped me.

30

It was raining.

For a long time that was all there was: the sound of rain. It beat down through darkness, through fever; now cool, now burning hot; now faint and remote, now closer, louder, stronger, beating down in great streaming waves into my brain. I tried to move, but the rain held me pinioned. I struggled to open my eyes—to see the treetops and the sky— but there was only dark walls and some sort of lid or screen poised motionless above them. The screen wavered, moved closer, stopped. I lay on my cot, looking up at the thatch roof of the infirmary. . . .

It may have been then, or much later, that I heard a voice. "Chris," it said. "Chris—" (It was my voice.)

"Yes, Mark?"

"Chris—"

That was all there was that first time. But it was enough.

The second time there was more. She was sitting beside me; I could see her. I put out my hand and touched her.

"Chris—"

"Yes, Mark?"

"Don't go away."

"I won't," she said.

Each time there was more. Or at least I could remember more. There was rain, sunlight, rain again. There was light

434

and dark; footsteps, voices; someone feeding me, someone bathing me. . . . Not someone. Christine. . . .

But the fever ebbed slowly. I could feel it rise and fall in dark waves. Sometimes I could hear her but not see her, sometimes see but not hear. Once I both saw and heard her, plain and clear beside me, but when I reached out she wasn't there. Once she was there all right, but, somehow, I wasn't. Lying there on the cot, I was no longer myself but John Mc-Hugh, and, beside Christine, there *I* was, looking down at me. I remember thinking it amusing and beginning to laugh. . . . And that's all I remember.

Then I was lying very still, and it seemed cold, and the rain was loud.

"He's gone, Chris," I said.

"Yes, Mark, I know."

"We were camped in a deep valley. There was a wall of rock and a ridge, and the Indians—"

"Yes, you've told me."

"Told you? When?"

"When you were awake before."

My mind went back, groping; but there was only darkness. Then, far behind the darkness, a lonely mudbank on a jungle river. . . .

"Tourinho—" I said suddenly. "He reached you?"

"Yes," she said, "he reached us."

"And—and then you made it back?"

"Yes."

"All of you?"

"Yes, all of us. Now go back to sleep again."

I closed my eyes. "If you give me your hand—"

She gave me her hand.

"I made it back too," I said.

Then there was the rain again. The web of fever. The web of the jungle. . . .

There had been neither days nor miles in my journey, but only forest—black river—more forest. Far overhead were the

435

rain and the sun, but, in the forest, only green twilight. Ahead, a liana: dark, twining, frozen. Beyond it, a maze of lianas, a maze of boles, branches, leaves, vines and ferns; now transfixed in utter clarity, now dissolving into a soft woven blur. . . . Stillness. Through the stillness, a humming. Through the humming, a screech. . . . Then stillness again, and, beyond the stillness, the glint of unseen eyes. Watching the alien, the intruder, as he creeps on through the jungle of his own fever and fear.

Here is a reach of the forest. Close, matted, suffocating. Underfoot there is slime, and around me spines and thorns that claw through my clothing into the flesh. I pass a tree that is black, twisted and dying. A choking vine is wrapped like wire around its trunk, and gray fungus oozes from its rotting pores. Farther on is another tree whose surface is not bark but a seething mass of red ants, and beyond that another covered with enormous white worms. On the ground nearby is a half-eaten putrid carcass. And more ants, more worms. . .

Here is another reach—a few yards distant. Above me are great cliffs of greenery, studded with the bright blooms of flowers. And in the soft air are flying flowers—butterflies—a thousand dazzling shimmering filaments of purple and gold. There is a single bird-call: high, clear and pure. In the shadows, under spreading branches, I can see row upon row of great hanging orchids, glowing as if with a deep inner light of their own.

Which is the real forest? Both. . . And neither. . . Reality is the next step, the rotted boot, the burning flesh, the throbbing brain. Reality is the thing deep within the brain that repeats itself endlessly: "Keep going, keep going, keep going. . . ." Once I caught a frog; once a lizard. I ate them raw, and my hands were red with thin cool blood. Then I moved on again. Through the web—the labyrinth. Through the obscure and fearful symmetry of blood and chlorophyll. . .

Then it was days later—weeks later?—and I had stopped. I was staring up, incredulous, no longer at the treetops but at the sky; at something that moved against the sky. . . . I closed my eyes. It is Barna, I thought—Barna on the ridge above you—and you have made no journey at all, but are back where you started—following Barna on, farther, deeper. . . . But when I looked again I saw that it was not Barna. It was not one shape, but many shapes; and they were not climbing, but flying, swooping, wheeling. . . . The tears ran down my cheeks and my body shook with sobs. . . There they were: brighter than Eden, brighter than the angels of God. So high. So beautiful. . .

The vultures.

Slowly the world came back. Voices became faces. Footsteps became bodies. Once I opened my eyes and saw Frei Ambrosio beside the cot. Once João Batista. Once Mordecai Cobb.

"Had a nice little outing, hey amigo?" asked Cobb, grinning. "Guess we got to give you your boy scout badge, first class."

The others came and went. But mostly I was alone with Christine. And as my fever waned and my strength slowly returned, I learned from her something of what had happened during my absence.

One thing was that the plane had returned. It had brought Moranda again, and the pilot da Silva, and with them food, supplies, messages. The Southern Cross people and the D.P.'s had meanwhile been preparing to leave Esperança. The *Fortaleza* had been ready, the river rising steadily. By now they were probably well up the Juruá and its tributaries.

What of McHugh?

According to Moranda he was all right. From Esperança he had been flown to Manãos, and from there to the hospital in Belem. After several weeks, when he was convalescent, they had arranged to send him home; but he had refused to go, and, as soon as he was able, returned up-river to Esperança. He had wanted to fly up to Graça de Deus with

Moranda, but Wooderson had finally dissuaded him. He would be on the *Fortaleza* with the others.

Hadn't Moranda wanted Christine to fly out with him?

Yes, he had wanted her to go. He had almost forced her to go.

"—Or at least tried to force me," Christine added.

Bit by bit, during those days, I too told the things *she* had to know. . . . Not everything. Not the darkest things. They could come later, perhaps. . . . But what she had to know, I told: briefly, almost dispassionately. And Christine listened, showing no outward emotion; not questioning me, not pressing me, but simply accepting the story in silence, as if it were one she had known all along.

One day she brought in a letter. It was a second message to Barna from Jakob Koppel, which Moranda had brought up and which she had succeeded in roughly translating. *They tell me you have gone into the forest,* it read; *but I am not surprised, for I know it has always been the forest that you love best of all. Soon I shall be joining you, dear friend, and it will be as if my life starts again. From the day of your miraculous escape I have hoped and prayed for this time. Through these terrible years it has been the memory of you that has given me the strength and hope to go on. . . .*

Tourinho Jackson visited me, perching like a brown monkey at the foot of my cot.

"All right, boy?" I asked.

"All right?" he repeated, as if it were a very foolish question indeed. "Yes, of course I am all right, Senhor Marco."

And that was the truth of it—the wonder of it: he *was* all right. His round elf's face was smiling. His eyes shone. There had been a time for grief and anger, but now they were gone. His father and mother were gone. Yesterday was gone. And what was left was today—and tomorrow; the day ahead, the adventures ahead, the life ahead; and it had nothing to do with selfishness or callousness or even forgetfulness, but simply with being a boy and being alive. And now, outside the hut there was the sound of running feet and voices shouting, and Tourinho jumped from the cot and shouted back.

"It is my friends," he explained, "and I have promised I will show them how the Tupari hunt for *tigre*."

Then he raced to the door, waved, and was gone.

After three weeks I left the infirmary: still thin and yellow-skinned, but otherwise not greatly the worse for wear. It was a world of rain into which I emerged—gray, sodden and almost cold in comparison to what it had been before. The clearing, once choked with dust, was now a sea of mud. The river flowed past, swift and swollen.

But the pattern of life had changed scarcely at all. The vultures still circled. The hammocks still creaked. The caboclos still trudged apathetically on their rounds and presented themselves at the staff shack with questions and complaints.

"The senhors in the aeroplano," they said "—they told us that the big ship is coming."

"That's right," I assured them.

"But it does not come. The river is high, and it does not come."

"It's on the way."

"You are sure?"

"Yes, sure."

"And when will it be here?"

"Cedo. . . . Soon."

Apparently they had stirred themselves to at least a slight amount of work, for the vegetable crop was finally on its way up and the weeds were under fair control. Frei Ambrosio seemed to have regained a certain measure of influence. But not once did I hear any of them so much as mention the name of O Touro.

One morning Cobb ambled into the staff shack.

The wound he had received from the Tupari javelin had not infected, and, apart from a slight stiffness in the shoulder, he was apparently again as fit as ever. Once or twice he had tried to pump me—about the black river, the hills, the Indians, Barna. But I had scarcely answered him. My only remaining interest in Mordecai Cobb was in terms of the day when I would be rid of him at last.

"Well?" I said, as he came in.

"I'm on my way again, amigo," he announced. "Just stopped in to wish you love and kisses."

"On your way? Where?"

"Where you think? After that perfessor, that's where. After that gold he's wise to, up there on the Rio do Sol." Cobb hawked and spat meditatively on the floor. "Horsing around here may be okay for the rest of you. But not for me, thanks. I got a little unfinished business out there in the bush."

"You can't go alone, man!"

"Who says I'm going alone?" He grinned and turned to the door. "Come in here, baby," he called. "Come say so long to the big chefé."

Serafima Batista appeared in the doorway.

For a moment I simply stared. Then I thought I was going to laugh. Then I looked back at Cobb sharply.

"You can't make her—"

"Take it easy, amigo—nobody's making her." He winked at the girl, "Are they, baby?"

Baby, no less. . . .

Serafima shook her head demurely. "No, senhor," she said to me. "It is I who have asked Senhor Mordecai to take me."

"But your father and mother—"

"They'll be tickled to get her off their necks," said Cobb. "Me, my neck's tough, I guess. . . . I told her it wasn't no Rio or São Paulo I'm going to; but she says she don't care where it is—she's getting off this mudbank."

The girl smiled at him, and her dark eyes glowed. "We will get to Rio too," she said. "You wait and see. With the

bags of gold we will get there. With the cruzeiros and contos." Her glance went to me, and she flicked the velveteen
pouch that still hung at her throat. "With the necklace of
jewels, Senhor Chefé, for my little *olho de boto.*"

She laughed, and Cobb grinned again and patted her
rump. "Guess mebbe she can't dance like that little Wop,"
he conceded. "But she cooks better."

Outside he slung on a huge pack (obviously filled with
company supplies) and adjusted a second smaller one on
Serafima. "Well, mebbe my luck will be better than yours,"
he said to me. "Don't be feeling too bad though, amigo.
You done all right for a tenderfoot."

He turned back to the girl. "Okay, baby, them million
bucks are getting tired of waiting—"

Then I stood in the doorway, watching them, while they
cut across the clearing toward the forest trail; and at its
entrance Cobb turned and waved a bony hand.

The crazy old bastard, I thought. . . .

But I wished him luck.

Usually there were four of us at the trestle table for supper: Frei Ambrosio, Tourinho, Christine and myself. The
boy would run off when the meal was over, and soon after
the padre would say goodnight, and Christine and I would
be left alone.

"Casino?" I would ask.

"Yes, of course, Mark."

And, more often than not, we would play late into the
night, while the insects whirred and clicked around the oil
lamp and the rain beat down on the thatch overhead. We
talked about the run of the game. . . . "Building nines—
three aces—sweeps—spades." . . . Or about the day-by-day
life in the clearing: from the condition of the vegetable crop,
to Tourinho's table manners, to the probable time of the
Fortaleza's arrival. But beyond that day we didn't go. Nor
did we go back beyond the day on which I had returned to
Graça de Deus. Instinctively, as if by unspoken agreement,

we existed in a hermetic transitional world between the future and the past.

. . . Until one night, very late, I paused suddenly in our playing, half-conscious that beyond the hum of insects and beat of rain I had heard another, more distant sound. I waited. I listened. And slowly the sound grew louder. Deep, hollow, reverberating—from far out within the jungle darkness—rose the wild chorus of the howlers. . . .

I looked at Christine. She was sitting motionless, hands palm-down on the table, eyes fixed on the cards that lay before her. The howling swelled until it seemed to fill the room. Then it faded, receded, became merely a murmur; and out of the murmur—just as I knew it would, just as it had before—came the single distant cry. In the next moment it was gone. Even the murmur was gone. There was only the clicking of insects and the beat of rain.

Christine's face was deathly pale. Getting up, I went around the table, stood beside her and put my arm around her; and, bending her head silently, she pressed it against me. For a long while we remained there, without moving, without speaking. Then we put the cards away, put out the lamp, and walked through the rain and darkness to our hammocks.

Forest of night and terror. . . .
Forest of growth and life. . . .

A morning came when the sun shone. The jungle was a green glittering ocean. The river flowed out of it, full and free, toward the greater rivers and the world beyond.

Leaving the clearing, Christine and I walked up to the high point near the head of the cachoeira and sat looking out over the treetops to the west. That was all there was: the treetops, the rain-washed sky—and between them, white and gleaming on the horizon, a slender scarf of clouds. There was no hint of hills or river. Nor of whatever else might be beyond them, remote and lost.

"Mark—" said Christine.

"Yes?"

"It's still there, Mark. The river. Your river. . . ."

I nodded silently. Then I felt her hand on mine.

"Some day you'll find it," she murmured. "I know that. You'll find it."

"We'll find it," I said.

Rising, we followed the path down from the knob, and soon, where stillness had been, there was the roaring of the rapids, and where sun and space had been was dim green twilight. Then the sound of the water faded, and there was only the forest and the familiar sounds of the forest. We walked without speaking, side by side, hand in hand; and when we came to a narrow path that branched off from the main trail, we still didn't speak, nor even pause nor exchange a glance, but followed it down between the twisting walls of fern and frond. We stood in a glade that was like a temple. We looked down at a black silver-glinting pool, and then across the pool at the trees beyond, and from a branch of one of the trees a small ring-tailed monkey looked back at us with a surprised inquisitive eye.

"He's still there," said Christine.

Yes, I thought, he was still there. . . . I looked back at the pool. . . . The piranhas were there, too. And somewhere, lying deep on the pool's bottom, a tiny white skull.

All right—they were there. They would always be there. If nothing else, I had learned that much about the forest-ocean. The piranha and the monkey: they were equally part of it. The skull and the soft sunlight were part of it. Fungus and orchid, mud and oil, mold and gold, scorpion and butterfly, fever and peace, prison and sanctuary, terror and beauty, endings and beginnings, death and life, black river and golden river—they were all part of it; they were all there; whatever existed in mind or heart was there, hidden and waiting beyond the emerald screens.

I glanced down at the tiny scar on the back of my hand. It was still there. It would always be there.

I looked at Christine. She was there too—beside me.

We sat on the mossy bank. Together. Alone.

. . . And then, suddenly, no longer alone, for there was a sound across the glade, and the figure of Tourinho emerged, running, from the trail.

"Senhor! Senhora!" he shouted. "I have been looking everywhere for you—" He came racing around the pool. "The ship—it is here!"

"The *Fortaleza?*"

"Yes, yes—the *Fortaleza*. It is coming up the river. It is around the last bend, and—" Before he had finished he was running again: around the pool, into the trail, out of sight.

Christine and I rose and followed him. We didn't hurry, but walked as we had before—silently, hand in hand—until we came out of the forest into the clearing. The clearing itself was deserted. Every human being in Graça de Deus was lined up on its far side, along the mudbank, staring out at the river. And beyond them—incredibly, fantastically— a ship was moving slowly in toward the shore.

In the little river it seemed enormous. Its funnel belched out a pall of smoke. Its steel sides loomed rigid and black against the trees on the farther shore. From its decks rose mountainous piles of crates, bales, tools and machinery, and its rails were lined with an unbroken sweep of watching faces. As we joined the crowd on the bank, I could see Mc-Hugh, standing on the bridge. Next to him was a short wiry-looking man with binoculars—Wooderson?—and, ranged around them, a group of other men wearing khaki and sun helmets. McHugh shouted. Some of the others waved. But along the rails below the long lines of immigrants stood motionless and silent, their eyes looking across the water at the Promised Land.

Which of them, I wondered, was Jakob Koppel . . . ?

The ship's side nudged the bank. Ropes spun down. A gangway fell. Then McHugh came down the gangway and shook hands, and the men in helmets and khaki came after him.

"Welcome to El Dorado, gentlemen," I said.